WELCOME TO CIVILIZATION

Zeeraum reached out casually with her front two manipulators, and picked up one of the little helper Vixa. She
cradled it in her left hand and patted it thoughtfully, like a
little old lady picking up her toy poodle to pet it. Suddenly
she lifted the little helper Vixa up over her heard and
dropped it into that gaping, obscene-looking mouth. The
sphincter abruptly shut, sealing the creature in.

Jamie could see the skin around the sides of the mouth-
chamber bulge out here and there as the helper struggled
inside, and he could hear what sounded like a tiny, high-
pitched scream that went on and on. Zeeraum scratched
herself absently.

It took all of his will to keep from screaming himself.
Hannah's hands were bunched up into fists, and her face
was an expressionless mask. Only the quiver at her jawline betrayed her emotions.

The muffled screams and the struggles inside Zeeraum's
mouth subsided. She made a low burbling noise that
might have been a laugh, or a belch, or even a rude comment in her own language. "Welcome," she said. "Welcome
to civilization."

NOVELS BY
Roger MacBride Allen

The Torch of Honor
Rogue Powers
Orphan of Creation
The Modular Man*
The War Machine (with David Drake)
Supernova (with Eric Kotani)
Farside Cannon
The Ring of Charon
The Shattered Sphere
Caliban
Inferno
Utopia
Ambush at Corellia*
Assault at Selonia*
Showdown at Centerpoint*
The Game of Worlds
The Depths of Time*
The Ocean of Years*
The Shores of Tomorrow*
BSI: Starside: The Cause of Death*
BSI: Starside: Death Sentence*
BSI: Starside: Final Inquiries*

NONFICTION

A Quick Guide to
Book-on-Demand Printing

The First Book of Hazel: A Quick Guide to the
Hazel Internet Merchandizing System

*Published by Bantam Books

BSI STARSIDE

Final
Inquiries

A NOVEL BY

Roger MacBride Allen

BANTAM • SPECTRA

BSI: STARSIDE: FINAL INQUIRIES
A Bantam Spectra Book / March 2008

Published by
Bantam Dell
A Division of Random House, Inc.
New York, New York

All rights reserved
Copyright © 2008 by Roger MacBride Allen
Cover illustration copyright © 2008 by Keith Birdsong
Cover design by Beverly Leung

Bantam Books and the rooster colophon are registered trademarks
and Spectra and the portrayal of a boxed "s" are trademarks of
Random House, Inc.

ISBN: 978-0-553-58728-9

Printed in the United States of America
Published simultaneously in Canada

www.bantamdell.com

OPM 10 9 8 7 6 5 4 3 2 1

To my sons'
two Grammies—Liz and Scottie—
in recognition of
the very least of their many gifts to me:
giving me the time to get this book done

ONE

NEED TO KNOW

Agents Jamie Mendez and Hannah Wolfson hurried across the BSI Bullpen toward the Commandant's office—and reached it just in time to see the door slammed shut in their faces.

Special Agent Boris Kosolov looked up from his cubicle just across the aisle from the office and laughed unpleasantly. "It's all backwards and forwards in there."

He watched as Hannah raised her hand to knock on the door. "I wouldn't do that," Kosolov said.

Hannah looked at him and frowned. "Why not, Boris?"

"Not such a good time to be disturb her, I think."

"She just called us on our pocket comms," Jamie said. "Told us to get here on the double."

"Yeah, but that was what, thirty second, forty second, ago?" Kosolov asked. "Something else come up since. More than on the double. On the triple, maybe. Double plus triple." He grinned. "She got a visitor. Is an outsider. They been talking. Friend of yours, I thinking."

For half a heartbeat, Hannah wondered if Kosolov was pulling their legs. He was an odd fish. Supposedly his Russian was as mangled as his English. She gave him a good hard look. *He knows who the visitor is,* she thought. *And knowing scares him, a little. But he also knows there's a pie in the face coming straight at Jamie and me—and he gets to watch.*

She was about to say something to him when the door to the Commandant's office swung open, and Kelly stuck her head out into the Bullpen. She spotted Jamie and Hannah in the waiting area, and gestured for them to come in. "Sorry about the hurry-up-and-wait," she said, "but I don't think I've ever had one pop this big or this fast. I'm juggling about three angles to this all at once." She looked at Kosolov and pointed a finger right at his heart. "And *you* didn't see anything."

The two agents followed her into her office as she shut the door behind them. Kelly didn't move to sit behind her own desk or gesture for Hannah and Jamie to sit. There was no one else in the room. "Agent Kosolov said you had a visitor," said Jamie.

"I do," said Kelly. "Two, in fact. They came in the back way, and they're in my inner conference room." She gestured toward a door in the side wall. Kelly used the inner room so rarely that Hannah had forgotten it was even there. "Kosolov only saw one of them," she went on. "Fortunately."

"Who are they?" Jamie asked.

"That's more of a *what* question than a *who* question," Kelly replied. "At least for one of them. But I can't risk keeping them waiting for more than a couple of minutes." She nodded toward the comm panel on her desk. "I've been on the horn with all kinds of brass and UniGov types and diplomatic liaison offices. The short form is that we do whatever our guests ask us to do and give them full, eager, absolute cooperation. I have been specifically instructed to quote, 'relay and emphasize the need for such cooperation to the assigned agents, and further emphasize the utter and grave seriousness of the situation,' unquote. Is that clear?"

"Would this be a bad time for me to use some of that back leave I've been accumulating?" Jamie asked.

"This is no time for jokes, Jamie," Hannah said sharply.

"If he's got any sense, he's not joking," said Kelly, "and I wouldn't mind tagging along with you on that leave. It might be a good time to get out of town. Or even out of the target area."

"Target area?" Hannah echoed.

"If you thought things were tense with the Kendari up to now, get ready to see what *real* tension is. And don't think the Elder Races would interfere if things got out of control. If the human race and the Kendari go to war, even the most sympathetic of them isn't going to wade in and stop us from wiping ourselves out. And a lot of races would be happy to hold our coats— or even egg us on."

"Commander—we just came off an assignment that came very close to blowing up in our faces," said Hannah. "We've barely gotten over that one—and we're both probably still a little twitchier than we should be. Can't you hand this to someone else?"

"I know. You two need to stand down for a while. I wish I *could* hand this off. I can't. You were specifically requested. The brass worked really hard to make sure that I understood I was to comply with that request at all costs. So let's get moving." Kelly made a move to open the inner door, but then stopped herself. "No. Wait a second. I've got a couple of details to cover first."

Kelly pulled out her own pocket comm and spoke into it. "Kosolov. Orders for you." Hannah heard Kosolov's muffled reply through the door and through the comm unit at the same time, though she couldn't make out the words. Kelly preferred yelling through open doorways. She had to be feeling extra security-conscious, and very eager to keep the door shut, if she chose to use a commlink to talk to a man ten feet away.

"Kosolov—don't worry about why," Kelly said into the comm. "Just do the following jobs yourself, personally, and do not delegate or discuss them. Grab Wolfson's and Mendez's Ready-To-Go duffels from their cubicles. Bring them to"— she paused to double-check a note on her desk—"Docking Bay 27. There should be an interorbit jeep-tug docked there by now. Put the duffels on board and leave. But before you do that, contact the quartermaster and have two full field-forensics kits, two field-ops kits, and thirty days of field rations for two delivered to Bay 27 and loaded aboard the jeep-tug."

Kelly thought for a second and looked at the two agents. "What else are you going to need?" she asked as she looked at them, plainly talking to herself. "And have the QM throw in a pair of sleeping bags and ground cushions as well. My authorization, and on the double-plus. That jeep needs to boost ten minutes ago. Confirm via text to my pocket comm when you're done, and have the quartermaster text-confirm to my comm—and only mine—when the items are loaded. And keep this *quiet*. If I hear about it at the water-cooler tomorrow, I'll establish a BSI office on Penitence just so I can assign you to it." Hannah heard Kosolov again on comm and through the door, and Kelly put away the comm unit. "*Now* we have to go in there. I don't dare keep them waiting any longer—or alone with each other, for that matter. Come on."

Hannah and Jamie exchanged looks with each

other. Hannah knew Jamie was trying to figure out the same thing she was. What kind of job would require the things on that list—but *not* the things that *weren't* on it? They weren't going to have much of a chance to figure it out. Things were moving too fast.

Kelly slid open the door to her private conference room and stepped through first instead of gesturing them to lead the way. That all by itself signaled a lot to Hannah: It was the action of a commander leading her forces against the opposition rather than that of a host showing deference to her visitors.

Hannah followed her in, with Jamie right behind.

The inner room was small, windowless, and spartan. There was a bland beige carpet on the floor, and four government-issue armchairs that sat, one in each corner, facing the center of the room. There were two doors—the one that led into Kelly's office and one on the opposite wall. Kelly immediately crossed the small room and stood by the closed door, folding her arms in front of her, making no move at all to sit down, making no signal that Hannah or Jamie should do so either. Another clear message: There was no time to get comfortable. They were going to be leaving very soon.

The passage behind that second door allowed visitors to come and go from Kelly's office discreetly, without being paraded through the Bullpen. And these visitors were definitely the sort that needed discreet handling.

Just seeing the first one made it hard for Hannah to keep from showing surprise. He was a being with a roughly centaurlike body plan; four legs and a muscular tail on the rear or horizontal torso, and a forward vertical torso that supported two arms and a vaguely wolflike head on a flexible neck. He was a Kendari—and not just any Kendari.

"Hello, Brox," Jamie said, speaking in Lesser Trade Speech. "It's been a while. It is pleasant to see you again."

"I can only wish it was under better circumstances, Special Agent Mendez," said Brox. "I greet you—and you as well, Senior Special Agent Wolfson."

"I greet you as well," said Hannah. Brox 231. What in space could have brought *him* to Kelly's private office? Brox. Senior Inquirist of the Kendari Inquiries Service—the rival counterpart of UniGov's Bureau of Special Investigations. In short, an enemy agent representing humanity's deadliest rival. But Brox had also been their partner on the Reqwar investigation. Wry, irascible, irritating—but also courageous, honorable, and honest, willing and able to act for the long-term benefit of all, rather than scoring short-term points for himself. Reqwar could easily have ended in disaster, in death for all of them, if not for Brox 231.

But Brox was not the only visitor in the room. At least maybe he wasn't. There was *something* else in the room, but it was hard to tell whether it was an object or a living being. It stood by the door. It was greyish pink, and consisted of an egg-shaped torso that had five projections sprouting from it, which roughly corresponded in size and position to the legs, arms, and head of a human being. It stood about one hundred eighty centimeters tall.

The five limbs or tentacles or growths or whatever they might be called were slightly flattened front to back, and the featureless "head" gently tapered to a point. On closer inspection, the head almost looked as if it was formed out of two limbs that had been fused together. The arms were little more than elongated flipperlike things, with no distinct fingers, hands, or joints. The legs ended in rounded-off, flat-bottomed stumps, with no distinct feet. The thing stood on its two leglike supports, swaying back and forth almost imperceptibly, its arms limp at its sides. It looked slightly potbellied somehow.

Its skin was very slightly translucent, and Hannah could just make out what looked like, not bones, exactly—more like a mechanical armature—in the hands. And there was something solid, roughly egg-shaped and skull-sized inside the head. If it was a head.

"Uh, what is that?" Jamie asked.

Hannah signaled for him to be quiet. It might well be a *who,* rather than a *what,* and there was no sense in giving needless offense to the—the whatever or whoever it was. A glance at Commander Kelly told Hannah that her boss wasn't going to be much help. Possibly Kelly wasn't much more certain of the situation herself. "Hello?" Hannah said in a tone of voice halfway to making it a question.

"This unit acknowledges you," said a flat, mechanical voice that didn't seem to come from any particular spot on the "unit's" body. The thing did not look toward Hannah, or shift its position or posture in any way. It simply continued to stand there, swaying back and forth ever so slightly.

"And we acknowledge you," said Hannah. "Please forgive us if we are uncertain how to behave. We have no experience of any beings similar to yourself." That was putting it mildly. But whatever it was, it would do no good to cause it offense.

"You are incorrect," the mechanical voice replied. "Humans have interacted many times with the Vixa."

"Then we must apologize again," said Hannah, speaking carefully. "We were unaware that you were a Vixan. You do not resemble the ones we have seen."

"This unit is not a Vixan," it replied, but made no other remark.

"The, ah, unit, has been provided by the Vixa to facilitate communication," Brox put in.

"Oh," said Hannah, resisting the temptation to say anything else.

Jamie was less tactful. "That's ah, not working out too well so far," he said.

"Ah, but give it time," said Brox. "At least that is what I am told. This is a Simulant Interlocutor between Vixa and Alien Humans, but it has only just been initiated, just started adapting itself to human behaviors and appearance. I was assigned a similar 'unit' some days ago—built so as to resemble a Kendari, of course—and already it has achieved a high degree of function." Brox paused and looked again at the simulant. "That is to say, higher than this," he added drily.

"You make it sound like we need it for an interpreter or something," said Jamie. "Humans communicate okay with Vixa. Heck, even *I've* talked to Vixa without any big problems. What do we need an, ah, Interlocutor for?"

"You don't, mostly," said Kelly. "And you likely won't on this mission. I'm not all the way clear on this, but as I understand it, the Vixa we'll be dealing with will need it. Very high-ranking fellows, and all that."

"Wait a second," Hannah protested. "You mean like, Sixes?"

"Not only Sixes," said the Kendari. "Quite possibly Threes as well."

"Okay, I'm lost," said Jamie. "Could someone just back up a little and explain this a bit more?"

"I can," said Kelly, "but we don't have time for more than the ten-second version. The Vixa that humans usually deal with are Nines—nine-limbed Vixa, or maybe even Twelves—middle-rankers and low-status types. The six-limbed Vixa are the elite—and the three-limbers are more or less their royalty. And the elite and the royals can't be seen dealing with grubby little Younger Race beings like us. So they use Simulant Interlocutors like this one as go-betweens."

"I've never heard of any such thing," Hannah objected.

"It is a new policy," Brox said. "A new Preeminent Director has taken over, and has set about making changes. It is claimed that he is merely reinstituting the right and just laws that were in place the last time Younger Races erupted out into the starlanes." Brox hesitated, and then spoke further. "I do not wish to contradict you, Commander Kelly, but the ranks of the Vixa biocastes are far more complex than what you have suggested. There are subcastes and subrankings of all sorts, such that it is possible—though rare—for, example, a Nine to outrank a Six."

"Umm, I don't want to seem rude," said Jamie as he looked at the gently swaying simulant. "But I don't quite see how we're going to get a lot of talking done if we're working through our new friend."

"The situation is complicated and somewhat unclear, but suffice it to say you will do your own talking. The simulant's role is largely ceremonial. Furthermore, the simulant will adapt to you," said Brox. "It's already started reshaping itself to resemble human form. It will learn social cues from you, and it will integrate the various data stores that have been pumped into it. It will get better and better at its job." Brox glanced over at the simulant. "And the sooner the better, so far as I'm concerned. I might add that accepting the simulant is an absolute requirement. Refuse it, or exclude it from observing your work, and the arrangements will be terminated."

Kelly nodded. "I'm not going to refuse, and I'm ordering you two to cooperate with the simulant. They might do you some good. After all, dealing with Vixan Sixes and Threes can be somewhat—challenging."

"Challenging enough that there's a standing order that BSI agents not do it," said Jamie. "Not unless they've done a six-month course on Vixan protocol and another course on resisting torture."

Hannah found herself wishing that Jamie hadn't known about that standing order. If he did, he'd likely seen the case report that had led to its being instituted. The file wasn't pleasant reading.

"Well, consider that standing order countermanded for the duration of this mission," said Kelly.

"So now we know we'll be dealing with high-ranking Vixa, even though we shouldn't," said Hannah, "and we'll be working with Brox here, even though he's an enemy agent. No offense intended, Brox."

"None taken," Brox said.

"Good," said Hannah. "But with all that established, could you please tell us what the assignment actually is?"

"No," said Kelly, obviously very unhappy. "Because I don't know myself."

"Security is very tight," said Brox.

"So *you* know what the assignment is?" asked Jamie.

"Oh, yes," said Brox. "However, I am authorized to say very little at this time. I am permitted to say that I have been given the task of conducting Final Inquiries regarding an incident that has just taken place."

Hannah crossed her arms and let out a low whistle. "Final Inquiries" was what the Kendari Inquiries

Service called a death investigation. But no one launched Final Inquiries if the victim had died at home in advanced old age in his, her, or its sleep. It was obvious that Brox wasn't supposed to come out and say it was a murder investigation, but apparently it was all right for him to give very broad hints.

Brox went on. "I can tell you that it was the humans involved in the negotiations who suggested we keep the circle of knowledgeable personnel as tight as possible. They were the ones who suggested the tightly controlled brief in the interests of not endangering any more beings than necessary."

"But it *was* deemed necessary to endanger Special Agent Mendez and me?"

"Regrettably, yes. I must refrain from saying more. Explaining the form of the danger in question would in and of itself release potentially dangerous information."

"I don't like this," said Kelly. "In fact, let's just say that's one of the great understatements of the year. But my orders were very clear, very specific, and very emphatic. It's you two they want, and it is you two that they're going to get." She checked her pocket comm. "Good. Kosolov and the Quartermaster's Office are both reporting task complete. We're clear to go."

"Wait a second," Jamie protested. "You mean, that's the briefing? We're done? We can't even go back to our desks?"

"Right on all counts, Agent Mendez," said Kelly. "There's no time, there's no more information anyway, and now that you know as much as you do, the more we keep you two out of sight, the better. And that goes double for our guests. Maybe triple. So you're leaving. Now."

She turned, opened the door behind her, and led the

way down the corridor. Brox trotted along behind her. The simulant stomped along behind Brox, struggling to keep its balance and working hard to keep up with him. It somehow gave the impression that it was traveling blind, navigating mostly by luck. Hannah and Jamie brought up the rear, neither of them eager to get too close to the simulant. Part of it was simply the desire to avoid collision with the clumsy simulant—but that was far from all of it.

Hannah's subconscious had already decided the sim was not an intelligent being, but instead a thing, an object. It was a machine, like a bicycle, a computer, or a coat hook. There was no need to treat it with the respect due to an Elder Race xeno. But it wasn't that simple. Echoes, whispers, of the old Frankenstein story flitted about in her memory as she watched the awkward, lumbering *thing* moving ahead of them. She wasn't so sure how much the sim would facilitate communications—but it was going to do just fine at giving them nightmares.

Kelly was taking them on a roundabout route through the maze of corridors that made up BSI's orbiting headquarters, no doubt doing her best to keep their two unusual guests out of sight. She was leading them at a brisk enough pace that Hannah nearly missed one or two turns. At last, Kelly hustled them all into an elevator. The simulant walked straight into the back of the elevator car and stopped, with its face—or where its face would have been—right up against the rear wall. All three humans, and Brox as well, managed to find ways to get as far away from it as possible.

They reached the docking-bay deck and the elevator doors opened. They got off—the simulant simply walking in reverse rather than turning around first. *We're going to be cooped up in a starship with this thing for a week?* Hannah asked herself as she watched it do a sort of three-point turn before following along behind Brox.

That was the usual routine, at any rate. Get the briefing, rush like hell for the docking bay, and boost off to the crime scene, who knows how many light-years away. The only snag was that the journey from one star system to another took days, sometimes weeks. That was the reason for the hurried departure. You had to hurry, precisely because the trip would take so long.

But this time, Commander Kelly was taking things to an extreme. No briefing at all. No time to gather data or ask any questions. Only as they arrived at Docking Bay 27 did it dawn on Hannah that Bay 27 wasn't even big enough to service the *Sherlock*-class ships, the smallest interstellar craft the BSI used.

No briefing and no starship, either, Hannah realized with a shock as they entered the bay and saw the vehicle in it. She had heard Kelly talk about it, but it hadn't really registered. They were going aboard a jeep-tug, a pocket-sized vehicle made for the interorbit transfers of cargo or personnel. It was designed so its interior could be configured to carry any needed combination of cargo and people. At the moment, it was rigged with four human passenger chairs, and a sort of couch or pad for Brox. A collection of gear and supplies was stowed in the back, held down by cargo netting. Kelly was already climbing aboard the little craft.

"Hold it a second," said Jamie, standing in the docking bay and peering through the hatch of the jeep-tug. "Ah, ma'am? Commander Kelly? *You're* going on this mission?"

Kelly looked startled. "Me? No. No, of course not. I'm going to chauffeur you to your long-distance ride.

That way we don't have to waste time or take chances by briefing a pilot. Come on. Get aboard."

Brox was already halfway up the ramp. Jamie and Hannah followed him inside, sat down, and strapped in. The simulant paused at the base of the ramp, standing stock-still for a moment. Then it very deliberately leaned forward at its ankles—or at least where its ankles would be—before heading up the ramp, adjusting its internal balance to compensate for moving up a ramp. It clomped aboard, straightened up, then paused and seemed to consider the sight of Hannah and Jamie seated in the forward pair of passenger seats. It then shifted to look forward at Commander Kelly in the pilot's seat.

It shuffled awkwardly toward the second pair of passenger seats and positioned itself so it was standing, facing forward, directly in front of the starboard seat. It paused for a moment again, then abruptly folded itself at the knees and waist and dropped heavily into the seat.

Brox laid himself down on his cushioning pad and strapped himself in. "You will observe that our new friend is already adapting to human behaviors. Although it has no visible eyes, it has started to point its face at things it needs to look at. And I am fairly certain that is the first time it has ever actually sat in any sort of human chair or seat or bench."

"How exciting," said Jamie. "Our little android is all grown-up."

"I suppose that's nice to know," Hannah said. "Though I don't see what good it does us."

"Not a great deal—yet. But it would be worth bearing in mind that our friend is changing, developing— and doing it rapidly. You would be wise not to take it for granted or underestimate it."

"So noted," said Hannah. Brox had a point. The simulant was, in effect, learning to move like a human being, to act like a human being. And the more it moved like a human, the more likely they were to accept it, ignore it, perhaps even speak openly in front of it. They would have to assume it was capable of remembering or recording vision and sound and could transmit it or play it back later for its masters.

"Time to get moving, people," said Kelly. "I'm going to close the hatch. Everyone strapped in? I mean, except for the simulant?"

"We're all secure. What about the sim?" Jamie asked. "Should I try to latch its belts? It's just got those flipper things where its hands should be. I don't think it could work the mechanism, even if we managed to give it the idea."

"No," said Kelly. "It would probably just sit there passively if you tried—but it might have some sort of hair-trigger self-defense programming. Get too close and it might go nuts on us. I'll just fly us nice and easy. With a little luck, it won't need a seat belt. Besides, it looks like it would be pretty hard to damage. Here we go. Sealing the hatch."

The ramp retracted, the hatch swung itself to and sealed itself, and Kelly cast the little craft off from the side of the Center Transit Station. She moved them slowly away, piloting with the self-conscious precision of a senior officer who was not only out of practice but also nervous about making a spectacular mistake in front of subordinates and visitors.

Hannah had one thing at least figured out. The normal procedure would have been for them to board a BSI interstellar-capable ship from one of the docking bays and depart directly for their transit-jump point.

But Brox 231 must have come from somewhere, on some sort of ship—presumably his own. And if Kelly had been a little twitchy about having a Kendari Inquirist in the BSI Bullpen, she no doubt would have been ten times as unhappy to have a Kendari Inquiry Service starship docking to BSI HQ. Brox must have left his ship in a parking orbit and come to the station on this or some other jeep-tug.

But Hannah didn't even know for sure that Brox had arrived via starship. There were Kendari installations on Center, the planet that Center Transit Station orbited. They might be about to dock with some sort of ground-to-orbit vehicle.

The jeep-tug boosted away from the station. Hannah checked the time. "Well, that's a new personal record for me," she said. "We're departing forty-two minutes after the completion of briefing."

"What briefing?" Jamie asked. "We haven't been told anything."

"All right," said Hannah. "*Two* personal records. Fastest departure, and departure with the least information."

"The second one is going to be tough to break," Jamie said sourly. "How can you get less than zero?" He swiveled around in his seat to look back toward Brox. "What more do you know that you can tell us?"

"I know a great deal more," said Brox. "In fact, it's safe to say that I know all there is to know at this stage. But I cannot tell you any of it—or even tell you why I cannot tell you. There was no time to work out a nuanced agreement that considered how much or how little information I could give out, or how much detail I could provide."

"All or nothing, huh?" Jamie said.

"Can you at least tell us when you'll be able to say more?" Hannah asked.

"No. Absurd, of course, but there it is. There simply was no chance to work out how I should respond to any such perfectly sensible questions. In fact, I was specifically instructed to make the most literal-minded possible interpretation of the agreement."

It was obvious that there wasn't any point in asking with whom Brox had negotiated, or when, or where. Hannah gave up—and shook her head to Jamie when he opened his mouth to prod further. No point in pushing Brox too far and getting him feeling put-upon and out of sorts before the case had even begun.

The only viewports on the jeep-tug were at the forward end, in the pilot's station, and Hannah couldn't see a great deal. She turned her head to look forward and peek over Kelly's shoulder through the pilot's viewport.

At first there was very little to see besides the background of stars rolling past as the jeep-tug came about to its new heading. Then the lateral movement stopped, and the stars stood still in the viewport. One bright dot of silvery light, right in the center of the field of view, seemed larger than the others. It had to be the ship that they were heading toward. Hannah was mildly surprised that she was able to spot it with her naked eye so easily. It must either be awfully close to Center Transit Station—a lot closer than they usually permitted uncleared ships—or else it had to be big. She craned her neck around to check Kelly's nav display and gasped. Very, very big. For it to be visible at their present range, the ship would have to be at least as big *as* Center Transit Station itself, and CTS was something like a kilometer across.

"Caught you peeking, Hannah," Kelly said, glancing over her shoulder. "That's enough backseat driving for now."

"Ah, yes, ma'am. Sorry."

"Don't apologize. I want my Senior Special Agents to be inquisitive. But I'm under some to-be-taken-literally orders myself. However, now that we're all safely aboard and clear of the Station, I *can* tell you a few things that aren't covered by those orders— information from sources other than those covered by the keep-quiet orders."

Kelly checked her controls, locked them, then swiveled around in her seat to face her passengers. "Seems that about three hours ago, Center System Defense Command got a QuickBeam message from a certain party, a trusted party, on Tifinda, the Vixan home world. All sorts of authenticators and encryption sequences and so on, to prove it was from who it claimed to be from, and warning us that a very big, very fast ship was about to arrive, and that it was not, repeat not, an attack. The message included coordinates for the ship's arrival in system and flight-path data for its transit through the system to planetary orbit around Center.

"It was obvious that there was some sort of mistake, as the data showed that the ship would arrive about five times closer to CenterStar than any possible transit point, and showed the ship accelerating to more than ninety percent of the speed of light just about instantaneously, heading straight for the planet Center, then stopping dead, decelerating to orbital velocity in less than a heartbeat.

"Then, sure enough, a ship arrived exactly at the predicted, utterly impossible, coordinates and flew right down the middle of the couldn't-be-right flight path—and, to make a long story short, it's the ship you see straight ahead of us. If not for the warning message from the certain party, Center System Defense Command would have—and should have—opened fire. My guess is that there were plenty of twitchy fingers near the triggers even with the warning." Kelly frowned thoughtfully. "It's damned lucky they didn't fire. Their weapons probably couldn't have hit anything moving that fast anyway, but just shooting at that ship could have made things about six times worse than they already are."

"More than six times worse, I assure you, Commander Kelly," said Brox. "It would likely have meant war with the—ah, owners of that ship. That war would not have lasted long, or gone well for you. It was likely lucky for my people as well. In my opinion, at least, whatever advantage there might have been for us Kendari, if humanity *were* eliminated, it could only have been short-term. It would have been a question of *where* and *when,* not *if,* there would be a flash-point incident for us as well."

That was a bit of cold-blooded analysis that Hannah could have done without hearing.

"You, ah, used the past tense there," said Jamie. "So if Defense Command had taken a potshot at that ship earlier today, humanity would already have been *eliminated*?"

"Oh, no. Not yet. Not so quickly. It would likely take the Elder Races almost a quarter of an Earth year, at the very least. But, as I said, that would do us Kendari little good if they next turned their attention toward us—and the odds of some peripheral incident or another getting out of hand and causing that would be very high indeed. Or else some Elder Race species might just decide on its own that getting rid of one

Younger Race species was really just a good start—and why not wipe out both of the dreary little nuisances, so long as they were at it?"

Jamie furrowed his eyebrows. "So you believe it's likely that both of our species avoided extinction this morning, and nobody knows about it?"

"A *few* beings know about it," said Brox, "and one can never be *certain* what would have happened, but yes, that is essentially the case."

"Well, no point, and no time, to worry about it now," said Hannah. She pointed out the viewport. "The Kendari don't have ships like that. Up until five minutes ago, I'd have said nobody does. Where did it come from?"

"It's a Vixan ship," said Kelly. "And nobody knew about it—except the Defense Command—until it showed up. Apparently, they don't use it much. They can't afford to. Requires too much energy expenditure. Too expensive to operate, except in emergencies."

"A ship the *Vixa* can't afford to fly?" Hannah asked. "Ouch." Both the Younger Races, humans and Kendari alike, had, over the years, come to assume that the myriad Elder Races had the technology to do whatever they wanted, whenever they wanted.

In a way, even the apparent exceptions proved the rule. The Reqwar Pavlat might be incapable of decrypting genetic kill switches—but only because they had deliberately renounced whole fields of knowledge in deference to their traditions. And it was not that the Metrans were unable to extend their own life spans, so much as that they so firmly believed it was impossible that they did not try—and once they did try, they succeeded.

And even those were examples of cultures that were *unwilling* to alter themselves—not unable. The belief in Elder Race omnipotence had more to do with outward-looking technology—physics, power generation, transportation, speed, manufacturing. The idea that any such thing might be difficult or expensive for *any* Elder Race species was startling, but for the Vixa, it was only more so.

If there was a superpower among the Elder Races, it would have to be the Vixa. Their ships, their machines, their cities, were the gleaming exemplars of what humans, at least, expected of a race of all-powerful aliens. The idea that any sort of spacecraft would be difficult for *them* to afford was daunting enough. That someone, presumably the Vixa themselves, had dispatched a Kendari aboard such a ship, and sent it to collect not just a couple of BSI agents, but, specifically and by name, Senior Special Agent Hannah Wolfson and Special Agent James Mendez, went well into the overwhelming and intimidating range.

The ship out there was getting closer—and larger. Hannah watched as it grew from a point of light to a fat dot to a featureless golden sphere, gleaming in the darkness. It was obvious that she had grossly underestimated its size. It was far, far bigger than any such paltry object as Center Transit Station. Some objects that size were classified as minor planets.

No one aboard the jeep-tug spoke as the Vixan ship swelled in the viewport, and filled it completely. There, at last, at its center, there was a tiny flicker of movement as an access hatch irised open. "Second time today I've had to fly into that little hole," Kelly grumbled as she swung her seat around, locked it down, and concentrated on her controls.

The "little hole" swelled larger and larger as the jeep-tug made its slow final approach, then flew straight into it and through a featureless tunnel, with walls the same satiny golden color of the spherical ship's outer hull. The tunnel was about a hundred meters or so long. The jeep-tug exited the tunnel's interior and arrived in a large compartment. Kelly extended the landing gear, engaged the vertical thrusters, and brought the little vehicle into a landing on the featureless golden deck.

"Checking external environment," Kelly announced, looking at her displays. "Air mix, air pressure, and gravity levels matched to Earth-normal. All the comforts of home."

"They *were* matched to Kendal standard when it was just me," Brox said, plainly amused. "It would seem our hosts are more concerned about making you comfortable now."

When it was just Brox? Hannah frowned. That was just the start of her questions. When had Brox come aboard? And where? And why were the high-and-mighty Vixa chauffeuring Younger Race nobodies around the Galaxy? "Hold it a second," she said. "If the briefing for this operation is supposed to be on a need-to-know basis, then, I think we're there now. I need to know."

"Yeah, but *I* don't need to know," said Kelly.

"The Commandant is quite right," said Brox. "She has been ordered to limit her own knowledge of the situation as much as possible. I can provide a limited briefing to you, soon, after her departure. I am not permitted to provide you full information until we have arrived at the—at our destination."

"So let's get you off this bus and get your gear out and let me be on my way," said Kelly. "That's the surest way to let all of us get what we want the fastest way possible."

Commander Kelly popped the hatch and led the way out onto the deck of the Vixan ship. Hannah and Jamie grabbed their Ready-To-Go duffels and got out as well, with the simulant following awkwardly, and Brox taking up the rear.

A pair of charcoal-grey platforms with rounded-off corners, roughly the size and shape of midsized mattresses, came floating up toward them as they disembarked. They stopped about five meters away from the jeep-tug, hanging in midair about a meter off the ground.

"Put on there," said the sim, directing a flipper-arm in the direction of what were obviously cargo carriers. Jamie shrugged at Hannah and dropped his RTG duffel on the closer of the two carriers, then went back for the rest of the stuff.

The three humans did the cargo-lugging, as Brox wasn't really the right size or shape to get in and out of the jeep-tug gracefully, and it was obvious that getting the sim to understand what to do would take far longer than just doing it themselves. It took a trip or two to get the small stack of supplies out of the jeep-tug, but the job was done in a couple of minutes.

Kelly came out with one last box of rations and handed them to Hannah. "Well," said Kelly, "I could make a long speech telling you how I'm not allowed to tell you anything, but—what's the point?"

"Agreed," said Hannah.

"I don't like this," said Kelly. "I've got a feeling that if I knew more, I'd like it even less. But what I do know for certain is that the stakes are high, that this is the right thing to do—and we don't have much choice in the matter anyway."

Kelly patted Hannah on the shoulder, nodded at

Jamie, then gave a mock salute to both of them. "Good luck," she said. "From here on in, you're on your own."

And she turned and climbed back aboard the jeep-tug.

TWO

POWER AND SPEED

Jamie watched as the jeep-tug lifted off, turned itself around, and flew silently into the access tunnel. The tunnel hatch irised shut so smoothly and perfectly that it was difficult to see where the hatch was after it closed.

They were standing roughly in the center of a large, cylindrical compartment, thirty meters in diameter and twenty meters high. The cylindrical wall, the deck, and the overhead bulkhead were all made of the same golden-bronze material. There were three large hatches equally spaced around the perimeter of the chamber. Smaller circular hatches were between the larger ones.

There was nothing, absolutely nothing in the chamber but themselves and their pile of supplies. Somehow, every sound seemed muffled and deadened, though the space was custom-made for echoes. Jamie found himself squinting, his eyes straining, as they struggled to find some sort of detail to focus on in all that featureless bronze. The room was lit by some unseen source of utterly diffuse and shadowless light. He had the odd sense that they were all floating in midair in a strange golden sky.

"I asked you once," Jamie said to Hannah, "if you ever got used to the sense of disorientation. I'm coming to realize just how dumb a question *that* was. If you asked me my own name right about now, I doubt I'd be able to tell you."

"Join the club," said Hannah. She turned to Brox. "Okay," she said. "We're here, wherever that is. We're about to get under way to where we're going, wherever *that* is. There is no way we can report back to anyone. So can you brief us now?"

"I can go so far as to confirm the various quite obvious conclusions you have no doubt reached already. A very serious crisis has arisen, under circumstances that involve not only your people, and mine—but the Vixa as well. Beyond that, I regret that I cannot go any further at this time," said Brox.

"Why not?" Jamie asked.

"Because there is, at least in theory, a way you *can* report back. Until we depart Center System, it is possible that you could be carrying some sort of transmitter. It is conceivable that a device hidden in your clothing or supplies is transmitting audio or video or some other sort of data back to BSI HQ." Brox held up his hands to stop Jamie's and Hannah's protests before they could begin. "*I* know and *you* know that any such idea is absurd. I *also* know that *you* know that it would be virtually impossible for a concealed miniature transmitter to punch a signal through the mass of the ship we are in. And so on, and so on. But there it is. Orders are orders."

"And paranoia is paranoia, and sometimes orders are absurd orders," said Jamie.

"I quite agree. But there are certain powerful parties involved," said Brox, and gestured toward the ship all around them. "I think it might be wise to humor them. And before you can ask, I am not so much as permitted to tell you *when* I can tell you more. For what it is worth, I will stretch a point far enough to say that all parties involved—and, I should add, most especially the human officials—urgently desire that news concerning the case be kept contained, compartmentalized, as long as possible. If certain details were to reach human news services prematurely, it could be very bad for everyone—but especially so for humans."

Brox hesitated, then spoke once again. "I would also ask you to consider that a failure to cooperate might not merely endanger yourselves."

Jamie's eyes widened. *In other words,* Brox was saying, *get them mad—whoever, exactly, they were—and they might blame me, or our people for it, and get very unpleasant.* "We get the point," he said. "You'll tell us as much as you can, as soon as you can. But that to one side—what do we do now?"

"You come me with," said a voice from behind them, speaking in an oddly accented, gravelly imitation of Brox's voice. Jamie and Hannah turned to see another Kendari—another Brox. Slightly distorted, not quite right in some subtle details, but Brox all the same. The shape was a little off. The neck was a trifle too short and stiff, and the legs too thick. It was pudgier than Brox, and it had a bulge, almost like a small camel's hump, on its back. At first Jamie thought there was something wrong with his eyes, that he was seeing double. But then he got it.

"Of course," said Hannah. "Your simulant. But yours is more developed than ours."

"Quite right," said Brox.

"You *all now* come me with," said Brox's sim.

"Yes, come you all," the humanoid sim agreed, walking stiffly forward to stand by his counterpart.

"Still working on syntax and word order, obviously," said Brox. "Odd they don't preprogram Lesser Trade Speech, but never mind. Let us follow."

"Do you think we should just leave all our gear on the floaters?" Jamie asked.

"No," said Hannah, in a very sarcastic tone. "We should take everything we just put on the floaters off, carry it ourselves, let the floaters follow us empty, then put everything back on them when we get where we're going."

"Brilliant repartee, partner," said Jamie. "But let's think about it before we leave our food and clothes and gear behind. We've lost all our luggage before—and we're not exactly communicating perfectly with the locals. Suppose that they carry it off to some storage locker and we don't see any of it again for two weeks? I'd feel better with a change of underwear and a toothbrush and a little something to eat in my pockets. Just to tide us over while the previously scheduled unforeseen circumstances are sorted out."

He went over to his RTG duffel, zipped it open, grabbed a couple of mealpacks and bottles of water from the crates of rations, and rummaged around inside the bag for a few other things. Next he pulled out a vest that was made mostly out of pockets into which he started stuffing his supplies. Hannah watched for a second, then went over to her own RTG and started to follow suit. "That is unlikely to be necessary," said Brox.

"No offense, Brox, but Jamie's got a point. We've gotten unpleasant surprises before."

"All set?" Jamie asked.

"How could I be when we don't know what comes next?" asked Hannah, stuffing a few more foodbars into her vest. "But let's go."

Jamie reached into his duffel one last time, as casually as he could, and hoped it looked like he was just squaring away the contents before closing it up. He managed to activate the hidden control without being obvious about it. *No, Brox,* he thought, *we don't have hidden transmitters. But you weren't all that far wrong.* He was nearly certain that Hannah had switched on the recorder hidden in her bag as well, but he wasn't about to ask.

The Kendarian and humanoid sims led the way down the corridor. It was about fifty meters long, and ended in a circular hatch that irised open as they approached. The sims stepped over the edge of the hatch and into a mazelike compartment full of intimidatingly complex fittings and gleaming equipment that was impossible to make sense of at first, other than gathering a general impression of silvery, mirror-bright metal and a whole constellation of glowing and blinking indicator lights. Jamie and Hannah followed cautiously, and Jamie turned to watch Brox entering last of all.

The hatch whispered shut the moment the Kendari's tail was through it, almost close enough to slice off a bit of it. He flicked it away, almost too late, and looked at Jamie. "Our host would seem to be in a hurry," he said in a low voice, before speaking again in louder tones, to the open air. "As you can see, we are arrived, SubPilot Greveltra. As per our agreement, I now give you formal permission to proceed."

"Conditions are not yet suitable," said a voice from somewhere inside the compartment. "The human's small transport vehicle ceased acceleration after reaching only a very limited relative velocity. It has not cleared the minimum safe operating distance standard."

"Then, obviously, proceed when all safety conditions are met," Brox said, a note of irritation in his voice.

"Your authorization is noted and accepted."

Brox looked toward Hannah and Jamie. "If you find rule-bound behavior and similar traits as irritating as I do, I fear you are in for an unpleasant journey. Come along."

The two sims stood—utterly inert, out of the way—by the outer wall of the compartment, drooping over a bit, almost like inflatable toys that had developed slow leaks. Whatever, exactly, they were and were for, they had plainly been deactivated for the moment, and Jamie dismissed them from his thoughts. There was plenty else to worry about.

He was starting to make a bit more sense of the compartment's interior. They were in a spherical chamber, maybe thirty meters in diameter, and the decking they were standing on cut right through its center. Jamie decided to think of the desk as the equator and the top of the sphere as the north pole. There were conduits and openings on the floor decking. Jamie could see bits of the lower, "southern," half of the sphere below. The skin of the sphere itself was a milky grey that Jamie had seen before on other Elder Race hardware. It was the "neutral" default-setting color of a material that could be adjusted to appear any color, or serve as a video display, or set to full or partial transparency.

Big, boxy, gleaming cubes and cylinders and other shapes, most about three meters tall or so, were bolted to the midway deck so as to form a series of narrow passageways between them. Jamie had no idea what the machines did, but they looked businesslike enough. Some hummed, one generated a static field powerful enough to set Jamie's hair on end, and several threw a fair amount of heat, while another was cold enough for frost to have formed on it. It struck

Jamie that they were in a place meant for machinery, not for people.

Brox led them out into a central open space, with what was obviously a pilot's station at the exact center of the sphere. Standing by the controls was a—a being of some sort.

Since they were aboard a Vixan ship, with two simulants that had been created by the Vixa, the xeno in front of them had to be a Vixan as well—but it didn't look like any sort of Vixan Jamie had ever seen or heard tell of.

The Vixa *he* had seen resembled giant nine-legged or twelve-legged starfish, though some said they looked more like a cross between a spider and an octopus.

That sort of Vixa looked enough like certain Stanlarr Consortia components that Jamie wondered if the Stanlarr had borrowed some Vixan genetic material to make them. But, for all Jamie knew, the Stanlarr might have visited Earth, captured some starfish, and used those instead. Radial symmetry was far from an unusual feature of biological design in the galaxy. It had evolved many times, in many places.

But Stanlarr components, spiders, octopi, and starfish, did not have internal skeletal structures. Vixa were simply too big to get along with just muscle power holding them up. Jamie had seen diagrams of Vixan skeletons. Each limb was supported by a central core of hinged-together bones that resembled a superflexible human spinal column. On a nine-limbed Vixa, the front three limbs served as arms, shorter and more flexible than the side and rear legs. Each arm ended in a three-fingered hand capable of very fine manipulation. On a twelve-legger, the front four limbs served as arms, and had similar three-fingered hands.

Vixa were also well equipped with eyes: There was one just above the point on the body where each leg joined to the central body—on the shoulder, if Vixa had had shoulders. There was another eye on the upper surface of each limb, more or less where the knees or elbows would have been. There were also eyes in the manipulator arms, in what corresponded to the wrists.

According to BSI's briefing books on the Vixa, the eyes on the shoulders and midjoint were barely more than light sensors, able to distinguish light and dark, but not much more than that. It would be very hard for anyone to sneak up on a Vixan, but the Vixan wouldn't be able to give a very good description of the attacker. The eyes in the wrists of the manipulator arms were much more acute, but were really best suited to close-in work. Vixa did not have particularly good distance vision.

The twelve-leggers were generally stronger and less graceful than the Nines, and their hands seemed better suited to heavy lifting than fine work. Sixes were the social betters of the Nines, an arrangement that both subspecies accepted completely.

But virtually none of all that general description applied to the being they now faced. It was as if someone had fished around in a bin full of standard Vixan parts and used them to build something else. At first Jamie thought it was three three-legged Vixa standing one on top of another, until he realized that it was all one creature, with a columnar central body core that sprouted three sets of three limbs each. The upper surfaces of the body were all a deep purple or violet, while the lower surfaces were all a pasty bluish white.

The lower three limbs were short, squat, and muscular, plainly dedicated to locomotion. The middle three were longer and more flexible, with much more developed three-fingered hands. The three upper limbs were shorter, but highly flexible, with the hand-eye structure modified into little more than oversized eyes on tentacles, the fingers short, stubby, almost vestigial. If on a "standard" Vixan the functions of movement, manipulation, and sight were all present on all the limbs, on this model Vixan the limbs had all been modified to specialize in one job each.

"I present SubPilot Greveltra, eighty-third known of that designation, of the Founder's Pillar Clanline, Tifinda," Brox said gravely. "He may be addressed as SubPilot."

"Ah, hello, SubPilot," said Hannah. "I present myself, Senior Special Agent Hannah Wolfson, and my colleague, Special Agent James Mendez. We may be addressed as Wolfson and Mendez."

There was a long silence, which lasted until Brox spoke. "Excuse me. My error. The SubPilot will not address you at all. My briefing on such matters of etiquette was quite rushed. By the standards of the Vixa, my species, the Kendari, is senior to yours, because it made contact with the Elder Races a few years earlier—but, of course, the Vixa are senior to the Kendari. The SubPilot does not have clearance to address anyone two levels of rank beneath himself."

"*That's* going to make it difficult to have much conversation with the natives," Jamie observed.

"Other Vixa will have greater latitude, or will be granted waivers for purposes of required contact. The prohibition does not apply if there is no one of intermediate rank present, or in the event of emergency."

"So if you weren't here, the SubPilot *would* speak to us," Hannah suggested.

"But I'm going to guess he wouldn't enjoy it," Jamie added.

"You are both correct," Brox replied, a tone of amusement in his voice. "However, if only one lower-ranking species is present, the SubPilot would address only those of the most senior rank within that species. He would speak with you, Agent Wolfson, but not with Agent Mendez."

"Right," said Jamie. "Tell me, Brox—do you ever wonder how it is the Elder Races ever get anything done? I mean, besides inventing rules and customs and traditions that prevent anything from happening?"

"I would remind you that the SubPilot can hear you perfectly well and understands your speech. He merely refuses to address you. Perhaps it would not be wise to insult him."

"Maybe it would be wise if he did not insult us," Jamie replied. "We've just been rousted out of our offices and hustled onto a starship the size of a midsized asteroid in order to rush to the scene of some unspecified crime. Someone would seem to need us very badly—and the Vixa are going to a lot of effort. But the first thing that happens is that we're told that we're not fit to speak with them."

He glanced at Hannah, half-expecting her to be signaling him to back down. But if anything, her expression seemed to be encouraging him. "If the Vixa want our help, they will have to provide us with sufficient support, cooperation—and respect."

"That is almost word for word the speech I made to a certain Vixan official not so many medium social duration units ago," Brox said. "Except, of course, I was telling them all those things about the Kendari."

"The small slow human vehicle has now achieved a safe distance from the *Eminent Concordance*," SubPilot

Greveltra announced, giving no sign at all that he heard any of what Jamie or Brox had said. "I will now commence maneuvers. Transport module to navigation station."

Greveltra's trio of midbody limbs whipped around with startling speed and flickered over the control panels. Suddenly the whole compartment lurched to one side, and Jamie felt the sickening drop in his stomach he got whenever he rode a high-speed elevator that was a little too high-speed.

"Perhaps it would be best to deopacify the hull to make the procedure clearer," said Brox.

Another midbody limb whipped over to another control on another panel—and suddenly the compartment hull vanished altogether. Looking up with a gasp, Jamie saw that they were moving, and fast. What he had assumed was a compartment with a fixed position inside the ship was in fact something closer to an elevator car—and they were riding it straight up a cylindrical shaft.

"I should explain," Brox said mildly. "The outer sphere we observed as we approached the *Eminent Concordance* is merely the propulsion unit, plus the power store for the ship and shielding. This smaller sphere comprises the crew compartment, the passenger space, life support, cargo space, the piloting systems, and so on."

Jamie thought for a moment, and recalled his history-of-technology classes, and the lectures on the early days of spaceflight, when they had to jettison everything the moment they were done with it in order to save weight. "So this little sphere here is the, ah, command module, and all the rest of this giant ship is the service module? All of it is nothing more than a way to carry this little sphere around?"

"That is it precisely."

"That's insane," said Hannah.

"Not in an emergency," said Brox. "Not to a species that has the technical and material resources that the Vixa have."

"Why does the ah, command sphere, move around inside the ship?"

Brox cocked his head to one side, obviously amused. "I should have made a transcript of my conversation with the SubPilot on the way here. I could have simply handed it to you to read. You are asking almost all the same questions I asked—and just about in the same order. The SubPilot explained that it is done to achieve a balance of safety and capability, with the sphere shifting positions as required by each phase of the mission. In order to achieve maximum safety from exterior radiation, to defend the command sphere against attack, and to permit the easy access of passengers and cargo, it is positioned in the center of the sphere whenever the combined vehicle is not actively maneuvering. During periods when precise navigation is required, and during periods when the high-velocity drive is active, the sphere is moved forward to the navigation blister."

"And that's where we're going now," Hannah suggested.

"Exactly."

At the moment, the command sphere came to a sudden halt with a rattly *bang*, lurching hard enough that Jamie was nearly knocked off his feet. Then the whole sphere took off again, moving sideways, starting up fast enough that Hannah had to grab at Jamie's arm to stay upright. They stayed braced together, and it was a good thing they did. A few seconds later, they came to another too-abrupt halt, then resumed their upward movement.

"They're not much for acceleration compensators, are they?" Hannah grumbled.

"Their compensators work on the ship as a whole. The Vixa are not much bothered by sudden, minor stops and starts, and, as a safety measure to avoid field interference difficulties, they often do not activate the command sphere's compensators."

"What did you do, Brox," Jamie asked, "memorize their technical manuals?"

"No. I am just trying to answer your questions as diplomatically as possible—having asked them myself not so long ago. And I have been dealing with the Vixa for some time now. I have learned something about their attitudes."

"What's had you dealing with the Vixa?" Jamie asked.

SubPilot Greveltra was directing two of his three eyestalks at Brox, and Brox tossed his head in the Vixan's direction. "I may have said little, but I have said too much already," said the Kendari.

"You may commence limited discussion soon," SubPilot Greveltra announced. "Our high-velocity drive will provide sufficient signal interference, and you will be able to provide a briefing on the general political situation."

"*Political* situation?"

"I think, perhaps, SubPilot Greveltra might also have said too much while saying too little," Brox replied. He looked up, through the overhead dome of the sphere. "But we are approaching the blister. There will not be much longer to wait."

Jamie and Hannah looked up as well. Overhead, they could see that the vertical shaft they were traveling through ended in another, larger hatch. Jamie half expected Greveltra to barrel on through at full speed, trusting the machinery to flick the hatch open at the last possible moment, but instead he brought their sphere to an abrupt halt well aft of the hatch, waited for it to open fully, then started up again with a lurch. There were two more hatches after the first one, and the command sphere followed the same pattern going through all of them. It was like riding on a rickety old antique manually operated tram at a transportation museum—on a day when the tram operator was in a bad mood.

Beyond the first hatch, and the second, was more vertical shaft. But beyond the third was—nothing. Just an empty hole, out into space.

The command sphere slowed to a crawl, and eased to a halt when the floor of the deck they were standing on was exactly flush with the hull outside. The clutter of machines and hardware around the perimeter of the sphere obscured the view toward the apparent horizon. But the view overhead was breathtaking. The outer dome itself was utterly, flawlessly transparent, with no smudge of dirt or shimmer of reflection to spoil the illusion that it was not there at all. The planet Center hung in darkness and glory before them, ten times, a hundred times, the size of the Moon as seen from Earth. The planet was almost in full phase, a gleaming ball of swirling blue water, shimmering white clouds framing the lush greens and sturdy browns and tans of the land surface.

Hanging in the middle distance, riding the rim of the world, was the dazzling, complex shape of Center Transit Station, home of BSI's orbital HQ, the Bullpen. Home, or the closest thing Jamie had to a home at the moment. Not much more than an hour before,

Hannah and he had been catching up on paperwork in the Bullpen. But that had been a very fast-moving hour. Things had changed, and then some.

"Commencing low-power acceleration safe-distancing maneuver," SubPilot Greveltra announced. Moments later, without any sensation of motion, without any shudder or vibration of any kind, the planet Center and Center Transit Station slid off to port side and rapidly receded out of view.

"Good Lord," said Hannah, speaking in a half whisper, and in English, with words meant for Jamie's ears alone. "And that's their *low*-power acceleration. How many gees do you think we're doing right now, to get past the whole planet in just a few seconds?"

With a start, Jamie realized that he had taken on the unconscious assumption that he was seeing something on the scale of a boat sailing past an island, or an aircraft passing over a city. They had just accelerated from near-zero relative velocity to a speed of many hundreds or maybe thousands of kilometers a second in less time than it would take him to walk once around the Bullpen. "This ship is big enough that it's got to be naked-eye visible from the surface of Center," Jamie said. "And it must be sending every radar system pegging off-scale high all over the CenterStar system. Can you imagine how much they must be freaking out down there?"

"Just about as much as we are up here," Hannah said, still more or less whispering. "Every once in a while it just gets rubbed in our faces, doesn't it? The sheer, effortless, incredible raw *power* that the Elder Races have."

"Indeed it has that effect," Brox said, speaking in pretty fair English himself. "Please note that I answer this rhetoric question to be good sport, and to remind you that many of my fellow Inquirists know English just finely."

"And to remind us you have good ears as well," said Jamie, shifting back to Lesser Trade Speech. *And recording devices so his people can play it all back later if need be.* He realized that Brox was doing something else as well—sending a signal that, this time at least, they were all on the same team.

But he was also putting them in the habit of deferring to him, turning to him for information, accepting him as their guide, even their leader. Jamie could have recited word for word the warnings that Hannah would have given him if they had been free to speak.

And though Brox was quite literally an enemy agent, Jamie and Hannah had every reason to believe he was also an honorable and trustworthy adversary. Until the moment came when they couldn't trust him any longer. *Just because things were complicated on the surface, that didn't mean they weren't even more complicated underneath,* Jamie told himself.

"Safe distance and thrust vector now achieved," SubPilot Greveltra announced. "Commencing primary acceleration maneuver."

"Look up," Brox said in a low voice. "You wouldn't want to miss this."

Jamie and Hannah turned their heads upward toward the gleaming stars, the swirling glory in the blackness—and watched as the sky began to melt.

It was the stars directly overhead, at the zenith, that first started to smear, to stretch, to blur, shift in color toward the blue, and fade to nothing. But the contagion spread outward from there, more and more stars smearing, spreading, growing dimmer and bluer.

After only a few minutes, all the overhead stars had

vanished altogether, and those near the horizon were mere compressed, misshapen blurs.

Jamie understood what was happening. As a spacecraft moved faster and faster, and got closer and closer to the speed of light, the light from stars directly in the line of travel was affected so strongly by blueshifting as to vanish altogether, while the light of stars that were merely close to the direction of travel were affected to a lesser degree. The closer your ship got to the speed of light, the more pronounced and dramatic the effect.

But on even the most powerful human-built ships, or for that matter, on any xeno-built ship Jamie had ever heard of, it took days, or at least hours, to generate enough velocity for the effect to be noticeable, let alone significant. The transition happened too slowly for the eye to notice. For any ship, to say nothing of a ship of this size, to accelerate from effectively motionless to a velocity this close to light-speed in a matter of a few seconds would require unspeakable amounts of power, power that they were expending in order to get James Mendez and Hannah Wolfson somewhere in one hell of a hurry.

What had happened? Why were they so short of time?

Time. Suddenly it struck him. Blueshifting wasn't the only effect of moving at near light-speed. "Time dilation," he said to Hannah. "A lot of it."

"Quite right," said Brox. "To an outside observer, measuring in human units, our whole journey will appear to take about seven hours. But so far as we are concerned, we'll be there in something like four hours."

Brox sat down on the deckplates, calmly folding his legs under himself and wrapping his tail around his body as if he were some giant, self-satisfied cat. "So," he said, "We are flying in a vehicle as massive as a small moon, we are shielded from all detectors by the full mass of the vehicle itself, as well as by the primary drive radiation—which is so intense the command sphere has shifted to the forward end to get as far from it as possible—and by the fact that we have just accelerated, in a matter of seconds, to roughly eight-ninths of the speed of light. I would expect there are all sorts of jamming and silencing systems running as well.

"However, as noted, our Vixa friends feel we are not yet *quite* secure enough for me to brief you on the specific situation. But perhaps you can suggest something else for us to talk about in the meanwhile, so as to pass the time away.

"Do you have any suggestions?"

THREE

THE PLANETS ON THE TABLE

Hannah smiled, shook her head, and sat down tailor fashion on the deck facing Brox. Jamie did the same. "I can't think of a single thing we need to talk about," said Hannah. "Maybe we should just stare at each other until we get there."

"It would be an unsuitable use of the time to stare at each other," SubPilot Greveltra announced. "Inquirist Brox must perform a briefing."

"It would appear that SubPilot Greveltra *can* acknowledge your existence," said Brox, "and also that he lacks a sense of irony. But before you warn *me* about insulting our powerful host, I would assure you he takes that last statement as a strong compliment." Brox paused thoughtfully for a moment. "If anything, he is unhappy about my *first* statement, that he can acknowledge you—but since it is self-evident that he did respond to your statement, even if he did not address you directly, and it is therefore a matter of fact, he is, by his own lights, forced to accept it. So he *can't* be insulted."

"I can think of plenty of humans who wouldn't be stopped by a little thing like that," said Hannah. "Anyway, the SubPilot does have a point, if not a sense of humor. You can at least brief us on the *general* situation now."

"And so I shall. But the *first* thing I will tell you is that you must not believe a single word I say. You will have the chance to get everything confirmed—or debunked—by your own people, and your own senses, your own efforts. Do so. Get all the facts—and all the versions of the facts—you can. The second thing I will tell you is that you might as well pay very strict attention to me, because I am certain that your own people will debrief you as carefully as they can, in an effort to squeeze out every drop of the information I am about to give you. *My* people will be doing more or less the same with me, concerning you two, Commander Kelly, and the other humans I've dealt with since the— event."

"In other words," said Hannah, "look forward to this being treated as a major situation. We'd gotten that impression already."

"So get on with it," said Jamie. "Start at the beginning, and let's go."

"Not the beginning," said Brox. "That might be a few million, even hundred million years ago. Back to when even the Elder Races weren't all that old. Leaving out a great deal of history, a star system, the Pentam System, has gone vacant. It is unusual for having not one, but two habitable planets, along with a number of other very attractive features. There have been meetings and negotiations going on since well before your race or mine came to the attention of the Elder Races, all revolving around who would be awarded the Pentam System—and who wouldn't. I won't propose going into the politics of the situation. To sum up, there were three or four shifting alliances, each made up of two or three Elder Races, each of which was mainly interested in making sure one or more of the other groups *didn't* get Pentam."

"*Two* habitable planets in *one* system?" Jamie

asked. "And you wouldn't *want* that for your own people?"

Brox shifted, unexpectedly, into his somewhat awkward English. "No. If you be Elder Race, you would not. Because having new worlds is too much trouble. Because things have been way they are long time, and change cause trouble. Because your species already is rich enough, has power enough. Elders say they *mature* enough not to want more just for sake of having." Brox paused briefly, then spoke again. "Kendari ask: What is maturity—What is decadence? Elder Races say things stay the same. Kendari ask—things stay the same or just *seem* the same? Kendari—and humans—say need new things, need challenge, to stay strong, stop decay."

Hannah knew what Brox was talking about. She and Jamie had seen it, and not so very long ago. An Elder Race could seem to have an utterly stable and secure society—and not even be aware of the slow rot setting in. It could be in a state of decline so slow it was undetectable. A species, like an individual being, never really stayed the same. If it did not evolve, it would decline. It had either to grow or contract, renew or decay. There was no middle ground.

A seemingly static society could become so utterly fragile, so unused to change, so incapable of adapting to it, that anything new or different could destroy it. Therefore, change of any sort—such as the arrival on the scene of the Younger Races, the humans and the Kendari—represented a very real threat. No wonder so many Elder Races were hostile to them. Hannah replied in English. "We view things in much the same way. Just bear in mind our hosts can record and translate, even if the SubPilot can't understand us."

Brox gestured dismissively. "I tell no secrets. Elder

Races know our opinions and laugh at them. Just not wish needlessly insult SubPilot to his face—if he can be said to have face."

"I thought you said he wouldn't be bothered by any statement that was factual," Jamie objected.

"Vixa find reason for anger if they need it. Be careful," Brox said, before shifting back to Lesser Trade Speech. "To continue, many alliances formed and broke up and shifted and so on. Ironically, they all accomplished their primary goals of preventing their rivals from taking over the Pentam System—but these were not permanent victories. Sooner or later, someone would settle Pentam, and undo the equilibrium. And then the Kendari emerged, followed not long after by the humans. Two small, weak races that posed no threat to anyone."

"Let me guess," said James. "They decided to give it to one of us—and *that* started the debate all over again."

"Exactly. But if any Elder Race that came to be seen as favoring the Kendari over the humans as regarding Pentam, or the humans over the Kendari, the other Elders would regard that as forming an alliance with that species, encouraging other Elder Races to support the other Younger Race, and so the whole weary cycle would begin again."

"My turn to fill in a few blanks," said Hannah. "The maneuvers, the deal-making, even to get things to the point where the various parties could negotiate about negotiating, took years, even decades. Since the ideal situation was for no one to have the Pentam System, there wasn't much incentive to hurry."

"Quite right."

"So the whole process was kept secret from all humans and Kendari until fairly recently, in order to keep the negotiations from becoming even more complex. At some very late, and very recent, point in the process, both Younger Races were informed of what was going on, and were politely told they could either participate under whatever conditions were dictated to them, or else the Pentam System would be awarded to the other race."

"Right again."

"And, finally, my guess would be, the Vixa were chosen to adjudicate the matter, because all sides trusted them and because they were known not to want the Pentam System for themselves."

"Your guesses begin to fail you. Half-correct, incorrect, and incorrect again," said Brox. "The Vixa weren't exactly chosen to decide the matter—they were chosen to preside over the decision and host the meeting. As you have no doubt gathered, we are en route to that meeting, on Tifinda, right now. But the Vixa were chosen for that role precisely because *no one* could trust them, because all sides knew, for certain, that the Vixa *did* want the Pentam System for themselves. You need to try harder to think like a member of an Elder Race."

Jamie laughed. "Which is what *she* tells *me* to do all the time. How does payback feel, Hannah?"

"I'll live with the pain, somehow," Hannah said mildly, before turning back to Brox. "*You* go ahead and explain how Elder Race beings think. Why put the Vixa in charge if no one trusted them?"

"Because then everyone else would be on the alert. They'd know to watch the Vixa and to be ready for tricks that would let the Vixa seize Pentam."

"But why would the Vixa accept the job?" Jamie asked. "What do they get out of it?"

"As I understand it, there are two main reasons.

First, it is an odd acknowledgment of their power, their prestige, and their skill at political maneuver. They enhanced their prestige merely by accepting the task. Secondly, it's a challenge to them as well. It would be a grand achievement indeed if, in spite of all the distrust and watchfulness, they somehow managed to get the Pentam System in the end."

"And 'the end' might be pretty far off," Hannah said. "An Elder Race can be patient. If they managed to set up a situation that would cause the Pentam System to come under their control a hundred years from now, that would probably suit them just fine."

"It would do more than that—it would enhance their prestige as schemers, plotters, diplomats tremendously," said Brox. "It is what most of the other Elder Races half expect the Vixa to attempt. It is something close to one of your sporting events, with the other Elder Races watching eagerly to see how the game is played and who will win."

"Right now, no one has the Pentam System, right?" Jamie asked.

"Correct."

"What happens if, somehow, the Vixa convinces both our people and yours *not* to take possession?"

"How would they manage that?" Hannah asked.

Jamie shrugged at Hannah. "Maybe with some real subtle politics. Maybe with bribes or threats—or by intimidating both sides by flying around a starship the size of an asteroid." He gestured back toward Brox. "Never mind how," he said. "Just suppose they managed it. What would happen?"

Brox grimaced. "I am, like yourselves, mainly a police officer, an investigator. All of us have had to play other roles as well, at times—including that of diplomat. But that does not make me an expert at such mat-

ters. I merely happen to know certain items of information you haven't learned yet. My somewhat-
informed guess would be that if, somehow, the Vixa
managed to chase both of us away—then, at the very
least, they would be in a very strong position to make
and enforce their own claim to the Pentam System.
Your question was astute, and on point. I am impressed that you thought to ask it."

"I don't get it," said Jamie. "All the Vixa I've ever
met before today have been very friendly, outgoing.
Quite pleasant. They aren't the sort of schemers you're
describing."

"Vixan diplomats are quite a different animal from
the Vixa we'll encounter," Brox said. "I speak literally.
Vixa are—well, let me just say they are highly variable,
and also remind you that you have met three different
Vixa—or at least Vixa-related creatures—today, and
they are quite different from one another."

"You have said enough!" Greveltra barked suddenly, in a voice loud enough to make them all jump.
"You have completed briefing on those matters you
are authorized to speak of before jump."

"Perhaps it was unwise to speak so much earlier in
a language the SubPilot does not understand," said
Brox. "It would appear to have made him suspicious.
But, no matter. I have already given the main points.
The rest can wait."

"People keep telling us that we can wait for the information in the middle of making us rush like mad,"
Jamie growled. "I don't suppose there would be any
objection if we mere lowly humans discussed matters
between ourselves? After all, if one thing is for certain,
it's that we don't have any information."

Jamie and Hannah both looked toward Greveltra,

but the SubPilot made no response. If anything, he was ignoring them as hard as he could.

"Silence equals consent," said Hannah.

"A dangerous assumption in general," said Brox. "But I think we can take it as such for the moment. Go. Talk. And, once again, my apologies for telling you so little. But I will feel much more comfortable if you arrived at the—ah—place we are going without having formed any preconceived notions."

Hannah and Jamie stood up and moved over to the corridor that led back to the hatch they had come through. They didn't know the half of it, not a quarter of it. Not yet. And the part they *did* know, the parts that they could guess at, were overwhelmingly big. But shaking all that off, pretending it wasn't there, wasn't just the professional way to act. In a situation like this, it was a survival skill. They simply couldn't afford to let their emotions kick in.

"Okay," Hannah said. "Evaluate. Cold and calm— and assume they can hear us, record us, translate later."

"We don't know anything secret," Jamie objected. "We don't know anything at all."

"Yeah, but let's keep good habits," Hannah said. "Maybe we know more than we know. Talk. Carefully."

"Okay," Jamie said. He paused for a moment. "Brox wouldn't have given us that history lesson if it didn't have anything to do with the case," he began. "And they—whoever 'they' are—wouldn't have sent Brox to brief us if the *Kendari* weren't involved—and they wouldn't have come to BSI—and us—if *humans* weren't involved."

"So," said Hannah, "the obvious conclusion is that whatever case we're meant to deal with involves humans and Kendari and the Pentam System—or at least it might affect negotiations about the Pentam System."

"Two *planets,* Hannah. Two whole habitable *planets.* Maybe a pair of Earth-plus tropical paradises—or maybe one is a frozen iceball that's barely warm enough at the equator, and the other is so hot that only the north and south poles are survivable. It doesn't matter. Two *worlds* that people can live on without building domes or underground habitats. Plus which, lots of people care who *doesn't* get Pentam. That tells me that, somehow, Pentam has strategic value. And Brox has as much as told us the list of candidates for who gets Pentam is down to humans and Kendari."

"So?"

"So what if solving the case—whatever the case is—gets in the way of humans claiming two whole worlds? Or suppose cracking the case gets in the way of keeping the *Kendari* from snatching them? And let's just bear in mind that our old dear honorable friend and enemy Brox 231 is playing the game for the same stakes we are—but he has a *lot* more information than we do. He's going to have all the same motives, or temptations, or whatever you might want to call it, to bend the case his way—and he's starting the game with a lot more chips and much better cards, than we have."

Hannah frowned. "Or if you really want to dream up nightmares, suppose the case concerns a minor infraction by our standards, by human standards. To them it's a crime against civilization—but to us it's a parking ticket. Would it really be the right choice to make if we did *everything* by the book—and cost the human race two planets? Would bending the rules enough to keep the Kendari from getting them, and endangering us, necessarily be wrong, bad, and evil?"

Jamie shook his head. "Listen to yourself. If *I* made that paranoid and worried a speech, what would you tell me?"

"Something like there's never any way of knowing for certain how things will play out in the long run—or even the short run. And that mostly things don't work out the way you expected anyway."

Jamie nodded and grinned back at her. "So you might as well play it all as straight as you can, because playing dirty might not work out as well as you think."

"Okay," she said. "So maybe the moral is there's no point in overthinking this thing."

"But let's not underthink it either," said Jamie. "We can't assume things will be what they seem to be."

"Agreed. But there's something else," said Hannah. "Brox is *scared*. And maybe more than that. In shock. He's hiding it well, and it's always tough to read a xeno's body language and expressions, and he's doing a terrific job of playing it cool—but even so, it's plain enough that something has him really, really worried. Something *bad* has already happened—and something worse might."

There was a sudden lurch, and a bump, then the command sphere was falling away from the navigation dome port. Both Hannah and Jamie dropped heavily onto the deck, Jamie falling forward and Hannah sitting down very abruptly. Cursing and grumbling, Jamie got up on his hands and knees, then shifted around to look up at the rapidly receding view of the stars. "Now what?" he asked.

In a moment, they were through the first hatch, and, as best Hannah could judge, heading back the way they had come. "Well, we moved forward to get as far as possible from the propulsion system when it lit, and to do a visual navigation check. Now the check is complete, and the engines are off, so the safest place to be is back where we were."

"If Greveltra is that worried about safety, maybe he should be a little more careful about knocking us over," said Jamie. He sat down on the deck facing Hannah as the command sphere banged and clattered its way through the system of shafts and hatches.

"The SubPilot is not worried about *our* safety," Hannah said. "Just his."

Brox came around the corner and looked from one of them to another. "Is your private conversation over? Am I intruding?" he asked in Lesser Trade Speech.

Hannah glanced at Jamie. He shrugged. "I think we're done," she said. "We sort of came to the conclusion that if we left out guessing, we wouldn't have much to talk about. Speculating too hard might do us more harm than good."

"I am glad to hear it," Brox replied. "It makes what I have to say at least somewhat easier. We will be making the transit-jump very soon. We had basically agreed that I would brief you on the case itself once we had completed the jump, were safely in the Tifinda System, and there was no longer even a theoretically possible way for anyone back in the Center System to monitor the conversation. On reflection, I feel it would be best for the case if I did not brief you at all before you examine the crime scene. I wish you to see it without any chance of your being influenced or unintentionally misled by something I said."

"Brox! Come on!" Jamie protested. "We're going crazy not knowing anything."

"I assure you that I sympathize. Even so, I ask you to endure this period of frustration. I believe you will understand and agree with my choice to let you perform a completely unbriefed examination of the crime scene evidence. Our transit through the Tifinda System to our destination will be somewhat shorter than our outward passage through the Center System. We will reach our destination in approximately another three hours."

"That's going to be a long time to wait," Hannah said.

"Not so long as it will seem," said Brox. "And I believe it will save time, and effort, in the long run. And, quite frankly, it will protect me from any later accusation of trying to influence you unduly."

Jamie was about to protest further, but Hannah caught his eye and shook her head. "Brox is right, Jamie. We just got done agreeing that we could get misled by our own speculations. If Brox wants to make sure we don't get pointed in the wrong direction because of something *he* says, that's just more of the same. Let's do a nice, clean, unprejudiced examination of the evidence. Go in cold, without preconceived notions."

Jamie frowned. "All right," he said. "But I'm not happy about it. I guess we just have to wait it out."

Hannah laughed. "So we'll sit in the dark with nothing to do and nothing to see while going at ninety-odd percent of the speed of light, and while setting the all-human record for transit between two planets in different star systems. Maybe between two planets, period. You ever hear of anyone getting from, say, Earth to Mars in under four hours?"

Jamie looked surprised. "No, come to think of it."

"Anyway, it's going to be a lot less boring than the one- or two-week flights we usually have to take," said Hannah. "That's got to count for something."

"I appreciate your understanding," said Brox.

"We'll ask a favor or two of you sometime," said Hannah, glad that she had been able to get Jamie more or less mollified. And, after all, Brox had given up some information. Either by accident, or because he saw no reason to deny the obvious any longer, he had at least admitted there was a crime scene—and therefore that a crime had been committed. And he had reinforced that admission by referring to evidence to be examined.

It was remarkably little to go on, but clearly it was all they were going to get. Hannah leaned back against one of the nameless machines that lined the corridor and shut her eyes. "Might as well get some rest, Jamie," she said. "Not much else to do. Besides, once we get there, I've got a feeling we're in for a long, hard day."

Hannah heard Brox snort in a Kendari sort of equivalent to a laugh, but she didn't bother opening her eyes.

"That much," said Brox, "I think I can confirm without prejudicing the case. We should all get some rest."

The *Eminent Concordance* raced through the darkness and toward the dangers and mysteries ahead.

FOUR

SHOUTS OF SILENCE

Hannah managed to make a sort of lumpy pillow out of her equipment vest. She then accomplished the even more unlikely feat of lying down, propping her head up on it, and dozing off right there on the deckplates.

It sometimes seemed to Jamie that Hannah and he took turns at being able to shut down and sleep. Jamie couldn't imagine sleeping right then and there, no matter how much sense it made to be rested for whatever lay ahead. Never mind. One of them ought to be awake to keep watch in any event. And if Hannah could sleep, and he couldn't, then it only made sense that he take the duty.

The minutes crawled by as Jamie sat on the deck, with nothing to do but think of all the questions that Brox wouldn't answer, all the guesses it wouldn't be smart to make.

"What's it like making a transit-jump on this ship?" Jamie asked Brox, more for the sake of conversation than anything else.

On a human-built ship, a jump was never completely routine. Transiting safely from one star system to another required incredible power and precision. The slightest inaccuracy in navigation could endanger the ship or disorient the crew. Transit-jumps could produce all sorts of strange effects, from weird lighting flooding the ship's interior to power surges that blew out equipment or scrambled computer systems. BSI ships tended to fly on poorly charted routes, which meant they ran into more severe effects more often. BSI ships flew jumps with as many systems as possible powered down, braced, as much as possible, for whatever trouble came their way.

"Transit-jump? I believe we have already made it," Brox replied evenly. He stood up and trotted a few steps closer to Greveltra's pilot station, then returned. "Yes. As best I can read the displays, we have already made the jump, and we are currently in the Tifinda System." He sat down again, tucking his four walking legs under him and wrapping his tail around his body. He stretched out his arms and twisted his neck one way, then the other, the very picture of bored patience. "We will be there soon enough," he said. "Based on what happened on my flight from Tifinda to Center, I can tell you that very little will happen until we are almost there—and then it will all happen at once, very quickly."

So. What was regarded as the most dangerous part of the trip for a human starship was so routine, so safe, so unremarkable on a Vixan ship that they didn't take any special precautions. You couldn't even tell that it had happened.

"If it's of any comfort to you," said Brox, "I find it all as intimidating as you do."

"I didn't know Kendari could read minds," Jamie said.

"We can't, as you know perfectly well. But I *have* been trained to read human expressions—and yours weren't exactly hard to read just now. The only difference between you and me at the moment is that I have already made one complete trip on this ship today, and we're getting close to the end of my second. And, of course, that I have been on Tifinda, and dealing with the Vixa, for some time. Even being stunned by the sheer power of this ship—and all their other technology—wears off after a while. Even being scared can get boring for a Kendari."

Jamie laughed. "For a human too, if it comes to that."

"It is a danger we must guard against," Brox said in a more serious tone. "Just because we have lost interest in a danger, that does not mean the danger has lost interest in us."

"Well, at least we'll never get bored being scared of each other," Jamie said. "Humans and Kendari, I mean."

"Are humans really frightened of us?" Brox asked, almost seeming surprised. "I suppose I knew that, intellectually, but it never really struck me as an emotional fact. We're frightened of *you*, of course—and also, I might add, very angry and annoyed."

"Annoyed? Why?"

"That isn't obvious? We arrived out in galactic society, or whatever you want to call it, just a few twelves of years before you did. We look back on that brief period as a lost golden age of promise. We weren't just one of two Younger Races. We were *the* Young Race among all the Elder Races, the *only* Young Race. Special. The first New Race of sentient starfaring beings to emerge in many thousands of years. In fact, it had been so long since a new sentient species was located that most of the Elder Races had assumed that the process of emergence was completed. We were unique, and of interest.

"Some of them took to calling us the Last Race. Their studies proved that 'the wave of evolutionary fervor'—that was their favorite phrase—that had produced all the sentient races had reached its end. We were the last dot on the graph, the last to appear. We were to be cherished, prized, protected.

"And then humans emerged, and the novelty was gone. Suddenly all their theories were wrong—and Elder Race scientists don't like to be proven wrong any more than Kendari scientists—or human ones, for that matter.

"Somehow or another, they seemed to take it out on your people, and mine, almost as if we had evolved, developed spaceflight, then star travel for no other reason than to make them look foolish.

"Since *you* appeared they have to explain away everything they got wrong. Some of them have decided you *humans* are merely the last aberration, the Last Race. Some have taken to assuming that there are any number of other Younger Races out there, bound to appear at any minute. But that position requires that they admit their mistake.

"So mostly the Elders have dealt with the problem by simply declaring that all Younger Races—humans, Kendari, and whoever else might suddenly pop up—are utterly insignificant. We are all so weak, so small, so behind in our technology that we simply do not matter. It doesn't matter if their theories are wrong, because the subjects of their theories aren't worth bothering about."

"That goes along with what our xenologists have concluded regarding the Elder Races in general," said Jamie. "The Elders figure that they know so much, and can do so much, have such superb science and technology and so forth, that anything they don't know or can't do is at the edges, unimportant."

Jamie had never really thought about the human-Kendari rivalry from the Kendari point of view. The human emergence into interstellar space must have upended any number of plans and hopes and expectations. It was just as irrational for the Kendari to resent the humans as it was for the Elders to resent both Younger Races for the crime of spoiling their nice neat theories.

There was a series of *clanks* and *thuds,* and Jamie sat up a little straighter. "Is our command sphere going to take another little ride?" he asked.

"I believe so," said Brox. "We are still traveling at something very close to light-speed, and will of course have to decelerate in order to match the orbit of Tifinda. Greveltra will want us as far from the propulsion system this time as he did the last time. Should we perhaps awaken Senior Special Agent Wolfson?"

"Huh? What?" Hannah came awake at the sound of her name. "Are we there yet?" she asked. "What's going on?"

The command sphere lurched forward before anyone could answer. They looked overhead to watch the sphere climb the vertical shaft system. "Brox says we're getting ready to slow down," Jamie half shouted, trying to make sure he was heard over the bangs and clatters of their transit.

"Thanks for the tip," Hannah said. "I never would have figured that out on my own."

The sphere crashed and banged through the various hatches and back up into the navigation-dome position.

The view overhead was utterly different. There was a muddled blob of reddened stars at the zenith, unnaturally crowded together, with only a sprinkling of smeared, distorted, off-color stars to fill up the sky between the horizon and the near zenith. It took Jamie a moment to figure it out. The *Eminent Concordance* had turned around, pointing her aft end toward the direction of travel in order to decelerate. The ship was flying backwards, and Jamie was looking back the way they had come. The view of the stars was *red*shifted when looking behind.

He barely had time to understand the spectacle before it disappeared. Suddenly the sky began to change, the stars spreading out from the center of the view, expanding out of their smeared distortion and color shifts, back toward the calm and familiar stars—but in a new pattern, the constellations of Center's sky completely gone. They had slowed down from near lightspeed in a matter of seconds. A human-built ship—or most Elder Race ships—would have required days or weeks.

Almost before the stars had regained their normal appearance, the *Eminent Concordance* pivoted around to a new heading.

At least the sight of the stars wheeling around in the sky was comprehensible. They might not have seen this sky before, but they had seen other skies do more or less the same thing. What they were not ready for was the sight of the planet Tifinda coming into view. The Vixa home world was a famously gaudy sight, and Jamie had seen endless images of it displayed in and on books, posters, video-walls, and so on. But none of those versions measured up to the real thing.

They were close, startlingly close to the planet. Jamie had assumed the paranoically safety-minded Greveltra would have vectored the massive ship into a high and distant parking orbit, just to keep that impossibly powerful propulsion system well away from populated areas. Instead, they were close enough to see the structure of the Stationary Ring on the daylight side of the planet, and the running lights of the Ring on Tifinda's nightside. They were directly over one of

Tifinda's poles—Jamie had no way of telling north or south—and therefore looking straight down at the planet, with the day- and nightsides visible. The nightside of black and deep blues, set with the glowing lights of cities, made a striking contrast with the blue-white-brown-and-green world of dayside. The gleaming silver-bright Ring hung round the planet like a gleaming diadem inset with glittering jewels.

The Ring encircled Tifinda precisely at the altitude of the planet's spin-stationary orbit, the point where the orbital velocity exactly matched the planet's rate of rotation. The engineering effort must have been immense, and hideously complex and expensive, but the result was simple: The Ring, as seen from the surface, was utterly motionless.

It was linked to the surface by the Six Columns, spaced equally around the planetary equator. The columns themselves were far too slender to be visible even at as close a range as this one, but it was easy to tell where they were. Gigantic, glittering domed-over space habitats were embedded in the Ring over each column, and huge, gleaming counterweights, metallic spheres the size of small asteroids, rode on extensions of the columns, several thousand kilometers farther out from the planet itself.

"Sort of makes the Grand Elevator at Metran look like nothing at all, doesn't it?" Jamie asked.

"It sure does," Hannah agreed. "And Metran's Elevator impressed the hell out of us not so long ago. I read up on elevators after that one, and of course, there was a lot of material about Tifinda. The overall structure is beyond huge. According to most calculations, the interior living spaces of the Stationary Ring, plus the Column Cities, plus all the other structures hanging off the Ring add up to a total habitable area substantially larger than what there is on the planet's surface."

"That's not just grandiose," said Jamie. "That's borderline insane. Why the devil could they possibly need that much space? Is their population that big? I thought the Elders sneered at us lowly humans for breeding to excess."

"They do, and they are right," said Brox. "You *do* breed too quickly. But that is beside the point. My information is that, even at the most generous definition of what constitutes a sentient Vixan, the total planetary population, including the Ring and Columns, is substantially below a billion."

"So why build that monstrosity?"

"A human I have had some dealings with called it 'keeping up with the Joneses,' if I am translating the English phrase properly into Lesser Trade. Competition through the acquisition and creation of status markers. Once one clan had an elevator, all the clans that could possibly manage had to have one too. But there was a practical strategic side to it as well. Once one elevator was in place, the clan that controlled it gained improved access to space, and the other clans needed to follow suit in order to match that capability. When the Ring was proposed, all the clans cooperated with the project to demonstrate their wealth, to keep parity with the other clans' capabilities, and show how unafraid and unintimidated they were."

"'We are strong enough that we have nothing to fear from connecting our column to yours,'" suggested Hannah.

"Precisely. All this was endless thousands of years ago, of course. The irony is, of course, that living in a Column City or a Ring segment is vastly different from living on the planet's surface. As a result, the communities on the Column Cities and the various sections of the Stationary Ring evolved long ago into essentially independent clans that form and split alliances with their ancestor clans and the rivals of those clans whenever they see fit—and the Column City Clans control the column elevators, and, therefore, most access to space. In terms of enhancing the security and space access of the clans that were the original builders, the whole project was massively counterproductive."

Brox looked thoughtfully out at the incredible structure. "Mind you, I am quoting the analysis of my own people—though it coincides closely with what your researchers have to say as well."

Jamie caught Hannah's eye. This close to where they were going, Brox was allowing himself to let a few details slip. There were humans on the planet— humans who spent time observing and studying the Vixan culture, humans with whom the Kendari were in contact.

"Arms-race theory," said Hannah. "Not all that far off from keeping up with the Joneses, really. The Red Queen, running as fast as she can to stay in one place."

"The Red What?" Brox asked.

"Hmm? Oh! An Earth legend. Not important. The point is that in an arms race, you expend a great deal of effort without gaining any advantage—but you *must* expend the effort or risk falling behind. All sides compete for advantage with such intensity that every achievement is canceled out or countered by the opposition before it can do any good. No clan benefited from the race."

"Except in this case, it was of benefit to *all* the clans as a whole," said Jamie. "Now the planet has six space elevators, six orbital cities, and the Ring itself. Those are pretty significant assets."

"The *first* elevator was a significant asset, and possibly the second—and perhaps even the third if you consider it as a backup system. But six is just a massive waste of resources," said Brox. "And that's not me opinionating. That's our embassy's economic staff doing some very thorough analysis. But the same analysts pointed out that we don't place the same values on things as species like the Vixa."

"'We' meaning Kendari?"

Brox looked a bit surprised. "No, actually, now that you ask, I realize what I meant by 'we' was individualist species, like yours and mine, as opposed to collectivist species, like the Vixa."

"You're not saying the Vixa don't have the concept of the individual," Hannah objected.

"No, of course not," said Brox. He gestured toward the SubPilot. "Obviously they do. Greveltra has a name, a status, a title. But the group is far more important. If I asked you who you were, you might say, 'I am Hannah Wolfson, Senior Special Agent of the BSI,' and leave it at that, and not even bother to say you were human, as that would be assumed. Greveltra would say 'I am of the Vixa, of the planet Tifinda, Founder's Pillar Clanline, of the rank SubPilot,' and might not even mention his name, thinking it unimportant.

"My point is that a collectivist species places very different values on things. Status of the group is important, but not individual status. A human or Kendari might want a large house or an important-sounding title to demonstrate his or her own wealth or value. A Vixan wouldn't bother much with that—but would want to work with others to build the biggest, grandest city or spacecraft or whatever to demonstrate the power and wealth of the *group*.

"You and I would see a huge, gleaming, near-empty Column City as a waste of resources that could have gone to improving the well-being of individuals. Greveltra would regard that same empty city as a worthy investment in staking out the territory of the Clanline, and in denying those resources to the competition. Those goals are not alien to your people or mine, of course—but the Vixa emphasize the group to such an extent, and downplay the individual so much, as to be quite jarring to Kendari—and humans. And many other species, for that matter."

Jamie glanced back at Greveltra. Had the SubPilot even heard Brox? Would he even care what a mere non-Vixan said or thought? But if Greveltra was a relatively low-ranking Vixan who could safely regard mere Younger Race types as beneath his interest—how did he square that with the frantic urgency of the effort he himself was expending to get those same Younger Race types to where they were going? Didn't the importance of their mission—whatever it was—confer any sort of status to them?

"Now at programmed and authorized station-keeping point," Greveltra announced. "Preparing for separation of vehicles."

"This is where everything starts to happen very quickly," said Brox.

Before Jamie or Hannah could ask what he meant, Jamie felt an odd, shivering vibration course through his body, a sensation he recognized as a new acceleration-compensation field powering up. He suddenly understood what Greveltra had meant by vehicle separation.

Just then, the world—or at least the command

sphere—began to turn upside down. Their view of Tifinda rolled away, to be replaced with a view down the shaft they had ridden before. Three lines of running lights came on, and Jamie could see some sort of mechanical motion far down the shaft. It looked as if something was retracting into the side wall. He realized it was the portal tube that had transferred them sideways between this vertical shaft and the one that they had been in originally.

With the way clear, he could see that the shaft they were in was a straight drop that went a lot farther down than he had realized.

There came a *bang* and a *thud*—but no sense of vibration or motion—and they were sliding down to the base of the shaft. The command sphere had rotated through a hundred and eighty degrees. They were looking straight *up* toward where *down* had been moments before—and they were moving toward it at an alarming rate of speed.

"I do not understand the process completely, but in essence the shaft we are traveling in right now will serve as a form of linear accelerator, using the interference patterns between the sphere's acceleration compensator and that of the propulsion module to throw us forward at great speed. The command sphere is inverted to maximize the desired interference reaction."

"Like a bullet out of a gun," said Jamie as the sphere hurtled to the end of the shaft. "First they have to load us into the chamber." They stopped with a *boom* and a *thud*. There was still not the slightest physical sensation of the command sphere moving at all, a stillness that was completely at odds with the sounds of big machine parts banging along and the sight of their craft being bashed and shuttled around.

"Activating launch sequence," said Greveltra in his bland, flat, expressionless voice.

There was a blinding flash of light and suddenly the shaft was filled with a storm of lightning bolts that flared around the sphere, engulfing it without touching it. The walls of the shaft flashed past in a blur, and, in less than a heartbeat, the sphere was flung into clear space.

They were looking upward and backwards along their line of flight at the massive spherical bulk of the *Eminent Concordance*—or at least the ninety-nine-point-ninety-five percent of her that was her massive propulsion module.

The sheets of lightning blazed up out of the launching shaft, seemingly unwilling to release the command sphere, their crackling fires dancing and reflecting on the polished golden surface of the great ship.

Greveltra swung the command sphere about, pointing it along its direction of travel, straight at the planet itself, directly overhead.

They were moving fast enough that Tifinda was growing visibly larger moment by moment. Jamie made a rough guess at their distance from the planet and realized they had to be moving at something like a hundred thousand kilometers an hour, straight at the planet. If Greveltra suddenly keeled over and the command sphere flew on as it was and impacted the surface at their present speed, at minimum the energy release would be comparable to a large nuclear weapon. He decided a few prayers for the health of their pilot and the continued proper functioning of their ship might be in order.

Jamie felt a few muscles straining and decided he had gotten tired of craning his neck to look directly overhead. He sat down on the deck, pulled off his gear vest, bunched it into a lumpy makeshift pillow the same way Hannah had, and lay down flat, his head on the vest. He could be astonished and overawed just as handily while flat on his back.

Hannah glanced down at him, saw what he had done, and lay down next to him, her head on her own vest. For a bizarre moment, Jamie was irresistibly reminded of camping trips in the mountains, lying back, looking up at the sky, and sharing the teenage equivalent of deep thoughts with his camping buddy. "What do you want to be when you grow up?" he half muttered, more to himself than to Hannah.

"Huh? What?"

Jamie chuckled and shook his head. "Nothing. Never mind."

"Glad you can find something to laugh about," Hannah said. "Do you have any idea how fast we must be going?"

"Yes," said Jamie. "But I don't see any point in discussing it." He glanced over at Brox, who had sat himself down and was calming watching the incoming planet. Jamie decided the Kendari was out of earshot and spoke to Hannah in low tones. "Do you have any useful guesses about what we're going to find down there?"

It was Hannah's turn to chuckle. "Yes, but I don't see any point in discussing it."

"Okay, you got me there."

"Seriously though—my guess is that there was some sort of bad accident involving humans and Kendari, and maybe Vixa or some other species." She gestured toward Greveltra. "The way *he* drives makes that easy to believe."

"Why do you say accident? Brox used the term 'crime scene.'"

"A bit of sloppy phrasing. I say accident because Brox is the enemy—but Brox isn't acting hostile. He's not angry at us, at humans. If anything, he's oddly sympathetic. So something caused us and them trouble, but no one is to blame. And it happened at exactly the wrong time, just when everybody is about to sit down and sign the deal. They want a joint investigation to smooth it all over, confirm no one was at fault, and have a nice signing ceremony."

"Hmmph. Well, maybe." The planet was getting bigger by the minute. Maybe a hundred thousand kilometers an hour was a low estimate. It looked as if they were heading for the daytime side, toward a part of the globe where it was roughly late afternoon. The cloud cover hid whatever was there. "I think that's optimistic. *Really* optimistic. The kind of rush they've put together here seems a little too panicky for that. And yeah, Brox seems friendly, but he's *scared* as well. I still get the sense not just that something bad *has* happened, but something even worse still *might* happen."

The planet had swollen to fill the entire upper hemisphere of the command sphere. Jamie had to turn his head to one side to catch a glimpse of the Great Ring, and even that vanished as he watched.

"Brox!" Hannah called, without getting up or taking her eyes off the terrifying view overhead. "Maybe now we're close enough that you could at least tell us where we're going. It's on the planet, not on the Great Ring. That much we've figured out. Give us something more."

"If for no other reason than to distract us from the view a little bit," Jamie suggested.

"Yes, certainly. We are headed toward what amounts to the planetary capital, though that's not exactly accurate. The city bears two names, which are not interchangeable, but are based on the city function to which one is referring. The correct name must be used at all times in order to avoid giving offense. The city is called Rivertide when referred to as a home, a place to live, and the Grand Warren of the Conclaves—or simply the Grand Warren—in the context of being the seat of power."

"And where in the Grand Warren are we going?" Jamie asked. "I mean, assuming we live through atmospheric entry?"

"I share your nervousness and discomfort. For what it is worth, Greveltra has a perfect safety record as a pilot. Our first destination is a building in the center of the city. You will submit yourself there."

"Submit ourselves for what? Approval? Accreditation?"

"Formally, you are submitting yourselves to the will of the Preeminent Director of Tifinda. 'Accreditation' is close enough. I have heard some of the humans refer to it as hazing or initiation—or ritual intimidation, which I gather is much the same thing in some human organizations. Think of it as a welcoming ceremony—though perhaps not the most enjoyable one you have ever attended.

"Once that formality is complete, we will travel in a smaller vehicle to the diplomatic quarter of the city—I should say *a* diplomatic quarter. It is an isolated section where the representatives of lower-ranking races are invited to house themselves. Perhaps 'diplomatic ghetto' would be a more descriptive term."

"Let me guess. The human and Kendari embassies are in that zone."

"Right next to each other," said Brox. "Each diplomatic mission has an assigned piece of land, in adjoining walled compounds."

"Why did they put us right next to each other?" Hannah asked. "They'd have to know your government and mine don't get along."

"You would have to ask the Vixa that question. For what it is worth, we do not inconvenience each other as much as you might think. The walls are high."

"How big are these compounds?" Hannah asked.

"I'm told the human compound is about the size of a city block in Center City. The Kendari compound is slightly larger."

"A city block is a pretty fair size," said Jamie.

"Not so large when you consider that both embassies have fairly large staffs, and that all personnel must be housed in that space, along with all provisions, equipment, and so on. And also consider that our hosts often confine the staffs of the embassies to their respective compounds for security reasons, or for no specified reason at all."

"And you've been posted to the Kendari embassy, right?" Jamie asked. It wasn't exactly much of a deductive leap, given the circumstances, and how much Brox knew about the situation on the ground.

"Yes. Thanks to you two."

"What?" *That* was a surprise. "How do you mean?"

"After I collaborated with the two of you on Reqwar, it was noted in my file that I had demonstrated a capacity—even an aptitude—for working with humans. And so when the Inquiries Service established a sort of Kendari-human security liaison office at this embassy, I was assigned to it."

"Kendari-human liaison office? To do what?"

"It is a joint office, staffed by Kendari Inquiries Service Inquirists and human Bureau of Special Investigations agents, who work together so as to prevent undesirable incidents."

"Hold it!" Hannah protested. She stabbed a finger up at the swelling bulk of the planet. "There are BSI agents at the human embassy already?"

"Yes," said Brox. "Three of them."

"Then why did you send for *us*?" Hannah demanded.

But Jamie knew. "Because they're all suspects," he said. "Or because they're all dead. Whatever happened killed them all."

Brox was silent for a moment before he answered, in a flat, careful, neutral voice. "They are not dead," he said.

"This just got worse, Brox," said Hannah. "Much, much worse."

"I agree," said Brox.

Jamie looked at Brox, at Hannah, at the planet looming ever larger overhead, and knew the question he had to ask. "But it's going to get even worse than this, isn't it, Brox? How much worse *will* it get?"

Brox said nothing, did nothing, showed nothing.

It was the loudest silence Jamie had ever heard.

FIVE

ESCORTS

Ambassador Berndt Stabmacher peered out the window—or more accurately the porthole—of his living quarters aboard the grounded United Human Government Embassy Ship *Kofi Annan*. Of course, "living quarters" wasn't quite accurate, either. What the devil *did* you call it when you ordered your entire staff—and yourself—into solitary confinement in the various small and impossibly cramped compartments aboard a grounded spacecraft that served as your embassy's emergency evacuation system?

Ignoring the spectacular view of the Grand Warren on the horizon, he scanned the skies instead. There wasn't any way to know from which direction they would come, or even if they would come at all—but what else was there to hope for? There wasn't any, *couldn't* be any, Plan B. He had barely been able to convince Diplomatic Xenologist Flexdal 2092 to accept the current proposal—or, as he had no doubt Senior Special Agent Milkowski would put it, the current humiliation.

Never mind. Stabmacher was more than willing to risk his career and his life—all their careers, *all* their lives—in exchange for preventing a war. To stop such wars was the very essence, the core purpose of diplomacy. Especially a needless and pointless war that would likely have no winners and many losers.

No winners? Maybe that wasn't quite true, if you

took into account the groups that sat back and watched the opposing sides cripple each other, possibly even destroy each other. No one could stop them from scooping up everything the combatants hadn't managed to destroy.

He turned from the porthole, sat down at the tiny foldout desk, and blinked vacantly. He was tired. Exhausted. Worn to a nub. He yawned mightily and scratched at his bristly chin. There were a fold-down sink, a fold-down couch, and some amazingly awkward sanitary arrangements in the compartment, none of them anywhere near satisfactory. He longed for a proper night's sleep, or even just a nap. He wanted a meal, a shower, and a shave, and not necessarily in that order. But such things were trivial. A day or two of confinement and discomfort would be a remarkably small price to pay, a real bargain, if it stopped a war before it started. *A very small price indeed,* Ambassador Stabmacher told himself.

But someone had already paid a far higher price.

The command sphere broke through the bottom of the highest cloud deck and flew into clear air at about ten thousand meters, though a lower layer of clouds hid the ground from view.

At Brox's suggestion the three of them had moved out to the perimeter of the sphere, where their view of the horizon would not be blocked by the banks of nameless machines. With the outer hull of the ship turned transparent, the world was on display at their feet. They could see everything—but at the moment, all "everything" amounted to was the layers of cloud above and below.

The sphere began to slow down as it approached

the lower cloud deck, then, in the blink of an eye, they were in the clouds, and the universe outside was a formless grey nothing. A heartbeat later, and they had broken through the last of the overcast, and the city of the Grand Warren, of Rivertide, was laid out before them. The command sphere paused where it was, about two thousand meters up, affording them a long and admiring look at the city.

It was Oz, Oz inside a three-quarters-sphere dome, a dome so graceful, transparent, and ethereal it barely seemed to be there at all. It was gleaming towers, lofty spires, broad avenues, elevated travelways linking the buildings, shimmering lights, the bustle of aircars and groundcars in purposeful motion—a full-scale, brought-to-life, all-expectations-met rendition of a city of the Elder Races, the archetype of what every schoolchild on every human world was convinced that every city on every xeno planet should be like, must be like.

Plenty of the Elder Race cities Hannah had seen were run-down affairs, almost as much partially–occupied archeological sites as they were functioning settlements. But the Grand Warren showed no signs of decrepitude. It was the very embodiment of vigor, confidence, power, and purpose.

"This is *their* capital city," said Brox. Then he pointed south toward a dusty quarter of low, flat buildings. "And that is *our* capital city. Or more accurately, that is the zone of their capital that *we* are allowed to move about in without excessive restrictions. But you will see more than enough of it soon enough."

The command sphere flew on toward the city. It entered the central-city dome through a portal midway up. Looking down from inside the dome, the Grand Warren reminded Hannah irresistibly of the canyoned streets of midtown Manhattan, with swooping ramps and elevated roadways and buzzing, darting aircars thrown into the mix. Everything about what she saw spoke of grandeur and power. The streets were full of life and activity, hustle and bustle—but all of it was strictly ordered. All the ground vehicles moved at precisely the same speed. The Vixa she could see walking along moved in packs, in groups, that marched along in more perfect unison than any precision drill team back on Earth.

But there was more to it than that. The groups—packs—swarms—none of the words seemed quite right—were sorted by color and size—and, as well as Hannah could judge from this distance, number of legs.

"If you view each cluster of Vixa as an aggregate individual, what you are seeing will make more sense—and, I expect, be less disturbing," said Brox. "At least it's less disturbing for me."

It did help, in a number of ways. Once Hannah starting thinking of each cluster as a unit, patterns jumped out at her. Clusters made up of larger, brighter-colored, and fewer-legged individuals seemed to take precedence over clusters of smaller, darker-colored, many-legged Vixa, which gave way to them whenever a group of one type encountered the other. The higher-ranking clusters also seemed to have fewer individual Vixa in them.

Hannah didn't have time to make any further sense of what she saw before the command sphere swept forward to a large building—or possibly a collection of buildings—that looked like a collection of giant, opaque, milky-white soap bubbles clustered together. Part of one bubble drew back somehow, and the command sphere flew inside.

"We have arrived," said Brox. "The hatch will open in a few moments, and we will disembark. You will see things that I have not the slightest doubt will disturb you greatly. As your Commander Kelly conceded, you are about to be in violation of standing orders against dealing directly with Vixa of these castes and ranks. All I can ask is that you make the best possible use of your training as to how to deal with surprises and unexpected situations—particularly unpleasant ones."

"Great," said Jamie. "That sounds just great."

The hatch irised open before anyone could say anything more. Brox led the way out into a large, utilitarian-looking room about the size and shape of a small airplane hangar. All was neat, all was orderly. Everything they could see was a tool, a machine, a device. There was no decoration, nothing done to indicate status or demonstrate wealth or taste or any sense of individual choice. There was a faint, slightly unpleasant smell in the air, just a whisper of something somewhere between overripe fruit and rotting meat.

A contingent of nine midsized, mauve-colored, nine-legged Vixa were lined up facing the command sphere. At a guess each had about the body mass of a smallish Saint Bernard. Hannah was doing her best to get used to the Vixa. She could more or less handle dealing with giant spiders, but she still found herself very much thrown off stride by the absence of anything that could serve as a face. There was no point on the Vixan anatomy that could serve as a focus point in conversation, nothing that provided any sort of cue or clue to the being's mood or reactions.

The two simulants immediately trotted off the ship and took their places at each end of the line. A voice came from somewhere—possibly from the Vixan at the center of the line, but there was no way to judge for sure. "You are now welcomed to the household of Zeeraum, Subhouseholder to the Preeminent Director, now and forever nameless," it said in flat-toned, nasal Lesser Trade Speech, if one could use that term in connection with a being with no nose. "This will be your only welcome. This guard will lead and escort you to the ceremony of submission. Be fearful in the presence of your superiors."

"Hello to you too," Jamie muttered.

"That's the last wisecrack out of *you*, Agent Mendez," said Hannah in a harsh whisper through clenched teeth. "Jokes could get us killed."

"Very true," said Brox. "Telling you—us—to be fearful was sound advice. Any Vixan superior to any other Vixan has the unquestioned right to destroy the inferior for any reason—or no reason. Occasionally, compensation must be paid to the victim's household, but that is rare—and it wouldn't do us much good."

"Ah, right," said Jamie. "Sorry."

The Vixan in the center of the formation pulled in its three forward manipulation arms and folded them out of the way, spun about on its six walking legs and started to move away from the ship. At a cue from Brox, Hannah and Jamie formed up directly behind the lead Vixan, with Brox bringing up the rear. The four Vixa on either side, and the two simulants, dropped in alongside to the left and the right, so their unit was marching along three abreast. The Nines walked in perfect synchronization with each other, moving their walking legs in double-ripple fashion from back to front, so that two pair of legs at a time were touching the floor. The procession moved forward at a speed that was almost, but not quite, too fast for the humans.

They moved out of the hangar, into an equally

utilitarian walkway, its floor made of something resembling bare concrete, with bundles of cable and conduit strapped to the barrel-vaulted ceiling. The lead Vixan turned this way and that when the corridor they were on intersected others, never varying its pace, never pausing to confirm that the visitors were still behind him.

Of course not, thought Hannah. *He's got eyes in the back of his head—if his central core counts as a head—plus the ones on his elbows and wrists.*

The lead Vixan made one last turn, and marched them down what seemed to be a dead end, with a blank wall directly ahead. It made no attempt to slacken its pace or prepare to stop, and neither did any of the other Vixa or the simulants. Then the entire unit—except for the humans and Brox—halted abruptly, with the leader's forward manipulator arms no more than a half meter from the wall in front. Hannah nearly crashed into the leader, and Jamie bumped into Hannah. Brox skidded to a halt a millimeter or two short of crashing into both of them.

A heartbeat or two after they had halted, there was a sudden faint vibration, and the blank wall in front of them started to move downward. It took Hannah a moment or two to realize that couldn't be right. They were moving *upward.* The section of dead-end corridor was in fact a long, wide, open-ended elevator car.

Either the Vixa expended the huge time and effort required to install acceleration compensators on interior elevators, or else they were merely superb engineers, but there was virtually no sense of motion or acceleration. *Why couldn't they do it that way on the* Eminent Concordance? Hannah had to watch the nearly featureless wall before her slide downward to be sure they were still moving. They passed one, two, three openings that gave them the briefest of glimpses of other levels, each seeming just a trifle more elegant, more decorated, and less like a factory floor, than the one below it.

At last they emerged at what had to be the top level of the structure. At least, when they started moving again and exited the elevator car, they were done with corridors of any sort—and walls too, for that matter. A vast, translucent, milky-white dome at least a hundred meters high formed the roof of the chamber they were in. The city outside could be dimly seen through the dome. It would appear that this one vast room took up the upper third or so of one of the soap-bubble structures they had seen on approach. A larger and higher dome was faintly visible outside. Perhaps that meant that this subhousehold was subordinate to that one—or perhaps not.

Their escort was immediately back on the move, making a beeline for the center of the vast chamber. But, as abruptly as it had done so for a solid wall, they stopped again after only about twenty meters. There was another cluster of Vixa moving toward them, apparently heading for the same elevator. Hannah instantly noted that this escort consisted of six, not nine, brighter-colored, larger nine-legged Vixa.

It took her a moment to realize that they were escorting a human. And, impossible as it seemed, a human she recognized—not through personal acquaintance but from seeing his picture on the news channels and newspads. Perhaps the last man Hannah would have expected to see on Tifinda, let alone being escorted by a half dozen Vixa Nines.

"Escort is respectfully requested to halt!" the man called out. The words might be a request, but the tone of voice made them an order—something more than an order. It was the voice a certain sort of man would use to call his dog, just to reinforce discipline. The escort stopped instantly, and the man stepped casually from inside it, with an air of self-possession that would have been more in place if the six Vixa were the horses pulling his carriage, or the body of the groundcar he was driving. His escort was an honor guard that he could put on oh-so-casual display. Hannah had the strong impression that their own escort was more of a security detail there to make sure they didn't run away. She wasn't quite sure what to do in response to his getting "out" of his escort. Things might get unpleasant if their escorting Vixa decided Hannah should stay where she was. It appeared that neither of her companions wanted to risk it either, so they simply stood awkwardly inside the space contained by their own escort.

"What in the stars, what in *hell*, is *he* doing here?" Jamie asked. "Brox—does *he* have anything to do with why we're here?"

"I cannot answer that," said Brox. "I knew he was on-planet, but I had not seen him face-to-face before now. Needless to say, that was fine with me. When I spoke of unpleasant surprises, I was thinking that *you* were likely to experience them. I was not speaking for myself. Clearly I should have been."

Tancredo Zamprohna, president of the Human Supremacy League, strode confidently toward them. He was a tall, thickly built man, with pockmarked skin, a jowly, ugly-handsome face, and a thick shock of red hair that was combed straight back on his head in a manner that had become one of his trademarks. Another was the perfectly tailored powder-blue business suit, always worn with an archaically wide necktie with a pattern of thick stripes—blue, white, and green as the colors of Earth, and then black, white, brown, and yellow to represent the races of humanity.

One joke was that just black and white, representing prison stripes, would have been just as appropriate. According to BSI intell reports, a good deal of money had changed hands in his native Brazil in order to prevent certain cases involving creative finance from being prosecuted.

"Ain't he a gaudy sight," said Jamie under his breath. "Sorry, Hannah, you said no jokes."

"It's all right, Jamie. You weren't joking."

"What have we here?" Zamprohna asked in a loud, booming voice that echoed slightly in the massive dome. He spoke in smooth, lightly accented Lesser Trade Speech. "Two humans and a Kendari. You're the Kendari Inquiries agent I have yet to meet. I am Tancredo Zamprohna. I acknowledge your presence."

"And I acknowledge yours," Brox replied, stiffly correct. "I am Brox 231. I should note that my service prefers the job title and ranking of Inquirist. I am a Senior Inquirist."

In Lesser Trade, one "acknowledged" an enemy met off the field of battle, or a rival, or anyone else one would not care to greet or welcome. Zamprohna's breezy, hail-fellow-well-met, backslapping-pol attitude made it a mere form of words. Brox's tone of voice carried exactly the intended subtext—perfectly understandable, as Zamprohna's Human Supremacy League advocated the eventual domination of humanity over all other sentient species in general, and looked with a certain degree of favor at the idea of exterminating the Kendari in particular—the sooner the better.

"And you're not the only one feeling inquisitive right now," Zamprohna said cheerfully. "Who are your companions?"

"I hereby present Senior Special Agent Hannah Wolfson of the Bureau of Special Investigations, and Special Agent James Mendez, likewise of the Bureau of Special Investigations," Brox said, speaking in the same formal, rigidly correct tone.

"More BSI here? Interesting. Very interesting indeed." Zamprohna shifted to English, and spoke it with somewhat more of a Brazilian accent than he had betrayed in Lesser Trade. "What has this character dragged you here for? Have the Ks managed to talk our people into doing more of the work?"

"I'm not at liberty to discuss our assignments," said Hannah. "But I would observe that your organization has created a great deal of often very unpleasant work for the BSI over the years—and that the Senior Inquirist understands English quite well."

"Have any of your friends along?" Jamie asked. "Maybe some of the ones with outstanding warrants against them?"

"Oh, you're out of luck there." Zamprohna laughed, completely unabashed. "I made it clear that was a condition of the deal when we were invited. None of my people are subject to arrest while here— and neither you nor your alien pals have any powers of arrest. *Maybe* you could slap the cuffs on us on the embassy grounds—but you'd have to set us free the moment we stepped out of the gate, or cleared embassy airspace."

"Well, stop by sometime when we're there," Jamie said. "We could just arrest you at the embassy and keep you there for all time. Though I suppose that might not be fair to the embassy staff."

"Wouldn't work either," Zamprohna said calmly, patting himself on the chest. "You're looking at a man with a clean rap sheet. All warrants dismissed, all charges dropped."

"Congratulations. I'm sure you must be very proud," said Hannah.

"Oh, I am," he said. "But listen here," he went on in a more businesslike tone. "What the devil goes *on* at the human embassy? It's shut down tighter than a drum. No calls answered, no access of any kind permitted, no one in or out." He hooked his thumb in Brox's direction. "My spies tell me his shop is in lockdown too. I need to know why. I was just up here trying to get the Grand Poobahs to tell me more. They've been real cooperative up to now—but they've clammed up too. What's going on?"

"No comment," said Hannah. "And let's just assume that's good until further notice."

"I've got a right to know what's going on!"

And I haven't the faintest idea myself what's going on, Hannah thought. "You show me a law, a regulation, a written order from my superior officers that tells me you've got that right—and after I double-check it, I'll comply with your request for information. I don't want to start any fights here, Dr. Zamprohna, but even if you've got a clean sheet right now, it wasn't more than six months ago that the Human Supremacy League came off the BSI list of terror-supporting organizations—and that was in spite of the protests of my direct superior."

"I wouldn't put too much stock in that," said Zamprohna. "Commander Kelly won't be in that job forever—and maybe not even all that much longer."

That was a nice, clear, indirect threat Hannah was going to have to report back as soon as possible. "I'll bear that in mind," said Hannah. *And tender my resignation the split second a commandant sympathetic to your outfit takes over the Bullpen.*

Zamprohna flashed an impossibly toothy smile and winked at her. "See that you do," he said. "Now I'm going to have to spend all of about ten minutes working my sources, and finding out what, exactly, you're doing here. My fellow humans, I bid you a fond farewell. And, *Senior Inquirist* Brox 231, I hereby inform you of my departure." He bowed to Hannah, nodded to Jamie, made no gesture at all toward Brox, and headed back to his escort.

"Real nice guy," said Jamie. "Hey, you think if his sources find out what we're doing here, then maybe we could get him to tell us?"

"Sure, for the right price," said Hannah. "By all accounts he's a very bribable fellow. Brox, what the hell *is* he doing here—on-planet, and paying calls on the powers that be?"

"You will learn the answer to the first part of your question soon, though you won't like it. As to the second part, I have no idea, beyond the motive he himself claimed."

They watched as his escort started moving again. Zamprohna moved off with them. His posture and attitude reminded her irresistibly of an old-time tycoon in top hat and tails, at his ease in the back of his limousine, puffing on a giant cartoon cigar. His escort group cleared theirs. Hannah was not in the least surprised when their own group started up again without warning.

It all had to be status, she reflected. The number of escorts a party received, the size and color and number of legs of the escorting group, the apparently intricate rules establishing who deferred to whom—all of it was, on the face of it, absurd posturing that accomplished nothing and used up labor and resources. It was of no more practical use than the Hall of Mirrors at Versailles, or the kilometer-long corridors of Hitler's Chancery, or the number of gold stars on an admiral's shoulder boards. But Vixan status display was different from what humans did. It was there to support the group, the clan, rather than to exalt an individual.

That played both ways, up and down the status scale. That little speech of welcome their escort leader had given them mentioned Subhouseholder Zeeraum, but also "the Preeminent Director, now and forever nameless." She remembered that part from the general briefing on the Vixa. When a Vixan ascended to the Preeminent Directorate, he or she gave up his or her name for all time, becoming as nameless as the subcaste Vixa in their escort, and was thereafter to be referred to merely by the title. The office was all, the power was all, the individual was nothing.

None of it, none of it at all, was even remotely like the Vixa she had met on Earth, on Center, and in the course of her BSI duties. Obviously, the Vixa sent off-world were very carefully trained to act as much like humans as possible, so as to keep the primitive Younger Race beings happy.

Hannah managed to study the Vixa that made up their escort in more detail as they moved along together. They appeared to be utterly identical to each other, down to the pattern of mottling on their bodies. They had to be clones, or something very much like clones.

The lead one and probably the others, could speak and understand speech, at least to some degree—but they had to use some other form of communication as well. Their feet were touching the floor exactly together, to within a hundredth, a thousandth, of a second. Their other body movements were likewise too perfectly synchronized. They couldn't be doing it by watching each other. It had to be that their bodies were all being operated by one unified central control system. Maybe it was embedded bioelectronics. Maybe it was some form of telepathy, if there even was such a thing in Vixan biology.

But if they were subject to central control, that either meant that the bodies themselves were essentially mindless, or else that they were configured so that higher-ranking Vixa—or perhaps even some automated control system, a computer—could take control of their bodies at will.

How odd—how terrifying—to become, at any time, a mere passive passenger in one's own body, incapable of controlling any movement at all, with someone or something else deciding what foot to move, what eye to open, how hard to breathe—perhaps even what to say. Maybe the lead Vixa of their escort *couldn't* speak—maybe it had just served as a sort of mobile, living remote mike and speaker system for some bored systems controller or artificial intelligence a kilometer away—or on the other side of the planet.

Well, Brox had warned them they would see disturbing things. Hannah had the feeling they had yet to scratch the surface.

SIX

SNACK TIME

Jamie walked along behind Hannah with his own set of worries, most of them centered, quite irrationally, on the question of how they could get out of there. He knew, as a matter of sense and logic, that they couldn't get "out." They were on an alien planet, a long, long way from home, flanked on both sides by giant face-less spiders who could undoubtedly outrun them but just as undoubtedly wouldn't need to, as the whole vast expanse they were crossing was alive with any number of other giant spiders who could head them off effortlessly. They had no tools, equipment, or weapons that would do any good, and no remotely plausible place to which they could retreat.

But by both training and inclination, Jamie tended to think in terms of tactics, moves and countermoves, strategies and plans. In an environment this strange, this alien and threatening, this downright *creepy,* it was no wonder that all the alarm bells were going off in his head.

Settle down, he told himself. *So you're surrounded by giant marching spiders and there's a smell of rotting flesh in the air and you have no idea why you're here or what happens next. Deal with it. Move on. Tell your paranoia to stop looking for lines of retreat that don't exist, and put it to work spotting information we can actually use.*

It helped. He looked around and starting taking

note of their surroundings as more than possible places to take cover in or move out from. The floor of the vast hemispherical dome they were in was dotted with smaller domes of various colors and sizes. Vixa—likewise of various colors and sizes—were moving about quite purposefully between the smaller domes. In every case that Jamie could see, a larger, brighter-colored six-legged Vixa was escorted by some number of smaller Vixa that might have six or nine or even twelve legs. After the encounter with Zamprohna, Jamie was not all that surprised to see various other aliens—humans, Kendari, Pavlat, Metrans, and a few others he couldn't immediately identify—moving thither and yon as well, each of them escorted by a phalanx of smaller Nines or Twelves.

He wondered briefly if there was any significance to seeing all these domed spaces inside this domed building that was inside a domed city—not at all unlike the ride they had just taken on a spherical ship inside a spherical ship. Did that speak of some deep-set Vixan need to have some physical space and yet not feel exposed? Did it reveal some Vixan obsession with domes and spheres—perhaps because they very roughly resembled the rounded main body of a Vixa? Or was it just a local, temporary, architectural fad?

Their escort came to another of its abrupt halts outside one of a cluster of domes near the center of the greater dome, then led them to a fire-engine-red sub-dome. As with the larger dome of which it was a part, it was not the largest—but it was *one* of the largest, and adjacent to the largest of all.

Great, Jamie thought. *I'm here less than an hour and they've already got me checking the size and positions of the buildings and the type of escort Vixa to determine status.* "It must be catching," he muttered.

"What?" said Hannah.

"Nothing. Nothing at all."

"We have arrived," said Brox. "We must wait until we are summoned. That could take thirty seconds, or three hours. We must be patient. I do not know what, exactly, will happen once we enter. The rituals vary, and I know nothing of this particular Subhouseholder. But I can assure you that you will not be harmed in this time, or in this place. I will escort you in. Speak only when spoken to, and only when a reply is truly required. Use no honorifics, such as 'sir' or 'madam' or 'Great One' or whatever. Only a Vixan may address a Grand Vixan of exalted rank in that manner. Keep your answers short, literal, and truthful. Make no attempt at humor. Ask no questions."

Even with those instructions, or perhaps in spite of them, Jamie felt sorely tempted to make a joke. But either Hannah was a mind reader, or they had been partners long enough for her to know him a little too well. The expression of warning on her face would have silenced anyone. He nodded his agreement and left it at that.

Their escort kept in formation around them, standing utterly still. Even the two simulants remained in line and motionless. There were two Sixes, with escort groups, to their left, obviously waiting to be summoned as well. Their escorts didn't move at all either, but the Vixa being escorted didn't seem obliged to freeze in place. They remained inside the perimeters of their escorts, but they were moving around inside the spaces, using their manipulator arms to work with what appeared to be the Vixan equivalent of datapads. *Reading the newspaper in the waiting room*, Jamie decided.

He was tempted to get "out" of their escort and

walk around a little, see what there was to be seen, but it didn't seem worth the risk of misunderstanding—or worse. So he stayed with Hannah and Brox, in an absurd caricature of waiting in the car.

Suddenly, without any signal that they could perceive, their escort started moving again. Jamie had expected that they would have to wait their turn behind the escort Vixa who were already present, but apparently their calculated status entitled them to jump the line. *That's a good thing,* Jamie told himself. *Probably.*

Their escort marched them toward the blank wall at the base of the dome. A door slid open at the last moment, and in they went, the door snapping shut behind them.

The interior was much dimmer than the outside, and it was hard to make out much detail immediately. The first things to hit Jamie were the heat, and the smell. It had to be at least thirty degrees Celsius, maybe higher, in the chamber, and, in those first few seconds, the sickly-sweet scent of decomposing flesh was almost overpowering. Jamie had to suppress the impulse to gasp, or cover his mouth. Hannah was having the same trouble. He glanced behind himself, and saw that Brox seemed not only unaffected, but slightly surprised by their reaction. Either the stink faded quickly or they had gotten used to it fast, but it didn't seem anywhere near as bad a few seconds later.

Their escort broke formation. It was, quite literally, as if a switch had been thrown. One moment they were all motionless, at absolutely rigid attention—and the next they were all going their separate ways—one of them stretching, another scuttling over to the edge of the dome and, if Jamie was any judge, curling up for a nap, two or three going over to what seemed to be a feeding trough to the left of the entrance. The two simulants, he noted, just stayed right where they were, and did their usual deflated-doll imitations. *Maybe that tells us that the others have at least some sort of volition to express when they're off duty,* he thought. *But not our two little pals.*

The red dome was just translucent enough from the inside to let him see the other domes that clustered nearby. It was difficult to tell whether the dim light in the room was being filtered in from the outside, or if there was some other, indirect source of illumination. Once his eyes adjusted, Jamie could see much more clearly—though his depth perception wasn't anything much.

The interior floor formed a shallow bowl formed out of some sort of darkish red material, roughened just enough to provide reasonable traction. The interior was about twenty meters in diameter. At its center was a low circular dais, about five meters across and raised enough to bring it almost up to the level of the floor by the doorway.

And on that dais sat a Vixan. A six-legged Vixan, easily four times the size of the ones in their escort, larger by far than any Vixan Jamie had ever seen. At a guess, it had to weigh five hundred kilos, if not more. Jamie had heard the term "Grand Vixan" somewhere along the way, and instantly decided the term must be intended to apply to specimens like this one. He also had a vague recollection from half-remembered briefing books that the Grand Vixa were all female but he wasn't sure that was right. Absent any other information, he decided to think of this one as female, in any event. *He* certainly couldn't tell by looking. In the dim red light of the audience chamber dome it was hard to judge the Grand Vixan's color, but it looked to be a red that matched the color of the dome itself on its upper or dorsal area, with its ventral surfaces dead white.

"Flaug glaw greaz whadaval trez?" the Grand Vixan demanded of them in a loud, booming voice that would have done a bull elephant proud. She was waving her left manipulator arm at them, and pointing her right arm so as to give its wrist and elbow eyes a good look at them. "Oh ho!" she shouted, shifting from whatever the first language was to Lesser Trade. "Humans! I shift to another speech you are capable of understanding. *Do* you understand me?"

Hannah found her voice before Jamie did. "Ah, yes," she said. "We are both fluent in Lesser Trade."

"Fluent indeed," snorted the Grand Vixan. "Know that I am Zeeraum, Subhouseholder to the Preeminent Director, now and forever nameless. You are subjected to a great honor in being brought directly to my presence. It is an honor I was reluctant to grant."

It seemed the sort of remark that called for a response, but Jamie remembered what Brox had said about only answering when necessary, and kept his mouth shut. In fact, he was perfectly happy to let Hannah do all the talking. And he wasn't even remotely tempted to try any smart remarks of any kind. Not in this place.

Zeeraum lifted a data display pad in her left manipulator and went on talking as she consulted it. "You are here to investigate the matter at the human embassy," she said. She stabbed her right manipulator again. "But there are two of you here. The arrangement was for only one human to come. You are commanded to explain."

"We—we were not informed of the details of the arrangement," said Hannah. "We were simply ordered by our superiors to come here and perform a task we would learn of upon arrival."

"But we agreed to only one! One of you must return! Reply!"

"We work as a unit. We are partners."

"Together, you are one investigator?"

"It is possible for us to work each alone, but we perform our duties much better when we work together."

"Ah. Very good. We are told always how apart, apart, apart you all are. Together is better. Very well. Both may stay."

Zeeraum seemed to consult her data display again, though it was hard to tell when she had eyes of one sort or another all over her body.

Jamie was having a harder time of this than he had imagined. It was impossible to determine where exactly her voice was coming from, and it was hugely disconcerting to have nothing like a face to look at. He suddenly noticed something crawling up Zeeraum's back—a pale-colored creature that looked like a Vixan Twelve, but only about the size of a small cat. It was a struggle to do so, but he managed to suppress the impulse to shout out a warning. He spotted another of the creatures moving around on the floor—and two more crawling from under Zeeraum's body. What were they?

"If you are partners, are you of equal ability?" Zeeraum demanded.

"Not precisely equal. Each of us is more skilled than the other in different areas, in ways that complement and amplify our combined ability."

Obviously, Hannah had latched on to Zeeraum's approving of togetherness and partnership, and was playing that up.

"Very sensible. The other one. Does the other one

speak? You! Other one. You are ordered to speak if you can!"

"I can speak," Jamie said, in a voice that was higher and squeakier than he would have wanted to admit.

"Good. Not that it matters. One may speak for all." Somehow, the way Zeeraum said that made it sound like an adage, a rule to live by. "What do you know of the matter at the embassies, other one?"

Embassies? Plural? That right there was more than Jamie knew. "Nothing whatsoever."

"But how can you investigate without knowledge? Reply!" There was a sort of soft plopping noise from the top of Zeeraum's body, and a rounded sheath or sphincter of skin about forty centimeters across relaxed and drew back. Jamie remembered the Vixan mouth—or at least its close analog to a mouth—was on top of its head—or least where its head would be. As the skin of the mouth drew back, it revealed what appeared to be a pile of small bones and bits of skin.

The small creature that had been crawling up Zeeraum's back started collecting the bones, gathering them up in two of its manipulator arms. Another of the smaller helper Vixa started climbing up the front of Zeeraum's body. The Grand Vixan patted it absently, the way one might a cat that was casually sauntering by, but otherwise paid no attention to any of its activities.

"We—we will gain knowledge when we arrive," Jamie said, trying not to watch but failing utterly. He was starting to feel distinctly queasy. "By limiting our knowledge before arrival, we avoid forming wrong impressions based on faulty or incomplete data."

"You talk too much, other one. Stop. First human. Other problem. The human ambassador is your superior. How can you investigate his other subordinates—

or him? The part cannot contend with the whole."
Again, the last statement sounded like an adage that
all were expected to know.

"The ambassador is not my superior. I—we—are
sent by *his* superiors, and ours. We can investigate,
accuse, arrest, and detain anyone at the embassy—
including the ambassador—if we find evidence of
crimes committed by that person." She paused, and
then risked a word or two more. "Please forgive my
long speech."

"Your apology is wrong. You provided required information." Zeeraum thought. "Strange idea, crime.
Only for individual-centered species. Vixa have no
crime. We have no problems. So you are outside embassy hierarchy? You are controlled by a superior, external hierarchy? Reply in very few words this time."

"Yes," said Hannah, and left it at that.

The two helper Vixa finished removing the small
pile of bones from Zeeraum's mouth, which was still
sagging open. Zeeraum pointed her manipulator at
Brox. "You there. You are not human. You are
Kendari. You are with the humans. You brought them
here." Zeeraum spoke with an attitude that implied
Brox would have been unaware of any of these facts if
she had not told him. "My briefing says you are all
three to make one investigation. Your peoples hate
each other. Don't you want to kill these humans?"

"No, I do not," Brox said evenly, though the twitching of his tail betrayed his agitation. He seemed
tempted to elaborate but followed his own instructions to keep his answers short.

"First human! Do you wish to kill this Kendari?
Don't you want to kill all Kendari? Can you work with
this one?"

"I don't want to kill this Kendari, or any Kendari.

We have worked with this Kendari before and can do so now."

"All of this is most surprising," said Zeeraum. She reached out casually with her front two manipulators and picked up one of the little helper Vixa. She cradled it in her left hand and patted it thoughtfully, like a little old lady picking up her toy poodle to pet it. "I am thinking," Zeeraum announced. Suddenly she lifted the little helper Vixa up over her head and dropped it into that gaping, obscene-looking mouth. The sphincter abruptly snapped shut, sealing the creature in.

Jamie could see the skin around the sides of the mouth-chamber bulge out here and there as the helper struggled inside, and he could hear what sounded like a tiny, high-pitched scream that went on and on. Zeeraum scratched herself absently, and the other helper Vixa trundled about their duties, displaying no reaction at all. None of the escort Vixa paid the slightest attention.

It took all of Jamie's will to keep from screaming himself. Hannah's hands were bunched up into fists, and her face was an expressionless mask. Only the quiver at her jawline betrayed her emotions.

"Very well," said Zeeraum, her voice unchanged. The muffled screams and the struggles inside her mouth subsided. "All is very odd and unusual, but your act of submission is accepted. You are granted permission to remain as independent investigators, not controlled by the embassy hierarchy. That is all." Zeeraum made a low burbling noise that might have been a laugh, or a belch, or even a rude comment in her own language. "Welcome," she said. "Welcome to civilization."

SEVEN

THE LAST DUTY

They got out of there, somehow. Their escort led them
to what was either the same landing bay or its identical
twin. SubPilot Greveltra was there, waiting to fly them
on in a smaller vehicle, a cylindrical aircar roughly the
size and shape of the jeep-tug they had started off
in, endless hours before. Their luggage was already
stowed on the craft. The two simulants, human and
Kendari, immediately collapsed back into rag-doll
mode the moment they were aboard. Hannah very
much felt like following suit.

None of them managed to say much of consequence
until they were airborne and on their way.

"I'm trying," Hannah said. "I'm trying as hard as I
can to remind myself they're xenos, aliens, totally different from us. They won't fit in our patterns, we can't
judge them by our standards. All of that. All of that.
But I still want to run away screaming from this
place."

"They are not like us," Brox agreed.

"That's an understatement," Jamie said. "Wait a
second—who's the 'us' in what you just said. Kendari?
You're not suggesting humans are like—"

"What? Oh, no! Forgive me, not at all. You are not
in the least like the Vixa. I meant—well, what did I
mean exactly? 'Species like ours,' I suppose. Species
that don't have biological castes. Species that have a
culture that permits broad individualism. Or perhaps

species that don't appear decadent, even morbidly degenerate, to Kendari sensibilities."

"'We Younger Race deadly-enemies-of-each-other have to stick together?'" Jamie suggested.

Brox tilted his head at Jamie and looked at him oddly. "Something like that. But Special Agent Wolfson is quite right. They *are* alien. Their ways are disturbing. We have just witnessed an act that would be regarded, at best, as the next thing to cannibalism in either of our cultures. It is the norm here. The superior may kill the inferior at any time."

"So they have one biological caste that combines the functions of the personal groomer, the pet, and the snack?" Jamie asked.

"Apparently. I had not personally witnessed that particular—ah, behavior before myself. But our rules, our laws, simply do not apply here. And even if they did, we do not have the power—or the right—to impose them."

"So let's leave it there," Hannah said. "We've got enough on our plate already. Brox. Where are we going now? To the human embassy?"

"Yes. And to the Kendari embassy, which is directly adjacent. We will be there very soon."

Hannah looked down on the quarter they were flying over. She instantly understood why Brox had called it a diplomatic ghetto. Below she could see dozens of walled compounds, arranged in a gridlike fashion, with access roads running between them.

The land itself was barren, a clumpy reddish soil dotted here and there with forlorn-looking plants that looked as if they had given up the struggle long ago. Everything was streaked or dotted or caked with dull red dust. The architecture of the structures inside the compounds varied tremendously, as if each was straining to stand out, make itself noticed, but the dulling red dust seemed to blot out all differences.

"How many embassies are there?" Jamie asked.

"Several hundred, at least," said Brox. "There are many less powerful Elder Races that have business before the Vixa of one sort or another. And then, of course, out at the very edge of things are the most junior and least deserving of all—the two Younger Races. And I should note that all that you see is quite old—and quite new. The capital-city designation 'Grand Warren' changes to conform with the residence of each new Preeminent Director. Until an Earth year or so ago, the various embassies were to be found in the Founder's Column City, out in space, where the Founder's Column meets the Stationary Ring. All the buildings and structures before you had been vacant for many long decades, since the last time Rivertide was the Grand Warren."

The aircar was flying over the roadways, and Hannah noticed that Greveltra seemed to be careful not to venture over the walls that separated the various embassy compounds from the roadways. "It looks like they are very careful about airspace around here," she said.

"An acute observation," said Brox. "Each embassy controls its own airspace up to something like twenty-two hundred and thirty meters, if I am converting measures properly. That's one reason we had to transfer out of the command sphere. It is simply too large to fly over the roads in the embassy quarter without impinging on xeno-sovereign airspace. And here we are, approaching our own homes away from home." Brox raised his voice. "SubPilot Greveltra, I ask that you hold this position for a brief time, so that the humans may view the area."

They eased to a halt at the far end of the block of walled compounds. The two compounds consisted of almost precisely square areas surrounded by four-meter walls made of something akin to concrete painted white. They were right up against each other, sharing a separating wall, so that the two of them together formed a rectangle twice as long as it was wide. There were access roads on all four sides of the two compounds, so that neither of them shared a common wall with any of the other nearby embassies.

"They put us right next to each other, and away from everyone else," Jamie observed. "Put two scorpions in a bottle, and hope they sting each other to death."

Hannah studied the view closely. Somewhere down there was a crime scene. From all the broad hints, it had to be a murder. Where, exactly, in which of the two compounds it had happened, Hannah had no idea. But it would unquestionably be useful to know the general layout of the place.

There was no one visible outside in either compound, but Hannah could tell at a glance that the one farther from the center of the city was the human embassy. The structures, the vehicles, all the things she could see were obviously human-built.

Hannah gave her first attention to the opposition, but the Kendari complex told her little from the air. The buildings were lower and wider than a human would have designed them. They were laid out in a precise and orderly pattern. No one building seemed particularly larger or more important than the others. Maybe a Kendari—or a BSI photo-interpreter—would have been able to read something from the layout, construction, and status of the buildings, but she couldn't see anything that would tell her much beyond that.

The human compound was another story. And, she realized with a start, the main structure, what she took to be the main embassy building, was actually a grounded spacecraft. Other structures had been built right alongside it and seemed to be joined to it, but it was a spacecraft all the same. It made sense in a way, especially given that you might have to do business where the air or the gravity or whatever didn't suit humans. Just land the ship, open the hatch, and your embassy was ready for business immediately. She had heard of the Diplomatic Service landing ships, but she had never seen an example of it.

From the utilitarian main buildings to the oversized communication shed to the heavy-duty ground vehicles and aircars, parked in precise rows, there was nothing gracious or elegant about the human compound. Everything—or almost everything—was rough-use grade, military-spec, field equipment.

The one exception was a most unlikely one: a garden, by the looks of it growing both vegetables and decorative flowers, directly in front of the main building.

But everything else was built to be ready for trouble. It wasn't just the complete absence of people outside. Hannah's practiced eye spotted the closed steel shutters, the portable barriers in place, and half a dozen other signs that the place was under lockdown. Everything down there shouted out that they weren't just *ready* for trouble. Trouble had arrived.

She turned back to the Kendari compound, and, now that she was looking for it, spotted what had to be their embassy ship, likewise connected to adjacent buildings—in what looked like a more planned and rational manner than was true on the human side.

"I call your attention to the building that straddles—or more accurately breaks through—the wall between the two compounds," said Brox. "That is our area of interest. Our crime scene."

Hannah nodded. "Now I see. I was reading that as *two* buildings, one on each side, each backing up against the wall. It seemed odd."

"Seems a lot odder to me that you'd bash a hole through the wall between you and your biggest competitor," said Jamie. "I take it you can enter that building from either compound?"

"Yes," said Brox. "But the security system is configured so that Kendari can only open the Kendari-side door, and humans can only open the human-side door. Furthermore, an interlock system allows only one set of doors—human or Kendari—to be used at a time."

"So, assuming everything is working right, everyone can meet in the middle, but no one can charge through to the other species' compound," said Hannah.

"Precisely." Brox looked down at the ground a moment more. "I think that tells you as much about the layout as we can learn from up here. Unless one of you wants to see more, or ask a question, of course."

"Yeah," said Jamie. "I've got a question. Who are they, and what are they doing here?" He pointed up the road to the north, back in the direction of the central city. There was a group of marchers—more like a mob, really—headed straight for the human and Kendari compounds.

And the marchers were *humans*. Hundreds of humans. Shouting, waving signs, kicking up a cloud of red dust, tussling with each other. "Where the hell did *they* come from?" Hannah asked. "And how did they show up, right on cue, when we arrive?"

Brox muttered something under his breath in his own language. "You met one of their leaders already. Our noble friend Zamprohna. Our Vixan hosts invited observer groups from both human and Kendari organizations. They are housed in temporary accommodations, in empty former embassies nearby. And somehow, they knew we were coming." He gestured toward another cloud of dust on the far side of the two compounds. "As did some of my compatriots."

A somewhat larger group of Kendari was coming down the road paralleling the one being used by the humans, moving along in quiet, orderly ranks, without any show or shouting or bluster. Somehow, that was even more unnerving than the shouts of the human mob. Hannah didn't understand why the two groups didn't try to get at each other, until she spotted the barriers that had been set up in all the cross streets between the two roads—and the Vixa with what appeared to be riot-control weapons who had suddenly appeared behind those barriers.

"This is as choreographed as a ballet," Hannah said flatly. "It's a setup. A riot—or at least a near riot—staged for our benefit."

"What are they in favor of?" Jamie asked. "Or what are they against?"

"I don't know," said Brox. "I left here—oh, in your measure, something like fourteen hours ago. There was no sign, no inkling, of anything like this. My guess is that it is not much more sophisticated than each species demanding that its own side win, and the other side lose, in the broadest and most general sense. As to how and why they are allowed to do this, I have no more information than you do," said Brox, "but I agree. Our hosts have all off-worlders, especially us Younger Races, under very tight control. At the very least, this could not possibly happen without the host government's tacit permission. I would regard it as much more likely that the Vixa in some way actively cooperated in the arrangements, or even organized the affair."

Jamie looked from the human mob to the Kendari marchers—then at the Vixan security forces separating them. "Okay," he said, "we get the message,"

"We do?" said Hannah. "What *is* the message? Who is telling us what?"

"I didn't mean to say we *understood* the message," said Jamie. "Just that we had received it. So far, I don't understand anything because I don't know anything."

"And it is time for you to learn more," said Brox. "Time for you to learn everything that I know." He spoke in a louder voice. "Take us in for a landing now, SubPilot Greveltra. In the Kendari compound, near the entrance to the joint operations building, if you please. As per the authority delegated to me by our Diplomatic Xenologist Flexdal 2092, I hereby grant permission for you to enter Kendari-embassy airspace, and land in the compound."

The aircar immediately moved sideways until it was directly over an empty spot of land in the Kendari compound, then translated straight down. Hannah could see a set of spindly-looking landing legs sprouting from the bottom of the craft. They set down almost before the legs were locked in place.

Then came the odd, shimmery sense of vibration as the command sphere's acceleration compensators shut down. Almost at the same moment, the humanoid and Kendarian sims, the two half-forgotten rag dolls, suddenly came back to life, straightening up and looking around alertly. It was instantly obvious that the humanoid sim's movements had become smoother and much more human-like than they had been only a few hours ago. And it didn't just look like a generic humanoid doll anymore. He—and Hannah decided she might as well think of the simulant as a "he" instead of an "it"—he now bore a noticeable, if sketchy, resemblance to Jamie.

"We are animated and ready for duty at our primary duty station," the two of them said in unison.

"Gee, we're glad to hear that," muttered Jamie. "That's what we're most worried about right now." His eyes were on the hatch, and Hannah spotted his hand twitching just a trifle, reaching for where his sidearm would be if he were carrying one. She couldn't blame him. She was just as jumpy herself.

The hatch opened, a ramp extruded, and they walked down to the ground. "Don't worry about your bags," said Brox. "The cargo floaters will follow with your luggage and equipment in a moment."

Hannah could hear the shouting and chanting from the demonstrators outside the walls, and even see the clouds of dust that both sides had kicked up. A volley of rocks came over the wall from the side where the humans were. The simulants didn't react, but Brox and the humans did, ducking, flinching, and shielding their heads with their hands. However, all of the rocks fell far short of the platform and landed harmlessly within a few meters of the wall.

"Nice welcoming committee," said Hannah.

Brox stepped away from the ramp, with Hannah, Jamie, and the simulants right behind him. "Come," said Brox. "This way."

Jamie started to follow, but Hannah didn't move and held up her hand, signaling Jamie to wait. "No," said Hannah. "We have to do this right. If we're headed to a crime scene, we need our crime scene kits first. We have to get them out of the gear on the cargo floaters."

Brox blinked in surprise. "My apologies. You are quite right. I will not say I am *eager* to get to the crime scene, but I am so *anxious* to do so that I am not thinking clearly." He turned to the simulants. "Request Greveltra to send down all the cargo and equipment the humans brought on board immediately."

"It has been done," both simulants said in unison.

Almost instantly, the cargo floaters emerged from the hatch and eased themselves to the ground—to the accompaniment of another badly aimed volley of rocks.

"What about all our other gear and supplies?" Jamie asked as he pulled out one of the two bright orange duffel bags that held the field-forensics kits.

"Leave them here, for the time being, I suppose," said Hannah.

"Right," said Jamie. He looked to Brox, slung the strap of the forensics kit over his shoulder, and patted it. "This kit should have everything we need to perform a two-agent examination of a crime scene. The other one is a spare. We won't need it. I hope. But I'd just as soon get it and ourselves out of this dust—and away from our rock-throwing friends—before we unpack and set up. Can we do that inside without disturbing the crime scene?"

"Yes," Brox replied. "There is a sort of anteroom just inside here where you can make your preparations without the dangers of dust or rocks, while not disturbing the scene of the crime itself."

"And what about you?" Hannah asked. "Do have the forensics gear you'll need?"

Brox gestured toward the entrance of the joint operations center. "I placed my equipment in the anteroom I just mentioned immediately before I sealed the building," he said.

"So *you* sealed this building—or at least this side of it—before you took off with Greveltra to come get us?" Hannah asked.

"Correct. I also placed tamper indicators on the Kendari-side exterior entrances of the building. If anyone tried to open or pass through those doors, it would be impossible for them to do so without leaving obvious traces and telltales."

"Good," said Jamie. "Next question—what goes on in this building? What *sort* of joint operations?"

Brox looked surprised once again. "How foolish of me. I have been so very careful not to tell you anything at all, and yet I am assuming that you are aware of all the local common knowledge. Joint security operations, conducted by Inquirists of the Kendari Inquiries Service and agents of the human Bureau of Special Investigations. Pooling information, coordinating travel routes and times for journeys back and forth to the negotiation site, monitoring troublemaking groups on both sides, that sort of thing. The prime mission of the operation was to prevent—well, exactly the sort of unrest that is going on right now, just outside the compound walls. I have no idea if it is by chance or by design that this disturbance is taking place immediately after the operations center was shut down."

"You're implying some sort of conspiracy there," said Hannah.

"So I am—and I should not be doing that. I have no information on that point at all, and I should not speculate about anything—especially before you have viewed the crime scene. I do not wish to prejudice you in any way."

Except you just did, thought Hannah. Was that accidental, an unintended hint at Brox's view of the case—or was he deliberately planting an idea, even as he denied having any such intent? "We'll do our best to remain uninfluenced," said Hannah, not even sure herself if she were being sarcastic.

"Excellent. Then let me get the door open." It was a sliding door, a big heavy slab of what looked like steel plating that rolled back and forth on a track. Someone with a powerful energy weapon, or a good-sized amount of heavy explosive, might be able to get through it, or blow it off its track, but it looked to be secure against anything less than a full-scale military assault. Brox examined some strips of elaborately patterned bright purple adhesive material that had been slapped over the door and the doorframe. "I call upon you both to witness and confirm that these tamper-indicator seals appear to be undisturbed."

Hannah got the distinct impression that Brox was speaking for the benefit of some sort of recording system. She couldn't see any sign of microphones or cameras, but that didn't mean they weren't there. She stepped forward and examined the seals, and tested one by pulling on it. It instantly turned from purple to orange, and the outline of her fingers, showing where she had touched it and pulled on it, appeared in screaming-bright green.

"We so witness and confirm," said Jamie.

Brox gave them the Kendari equivalent of a nod, and then pulled off the rest of the seals. Each of them turned a different garishly bright color as he removed it. Brox did not attempt to explain the lock system, and they did not inquire. Whatever he did caused a panel next to the door to throb blue for a minute, which seemed to satisfy Brox. He grabbed at a handle set into the door a bit lower than would be comfortable for a human and pulled it hard to the left.

The blast door rumbled back along its track, and Hannah was not the least surprised to see another door, identical to the first one, but hung so it rolled open from the opposite side. The space between the inner and outer doors formed an antechamber about two meters wide.

Brox gestured for them to step through, and they did so, the two simulants right behind them. He immediately pulled the outer door shut and locked it from the outside. Hannah tried not to think too hard about the fact that Brox knew how to get out, but they didn't. Either they trusted him, or they didn't—and they were in so deep that, if he decided to betray them, it wouldn't much matter what side of the door they were on.

Brox went immediately to a container that sat in the middle of the chamber, opened it, and began pulling out Kendari forensics equipment.

It was obvious that Brox was extremely anxious to get on with the job at hand. The endless delays, the long hours, the incredibly long round-trip that had been required of him—all of that must have been far more of a strain than he had admitted. Now, just a few meters and a few moments from the end of all that, he was allowing himself the luxury of letting the mask slip, just a little.

But even so, Hannah observed, he did not let himself rush. His preparations were deliberate, organized, carefully thought-out in advance. He opened the container, laid out his equipment, extracted his isolation suit, stepped into it, and sealed it up without a single wasted motion, and even got the suit's awkward hood over his head and ears, and the breathing filter slid down over his muzzle, with something approaching grace.

Hannah felt herself catching Brox's mood as she made her own preparations, unpacked her own iso-suit, laid out her own gear. She was the bullfighter dressing for the ring, the duelist making sure that everything was just as it should be so that the deadly event would be carried out properly, the knight girding himself for battle. What was usually done by habit and rote motion somehow became ritualized, a ceremony of preparation. She half expected to hear stirring background music rising to a climax as she strapped on the last recorder and clipped on the final measuring device, then pulled the absurd little booties on over her shoes and slithered the surgical gloves onto her hands.

The iso-suits, the gloves, the booties, the face masks were meant to keep a bit of dried skin, a bit of hair from Jamie or Hannah, a bit of body felt from Brox, a droplet of spittle transported by a cough or a sneeze, from contaminating the crime scene, destroying or masking some vital bit of evidence.

Brox drew on his gloves just as Hannah finished, with Jamie done just a little ahead of them both. Hannah felt a completely irrational flash of annoyance that they didn't all finish in unison.

Finally they were ready.

Brox stripped the tamper indicators off the inner door, released the lock, and pulled it open. He did not step through the door, but instead gestured for the two humans to go first. *One last effort to keep us unbiased,* Hannah told herself. Or was it just that Brox wanted it to appear that way? This could all be stage manage-

ment to prime them for some bit of manipulation yet
to come.

If so, it was too deep a scheme for Hannah to perceive. She and Jamie collected their gear and stepped
through the door. Whatever they had been summoned
to see, whatever had set off this interstellar, interspecies furor, whatever had caused two embassies to
lock down altogether and summoned two mobs, was
just inside. Hannah felt her gut tighten.

They stepped into a large central room that took up
much of the structure's interior. The lights were off,
and the only illumination came dimly through a large
overhead skylight. The room was stuffy, the air stale,
with a faint musty scent overlaid with a hint of an unpleasant sickly-sweet odor, a smell that every police investigator knew to link with death. The two simulants
followed the humans and Brox inside, but they made
no effort to move forward, or to participate. Brox
seemed barely aware of their presence as he pulled the
inner door shut and locked it down. "Give me just a
brief moment," he said. "Part of the agreement was
that all power be cut until our arrival."

Jamie stood by Hannah as she waited and looked
the place over. Out of the corner of her eye, she saw
Brox working at some sort of control panel. They
were in what was plainly a room divided in two, with
the furniture and equipment in the half they were in
designed for Kendari use, while the other side was
equipped with human-style desks and chairs.

There was a row of three Kendari workstalls—
basically low desks with sling arrangements instead of
chairs—facing a row of three banged-up government-
issue-style human desks. The space between the workstalls and the desks was very obviously a neutral zone,
a border, between the two sides. Indeed, the border be-

tween the two compounds was very clearly visible: the Kendari side of the floor was covered with a bright orange carpet, while the human side was slate-grey government-issue linoleum. Hannah had not the slightest doubt that the precise border between the two compounds ran right along the line where carpet met flooring tile.

All that she saw in a single glance. Then Brox got the environmental systems going. The room turned dazzling bright and the ventilation system whisked away the worst of the sickly-sweet scent of decay. Hannah's attention was utterly and instantly focused on what they had plainly come to see.

"I told you I was performing Final Inquiries," said Brox, standing in the far corner. "In other words, a death investigation. We Kendari tend to use overly polite, unemotional, perhaps even clinical terms for anything we find upsetting. What humans call 'dying in the line of duty,' we call 'performing one's final duty,' as if the death itself were the duty to be fulfilled—instead of being the disaster that *prevents* completion and fulfillment."

Brox walked toward the center of the room, and paused a few paces away from the motionless form that lay there, collapsed directly over the dividing line between human territory and Kendari.

The body lay on its side, the neck, the spine, and the long tail all arced inward, the four walking legs rigid and extended, the arms stretched out forward, the hands clenched in fists. The muzzle was frozen in a grimace, the lips drawn back from the teeth. The eyes were shut, almost peaceful, but the expression frozen on the face was one of fear and pain. There was what looked to be burn marks on the skin around the back of the mouth, and the gum tissue visible inside the mouth was badly inflamed. There was some sign of discharge and irritation around the visible eye and ear, and around the nose as well.

Hannah flashed back to the training photo they had shown her on the opening day of the mandatory xeno-forensics class every trainee agent sat through. It was almost a textbook case of caffeine poisoning. Any human who came in contact with Kendari was warned endlessly not to use any caffeine product near them. This was why. On the floor, not twenty centimeters from the dead Kendari's clenched fists, was a human-style white-china coffee mug, the twin of one Hannah kept on her desk back at the Bullpen—down to the BSI logo emblazoned boldly on its side. It was slightly cracked, and a chip off the rim, a sharp, curved triangle of ceramic material about two centimeters on a side, lay on the floor next to it. There was a dried whitish residue on the linoleum around it. There were a few whitish spots on the Kendari carpet, and a wider, fainter pool of similar residue around the dead xeno's head, roughly centered around the jawline.

Jamie came around to the other side and stepped forward, gingerly, carefully, respectfully, kneeling down by the head, not coming close to touching anything. "Who is this, Brox?" he asked in a quiet voice, almost a whisper.

Brox hung back from the corpse, standing well to the rear of Hannah. He gestured vaguely toward the body, knotted his fingers together, and shifted back and forth on his walking limbs as his tail twitched, ever so slightly. "There is a tradition—a common way of doing things among Kendari of my age and social class. Some of your cultures have arranged marriages. We have a similar but not identical procedure—proposed marriages. Families will seek out eligible and suitable partners for their adult offspring. It would be arranged for the potential partners to spend time together, work together. If the two work in the same profession, that is all to the good."

Hannah looked up at Brox. It was not like him to speak so obliquely, to say things in such an indirect, unfocused way. *You're wrong,* Hannah told herself. *It is like Brox. It's like Brox when he's in shock, in mourning, straining to deal with a hurricane of personal emotions and professional crises that all come at once.*

"Go on, Brox," said Jamie. The two humans glanced at each other, in silent agreement that Brox had to say it, had to get the words out there. No one could perform this last part of his current duty for him.

"Her name is—was—Emelza 401. She—she was an Inquirist, approximately one-quarter of a ranking level above me in the Inquiries Service. And she was my prospective mate. My fiancée, I suppose you would call her."

Neither Jamie nor Hannah pushed any harder. *We know the rest,* thought Hannah. *You were going to marry her. You were here together working to keep the peace between humans and Kendari. And approximately sixteen hours ago, she was found dead of caffeine poisoning.* It was unquestionably a murder. And she died in the office she shared with three BSI agents, with a BSI coffee mug next to her head.

EIGHT

DOCUMENT OF DEATH

Now we know, thought Jamie as he worked the crime scene. *Now we know why it had to be this way.*

Why the BSI agents on the scene couldn't take on the investigation. That coffee mug—and the fact that the body was found in their workplace—made them prime suspects.

Why Brox couldn't do the job all by himself. He was not only too close to the case emotionally—he also had to be considered a suspect. Jamie didn't know anything about Kendari crime statistics, but it was at least a reasonable bet that the percentage of murders that turned out to be domestic disputes wouldn't be that different than the rate for humans—and an awful lot of human murders were committed by spouses, intended spouses, and ex-spouses.

Why no human—or Kendari—on the scene could do the job. Why both the Kendari and human embassies were in lockdown until Hannah and he could examine the crime scene. *Every* human and every Kendari, in both embassies, had to be considered a suspect. Emelza 401 had died in the midst of a diplomatic battle for the control of two whole planets. If the murder of one enemy xeno—or, indeed, the murder of one of your own people, staged so as to discredit the opposition—could win that battle for one side or the other, was there a government anywhere, at any time, that wouldn't at least have been tempted by such a prospect?

Or had Emelza known something, said something, possessed something that could have led to her death? Was she merely a passive victim? Or had she, in some way, been playing the game of worlds herself—and taken one risk too far?

The worklights from their crime scene kit were powered up and casting harsh cones of cold and clinical brightness down on the sad little scene of death, illuminating the dark corners, making the shadows sharp and hard. Nothing could look right, or natural, or simple in light that hard.

They decided to examine the nonmedical physical evidence first. The big, obvious item was the coffee mug—but it was rarely a good idea to go for the big, obvious thing first. Hannah and Jamie pulled samples from the dried-up spill off the hard flooring on the human side and the carpeting on the Kendari side. They snipped fabric and did adhesive-tape lift-samples of every nearby surface, but all of that was more or less pro forma. If there was anything there to find, they'd find it—but there wasn't going to be anything there.

They photographed the rest of the room as well, from the desk chairs placed neatly behind the remarkably tidy human desks and the equally tidy Kendari workstalls to the plain, undecorated walls and doors. Probably pointless, all of it, but there was always the off chance that some mark, some small item might be a clue. Later, they would have the photographs to check.

Thinking about it for a moment, Jamie wasn't much astonished by the compulsively clean work areas. You wouldn't want to risk leaving anything around for your counterparts to see—not when those counterparts were onetime enemy agents and likely would be so again in the future.

The three human desks were arranged identically. On each sat a pencil cup, holding three pencils and three pens, a plastic deskpad writing surface, a stack of blank writing paper, and a set of sockets for a desktop data display and input system. If the agents here had been using anything like standard BSI security procedures—and they plainly had been—the data units were taken away and locked up when not in use. Faint scuff marks on the desk showed where the data system units had sat.

Once the surrounding area had been examined and recorded, they focused in on the areas of central interest—the victim, and the coffee cup that was the apparent murder weapon.

Jamie photographed Emelza. Overall views from all angles, close-ups of her head, her feet, her hands clenched into fists. He moved through the process systematically, methodically. One shot after the next. He shifted position to get another angle—and caught himself a moment later, just crouching there, motionless, lost in thought, staring at nothing at all.

"Jamie?" Hannah called out. "Stay with us, okay? It's bad enough we're nearly losing Brox. You need to keep sharp."

"Huh? What? Oh—okay." He blinked and forced himself to concentrate on the task at hand. Measure. Photograph. Evaluate. Seek for the small thing, the tiny detail that would speak and tell them big things. Study the corpse as a record, a result, a document that displayed the physical results, the defining marks, of whatever it had experienced, and therefore would show, to a discerning eye, how death occurred.

Think of the corpse as a *thing,* an it—not a she, not

a person, not the intended spouse of your friend, your enemy, your colleague. Think of the corpse as a puzzle piece, a crossword to be solved, a part of an intellectual game—and not as the centerpiece of an interstellar, interspecies crisis.

Keep it clean. Keep it simple, Jamie told himself. *Solve the crime. Let the victim, and the victim's intended, and the politics, take care of themselves.*

"It'd be nice if it were that easy, wouldn't it?" he said to himself, speaking out loud.

"What?" Hannah asked, busy herself, doing a quick pencil sketch of the scene. "Were you talking to me?"

"No," said Jamie. "Not to you." He was going to have a hell of a time keeping things clean, simple, and impersonal if he started out by talking to the dead victim.

"Okay," Hannah said absently, not really listening as she finished up her drawing. "You just about done with the initial photography of the victim?"

"Yeah," said Jamie, his voice close to a whisper. "But I'm not in any hurry to finish. I don't know what, exactly, we do next."

"What do you mean?"

"What I'm thinking is if this was a—a *regular* murder, and we had more or less normal facilities, some sort of trained tech would magically appear and draw samples here in the field for analysis, then take the body away to a lab to run tests. We might never see the body again, but we'd get a nice fat data file full of medical evidence. But we don't get that this time—and I don't know how to draw Kendari blood or take tissue samples for toxicology and so on. What happens instead?"

Hannah glanced over at Brox. He was standing, his

back to the crime scene, staring blankly at a patch of very blank wall. He was acting one hell of a lot like a human who had held together until his job was complete, his duty performed, and then fallen apart. It had been an act of sheer will to keep moving forward, get the job done—but now the job *was* done. He had delivered the human investigators he had been told to retrieve. Now he could let go, unravel, at least a little bit, for a little while.

"Well," said Hannah, "the obvious answer would be to get someone from the same species, preferably someone who has some expertise in crime scenes, to do the job—and that's Brox. But Brox *can't*. He's the grieving intended mate—and, let's face it—a suspect. Don't get me wrong. *Every*body in both embassies is a suspect, and that BSI coffee mug and the three desks for BSI agents three meters from the corpse don't make it look good for our side. But the whole point of our being dragged in here was to keep from having Brox investigate this one by himself. Even if he wasn't half in shock, even if we were ready to ask him to draw samples from his fiancée's dead body—it would taint the whole case to have him do the work."

"Then it's up to us," said Jamie. "But I don't know what sorts of samples to take, or how to take them. And that brings us right back to Brox. He's the only one who can walk us through this."

"No he isn't," Hannah said. "Medical officer. The Kendari diplomatic mission must have *some* sort of medical officer. So would the human mission."

"Both of whom are also suspects," Jamie objected. "More so than most of the other embassy personnel, given that this a *prima facie* poisoning case."

Hannah gestured to Emelza. "If we found her dead from a blow on the head, would you say that carpenters had to be prime suspects because only a carpenter would know how to use hammers?"

"I don't see your point."

"*Everyone* knows that caffeine is deadly poison to Kendari. They train and train and train every human who comes into contact with Kendari, exactly because it's in such common use with us and it kills them. We all know what the symptoms are, how small the dose has to be, what a Kendari caffeine case looks like. You don't need to be a doctor to know poison will kill you."

"Point taken. They aren't stronger or weaker suspects than anyone else."

"Right," said Hannah.

"So you're saying we pull both medical officers out of solitary?" Jamie asked. "Let them watch each other, and we watch both of them—and maybe Brox will snap out of it enough to watch us watch them?"

"Right. Brox will know how to contact his side, and have them contact our people."

"Let's do it."

But, of course, it was never that easy.

Ambassador Stabmacher splashed some water on his face, smoothed his hair back with the damp palm of his hand, and did his best to straighten up and smooth over the rumpled clothes he had been in for more hours than he cared to admit. He didn't much worry about his appearance for his own sake, but he knew full well the importance of looking his best for the sake of those he represented. And when that hatch opened in a moment, he would be the visible face of the human embassy on Tifinda.

The annunciator chimed, and the ambassador

folded up the sink, made one last check of his appearance in the mirror, and went to the door. He pushed the intercom button. "Hello," he said.

"I'm here to escort you," said a voice he heard from the intercom, and also, in more muffled tones, coming through the hatch.

"Very good," he said. "You'll see what I believe are called tamper-indicator tapes over the seam of the hatch and the hatchway and so on. I'm told that those need to be removed before the hatch is opened, to prevent them from getting jammed in the mechanism."

"Yes, sir," said the voice once again, in a tone that managed to suggest both due respect for the ambassador, but also a slight weariness at being told how to do your own job by someone who knew far less about it than you did. "I'm photographing the tamper strips now, to demonstrate they were intact, just in case that comes up."

There was a slight pause, and then a few quiet rustles and scraping noises. "All right, sir. Ready for you on this side."

The ambassador undid the lock from the inside, and the door slid back into its recess. Ambassador Stabmacher put a smile on his face while at the same time trying to mask his very genuine sense of relief—and then decided there was no point in masking it at all. Who *wouldn't* be glad to get out? And why not, at least once in a while, let his expression and his voice show the way he really felt, instead of the way he *ought* to feel?

"Hello," he said, putting out his hand. "Ambassador Berndt Stabmacher, representing the United Human Governments to the Eminent Masters and the Preeminent Director of the Grand Warrens of the

Conclave of Tifinda." He grinned again and shook his head slightly. "How's that for a mouthful?"

"Senior Special Agent Hannah Wolfson, BSI," said the woman as she took his hand. "Very glad to see you, sir. This is a bad situation. But you know that better than I do."

"Maybe not. I've been cooped up here quite a while. Things might have changed without my knowing," said the ambassador. He gestured around the small compartment. "Negotiating from voluntary solitary confinement is difficult."

"There was a lot of negotiating, yes, sir. It took a lot of dickering with the Kendari just to get a deal that would allow me to go through the door on the human-embassy side of the joint operations center."

"Let me be sure from you that I understand the agreement. The medical officers from the two embassies are to perform the, ah, actual *handling* of the body, and the two ambassadors, and Inquirist Brox 231, and you and your partner are to observe? Plenty of witnesses all around?"

"That's about it, sir. Except I believe the Kendari medical officer will be the one doing most of the work. Obviously their medical people will know more about handling one of their corpses. And my partner is watching the body while Inquirist Brox and I collect everyone else."

"Yes, I suppose that makes sense. Well, let's go pick up our doctor and get on with it. I promise you there are a great number of people who don't want to be kept waiting any longer."

"We've gathered that much, sir, but I think it might be best if you didn't say anything more until after we have dealt with the primary evidence. I think it would

be wise if we waited for a formal interrogation—or de-
briefing, if you prefer that word."

"'Hearing,' would come closest, I think. But let's get
on with it, shall we?"

Jamie stood alone—or nearly alone—in the harshly lit
center of the joint operations center. He did, after all,
have the simulants for company, for whatever that was
worth. And, of course, Emelza 401 was there as well.

He knelt in front of her body and considered it
thoughtfully. He knew nothing about her, really. She
had been an Inquirist, she was young, and somehow, a
group of family members from both sides had concluded she and Brox would be a good match. That was
all.

In the cold, grim world they were working in, it
didn't matter if he knew much else, unless it bore directly on how and why she was murdered. He, Jamie
Mendez, and Hannah Wolfson, Commander Kelly,
and Ambassador Stabmacher, and the BSI, and even
Greveltra and his monster ship, had been pulled into
all this not because of who she was, or what she did, or
thought, or felt, or who did or did not love her, or even
because she had died—but simply because of *how* she
had died, and when, and where, and what was going
on around her death. All that really mattered about
her, to any of them, was that she had been murdered in
the midst of delicate negotiations, and in a way that
threw suspicion on humans in general, and BSI agents
in particular. She had been reduced to a token, a symbol, an excuse.

"I'm sorry," Jamie said to Emelza. "I'm sorry
you're in the middle of all this." In the middle, and yet
just about forgotten. Which brought him back to the

simulants—over at the edge, and likewise just about forgotten.

He stood up and walked over to them, stared at them both again. They were doing their deflated-beach-toy routine. But it would be a mistake to under-estimate them. Whatever they were, exactly—robots, living beings, some weird amalgam of the two—they were here, in this room, because the Vixa were power-ful enough to insist upon it and get their way. Odd to realize that he had more contact with them than any of the other Vixa. Unless Greveltra counted—and Jamie had gotten the very distinct impression from Brox that Greveltra, to some extent, *didn't* count. Jamie had barely said five words to Zeeraum.

And if *he* didn't count, these two—beings, objects, machines, animals—certainly didn't. And what did that say about the "real" Vixa if they surrounded themselves with lesser forms?

"What are you here for?" Jamie asked the two sim-ulants.

The two of them stirred and came to life. The hu-manoid one was moving much faster and more smoothly than he had before. The thing had started out as a cartoonish blob-shaped approximation of the human body, so poorly programmed that it didn't even know to face the person he was speaking to. But it had learned to look up at him and establish eye contact.

For that matter, Jamie realized, the simulant had grown *eyes* along with a mouth, nose, and ears—or at least simulations of them. They all looked painted on, like the features on a doll or a mannequin. He had a sort of a mop of hair on his head—no, strike that—there were bulges growing out of his head that were colored and textured to approximate a thick mop of hair. "We are here to observe and assist," said the simulant. The words came out of the general region of the mouth, but the mouth itself did not move—nor did any other part of the head. But Jamie recognized the voice—his own voice—all the same.

Jamie felt as if he were looking through a mirror that produced a blurred and slightly distorted reflection. It was more obvious by the hour that this simulant was making himself over into a copy of Jamie Mendez.

"For whom do you observe? What are you here to observe?" he asked in Lesser Trade. "And how do you assist? You have not been of any great help so far."

"We observe on behalf of those who sent us. Our assistance will be provided at a later time and will be of significant help to you."

"Those answers, I must tell you, are of no help at all."

"They are the answers we provide. Our assistance will be provided at a—"

"That's enough," said Jamie. "Quiet."

He turned his attention to the Kendarian simulant, who pointed his muzzle at Jamie and cocked his head slightly to one side in a startlingly good imitation of one of Brox's mannerisms. "You have had more time to develop and observe than your companion. Will your responses be any more helpful?"

"We observe on behalf of—"

"Quiet," said Jamie. It didn't make any sense. Jamie was no expert on diplomatic niceties, but BSI agents had to know the basics. The principles of diplomatic immunity and of extraterritoriality, of an embassy being outside the territory and control of the host government, were to all intents universal. The Elder Race traditions and laws controlling those concepts were virtually identical to human practices.

It was a huge breach of those standards for the Vixa to require these simulants to accompany them on this mission, and into Kendari and human sovereign territory. Legally, the spot of ground he was on was, for most purposes, to be treated as if it were physically part of the planet Kendal. If he walked three meters to the BSI side of the main room, legally speaking, he'd be on Earth—or possibly Center. He was a little fuzzy on that detail.

What he did understand was that the cartoon version of diplomatic immunity—a drunken ambassador running over five people in the host country's capital, and not being punished for it—wasn't the reality. Diplomats and embassies weren't supposed to be immune from the law, or above it. The whole idea was that they were to be governed by the laws of their home governments. That was why this case wasn't being investigated by Vixan cops. And an embassy was supposed to be a place of safety, sanctuary, privacy. Access to it should be completely under the control of the embassy itself, with no reference to the host government.

Of course, nothing in life was absolute. There were practical limits and exceptions to that principle, and the rules had been broken many times by both host and guest governments. But the rules were there because they had to be there. Without such protections, every ambassador, every diplomat, was little more than a volunteer hostage, controlled by the whim of his or her hosts—with his or her opposite number the obvious target for reprisal by the folks back home. When one side or the other started playing that game—and it happened from time to time—relations between the two governments rapidly ground to a halt. Diplomats *had* to be safe. Embassies *had* to be extraterritorial, or else the whole system would collapse. The principle was universal because it was so basic, so fundamental.

And yet here were these two simulants, given the run of the Kendari/human joint operations center, and, apparently, both embassy compounds. The Vixa would have had to force that down the throats of the two ambassadors. It must have been the subject of huge protests, big arguments, complicated negotiations.

And for what? So a pair of rubber-faced copies of the real investigators could sit at the edge of the room and stare blankly at nothing at all. Why cause so much ill will for so little gain? It didn't make sense.

The inescapable conclusion was that the simulants were there for some other reason. But what the devil could it be?

He decided to try one more thing. The simulants had picked up Lesser Trade very rapidly. So fast that Jamie figured that it *had* been preprogrammed in them, but that the programming was latent in some way. It was in there, stored away, but it had to be *activated,* in something like the way a simulant apparently had to be near to and observing a subject before it started mimicking it. At a guess, hearing Lesser Trade spoken stimulated the memory centers that held the language, causing them to activate and feed their language skills to the simulant's brain, or its central processor, or whatever it had.

Maybe English was in there in some sort of latent state as well. If the Vixa had gone to all the trouble to create a human simulant, they should have had the sense to include some sort of language module that would enable it to talk with humans—or listen in on them.

They had spoken some English in the simulants' presence. Maybe enough to stimulate at least limited activation of that module, if it was there.

It was guess upon guess upon guess. But if he were right, the simulants would have only limited English skills, and they likely wouldn't be programmed with pat answers for everything. Maybe a little truth would come out, if he got lucky.

"I ask again," he said, speaking in slow and careful English. "I urge you to answer fully. What are you here to observe?"

Jamie was facing the humanoid sim, his own fun-house mirror image, but it was the Kendarian who replied. "We here to watch you investigate go bad, fail," he said. "Then the Eminent can stop Pentam tal—"

The simulant's voice cut off suddenly, and he froze into immobility.

"My—my—my colleague has said too much and spoken in error," the humanoid said in Lesser Trade, stuttering, and his voice oddly wooden at first, then smoothing out. "He is being reset."

Jamie nodded, feeling a bit wooden and stuttery himself. The simulant had a point. That *was* too much. Way too much. There were days, and this was one of them, when he felt as if he could do with a reset himself.

Hannah's first impression of Ambassador Stabmacher was Ichabod Crane with perfect manners—but it took only a minute to realize that Stabmacher was canny enough to use his angular physique and boyish gawkiness as a social tool, a way to put others at ease—and to guide them in the way he wanted to go.

By the time they reached the compartment where the medical officer was under voluntary confinement, Hannah realized that Stabmacher had already drawn her in. She felt like a member of the team, *his* team, ready to go forward and do what needed to be done.

It took some real skills to pull off that style of leadership, and Hannah couldn't help but admire him. But she had to keep her distance. As even Grand Vixan Zeeraum had understood, Stabmacher needed her, and Jamie, exactly because they *weren't* on his team. Conflicting allegiances would do none of them any good.

They reached the med officer's cabin. Hannah pressed the annunciator button but got no answer. She looked to the ambassador, but he merely shrugged and smiled, obviously amused rather than worried. She pressed the button again, and then pounded loudly on the metal hatch with the flat of her hand. "Dr. Zhen?" she called. "Are you there?"

"Of course I'm here," said a muffled voice through the hatch. It would seem Dr. Zhen couldn't be bothered with using the intercom. "I'm sealed in with tamper strips on the door. Where *else* would I be? Give me a second."

Hannah looked again at Stabmacher, but he had gone all poker-faced. She set to work peeling off the tamper strips, and just barely got done when the hatch slid open without warning.

Hannah hadn't really given much thought as to what to expect of the M.O., beyond the clichéd idea that embassy doctors and civilian shipboard doctors were usually washed-up old wrecks marking time until retirement. But any trace of that idea went away the moment the hatch opened. "What in the world is going on now?" said the pigtailed woman who opened the door.

Hannah's first impression was of an Asian Dorothy Gale, complete with pigtails, there in the thick of it, doing her best to deal with everything the land of Oz could throw at her. She was black-haired and olive-skinned, and her oval face seemed to fall into an open and frank expression that made her look perpetually surprised. She was dressed in pale blue surgical scrubs. She seemed very young, very determined, very sure of herself—but with a fragility, a sense of uncertainty as well. "We're here to collect you for the exam. The examination and removal of the remains," Hannah said.

"Oh, right," said the other woman. "I'm sorry. I was taking a nap. Sometimes I'm a little woozy if I get awakened suddenly. And I'm bad on names. Who are you?"

"Dr. Zhen Chi, allow me to present Senior Special Agent Hannah Wolfson," said the ambassador, who was making no effort at all to mask his amusement, even as he went through the very proper forms of introduction. "Agent Wolfson, Dr. Zhen."

"You can skip the 'Dr. Zhen' stuff. Just call me Zhen Chi or Zhen. Everyone does. I prefer it. Lemme grab my bag." She stepped back into the compartment, collected a medical kit, and stepped back out. "Let's go."

The ambassador led the way, with the two women walking side by side behind him. "Forgive the personal question," said Hannah, "but how in the world did you manage to fall that soundly asleep in the time since we got the exam arrangements worked out?"

"Force of habit that I picked up in med school and my internship," said Zhen Chi. "If you're just sitting and waiting, doze if you can, because you probably won't have the chance later. It's almost a job skill. Sorry if I was rude making you wait like that."

"Oh I wasn't offended," said Hannah. "I was *jealous*. It's a job skill for BSI agents too—and you're better at it than I am."

Minutes later they were back on the human side of the joint operations center. Jamie was still there, the simulants standing alongside him, almost as if the two of them had been in conversation. Hannah looked at him and got a raised eyebrow and a shrug in return. She had spent enough case time with Jamie to read that pretty clearly: Something interesting had come up, but he couldn't tell her now.

Almost at the same time, the Kendari contingent arrived, led in by Brox, who got straight to the point. "I present Diplomatic Xenologist Flexdal 2092 and Medical Technist Remdex 290, as per our agreement."

Ambassador Stabmacher spoke, recapping the agreement for the benefit of the various recording devices that would bear witness that Flexdal had agreed to the arrangements, but Hannah tuned him out.

She studied the newly arrived Kendari instead, to try and get some sense of how they felt about the situation. But either she wasn't all that good at reading Kendari emotional reactions, or else the medical technist and the xenologists had the makings of excellent poker players.

She tuned back in to what the ambassador was saying just as he was concluding. "To sum up, in deference to your medical technist's far greater experience with Kendari medical matters, Technist Remdex will perform the postmortem exam and removal of tissue and fluid samples, while our medical officer and the BSI agents—and you and I—serve as witnesses."

"Agreed," said Flexdal. He turned to Remdex. "You will proceed."

"I act as instructed," said Remdex in a tone of voice that suggested Remdex wasn't happy about the situation.

But then, thought Hannah, *who is?*

The obvious next step was to deal with the coffee mug. After subjecting it to endless additional photography from every angle, including extreme close-ups, they were ready to pick it up and move it.

There was only one thing slightly unusual about the cup. The word "Milk" had been written in some sort of indelible marker across the base of it—at a guess, to remind whoever made the coffee what that person liked in his brew. The lettering was verging on the dim and fading, as if the cup had been washed many times since it had been marked. The BSI logo on the side was still new, all bright and shiny. It had some sort of protective overcoating, though that overcoating seemed just to have been very slightly roughened. Jamie noticed one other thing—that something about the lettering seemed to bother, even worry, Hannah.

After a certain amount of dreary debate, it was agreed that the Kendari could have the main part of the cup, while the humans had to settle for the chip— but each side was allowed to run a sterile swab on the interior surface of the other's piece—then run a second swab to be held by the possessors of the piece.

As bickering between cops from two jurisdictions went, it was actually pretty tame. They got the coffee mug and all the related items into sealed containers and duly labeled and witnessed in fairly short order.

Then came the far tougher, far grimmer job of dealing with the body itself. Jamie was not in the least bit sorry to step back and let the medical specialists deal with that part of the job.

Jamie stood as patiently as he could, watching the watchers watch, trying his best to learn something from the procedure, if nothing else, something about Kendari procedure that might come in handy on some future case. The exam went on with the endless attention to detail that such matters required. Given the utterly obvious cause of death, it almost seemed pointless for Remdex to be as compulsively thorough as he was. But the body of a murder victim was a document that could likely only be read once. The processes of decay, and the very action of examining the body, could degrade, conceal, or completely destroy some vital piece of evidence. You had to get every bit of information out the first time, because there might not be a second.

Unless, of course, the obvious answer was the correct answer, and the whole rigmarole was a complete waste of time. But you never knew that until later. So Remdex carefully removed samples of Emelza 401's body felt and circulatory fluid, took swab samples of her eyes, ears, mouth, and nose. He carefully examined her feet and tail—Jamie had no idea why. Zhen Chi watched Remdex's every move and assisted him as best she could, handing him sample containers and sealing them once they were filled. They took three samples of each type—one for the Kendari, one for the humans, and one to be sealed away and preserved to provide a reference point in case of future disputes.

Brox, in theory, was supposed to be one of the

official witnesses, but he hung well back from the proceedings, staying inside his own workstall on the southeast corner of the room. It was plain that no one on the Kendari side of the job was going to reproach him for that, and Jamie certainly had no desire to intrude. Nor, he felt sure, did any of the other humans. There were enough layers of observation and evidence protection that the investigation team could spare him the sight of his own espoused's field postmortem.

The simulants, on the other hand, were very much front and center, carefully observing the whole procedure—though Jamie was not at all certain why, or for whom, they were watching.

"I am think we are done," Remdex announced at last, speaking rather sketchy Lesser Trade Speech, arching his long neck up and stretching it back and forth to get the kinks out. "Now we ready place body in holding container, place in freeze place." The Kendari had decided to clear out some sort of food-storage freezer to hold the remains for the time being. "Is you agree, Med-Tech Chi?"

Zhen Chi glared at Remdex and Jamie grimaced. It was obvious that Remdex's grasp of Lesser Trade Speech was pretty weak—weak enough that deliberately making a clumsy rhyme out of Zhen Chi's name was well beyond his powers. But it was obvious that Zhen Chi was annoyed by it all the same.

"Oh, yes, Med-Tech Remdex," said Zhen Chi. "We are all the way done. Get her into a body bag and pop her into the freezer whenever you like."

"I like do move now," said Remdex, his attention on the body and completely unaware that he had given offense. "But first request additional images of that," he said, and pointed to the right shoulder area of the body.

"Of what?" Jamie asked. He hadn't noticed anything special in that area. He looked at Hannah, but she just frowned and shook her head. Neither had she.

"At *that*," said Remdex. "Is very clear now. All developed." He grabbed a pocket light and held it low and pointed across the surface of the body, so as to produce stronger and more distinct shadows.

Hannah drew in her breath in shock, surprise. "How the hell did we miss *that*?" she asked.

"I don't know," said Jamie. "I haven't the least idea in the world." But he did know, immediately, that something had gone very, very wrong. They *couldn't* have missed something that obvious. But it was just as obvious that they had.

There, in the shoulder area, was a rumpled series of indentations, almost as if the dead Kendari's flesh was soft clay that someone had poked at.

Someone who had poked at the body with one finger, then two, then pushed at it with the whole hand, leaving behind a well-formed, absolutely clear handprint. The print of a left hand.

A human left hand.

NINE

INTERVIEW WITH AN AMBASSADOR

"You can check for yourself, Ambassador," said the younger, male Special Agent, reaching across his desk to hand him a datapad.

Ambassador Stabmacher took pride in his ability to remember names and faces, but it had been a damnably hard couple of days, with far too little rest, let alone sleep. *Mendez,* that was it. The ambassador accepted the datapad and resisted the temptation to toss it to one side, unexamined. He could at least retain his skill in managing his temper.

He leaned back in his chair and studied the images carefully, then glanced out the window at the compound, and at the embassy ship, thirty meters away. They were meeting in his formal office, and it was a distinct relief to get out of his ship-side quarters and get some elbow room. No doubt the rest of the embassy staff was itching to get out as well. He realized that his thoughts had wandered, and forced his concentration back to the images.

"Those are from our cameras and Brox's as well," said Mendez. "No chance of the photos being retouched."

"And I quite agree that there is no sign of the finger marks or the handprint," the ambassador agreed. "But I hardly think that improves the situation. If the handprint wasn't there when you took those photos at the start of the crime scene examinations, it must have been created during the time when the corpse was continuously under watch. Under *your* watch. Possibly during the period you were there by yourself while Inquirist Brox and *Senior* Special Agent Wolfson"— there! *Her* name he had remembered without effort— "were collecting the rest of us."

Mendez stood uncomfortably and shifted from one foot to the other. "Sir, I can't say that my eyes never left the body. They did. But it's impossible, absolutely impossible, that someone came in, poked at the corpse, then left the room without my noticing it. And, ah, for what it is worth, I wasn't exactly alone, sir. There were the two simulants, the human and Kendari ones, there the whole—"

"No!" Stabmacher almost bellowed; loud enough that he almost frightened himself. "It's bad enough, humiliating enough that we have been required to tolerate those—those *things* having virtually free range of the compound. I will *not* allow them to become witnesses, or active participants of any sort, in the investigation."

"We take your point, sir," said Special Agent Wolfson. "But witnesses or not, we can't lay this on Mendez. And that's not me defending him. It's plain common sense. No remotely competent human being could have missed someone coming in and poking at the corpse, then sneaking out. I think we're only focusing on the time period when he was alone with the body because it's even *more* improbable it could have happened while Brox and I were there—or when we returned with you and the others. It *couldn't* have happened when we were all there, and therefore it must have been when it was just Mendez. But he'd have to be deaf and blind to miss such a thing. It *couldn't* have happened when he was alone on watch, either. There must be some other explanation."

Ambassador Stabmacher took a mo ent to calm himself. He had to admit the woma had a point. You'd have to be blind drunk or dead to miss someone coming in, poking at the corpse, and running away. Jumping up and down and yelling wouldn't change that, or get them any further forward. "You're right," he said, trying to sound calm and reasonable. Perhaps a note of humor would help. "You're absolutely right. I can't imagine what the explanation might be, but there's that old Sherlock Holmes rule, isn't there? 'When you have excluded the impossible, whatever remains, however improbable, must be the truth.'"

The two BSI agents exchanged a glance, and muttered some sort of agreement. The ambassador suddenly realized they must have had that line quoted back at them a hundred times before. It must be as old to them as all the lame jokes about diplomatic immunity were to him. He cleared his throat uncertainly and went on. "In any event, Agent Wolfson, your point is well taken. My apologies to you both."

"Sir?" Mendez was speaking. "Pardon me, and I'm not trying to defend or excuse myself. But if we do exclude the possibility of my going crazy, or lying, or the Kendari messing with my mind, obviously *something* must have happened to make that handprint in some way we don't know about. And for whatever it's worth, the Kendari didn't seem all that surprised or bent out of shape when they spotted the handprint. *Their* side didn't start jumping up and down. *Ours* did."

"So you think they were *expecting* that handprint?"

"N-n-nooo. Not exactly. But they didn't seem to regard it as out of the ordinary."

The ambassador considered. "Yes," he conceded. "You're right about that." He thought for a moment. "Some of their people—and ours—are less than happy about all the interspecies cooperation on this investigation. Consorting with the enemy and so on. If the roles were reversed, I could very easily imagine one of our less, ah, cooperative people letting the Kendari sweat for a while, instead of immediately volunteering information that could clear up just this sort of misunderstanding. If our people can behave badly, why not theirs?"

He drummed his fingers on his desktop for a moment. "All right then. We'll leave it there for the moment until the Kendari are more forthcoming. I expect Dr. Zhen Chi is also researching the point. Let's move on to other matters. I would say our next and immediate priority is going to be getting all our people out of confinement."

"Sir?" asked Wolfson. "We never have gotten a clear explanation of all that. I for one am not sure why they *were* confined. Could you go back a few steps and tell us about how and why exactly everyone was locked up? It's possible that Jamie—Agent Mendez—and I—have gotten the wrong idea. It might be better to get the whole story on that from beginning to end. And there are a number of other areas we need to discuss. You said something that suggested there are more simulants around, and I think we need to know more about the mobs—the ah, *groups* of humans and Kendari outside the compound."

Ambassador Stabmacher glanced out his picture window again. It was the sort of window that ambassadors got so they could look out on whatever magnificent view might be on offer. In this place, all he could see was the embassy ship, the compound wall, and a thin pall of red dust floating up from just outside it. And that cloud of dust indicated that the demonstrators were still there. If he strained his ears, he could at least imagine he could hear them shouting and chanting. "Several topics," he said meaninglessly. "Of course, of course."

The ambassador realized that his visitors were still standing. That was all right when he was bawling them out, but not when they had shifted gears into a more conventional sort of meeting. "Please, both of you, take a seat. I suppose this will be part of the official case. Use whatever recording system or whatever you want."

He was a bit surprised to see both of them pull out paper notebooks, though at least the younger one also pulled out a semiobsolete datapad and flipped on its record function. He would have thought they would been more likely to reach for the latest and greatest gadgets.

"For the present," said Agent Wolfson, "I'd like to concentrate on what you saw and did—not about what others told you. As per our previous discussions, I want to leave out any discussion of the crime itself, the crime scene, and the discovery of the crime. I don't want to start out with hearsay—uh, secondhand accounts on those matters."

"A more diplomatic way of saying the same thing," said the ambassador with a smile.

"Yes sir. That is, unless, ah, *you* discovered the crime scene—"

"Me? Oh, good heavens, no. It was Special Agent Milkowski."

Wolfson made a small frown. "Would that be Special Agent *Frank* Milkowski?"

"Yes. You know him?"

"Slightly," she said, obviously not too happy about it. "Not enough to complicate matters, if that's what you're concerned about."

"Thank God for that. I don't know what your term for it is, but if you had to recuse yourself, or withdraw from the case or whatever—well," he said, turning toward Mendez. "You'd have had a lot more on your plate."

"Yes, sir," said Mendez, in a tone that was both respectful and a trifle impatient. "Getting back to how the lockdown happened. You say Milkowski found the body."

"That's right. I suppose I have to at least start with a bit of hearsay to set the scene. Late yesterday evening, about two hours after dark. About 2200 hours. He went back into the joint ops center to do some paperwork."

"That seems a bit late to start working," Mendez suggested.

"Not so late as you might think. We run on a sort of ad hoc clock here that runs from 0000 hours to 2700 hours. The planetary day is near enough to twenty-seven hours long that we run on a clock that long, and just restart our embassy clocks at 0000 hours whenever we start getting too far out of sync with the local day reckoning. So you might think of 2200 hours as five hours before midnight—call it 7:00 P.M. People adjust to the longer day in different ways. Milkowski liked—likes—to catch a quick late-afternoon nap after official hours, then go and do a little catch-up work before going to bed for the night."

"You know his daily routine that well?"

The ambassador gestured to indicate the space around them. "This compound is a pretty small place, and there aren't that many places to go. We're pretty much right in each other's laps. It would be pretty hard not to learn each other's habits. Besides, Milkowski and the other BSI agents provided—provide—outside security for me, and that put us even more in each other's lives."

"So he goes into the ops center," Wolfson said. "What happens next?"

"He found the body and immediately withdrew from the ops center."

"Pardon me, Ambassador, and I know it's tricky, but so far this is nothing *but* secondhand evidence," said Mendez. "I understand that it's necessary to give your own actions some context, but even so. Just to be absolutely clear, you weren't a witness to any of this, were you?"

"Well, no, I didn't see him go in, and I certainly didn't see him find the body."

"Is there any way of confirming his movements?" asked Mendez. "Maybe an enter-exit log tracker on the ops center entryway?"

"I beg your pardon?"

"We have to think in alibis and evidence," said Wolfson. "Particularly for whoever found the body."

"There *is* an automatic entry-log system, in the joint ops center and for all the secure buildings in the compound. But I expect you know as well as I do those sorts of systems aren't always utterly reliable. Sometimes something as simple as two people going through the door at once, or someone leaving his tracker-badge on his desk, can be enough to throw them off."

"Yes, sir. But even so, we'll want to secure that tracker data at once."

"There might be a problem there, too, then. One we're going to run into over and over again. Milkowski was—is—responsible for that data." It was damnable the way he was falling into the trick of speaking of them all in the past tense. "But since everyone in the compound—including me—has to be treated as a suspect— virtually *all* the information you're going to get from any of us is going to be suspect to one degree or another."

"It's a challenging problem," said Mendez. "But it sort of helps make the point I was about to make—it might be best if you speak of what you know, rather than what you assume, or what someone told you he did."

"Hmmm? Ah! For example, Agent Milkowski *said* he went in, found the body, and immediately sealed the human-side doors. That is what he *told* me, and I was a direct witness of his saying all that. But I don't know for myself whether he actually did it or not."

"Exactly," said Mendez. "Please do go on, keeping that idea in mind. How, precisely, did he contact you?"

"Well, he called me on his commlink, and I of course went right over to the human-side entrance of the joint ops center."

"Why didn't he come to your office?"

"Because he—well, he didn't say why, now that I come to think of it, but I assume it was because he didn't want to leave the entrance unguarded."

"Why call you first?" asked Agent Mendez. "Why not one of his colleagues?"

Because he already suspected one of his fellow BSI agents, the ambassador thought. That was the clear implication of the question. *Or else, even worse, because he had done the murder himself and saw calling in the highest possible local authority immediately as a good cover.* It was amazing how one short question could stir up so many suspicions out of nothing. Ambassador Stabmacher found himself starting to get nervous. "Because I am the ambassador, and a murder had been committed, and he felt I should know about it first," he said in a voice that was a trifle more defensive than he intended.

"Of course," said Mendez. "What did he say?"

"He told me that he had found the dead body of Inquirist Emelza 401, and described it to me."

"Had he thought to take any photographs, or anything like that? Did he have anything to show you?"

"No," said the ambassador. *And why didn't he take such a perfectly obvious step?* "He wasn't walking around the compound carrying one of your crime scene bags, after all. He was working a straight desk job. Why would he be carrying a crime scene camera?"

"All right. How did you respond, and what did you do next?"

The ambassador noticed that it was the junior agent interviewing him—no, questioning him, interrogating him, while the senior agent just sat back and watched. Was she the one he should be nervous about? Perhaps Mendez's job was to keep him distracted while she watched and analyzed without being noticed. "I, ah, ordered him to lock down our side of the ops center, put tamper-indicator seals on all the doors, and summon the other BSI agents."

"Which did you have him do first?"

And putting it that way reminds me that I took over command of the crime scene at that moment. "I had him summon the other agents by commlink in order to witness the lockdown and the seals going up, and to tell them what was going on."

"How long did it take to get them over there?"

"Not long. Three or four minutes—though that seemed very long at the time. The compound is a small place, and neither of them had gone to bed."

"Did you order them to bring the seals with them?"

"Ah, yes."

"Then what?"

Ambassador Stabmacher realized that he was sweating. "Then I had them put the seals up. Then I started thinking about the old story about how you catch a skunk. All you need is a big bucket. You sneak up on the skunk, turn the bucket over, drop the bucket down over it—and then you can use the bucket as a place to sit and think while you try to figure out what to do next." It wasn't all that funny a story, or perhaps in the best taste under the circumstances, but the fact remained that he *had* thought of it the moment the seals went up.

"I'm not sure I follow," said Mendez.

"Well, we had the place sealed up, at least from our end—but things were bound to explode at any time. If the Kendari had gone in at that moment, and found the body and found the doors to our side locked down and sealed, I don't like to think what might have happened. They could easily have interpreted it as a deliberately staged provocation. We might be at war right now."

"Things are that tense?" Wolfson asked, interrupting the flow of the questioning.

"We've made great progress in the Pentam negotiations, but, yes. All that we have built up is still quite fragile. It all relies on trust—and there is precious little trust between the two species. You might say the trust we've built up here isn't between humans and Kendari, or even the human and Kendari governments—it is between the two staffs, the two embassy compounds—and it runs—or at least ran—through the joint operations center." The ambassador frowned. That answer was too high-flown, too much like a speech meant to rally the troops. Not at all the right tone for this situation.

"So that an attack on someone in the joint ops center was more or less literally an attack on the relationship between the two sides," Wolfson suggested.

"That's right," he agreed, resisting the temptation to elaborate.

"Let me edge over into speculation for a moment," she went on. "Might that just possibly be the motive for the crime? Not dislike of the victim, or any personal motive—but a deliberate attempt to derail the Pentam negotiations? Perhaps to force us to withdraw?"

"The short answer is yes," said the ambassador. It was exactly the point he had been stewing over since the first moment of this nightmare, and he had no desire to discuss it further—particularly with a pair of intrusive police officers.

"I see," said Mendez. "All right then. Getting back to our chronology, you and Flexdal speak on the phone. What sort of record is there of that call? Once again, a time and date stamp, or a call duration, would come in very handy."

"I can do better than that," said the ambassador. "I recorded the call at my end. I'll get you the full recording whenever you like."

"Excellent," said Mendez. "For the moment, however, can you give us a quick summing-up of that conversation?"

"Well, yes," said the ambassador, and hesitated for a moment. "But I believe it would be best if I gave you some background to the situation. First off, you must understand that we might be very close to settling the Pentam issue."

"Who's going to get the Pentam System, then?" asked Wolfson.

The ambassador smiled wearily. "I haven't the faintest idea. We haven't even gotten close to *that* issue yet. What I should have said is that we're close to settling on the procedure for *negotiating* the Pentam issue. You might say we're having talks about the talks. To put it very crudely, we, the Kendari, and the Vixa, and the other interested parties have just about agreed on the rules for how the humans and Kendari will state their cases. What we can and cannot do and say to convince the Elder Races in general—and the Vixa in particular—that we are the species that should take over the Pentam System. To use an old diplomatic expression, we've finally agreed as to what size and shape of table we're going to use. We're just about ready to get it built and sit down at it."

"Do you have to convince them that we're more deserving, or that we'll do a better job, or what?"

"We don't know for sure. Part of the procedure—or, if you will, part of the game—is that neither side is to be told what, exactly, the decision criteria will be."

Mendez smiled at that himself. "Great. So long as they don't make it too hard on you."

"Precisely. But the point is that neither Flexdal nor I wants to wreck the progress we've made. If, God forbid, we had to start over from scratch, it might be years or decades, even centuries, before we got back to this point. This death—this murder—is a terrible thing, but it must not be allowed to interfere with the negotiations—especially given that, as Agent Wolfson suggested, upending the negotiations might well have been the motive for the crime. I called Flexdal, told him what had happened, and the steps I had taken. Flexdal got off the line and called me back a few

minutes later. I expect—but I can't say for certain—
that he was having his people check on the situation.
He immediately suggested that, rather than risk
wrecking the negotiations, we initiate a rush investigation and call in outside investigators if at all possible.
He suggested that we request the use of one of the
Vixa's hyperfast ships.

"We placed a conference call to the Preeminent
Director's household to advise him of the situation and
request assistance. The Vixa haven't exactly fallen
over themselves to be helpful in the past, so we weren't
expecting it would be easy to convince them. I'd bet
that Flexdal was as surprised as I was when the
Director immediately offered the use of the *Eminent
Concordance* for the purpose of collecting an investigator who wasn't a suspect in the case."

"Why us?" Mendez asked.

The ambassador smiled slightly. "Why human BSI
agents, and not Kendari Inquirists, or why you two in
particular?"

"Both, I suppose. My impression was that Brox requested the two of us specifically."

"He did indeed, shortly after the Preeminent
Director finished speaking with us. As for why the BSI,
it was of course the obvious choice after the decision
was made to request a human rather than a Kendari
investigator."

"But why *not* a Kendari investigator? Why didn't
they insist on that? After all, it was a Kendari that had
been killed."

Ambassador Stabmacher frowned, sat up straight in
his chair, and needlessly tidied up a few papers on his
desk. "You'll have to ask them that, to get a definitive
answer—and good luck to you. However, I can offer
some guesses.

"First off, we know nothing of the actual relationship between Inquirist Brox 231 and the deceased. For all we know, they could have been seen fighting loudly an hour before. There might be some other evidence of which we are unaware that would cast suspicion on Brox, or on someone else on that side of the wall. Perhaps they were hoping that human investigators would have more difficulty proving a case against a Kendari.

"Or there might be some political issue back on Kendal that would make it impossible to dispatch any Inquirists. Perhaps the whole affair is so scandalous—a lover's quarrel, a murder in front of outsiders—that Flexdal didn't even want to try to get support from back home. Perhaps some other reason that isn't remotely close to my guesses. All I knew for certain was that I wanted BSI, and not the Kendari Inquiries Service—and when the other side agreed, I wasn't going to ask why. I was the one who suggested dispatching Brox to collect you. I pointed out we wanted to keep the knowledge closely held, that he knew as much as anyone, and that our people had a high regard for him." The ambassador cocked his head slightly to one side. "All that is true, so far as it went—but there was more to it, of course. It was a way of my paying a compliment to the Kendari, and conceding that harm had been done to them and not us. And it said we trusted that Brox wouldn't try to escape—but Brox was going to be on a Vixa ship, then in BSI custody, then returning on the same ship. For all practical purposes, he was just as confined to quarters as the rest of us—even if he was traveling the devil knows how many light-years in one day."

"Whose idea was the lockdown?" Mendez asked.

"Well, Flexdal suggested it to me," said the ambassador. "I can't say he thought of it—but someone on that side of the wall did."

Mendez smiled. "I think you're starting to get the hang of this, sir."

"What reason did Flexdal give for wanting it?" Wolfson asked.

"Protection of evidence."

"But the joint operations room was locked down and had tamper indicators all over it. Why lock down both entire compounds as well?"

"Whoever committed this crime would have every motive to find a way past the seals on the joint ops center without disturbing them, so as to get in there and destroy the evidence before an outside investigator could arrive. For that matter, the killer might decide to get into the ops center no matter what, even if he or she did wreck the seals. Locking down the compounds was a way to prevent that."

"But wouldn't anyone going into the ops center be caught, or at least spotted?" Wolfson asked.

"Someone got into the ops center, somehow managed to get a cup of coffee into a Kendari, and got away. Someone else—or more likely the same person—got in there and left a handprint and, once again, got away. Maybe they could do it again in order to remove or destroy the evidence, or maybe the guilty party would be up to some other mischief. Maybe the killer wasn't from the embassy, but was instead from the human interest-groups encampment just up the road. If so, he or she would just want to get over the wall and get away."

"I can see why you wouldn't want anyone leaving the compound, or entering the joint ops center, but why order everyone into solitary?"

"Witnesses," said the ambassador. "And the prevention of witness tampering—and to keep everyone from gossiping among themselves, being influenced by each other, starting to spin theories or looking for evidence themselves—or even getting ideas about who must have done it, and telling each other about them. And, of course, if it *was* one of us who did it, that person would be doing his or her best to muddy the waters, throw people off the scent."

"But wasn't locking everybody in an extreme measure? And what would you do if there had been an emergency? A fire, or a riot? And, just by the way, who locked in the last of you?"

"This crime was exposing us to the very significant risk of losing humanity's chance to claim two habitable planets," the ambassador said stiffly. "Earth times two. Consider the amount of wealth involved in gaining us a new planet—and then double it. The continents. The oceans. The mineral wealth, the living things. *Two* Earth-like planets—plus all the other resources in that Pentam System, plus the benefits of controlling a strategic position in space.

"Asking twenty-odd people who had been working toward that goal, many of them for years, to allow themselves to be confined in relatively comfortable quarters for a day or two does not seem extreme to me in that context. And, I might add, that they *weren't* locked in. They were told to remain in their quarters in the embassy ship, and tamper-indicator seals were placed over the hatches.

"The worst-case scenario would be that a few hatches might be jammed open if the seals weren't removed carefully first. If there had been an emergency—more accurately, a *further* emergency—the necessary people could have been pulled out and put to work. And the chief engineer actually did lock himself into the embassy ship's engine room. He adjusted the entry hatch's lock so it could only be opened from the outside—then stepped inside and pulled the hatch shut."

"We'll need to check on him soon," said Mendez.

"I'll see to it myself, this evening as soon as we are done," said the ambassador. "I'm planning to release him, escort him to his own quarters on the ship, close his door, and use tamper strips on it as well. Unless you feel that you should do it, or that I should be reconfined until morning, or whatever."

"No," said Mendez, with a deadpan expression. "You've done things your way so far. You carry on. That way the results will be consistent."

It was hard to miss the sarcasm in his voice, but the ambassador was a diplomat, and a past master at pretending not to notice things. "Very well then," he said.

"Where, exactly, did you put everyone else?" Mendez went on.

The ambassador gestured out the window. "In the embassy ship, of course. Regulations require us to have accommodation for all of us on board, so that the entire contingent can be evacuated just by launching the ship. Given that an evacuation would very likely result in everyone's having to spend two or three weeks in transit home, under the best conditions, regulations also require that there be separate cabins for each single person, and for each family.

"This being viewed as a danger post, there are no children and no dependent spouses. There are four married couples, but in all cases both husband and wife work for the embassy. None of that is by chance, of course. An embassy this small, and with an enemy species literally right next door—plus a sometimes less-than-friendly host species—has to be a no-children, no-dependents post. This ship is designed to accommodate a slightly larger staff than we have. There are thirty cabins in all, so there was little difficulty. The cabins are very small, and rather spartan, and of course everyone normally lives in the prefab structures we've put up in the rest of the compound, so they all had to gather their personal items and bring them in—but it all worked pretty smoothly."

"We spent all of about two minutes in the Kendari compound, but it seemed more or less deserted. Did they agree to the same sort of voluntary lockdown for themselves?"

"Yes, of course."

"Was there any sort of verification agreement?" Wolfson asked.

It was clear Wolfson was asking the big-picture questions, and Mendez was focusing on details. *One for strategy, and one for tactics?* "No," he admitted. "The arrangements were made very quickly, under difficult conditions. You have to imagine my managing four calls at a time, with my staff all getting ready to confine themselves for what might turn out to be several days, and everyone working in the middle of the night. We had to work out all sorts of things very fast. Just to pick one, we needed to sort out communications—we needed, for example, for Dr. Zhen Chi to be able to receive medical emergency calls, but we also needed to make sure people didn't use their commlinks or the intercom system to talk among themselves. We solved that problem, but there were any number of such issues to sort out, in the dark, in a rush, and with the knowledge that any one of us could have been the one who killed Emelza 401."

"We can appreciate the difficulty," said Wolfson. "We've been in situations that weren't any easier."

"I sincerely hope that you are never in one that is any harder."

"I haven't seen any sign of the embassy staff coming out of confinement," said Jamie. "Have you informed them that they can come out now?"

"No, of course not," said the ambassador, slightly surprised.

"But why not?"

"Because you two haven't interrogated any of them yet," he said.

There was a moment's silence before Mendez spoke again. "Excuse me?"

"Interrogate them. They're all waiting for you to interrogate them. That's the whole point of their still being confined." He glanced at his watch. "In fact," he said, "given how long they've been waiting, I suggest you get started right away."

TEN

IN THE DARK

Ambassador Stabmacher frowned, and looked from Wolfson to Mendez. There was a dead silence that lasted for a long time. The two agents were expressionless. They looked at Ambassador Stabmacher, then at each other, without speaking. Something in the room changed in that moment. Suddenly the two BSI agents weren't the ambassador's colleagues. They had become something else—his opponents, his adversaries, the cops that were on his tail. He had the general impression that these two agents thought he had done something idiotic and were straining to keep their tempers.

"Ambassador Stabmacher," Wolfson said at last, in a very slow, artificially calm voice, "we started the day in another star system, and we've gone through a period of relativistic time dilation, and changed not only time zones, but shifted to a different planet with a different rotation period and day-night cycle. Part of what that means is that we're exhausted—but it also means that Special Agent Mendez and I are more than a little disoriented as to time. How long ago, exactly, did Special Agent Milkowski contact you and tell you that he had found the body?"

Not when the murder was, or when Milkowski found the body, because you didn't witness those things, the ambassador told himself. It was a very carefully phrased question. "I can't give it to you to within the exact second without checking the time-date stamps on my commlink log, but it was roughly twenty-one hours ago."

"And how long did it take to get everyone organized, get them into voluntary confinement?"

"I was the last one sealed in by the chief engineer, then of course he went below and locked himself in. That was about three hours after Milkowski called me."

"How long between his call and the *first* person being confined?"

"I would say about two hours."

"Was there any real degree of control over everyone during those two hours?" Mendez asked. "Were they kept in one place where someone could keep an eye on them?"

"N-n-nooo. Not especially."

"How did you do surveillance over the compound once everyone was locked down? I would assume there were watch cameras on and recording?"

The ambassador grimaced and shook his head. "No, I'm afraid not. The entire surveillance camera recording system was inoperative. The BSI agents managed it. The system is designed to do forty-eight hours of recording of all cameras. Then the recording media has to be switched out. There are security requirements that require us to change out the recording media manually. The procedure requires two people— again, for security purposes. A watch-me, watch-you protocol. If the media fills up, then the system stops recording and just presents live views to the security-pod monitors. And with the agents locked up—well, they couldn't do that job."

"And the recording media filled up when?"

"About an hour after Milkowski contacted me.

Everyone just forgot about it until about four hours until the lockdown was complete."

"Who remembered about it, and what was done?"

"Special Agent Singh contacted me and told me that he had been assigned to do the change-out and had forgotten about it."

"And what did you do?"

Another long silence. "Nothing," the ambassador admitted. "I concluded that the damage had been done. In order to restart the system, we'd have to have one of the BSI agents come out of confinement, and I'd have to come out to observe him, and we'd probably have to get the chief engineer out in order to witness the work and to lock us both back up again. The odds of creating more and worse problems in the process, adding more variables, seemed very high. The decision at that point was mine, and I take full responsibility for it."

"Unfortunately, taking full responsibility doesn't get us usable surveillance recordings," said Mendez, allowing a bit of temper to show. "From where we're sitting, Ambassador, you've handed us twenty or so witnesses, all of whom were given two to three hours to confer together, then eighteen or so hours to cool their heels, rest up, and think things over without being disturbed. And the number of ways a comm system or a computer system can be diddled to allow unrecorded conversation is almost unlimited. Furthermore, unless they were designed as holding cells, which they weren't, I'd be willing to bet that half of the cabins in the embassy ship have some other way out, via access panels or servicing hatches or escape chutes or whatever. And I'd make another bet that there are ways to communicate between cabins even if the intercom isn't used. Just whisper into an air duct, or shout loud enough, or tap on the wall to do Morse code, or one tap for yes and two for no."

Mendez rubbed his face, let out a weary sigh, and went on. "You've given us an entire compound that has no visual record of people coming and going. Because you had the joint operations center sealed from *this* side before anyone else could view the body or photograph it, the only description we're going to get of the state of the body as it was when it was found is going to have to come from Milkowski, who has to be considered one of the prime suspects.

"And, since you mentioned the enemy right next door, let me remind you that we only have *their* word for it that they sealed the ops center from their side when they said they did, that they kept the seals on, instead of peeling them off, going in, doing whatever they wanted, then leaving and installing fresh seals. I've got several more points on my list. Do you see what I'm driving at? Do I need to go on?"

"Um, ah, ah, no. I see. I believe I do see." The ambassador discovered he was sweating.

"The further problem," said Special Agent Wolfson, "is that neither Special Agent Mendez nor I is in any shape to do one interrogation—let alone twenty interrogations. We need some sleep, we need some food, and we need some sort of chance to evaluate the information we have so far—or we won't know what to ask questions about."

"And there's another problem," said Agent Mendez. "The three BSI agents. We can't use them on the investigation, obviously. Not unless we're able to clear one or more of them absolutely, and I don't quite see a way to do that."

"I agree," said Agent Wolfson.

Mendez turned and looked the ambassador straight

in the eye. "But let's go further. They can't do *any* work, can they?" he asked. "They're in charge of security—but at the same time, they have to be regarded as a major security threat. Last to see the deceased, and the persons with best access to her. I speak no ill of the agents themselves here, but it's just simple investigative doctrine. If there's prima facie evidence, even if it's just circumstantial, that a cop, any cop, committed a crime, you pull them off any sort of duty that involves criminal investigation work or security responsibility. You put them to work in the personnel office or something. But there's no way to do that here, is there? No job they could do here that isn't being done, that needs doing, that doesn't have a security element?"

The ambassador saw the point Mendez was making, and he didn't like it. "No," he said, and left it at that.

"Let me go a little further," Mendez went on. "In a post this small, and in this high-risk an assignment, is there *any* desk job at all that doesn't involve exposure to secured material of one sort or another? Sooner or later—probably sooner—something that is classified in one way or another gets to just about everyone, right?"

The ambassador frowned. "I suppose I could find something for them to do, but it would be about on the pick-up-sticks-and-lay-them-straight level."

"But even that level of paper shuffling would have to be set up in, what would you call it, a quarantine area where nothing sensitive could go in or out. Plus which it would probably have to be the BSI agents themselves who would set that up, wouldn't it? And it would have to be done *now,* while the whole embassy is in an uproar already, wouldn't it?"

"I haven't had the opportunity to think that

through," said the ambassador. "But I suspect you are correct."

"And who is going to do that work?" Mendez asked. "Who is going to run security at this place, handle travel security, and run this investigation, all at once? Care to make a wild guess?"

Mendez was plainly angry—and he was just as plainly someone that the ambassador didn't want to have angry at him. He found himself wondering whether or not the BSI agents' powers of arrest extended to ambassadors. And perhaps arrest was really the least of his worries.

Senior Special Agent Wolfson spoke hurriedly, as if she wanted to do so before Mendez had a chance to explode. "We'll deal with all that, Jamie. Somehow. Frankly, I don't know how, but we will." She turned back to the ambassador, and he felt nothing but relief that he had her to deal with, and gratitude for the way she had intervened with Mendez.

The ambassador couldn't quite tell if it was all authentic emotion, or just good-cop bad-cop theater, but he didn't care anymore. If it was theater, it had him thoroughly convinced. "Thank you," he said.

"Let's focus on one problem at a time. As regards the interrogations—under normal circumstances, I think we'd be lucky to do a dozen a day. Obviously, we can't keep the staff on hold that long—some might not get out until two or three days from now. It might be tempting to get a start on it this evening, but, as I said, we're just too tired to do the job properly, and we haven't had any chance at all to review the information we have. So as long as all members of the embassy staff are voluntarily confined, I think we might as well let them spend one more night there. We'll have to tackle all of them tomorrow—somehow."

Wolfson smiled sadly. "I seem to be using that word 'somehow' a lot. In any event, we're going to bed down somewhere and get some rest, and I suggest you do the same. But first, I do want to cover a couple of other points. One, the simulants and two, the Kendari and human groups that seem to be on-planet. I suppose I have the same general questions regarding both. Who are they, how many are there, where are they, what are they doing here, and how did they get here? Let's cover the simulants first."

Ambassador Stabmacher nodded eagerly, glad to talk on another subject, any other subject. "They got here because the Vixa insisted on them. It was a flat-out condition of their hosting the next phase of the negotiations. We were to accept them and allow them, quote, 'to perform their initial functions' unquote, or else there would be no negotiations, and the Vixa would shut down the human embassy."

"So they haven't been here long?"

"No. The first—mine—arrived about four months ago. There are five of them in the compound at the moment, not counting the one that came with you. You've noted that they seem to imprint on a person—it would appear that your simulant has imprinted on Agent Mendez. The five here imprinted on me, the three BSI agents, and Dr. Zhen Chi. They have arrived one by one, and we are told that more will be arriving as we go along until every member of the embassy staff has one."

"But what are they for? What good do they do?" asked Mendez. "I spoke to the one imprinted on me, and the one imprinted on Brox, but didn't really seem to get much out of them." He turned to Wolfson. "Nothing that made sense, anyway. There were a few details I'll talk over with you later."

"The Vixa really haven't told us what they are for," said the ambassador. "Or at least, when they have, the answer isn't much help."

Mendez flipped through his notes and read from them. "'We observe on behalf of those who sent us. Our assistance will be provided at a later time, and will be of significant help to you.' That sound familiar? Or how about 'We are here to observe and assist.'"

The ambassador nodded. "We've all heard that many times. And the subhouseholders of the Preeminent Director tell us pretty much the same thing."

"They certainly aren't the most efficient observation or monitoring devices," said Wolfson. "It would be a lot easier just to send in a bunch of cameras on floaters, or blanket the embassy with whatever sort of covert spycams or listening devices they might like to use. Are the sims in fact recording or transmitting video or audio signals?"

"We've checked every frequency and transmission system we have the gear to test, and haven't found a thing. They do seem to send and receive encoded messages via a short-range variant of QuickBeam that the Vixa use, but those messages are short and very intermittent. We can't read the content of those messages, but we can measure their characteristics pretty well. The transmissions *might* be highly compressed summings-up of observations, but it seems very unlikely. I'm told that something called the information density of the signal just wasn't high enough for that. Our signals specialist said the structure of the messages looked a lot more like the simulants receiving commands and sending 'yes I got it' confirmation messages. And, just by the way, the Vixa *do* send in spy devices. Finding them and disabling takes up a lot of the time of our signals and comm specialist."

"Those five people who have gotten simulants," said Mendez. "Is there any rhyme or reason to why you five were the first to get them?"

"Yes, actually. We're the people here who have had the most frequent direct face-to-face contact with the Vixa."

"And where are the simulants now? We haven't seen them."

"In a storage shed over by the motor pool," said the ambassador. "They have their feeding stations there. The agreement with the Vixa states that we only have to allow them to be up and about during official duty hours—and I assure you, we keep to that agreement very closely."

"What are they exactly?" Mendez asked. "I haven't been able to decide if they're machines or not. You mentioned a feeding station. That suggests they are living creatures. Are they a subspecies of the Vixa? A sort of domestic animal?"

"The short answer is all of the above. They certainly have some sort of integral electronics, or something closely equivalent to electronics, that is part of them. They appear to be related to the main Vixan castes— but they certainly aren't full-fledged citizens, if that concept even has any meaning for the Vixa. I would suggest you discuss that area with Dr. Zhen Chi. It's far more her area of expertise than mine. I can tell you that she is of the opinion that the human and Kendari simulants are actually the same sort of creature or being or whatever term you might use. They seem to be based on the Vixan six-legger's body plan, but are capable of fusing and merging body parts to mimic whatever being they're imprinted on, and of course, altering their skin coloring and texture to mimic the skin or clothing of their imprinting target."

"That reminds me. What about the Kendari?" asked Wolfson. "We've seen that Brox has a simulant. Is it about the same pattern with them?"

"Oddly enough, no. The Vixa don't seem to be much worried about parity—they don't much worry about treating both sides exactly the same way. The Kendari certainly don't tell us everything—but so far as we are able to tell, Brox has the only Kendari simulant, and his was only assigned very recently. He does provide transit security for Flexdal, so it fits the pattern of giving them to those who have frequent contact with the Vixa, but Flexdal doesn't have one, and neither does anyone else over there.

"I don't give it much weight, but I have one theory that the Vixa expected us to view the simulants as a status symbol. A substitute for the escort Vixa. Flexdal was supposed to be jealous that I had one, perhaps, or maybe he is supposed to feel *superior* to me because simulants are only for the lower orders. Maybe they are a fashion accessory. We have no idea what, if any, meaning they have for social status, or anything else, in Vixa society."

"What do they do, exactly?" asked Wolfson. "We haven't seen them in action yet."

"I don't think I'd use the word 'action' to describe their behavior," said Stabmacher. "They stand around. They follow you from place to place. They go everywhere you go until specifically told to wait outside. They can be told to run very simple errands—carry this note to the comm office, go get my sweater from my bedroom and bring it back—but nine times out of ten, it's more trouble to get them to do the job than to do it yourself. At the close of official business hours, we herd them into their storage shed, and leave them there until the next morning, when they can start cluttering the place up again."

"I thought the Vixa signed up to the idea that an embassy was the sovereign territory of the guest government. Isn't forcing you to accept the simulants a huge violation of that principle?"

"In a word, yes, and you've just said in ten or twenty words what I have said dozens of times, in hundreds or thousands of words in letters back to the UniGov Ministry of External Affairs. They agreed that it was a violation of principle, but the chance to win the Pentam System trumped everything. And, as you pointed out, the simulants aren't the most efficient spy system going, especially for an Elder Race that has every conceivable form of technology going for it. We work on the assumption that the Vixa can hear, and probably see, everything we're doing, if they want to go to the trouble.

"The Ministry argued that the simulants wouldn't be able to do any spying that the Vixa couldn't do better some other way, and they were full of all sorts of other arguments to the effect that they weren't going to do any particular harm, so why not go against a universal precedent that was thousands of years old? The long and the short of it was that I was expressly ordered to accept the simulants for the duration of the negotiations. The Vixa seemed to be satisfied with that agreement. I insisted that it be noted in my file that I was obeying under protest, and the Ministry noted that down—and that was that."

"Very well then, we'll mark that down as your not having gotten any better an explanation than we had to start with. What about the large number of humans and Kendari that seem to be here for no apparent reason?"

The ambassador sighed. "Another bit of excessively helpful interference from our Vixa friends. Some time ago, the Preeminent Director's household got it in their heads—if they can strictly be said to have heads—that the Pentam decision was going to be very important for all concerned, and that all sides of the question must be discussed, and all points of view heard. We of course pointed out that the United Human Government, UniGov, was the sole representative of the human race in all dealing with xeno species, and all the standard arguments.

"We also pointed out that we were trying to keep the Pentam discussions secret from the general population, for fear of complicating matters even further, and that inviting some unspecified but large number of people from organizations that thrived on publicity wasn't going to help matters. The Vixa insisted that they could manage to keep the Pentam story from leaking out, and just told the delegates—that's what the Vixa called them—that they were to attend a general meeting regarding outstanding issues between humans and Kendari, and would be transported and housed at Vixa expense—but kept here for the duration of the meeting."

"Which groups are they, exactly?" Mendez asked.

"There are any number of them," said the ambassador. "And they certainly represent a wide range of views. Pax Humana, the Refusalists, Xeno-Deniers, the Human Supremacy League—that's Tancredo Zamprohna and Helga Zamprohna-Weldon's group—the Alien Friendship Council, the Society for Total Amalgamation of Humans into Galactic Society, and on and on. They are all housed together, about two kilometers from here, in really a quite pleasant group of compounds, and are well taken care of. But you can just imagine what the arguments are like with Refusalists and Amalgamationists living more or less right next door to each other."

"They should have put the Pax Humana people in between," said Wolfson.

"They did. The Paxers insisted on being moved to other accommodations."

"The groups you've just rattled off are all way off on the fringes, either extreme pro-xeno or extreme anti-xeno," said Mendez. "I know we're not supposed to get involved in human politics, but those are all either nut groups, or close to it. Everybody but the League of Irresponsible People."

"The one thing they all have in common is that none of those organizations have much love for the Kendari," said Hannah. "Anyone from the rational middle ground?"

"What few there were left some time ago," said the ambassador. "They weren't allowed to go home, in order to keep the Pentam negotiations quiet. Instead the Vixa put them up in what amounts to a custom-built luxury resort in the tropical regions of this planet. I've visited it—and I have to admit I was tempted to stay. All the finest food and wine and books and films and what have you imported from Earth, very comfortable accommodations and a magnificent beach right outside your front door. Imagine being forced to choose between staying at the finest hotel on Hawaii free of charge, with no duties, and living between the Xeno-Deniers and the Alien Friendship Council. I can't blame them for leaving."

"We saw what appeared to be a good-sized Kendari mob as well," said Mendez. "Is it more or less the same story with them?"

"In broad strokes. Kendari political groups tend to

be more clan-based—almost as if you inherited the family politics along with the family number. If Zogham 43139 is a strict antineofeualdist, or whatever, you can bet that every other 43139 feels the same way. But yes, the Vixa did invite their various political factions, and it seems to be mainly the extremists on both sides who have stuck around."

"Do you know why, exactly, the various groups are protesting outside the two compounds?"

The ambassador laughed. "You mean, today? I have no idea. There have been so many protests, on so many subjects that are and are not related to the Pentam conference that I have completely lost track. Besides which, today I was rather too busy to receive a delegation—especially from a group that has a habit of hanging me in effigy."

"Very well, Ambassador," said Wolfson, closing her notepad. Mendez took that as a cue and started putting away his own gear. "That will do it, I think," Wolfson said as she stood up. "At least for now. We're going to have a lot to talk about in the days to come. You can count on it."

"I know I can count on it," the ambassador said, rising to see his guests or subordinates or inquisitors or whatever they were, out of his office. He smiled one last time and gave himself the luxury of allowing the smile to be utterly, transparently, false, of allowing all his fear, his weariness, his anger shine right through. "I just don't think I'm likely to enjoy it."

Jamie and Hannah left the ambassador's office and went down the stairs to the ground floor, then outside to the scruffy, dusty grounds of the compound. Night was coming on, and it was cool and quiet. Glowlamps were hung here and there and gave a fair amount of illumination, but not so much that the comforting darkness was chased away. There was a park bench set up just outside the building, and Jamie dropped down wearily onto it. "Boy oh boy oh boy," he said, shifting over to make room for Hannah. "*That* was a hell of a session."

"It's been a hell of a day," said Hannah. "If it has only been a day. It seems more like a year." She looked around thoughtfully at the compound. "I guess our gear is still where we dumped it after we brought it through the human side of the joint ops center—and with everyone but the ambassador and Dr. Zhen Chi still confined, I guess there isn't going to be anyone around to tuck us in—or tell us where to sleep, or whatever. I'm all of a sudden really glad that Commander Kelly thought to have us bring sleeping bags and ground cushions. We could probably commandeer somebody or other's bedroom, but that seems pretty pushy. Sleeping bags and ground cushions in the main level of the embassy ship?"

"And if it just so happens we're sleeping in front of the main hatch if any of our little confinee friends tries sneaking out during the night? Sure." Jamie shifted as if to get up and get started, but he didn't quite make it. "Three more minutes," he said. "Then I'll get moving."

"Fine. I don't have to until you do."

They sat in silence for a moment, looking out over the scruffy little compound and the magnificent city of glorious towers and triumphant architecture, glittering and gleaming with a million lights aglow, all visible from where they sat.

"I was just thinking about what you said this morning, however long ago that was," said Hannah.

"About whether or not you ever got used to being disoriented. I think maybe part of the answer is that right now I'm too tired to feel anything—disoriented, happy, sad, scared—anything. It helps, in a weird way."

They were both quiet for a moment, looking at the strange and alien night that surrounded the scruffy little human enclave. "Did you see anything much wrong with the physical evidence?" Jamie asked.

"Plenty. And so did you," said Hannah. "Nice try on the innocent-sounding leading question. But we'll talk about it tomorrow."

"Fair enough. But there's one thing I sorta feel I've gotta hear about tonight—partner-to-partner stuff, not BSI Special Agent stuff, strictly speaking."

"You noticed my reaction to hearing Milkowski's name." It wasn't a question.

"Yeah. I think I need to know the backstory there, before I talk to him."

Hannah sighed and leaned forward to rest her elbows on her knees. "You're right. You do. Frank Milkowski. Frank Milkowski is—well, let me put it this way. Before I saw her, I pictured Zhen Chi as being the sort of doctor that usually ends up being posted to a small remote embassy or a small, semiobsolete warship that's given really routine patrol assignments so the *real* UniGov Navy is freed up for real work. Old, tired, last-tour-before-retirement, maybe with one or two reprimands more than usual in her personnel file, marking the days on the calendar before she's posted home. That's *not* Zhen Chi, obviously. But it *is* Frank Milkowski. Old-school guy, middling-good-enough agent, did what he needed to do to do the job, but no more. But Frank's maybe just a bit worse than that.

"We call ourselves Special Agents and tell ourselves we really *are* something special. But really, we're just another kind of cop—and sometimes cops turn sour. Maybe they start out telling themselves they're entitled just this once to bend the rules because of all the hard work, all the sacrifices, all the effort that came to nothing when the case fell apart or the jury let the creep go. Then they're entitled to bend the rules more often, just because they work so hard. And then maybe they bend them just because they can, because cops have a certain kind of power.

"They bend the rules so hard the rules stay bent. Sooner or later, some captain or watch commander or Commandant is pretty much forced to take notice. Maybe a few free doughnuts has turned into grand larceny out of the evidence room, or you go from fixing a traffic ticket for your brother-in-law to getting half your family jobs they never show up for. Or maybe you're a BSI Special Agent who never did like aliens much and tends to give human suspects a break when he can, even if it takes manufacturing this evidence and suppressing that evidence—and it turns out one of those suspects—a murder suspect—didn't deserve that break when some Kendari merchant wound up dead."

"Oh," said Jamie. "That's not good."

"It's all rumors—the sort of stuff everyone knows for sure is true but can't actually be proven. Dig too deep, and you know you'll do a lot of harm without doing much good. Maybe get a hundred perfectly legitimate convictions thrown out and let some really bad guys go free because the same cop who nailed them bent the rules a little on their cases too, before he broke them all the way. And the guy has put in his time and done some good before he screwed up. You can't fire him, you can't prosecute him, and you can't just set him loose to do more, and worse." She gestured toward the compound. "So you dump him on some out-of-the-way embassy as security liaison or whatever, because nothing will ever happen there and he can't do any harm—and three months after he's posted there, all of a sudden the embassy is in the middle of a huge interstellar conference."

"And that's Frank Milkowski?"

"That's Frank," Hannah said. "And we're going to have to tackle him first thing." She stood up, stretched, and yawned mightily. "First thing tomorrow, after I have a chance to sleep on it and figure out how to do it. And we're going to have to consult with Brox, of course, before we get much further. Maybe he should have been in on our chat with Ambassador Stabmacher—but probably everyone would have started jumping up and down about establishing a very bad precedent or something. A Kendari interrogating a UniGov ambassador, and all that."

Hannah yawned again, even more hugely, and shook her head in an effort to rouse herself. "Come on," she said. "Let's go find someplace to sleep."

Ambassador Berndt Stabmacher felt massively undignified, peeking out the edge of his window to see if the two BSI agents had gone away yet. But as ridiculous as he felt, it would be a thousand times more awkward for him to go down the stairs, go outside, and encounter them again, after the grilling he had just endured. What would they do? Chat about the weather?

Five more minutes. He would give them five more minutes, then, absurd or not, he would leave. It had been a long, hard day for him, as well, and he wished devoutly to get out of the clothes he had been wearing since the day before, to get himself cleaned up and into his proper bed for a proper night's sleep.

He glanced over at the embassy ship and felt a pang of guilt. If he was suffering from cabin fever, what must all of his people be going through? Under the protocols he had agreed to with the Kendari, he couldn't even send them any sort of update on the status of the situation. They were to remain incommunicado until such time as Brox 231, Wolfson, and Mendez jointly agreed to let them go. And then, there was a whole other supply of locked-down diplomats just across the way. He couldn't help but wonder, a trifle maliciously, if Wolfson and Mendez had realized yet that they might have to contend with interrogating the Kendari as well as the humans.

Perhaps it wasn't worthy of an ambassador with such heavy responsibilities, but he couldn't deny a small flicker of pleasure at anticipating their reaction when they got that news. But then, he had not enjoyed his little chat with them. Not one little bit. Petty of him, perhaps, but any career diplomat who managed to elbow his way up to the rank of ambassador did not do it because he or she liked being pushed around. And the Vixa were pushy enough customers that he certainly didn't need it coming from another angle.

He took another peek down at Mendez and Wolfson. It looked as if they were planning to settle in for the night down there. Maybe there was *some* sort of paperwork he could still get done, even in his present state. He went back to his desk and sat down smoothly and gracefully. Even at this hour of the night, with no one else present, it paid to keep the habit of always looking poised and in control. No plopping heavily into the chair with a theatrical grunt for him.

They still called it paperwork, though of course the vast majority of it never left the computer systems or datastream. But it was still the same old routine of approvals, authorizations, memos for the files, cables to be drafted—and how many centuries had it been since the messages sent by that name had been sent over a cable! Those and other such minutiae seemed to be the fate of the diplomat. No one element of it was vital, or perhaps even all that important—but taken all in all, these bits and pieces of trivia were the lifeblood of the whole operation. Stop dealing with them, let them pile up, and the whole embassy would rapidly grind to a halt.

There was something almost soothing about working his way through the accumulated collection of routine matters. Even once he heard the two BSI agents finally stand up and walk away, he couldn't resist staying where he was to finish up two or three last items. His office was usually a bustling place, with subordinates coming and going, one meeting scheduled on top of another, his assistant popping in every five minutes with another new item. There was an odd sort of luxury in having the place entirely to himself, with the chance to concentrate on one thing at a time without interruption.

It didn't last. The chime on his commlink went off, loud enough in the quiet of that moment that he nearly jumped out of his skin—though he managed to repress his reaction well enough that anyone watching wouldn't have noticed it at all. He pulled the link out with a sense of irritation. Who could possibly be calling at this hour, with the embassy in lockdown?

He figured out the answer in the split second before he saw it on the commlink's ID display. "Zhen Chi," he said into the phone. *Of course. There was no one else available who could call.* "A good evening to you, Doctor."

"You've got a funny idea of good, Mr. Ambassador.

But I do have some news for you. I've been searching all the sources I have access to that talk at all about Kendari medicine and postmortem phenomena. I'm sending it through to your datapad now with the key items highlighted. I'll let you draw your own conclusions. I'm going to bed. Zhen Chi out."

Ambassador Stabmacher often felt annoyed by Zhen Chi's abrupt manner, but the moment he reached for his datapad and started reading what she had found, he was ready to forgive everything. He reached for his commlink so he could call Wolfson and Mendez—but then he stopped. They were no doubt headed for bed as well—and there was nothing they could do about it before morning, anyway. Everything was locked down. It could wait until morning. If they could even deal with it then. They were bound to have their hands full for a long time.

And besides, after what they had just put him through, he wasn't going to feel particularly guilty if his perfectly reasonable decision to hold off on this a bit made the two BSI agents sweat a little.

Or even more than a little.

It didn't take long for Jamie and Hannah to get their sleeping bags and ground pads out and get ready for bed. It took even less time for Hannah to fall into a profoundly deep sleep.

It took only a little bit longer for Jamie to realize that he wasn't going to sleep any time soon. Too many things were running through his head—and there were too many things they were going to have to handle in the morning.

Might as well deal with some of them now, Jamie thought. Muttering to himself, he fumbled his way back out of his sleeping bag, found his handlight, and got up, being careful to avoid making too much noise—but not too careful. He knew from experience how hard it was to wake up Hannah when she was under this deep.

He made his way outside and stood there in the dark for a minute, savoring the cold, fresh air and admiring the view. The domes of the Grand Warren glowed on the northern horizon. To the south, the Stationary Ring arced across the sky. The Vixa might be strange and scary as hell, but they sure knew how to build big, impressive ships, buildings, and structures.

But to do big things, you had to start with little things—even if that just meant clearing the ground clutter out of the way. He switched on his handlight and walked over to the main building of the embassy. He punched in the entry code and found his way to the BSI's office area. He turned on the light and dropped heavily into the chair behind the desk closest to the door.

Since the far-off and ill-fated day, lost in the mists of time, when some fiend had invented the in-box, office workers everywhere had learned to dread getting back to their work after being away for any length of time. Paper messages, voice mail, e-mail, commlink echoes, and all the rest accumulated whenever people were away—and made the return to work a dreary slog through whatever minutiae had rained down during one's absence.

All of that would be especially true for the BSI office at this particular embassy, as the BSI office had been designated the local security liaison office. And with all three BSI agents locked down, it was obvious that (a) Jamie and Hannah were bound to get stuck covering for them and (b) there was bound to be a lot of clutter accumulating already. And, just by the way, it was at least possible that (c) there might be some sort of report or message that would have some bearing on the case. *And if I deal with it now,* he told himself, *I won't have to deal with it in the morning. Besides, maybe plowing through the reports will be boring enough to let me get to sleep.*

Jamie powered up the comm system and started chugging his way through it all. He quickly decided that possibility (c) was going to be a washout. Fortunately, the comm system included an artificial intelligence system that was competent to listen to audio messages, read through text messages, and evaluate nearly all the other sorts of messages, then categorize them and present their contents in a standardized form. That allowed him to work through it all much faster. Nearly all of what he saw amounted to police-blotter reports from the human groups Stabmacher had told them about. It would seem that the human settlement had improvised some sort of self-policing system that could deal with most minor incidents but their system automatically copied all reports to the embassy. Sensible arrangement.

Jamie scanned the list of incidents. Domestic dispute—wife vs. husband, crockery thrown. Tashland, Franz reported drunk and disorderly, particulars as follows. Abe, Sezio drunk and disorderly, particulars as follows. Tashland, Franz, D&D for the second time on the same night. Reading between the lines, old Franz didn't listen the first time someone told him to stop singing at the top of his lungs and go home. Trash fire extinguished. Missing person report on Weldon, Linda, age eighteen. Description as follows, notation: reported missing and returned safely on three previous occasions. *Someone* had a mother or father who worried too much—or maybe, not enough, if she kept managing to sneak off like that. He wouldn't want to be the boyfriend when Daddy finally caught up with them.

A broken window. A scuffle with a pair of Kendari, scratches and bruises. A teenage male took a sting from a Vixa security guard, treated and released.

Or, to sum up, *isolated human settlement displays all the symptoms of boredom and frustration,* Jamie thought. He scrolled through the rest of it, but there was nothing that had anything to do with the embassy and nothing that rose to the level of requiring a BSI response.

He yawned mightily. Enough. He had been hoping to find something from the Kendari embassy, or some report directly connected to one of the BSI agents at the human embassy.

Something that might provide an alibi, or at least document someone's movements. Something written, date-stamped, firm and certain that could confirm or contradict some fact in one of the statements they would have to start taking in the morning. But there was nothing there.

Which sort of summed up the whole case, so far.

He powered down the system, shut the office down, locked up, and went back to collapse into his sleeping bag.

ELEVEN

SUSPECT BEHAVIOR

Diplomatic Xenologist Flexdal 2092 lashed his tail back and forth and paced angrily across the length of his office. "This is intolerable," he half snarled at Brox 231. "It has barely begun, and yet it has already gone on far too long. The case against the human spy-agent Milkowski is obvious and strong. I want him named as the murderer and in custody by the end of the day."

"Very well, sir. And would you like the subsequent war with the humans to start here, or would the Pentam System be more convenient?" Brox asked, placidly sitting back on his haunches with his arms folded over each other. He glanced around the office in a casual manner, as if the matter under discussion were of no great importance to him. He found himself glad to be back inside architecture that was properly proportioned for Kendari—but also found himself, for the first time, noticing how very much the *same* everything was. This long, low, dimly lit office could be any office of any person of moderately high status, on any Kendari world.

"Do not dare to speak to me in such a manner!"

Brox went on in a conversational tone, as if he had not heard Flexdal. "Seizing one of their officers on insufficient evidence on Vixan territory might well be enough to tilt the choice of who gets Pentam toward the humans, so that might be more appropriate on the whole."

"Blast you to atoms!"

"And they will likely blast you as well, My Superior. And all the rest of us. Of course, who 'they' would be is not yet certain. It might be the Vixa, it might be the humans, it might be some other alien race—or it might be your superiors, if they judge that destroying this embassy might mollify those you enrage. But whoever it is, there will be violence enough to engulf us all."

"Insolence! How do you dare speak to me this way?" Flexdal demanded.

"Because you are wrong," Brox said coldly. "Because if I follow your orders, disaster will follow. Because Family Number 2092 is a remote and low-ranking offshoot of Family Number 231, and, whatever your political and professional rank, however lowly and insignificant a mere Inquirist might be, my *social* rank is far above yours. I pause to note that I would not inject my family status in this matter if I did not believe it was essential that *you* listen to *me*. And I dare to speak because it was *my* espoused one who was killed, and I will *not* be involved in the massive dishonor of blaming the wrong being for her death, simply because it will save a few hours of your time."

"You claim the spy-agent Milkowski is innocent?"

"I claim nothing of the kind. I grant the obvious, that the first evidence points toward it being one of the BSI agents," he said, careful to pronounce the three-letter abbreviation in the manner that the humans did, and not, as was fashionable in Kendari government circles, as "spy." The human's pejorative term for intelligence agent was one of the few English loan-words that had come into use in Maximum Kendari.

"What I do not grant," Brox went on, "is that the obvious is always, or even generally, correct. While the BSI Agent Milkowski is not well-disposed to us, and while he is belligerent and aggressive, he is not a fool. It seemed unlikely to me from the start that any police officer would arrange matters so as to commit what was obviously a deliberate murder—how could a poisoning case be anything else?—so that the victim's corpse is found at the killer's place of work, with what might as well be the killer's identity document left at the scene."

"The beverage container? There is proof that it was his?"

"Not proof, perhaps, but evidence. You do not read English characters. There is a faded inscription on the bottom of the container—four characters that correspond to the first portion of the name 'Milkowski.' There is at least one other possible interpretation of that inscription, but it is at least highly suggestive."

"Yes! It suggests—it shouts out—that the spy agent Milkowski is the killer."

"It shouts it at such deafening volume that I have trouble believing it. We are talking about a professional investigator leaving his name at the scene of the crime. Either he is, in some way, insane—perhaps in a way that is unique to humans and is not known to us—or the actual killer has manufactured evidence that points to him. I see no plausible third explanation."

"A trap by the humans, then. We accuse the wrong human, they prove his innocence—and do it in a manner that makes it impossible for us to make a second accusation without losing face."

"If that is the case—though it seems a wildly risky plan for the humans to try—then, moments ago, you were demanding with great violence that we fall for it."

"Well perhaps then the spy agent Milkowski did do it—though there is something in what you say."

"Quite right, My Superior," Brox said with sarcasm as thick as half-melted tar. "We can be absolutely certain that Special Agent Milkowski is either guilty—or innocent." He rose to stand in a position of respectful submission. "Give it time, My Superior. Give it just a little time, and we will plow our way clear of this field overgrown with muddle and uncertainty, and move forward to better-tended pasture."

"Time," said Diplomatic Xenologist Flexdal 2091, "is the item that is in shortest supply. Do your job then—but do not expend a single needless duration unit of that precious commodity."

Hannah's eyes snapped open, and she found herself staring up at a ceiling she had never before seen in daylight. Fear flickered through her mind, but she shoved it aside. She had been on too many assignments on too many planets, experienced the same sort of thing too many times before to be thrown off by it. It took her only a few seconds to go from *where am I/what am I doing here* and utter disorientation to getting herself fully grounded back in the facts of the case and her own situation.

They had bedded down in the main entry hallway of the embassy ship. They had chosen the spot for a number of reasons, not least of which was that it was also the main access hatch for the ship and the only hatch at ground level. Any of the people in confinement who decided to leave the ship for whatever reason would have found themselves unexpectedly stepping over two BSI agents, one on either side of the inner air-lock door.

She peeked through the locked door and into the lock chamber itself. There was Jamie, as dead to the world as she herself must have been little more than sixty seconds before. Hannah decided to play a little game with herself and started to count silently.

Before she got to thirty, Jamie's eyes came open, and it was plain from the look on his face that *he* knew exactly where he was and why. No frown of puzzlement for him.

"Good morning," she said to him through the open air-lock door. How he always managed to wake up within one minute of her when they were on a case was beyond Hannah, but he always did.

"Morning, anyway," he said. "We'll have to go and check before we find out how good it is."

She heard something of the fierce, innocent courage of a six-year-old out to chase the imaginary monsters in the backyard in his voice, and saw it on his face as well. *That's my boy,* Hannah told herself, not certain if she felt more motherly or big sisterish just then, but knowing for sure to keep her feelings to herself. Hannah was careful to hide her affectionate smile from Jamie as they both wordlessly got up and went through the routine of stowing their gear. It was a matter of reflex for both of them to step out of view of the other and turn their backs on each other as they got up and got ready for the day.

"Tell you what," said Jamie. "I'm just about ready to go. I'm going to wander outside and give you a little time and space for getting organized."

"Okay," Hannah said, being careful not to thank him. It might embarrass him to bring too much attention to his attempt to prevent her embarrassment.

Working in a split-gender partner setup with a partner who sometimes seemed almost young enough to be her son wasn't always easy. There were times when it required a certain amount of dancing around each other to keep embarrassing sights and emotions from being displayed. But it was a dance they had both gotten pretty good at.

Jamie shouldn't have been surprised to see Zhen Chi outside, working in the embassy garden. After all, she was formally released from confinement—and keeping Earth-based plants alive in this place had to be a job that required constant attention—especially with all the very reasonable and proper precautions that were imposed to keep the Earthside plant life from escaping and establishing itself in the wild.

"At least I don't have weeds to deal with," Zhen Chi said, when she saw Jamie. She was kneeling in one of the flower beds, doing something or other to the plants. Jamie wasn't remotely experienced enough to say what. "We didn't bring them along, so we don't have to pull them up. I could certainly do with bees, though."

"Aren't the Vixa close enough?" asked Jamie. "I thought they were supposed to be hive animals."

Zhen Chi stood up, peeled off her very petite gardening gloves, and carefully shook the dirt off them. "Come sit," she said, indicating a bench off to one side of the flower bed. Jamie followed her over and sat next to her and stared fixedly at the flowers.

"Nice to see some life-forms I'm sort of familiar with," he said. "Even if I don't know much about them."

"Let me guess," she said. "You had a pretty rough ritual of submission."

"I don't remember submitting to anything."

"Yeah, but they call it that. What happened?"

"We went in to see a Grand Vixan named Zeeraum. While we were standing there, she opened the, whatever you call it, her mouth sphincter." Jamie gestured toward the top of his own head to show where he meant. "There were some bones and things there. Some cute little helper Vixa scuttled up there to clean out the debris. Once it was done, Zeeraum picked up one of the helpers, cuddled it for a second, then tossed it into her mouth and swallowed it whole. We could hear it screaming from inside the mouth—and even saw it struggling."

"If it's any help, which it probably isn't, I very much doubt that's what you saw. When Zeeraum was finished cuddling the helper, she would have paralyzed it by using one of her manipulator-arm stings. The Vixan digestive acids and enzymes are very powerful and fast-acting. The flesh dissolves fast and produces a lot of gas, which can form bubbles and odd noises as it dissipates."

"I saw what I saw, and heard what I heard," said Jamie.

"Then, by the lights of her own culture, Zeeraum was guilty of deviant behavior. Forgive me for putting it in such flippant terms, but the Vixa view it as very poor form to play with their food. If she's caught doing that, she'll be punished."

"Oh, good. Now I feel much better about Zeeraum's swallowing her relative whole."

"I know these aren't the points you're worried about," said Zhen Chi, "but Vixa don't swallow. That mouth is really just the opening to a sort of predigestion chamber. The food goes in, and the digestive juices start flowing, and everything edible is dissolved off the food object. The liquefied food flows down into the main body for further digestion, leaving the solid remains behind to be spat out or cleaned up or whatever. The predigestion chamber is normally kept full and working at all times."

"And all that makes cannibalism all right?"

"No. But, by their lights—and as a piece of brutal logic—what you saw wasn't cannibalism, or any more or less wrong than your eating a hamburger. The only difference is the cow is killed and slaughtered and chopped into little pieces for you, off where no one has to see it."

"After yesterday, I'd have to say that's a pretty big difference," said Jamie. "But one Vixa ate another. How is that not cannibalism?"

"We don't even know how many Vixa biological castes there are," she answered. "We're reasonably certain that the smaller ones are maybe as smart as say, dogs or rats. Not smart enough to talk, or think—but smart enough to be programmed to perform simple tasks. Some of them don't have minds at all, in any sense we'd understand. They just have what amount to remote-control systems."

"And they didn't get those from Mother Nature," Jamie said. "It had to be that our escort Vixa were being operated by some sort of centralized system. Were they all lobotomized and equipped with two-way radios?"

"Possibly, but unlikely. They can function independently, so their brains haven't been altogether removed."

"Yeah, I saw behavior to confirm that. But my point is that not all of these castes and variants and so on evolved naturally. They've been bred, or genetically engineered. I take your point that there's not really any logical distinction between me eating a cow in pieces and a Vixan eating another critter in one bite—but taking my cousin, or my child, and genetically engineering him so his ancestors are not only mindless, but delicious—maybe even breeding them so they don't mind being eaten—*that's* different. That's wrong."

"Yes," said Zhen Chi. "It is wrong, horribly wrong and evil—for us. It's decadent, degenerate—for us. I certainly don't approve of their culture. I find it as repellent as you do. But we come from a species where we really *are* all the same—and a species that just recently stopped treating people who looked slightly different from them like animals. It's still a wound, a raw wound, with us. And seeing a species where all the lies told about human slaves are *true*—the lower-end castes *are* happy, they *aren't* capable of taking care of themselves, they *love* taking care of us, we *are* better than they, and we *were* born to rule them—just saying those words makes me feel a little bit sick. And yet, here, *they are all true*." She shuddered. "Brrr. It makes us all twitchy. But I'll tell you what might be the deeper truth—the thing that makes us wonder if the Vixa really are decadent, maybe even degenerate, as a culture. It's the *waste*."

"The waste of what? And what does it matter what they waste? They're infinitely richer than us."

"The waste of their own potential, if you come right down to it. There were some xenoanthropologists through here a while ago, doing some very basic observations on the Vixa. They estimated that the majority—that's more than fifty percent—of their economic activity revolves around demonstrating and establishing status. The specially bred escorts. The huge, uselessly redundant space elevators. The whole Stationary Ring. The massive cities that have to be built to hold all the escorts and aides and assistants and what have you, billions of them, to dance attendance on, at most, a few million Grand Vixa and other fully sentient castes. *Think* what they could accomplish with the energy and skills and resources that are burned up by status display."

"Could they do that?" Jamie asked. "Could they break free? Would they want to, or need to?"

"You mean, so they could start acting sensible, like us?" Zhen Chi smiled sadly, and shook her head. "I doubt it," she said. "I know you've heard it a million times, but biology is destiny. I don't care *how* Elder the Race is—*every* species is shaped by the way it evolved, what its nonsentient ancestors did for a living. There is no strong link between the complexity of the physical, biological organism and the sophistication or level of advancement of the culture. There are some sentient species that are way beyond humans in terms of biocomplexity and sophistication—but insofar as their culture—to use the technical term, they're a bunch of slobs. What they've got, those races inherited from other races. On their own, they really don't have that much to offer.

"The Vixa are somewhere between highly evolved trilobites and the first chordates, with much larger brains, of course. We're *much* more biologically complex—but simple designs can be very advanced and efficient. And there is nothing second-class at all about their minds. Take a look at their technology and you can see that.

"The Vixa have made simplicity work for them in lots of ways, made it into a huge advantage. It's easier to make changes to a simpler machine. That right there explains a lot of their ability to modify themselves into so many variants with so little apparent effort. Their stingers and toxins, for example. There's a stinger at the end of each arm, and the Vixa have engineered themselves so that each stinger injects a different toxin. Their med-specialist castes don't have toxins in their stingers—they've got various injectable medicines.

"But it's not even about evolution or biological complexity. It's about how they reproduce. Think ants, think termites, think naked mole rats. Have you ever read *Brave New World*? Aldous Huxley? Early twentieth century—pre just about everything. Precloning. Pre–behavioral science. Pre discovery of DNA, for that matter. All the science, all the technology wrong—but the basic idea of a society that mass-produces people— that part Huxley got right. If I were the ambassador, I don't know if I'd make that book required reading for everyone at the embassy—or else ban it from the embassy library as too disturbing and a threat to morale."

"You've gotten ahead of me," Jamie said.

"Okay. Sorry. I do that. I get involved, and I just take off with it, whatever it is. Okay. Lemme back up. Hive species. Like ants and termites and bees. One thing they have in common is that they limit reproduction. The queen bee is the only one who lays eggs. *All* the bees in the hive are her children. Nearly all of them are sterile females. Worker bees. Naked mole rats are mammals, but they have a lot of behaviors in common with ants and termites. They have a queen that does all the reproducing. They build an underground burrow and pretty much never leave it. They create, control— and are confined by, controlled by, the limits of the burrow."

"That's not like the Vixa," Jamie protested.

"It isn't?" Zhen Chi gestured at the blue sky above, the garden by the embassy, the world all around. The breeze blew a few strands of hair into her eyes and she brushed them away. "Aside from cops and security types, have you seen one Vixa outside, not in a vehicle or a structure, but outside, exposed to the sky and the wind and the air, since you got here?"

"Well, now that you mention it, no. But I've seen diplomats, trade representatives, even Vixan police investigators on human worlds. I've talked to them. They went outside. Sometimes." Thinking back on it, Jamie realized the Vixa he had met did seem to find a lot of reasons to stay inside.

"If they were outside, I promise they didn't enjoy it," said Zhen Chi. "There are worker castes and soldier-police castes and so on modified to tolerate exposure to the outside, but that's considered very low-class behavior. And I promise you, as certain as I'm sitting here with you, that those diplomats and representatives and investigators were specially bred—no, more than that, specially *engineered* from prebred stock, then specially raised and indoctrinated for the job they were doing. And, my guess would be, they were heavily medicated at all times. Remember what I said about the medical castes having injectable meds in their stingers? Some of our more excessively imaginative intell types think that the Vixa bred and engineered for off-planet work have their stinger glands modified to provide various tranquilizers for self-injection!

"Believe me, one of the things that the Vixa sneer at us for is that we *like* to go outside—and they think the concept of privacy is a downright deviation. And I can bet you whatever you like that you never saw a Vixa alone—"

"SubPilot Greveltra! The one who flew us here!"

"I was about to say, *except* for a spacecraft pilot or

subpilot. They're crazy already so it doesn't matter. And I think they're crazy *because* they are bred and engineered to be alone. Every other caste or breed of Vixa actively needs company. At least one companion, preferably dozens. That's probably where a lot of the escort tradition came from. Aside from the pilot castes, my rough measure is that an hour or so alone for a Vixa is like a month in solitary confinement for us."

"What about the simulants?" Jamie asked. "My sim was alone with us for a while."

"They need to do that for imprinting, I think. There's a lot of guesswork. The simulants are new to us, and we know almost nothing about them. But I'd bet a week's pay that as soon as your simulant had the chance, it linked up with a Vixa or another simulant— and, if it had the chance, it stayed away from the SubPilot."

"Well, yeah. You're right."

"My guess—and it's just a guess—is that they regard space travel as such a high-risk profession that they design the whole system to expose as few Vixa as possible to it. Not for the sake of the individual's safety. That wouldn't matter so much. But to limit contamination. Exposure. To keep from having to contemplate sending ten or twenty Vixa, or a whole subhive, some socially significant grouping, outside the group. It's a very disturbing idea to them. Risking one SubPilot would be like risking a fingernail. Not a much bigger deal than expending a simulant. But ten or twenty six-limbers, or even nine-limbers—a *group* of connected, related, individuals is something very different. That is perceived as a significant part of the whole."

"But if there's a hive mentality, why should the hive care about individuals?"

"They—it, the hive—doesn't care about individuals. It's fear. Like giving someone a chance to chop off your hand, or poke your eye out. Plus, maybe, that chopped-off hand could grow itself a new body—and then come looking for you."

"Huh?"

"In theory, at least, a large enough group could be the nucleus, the starting point for a new hive that would compete with the old one. So the old hive not only doesn't *want* a large number of its members to die—it also doesn't want them cut off, given a chance to escape and grow on their own."

"But how could they form a new hive if they're all sterile?"

"In honey bees, if the queen lays an unfertilized egg, that egg still grows into a bee—a male, a drone. That drone could then mate with the queen and fertilize her eggs, so they would grow into worker bees. Feed one of those workers royal jelly long enough, and it will grow into a queen who might be able to start her own hive—but she'd be the descendent of a drone hatched from an unfertilized egg. We don't know the details of Vixan biology very well at all, and I'm sure it doesn't work quite that way—but if bees can reproduce without a queen, why not Vixa? Besides, bees don't have labs and test tubes and gene sequencers and cloning labs—but Vixa do. And maybe they aren't so good at doing biology or genetics on anybody *else*, but believe me, the Vixa are good at working with their *own* genetic material. Any group of twenty or forty or so Vixa that included a few six-limbers could be presumed to have the capability of forming a new hive."

"And they've used that same skill at genetics to breed themselves some castes for use as snacks?"

Zhen Chi frowned. "Possibly. We don't know. More

than likely, those helpers you saw eaten were developed from some naturally occurring nonsentient caste. The same with the other slave castes—the escorts, the laborers, and so forth."

"So you'd go ahead and use the word 'slave.'"

"Slavery is wrong for humans because it means taking people as sentient as you are and treating them like animals. Most people have no problem with making a horse or a dog or a camel work, but there *are* some people who say it's wrong. You're forcing the animal to work, and breeding away its desire for freedom."

"Dogs and horses aren't slaves," Jamie said stubbornly.

"Why not? Forced to work, no pay, no freedom— and deliberately bred for the work, to boot. How do they not fit the definition?"

"I don't know. I haven't thought about it a lot."

"The Vixa modified their equivalents of dogs and horses and cows, and used *them* as the raw materials to make new species, new subordinate biocastes. They breed *them* for work—or for food. Not so different than what humans do. We think—or at least hope— the Vixa don't modify themselves into born slaves."

"It still freaks me out. What I saw is going to give me bad dreams for a long time."

"Pretty much everyone at this embassy has those dreams," Zhen Chi said quietly. "Just being on the same planet with the Vixa forces us to ask a lot of uncomfortable questions. But in the available universe, we have no choice but to deal with the Vixa."

"There you are!" called a voice from a short way off.

Jamie looked up. It was Hannah. "I've been looking for you," she said as she walked up. "Good morning, Zhen Chi."

"Good morning."

"Anything going on?" Hannah asked.

"Just getting a quick biology lesson," said Jamie.

"Well, class is over for now. Come on. We've got a lot to do."

Jamie stood up and turned to Zhen Chi. "Thanks," he said. "I think that helped. At least I hope so."

"Me too," she said gravely. "But fair warning— nothing does, very much. Nothing will, as long as the Vixa are the Vixa."

TWELVE

CAFFEINATED SOCIOLOGY

Hannah and Jamie found the canteen without much trouble. It was the utilitarian building with the excessively cheerful, brightly colored handmade sign reading SNACK SHACK. Just by virtue of being one of the very few splashes of cheerful color, the sign served as a reminder that everything around it was government-issue beige, utilitarian, and serious. Hannah made the private observation that officially mandated morale-raising efforts at fun and informality never did work very well.

She flatly vetoed Jamie's suggestion that they conserve their own mealpacks and make use of embassy supplies. Food became very important in a small, remote post. Hannah knew that rummaging around in the supplies could throw off the menu planning for the week, or even the year. They might accidentally gorge on the one item that was in short supply, or blunder into some existing feud about what food belonged to whom—or worst of all, touch off a *new* feud that would set the two of them against the embassy staff.

But that didn't mean they couldn't eat their own food there. Even long-store meals just tasted better eaten off a real plate with a real knife and fork. Therefore they satisfied themselves with borrowing plates, forks, utensils, and so forth—being *very* careful to clean up after themselves. But no matter how careful they were, they were plainly intruding on a very small club, run on a very personal basis. Hannah could see that, in a dozen little details of arrangement.

Hannah was starting to get some ideas about how they might make use of what the Snack Shack was telling her. She left Jamie to rustle up whatever sort of meal he could from their own mealpacks while she took a look around the interior of the small canteen. It wasn't a large place, and she had seen similar layouts in any number of remote posts where people tended to stay on base a lot for whatever reason.

There was a cooking area with stoves, ovens, freezers, refrigerators, and the like along the back wall, and an auto dishwasher in the right rear corner. A serving line ran down the center of the room, and the front half of the place was taken up with just enough seating for everyone at the embassy to squeeze in at once.

There was an accordion-pleated flexible folding partition that could be drawn across the room, dividing it in two, and thus turning the right-hand side into a private dining room that could be reached from the outside from its own door.

In the front left-hand corner of the lunchroom were two large coffee urns, marked with official-looking stick-on signs marked REGULAR and DECAFFEINATED.

Hanging on a pair of chains from the ceiling above was another sign, also quite official in appearance.

ALL EMPLOYEES WITH KENDARI CONTACTS MUST OBEY CAFFEINE SAFETY PROTOCOLS AT ALL TIMES.

A typed note on embassy stationery was taped to that sign. The paper looked like it had been there a while. It had browned a little at the edges, and dried splashes of what could only be coffee marked the lower right-hand corner. It was all in capital letters, and read:

REMINDER, PEOPLE—CAFFEINE SAFETY PROTS
EXTEND TO ALL UNUSED REG & DECAF COFFEE
GROUNDS, USED COFFEE GROUNDS, USED AND
UNUSED LOOSE TEA, TEABAGS (INCLUDING
HERBAL—BETTER SAFE THAN SORRY) ALL OTHER
CAFFEINATED BEVERAGES, ALL DECAF VERSIONS
OF CAFFEINATED PRODUCTS, *AND ALL
CONTAINERS THAT DO OR EVER DID HOLD THE
ABOVE OBJECTS!!!*

Dr. Zhen Chi, Med. Off.

The ink scribble over Zhen Chi's typed name had to be her signature, but Hannah couldn't make out a single legible letter in it. Hannah had long ago observed that the stereotype about doctors and their handwriting was far better deserved than most.

A final, smaller, handwritten note in neat block letters was taped to the other corner of the ALL EMPLOY-EES sign. It was newer-looking, and cleaner.

PLEASE REMEMBER TO WASH, NOT JUST RINSE,
MUGS BEFORE RETURNING THEM TO RACK.

THANKS!
SNACK SHACK STAFF

And, there, on the wall to the left of the coffee urns, were two sets of open shelves just deep enough to hold a single row of cups or glasses. The first shelf was filled with about thirty identical standard UniGov-issue coffee cups, each on its own saucer.

The second set of shelves was plainly someone's well-intentioned but doomed effort to organize everyone's personal cups and mugs. There were neat little labels under each section of shelf, each with a person's name or title. There were about twenty of the labels. Most, but not all, had cups or mugs parked in their assigned spots. They were of all sorts—insulated mugs with lids, handmade ceramic ones purchased at this or that crafts fair at some previous posting, others with the logos of businesses or government departments, and a few with jokes or sayings. One showed a cartoon of a bureaucrat dozing at his desk over the caption *Visit Fabulous Center—The Capital Planet on the Edge.* Hannah was pretty sure she knew what gift shop that had come from.

One bothersome fact was that no fewer than four of the mugs had the BSI logo—one of these was dark blue, but three were white, and identical to the one found at the crime scene. She checked the white ones, and found that all of them had names written on the bottom in black marker that looked to be quite recent. It looked as if the same person had written in all the names, but she couldn't be quite sure the handwriting was identical, judging only from lettering scribbled on the bottom of cups.

She skimmed her eye over some of the other labels. *Groppe, Lindermann, Bonkofski, Mtombe, Smith, DCM*—that had to mean Deputy Chief of Mission, the officer second-in-command under the ambassador— *Halloran, Med. Off., Singh, Farrell*, and, inevitably, one just labeled *The Ambassador.*

Stabmacher's cup wasn't in either of the spots one might choose as the highest-status spot, either first in line at the top, or in the center of the center row. It was instead democratically positioned off to one side of the second row. It was deep red, with the UniGov Diplomatic Corps logo printed on it. There was just the faintest film of undisturbed dust on its rim and handle, and around the base of the cup, making it clear that that cup was never used, or moved.

The bottom row and a half of shelves gave mute and eloquent testimony to the limits of organization. Two labels had been peeled off incompletely, but cups still sat over where the labels had been. On another label, the original name had simply been scribbled over, and the words *Fred's Cup* awkwardly written in underneath.

Down in the corner was one marked *Linda* in an aggressively cheerful, youthful-looking handwriting that was almost elaborate enough to be called calligraphy. The cup over it was blue and gold, and looked to have some sort of college crest emblazoned on it. It looked brand-new.

Two or three of the empty spots over the name labels were a bit scuffed and scarred, and showed the remains of water rings. Other spots showed no sign of ever having been used.

Hannah didn't have any trouble reading the story that the shelf told. Someone at the embassy was a great believer in the blessings of being organized and had decided the previous arrangements for storing cups just wasn't good enough.

So that person—at a guess, judging from the handwriting on the original labels, that female person—had taken it upon herself to do the thing properly, and set up the shelf, done up the original labels, and busily typed up memos for distribution urging everyone to follow the new arrangements.

Ambassador Stabmacher had dutifully gone along. Probably he was the second person to shelve his cup, right after whoever had set the thing up. It showed he was just part of the gang, a team player, just as likely as anyone else to wander down to the Snack Shack for a cup of coffee and a chat. Everyone joined him in pretending that was true, but everyone knew just as well as he did that it simply wasn't the way he ran the show. Hannah had seen his *real* personal cup, and his private coffee service, in a service alcove just outside his office.

She judged that personal-cup shelf system was already well off its peak of compliance and had entered into a gentle decline. People were still putting up with it, mainly for the sake of humoring the person who had started it, but a few malcontents had never cooperated, and it would appear there had been a few backsliders in recent months.

Silly, trivial stuff—except that it told her a lot about the community they were in, how it worked, what things were important to people. No doubt the fact that care had to be taken to protect the Kendari from caffeine had, all by itself, raised the social, and even political, importance of what a person chose to drink, what cup a person used, and even where one put the cup when done.

She had the distinct sense that, given just one or two more outside facts, this collection of cups and mugs could tell her a lot about the recent social history of the place—and, just possibly, a great deal more. Her ideas were starting to take firmer shape. There were things that could be used here.

"I take it the choice of murder weapon causes you to study this," Jamie said as he came up behind her. "Speaking of which—" He handed her a cup of coffee for herself. "Here you go. Our instant stuff mixed with their water in one of their generic cups. Let's see us get in trouble for that."

"Thanks. The *apparent* choice of weapon causes me to study this, yes," said Hannah. "But the Frank Milkowski I knew was no fool, even if the crime scene would have us believe that Milkowski did it, then did the next best thing to hanging up a big neon sign that flashed on and off with the message 'I DID IT!' It makes no sense. No more sense than a handprint that appears out of nowhere."

"And therefore it must be a setup—but who did the setting up and why?"

"No data," said Hannah as she followed Jamie back to the table he had colonized. "Therefore, no comment. Hey, our mealpacks must have gotten better again. These almost look like real pancakes."

"Yeah, but don't look too hard at the bacon." They both sat down and started to eat. "Okay, if you don't want to discuss things we don't have data on," said Jamie, "maybe we can talk about data that makes no sense—and I mean *besides* the coffee mug and the handprint."

"Fine. That leaves us with plenty to talk about. For starters—either someone is not playing straight with us, or there's something odd about the discovery of the body."

"Yeah," said Jamie. "I assumed you caught that too, but I didn't want to do any follow-up that might tell the ambassador we were especially interested in that point."

"He's on your suspect list?"

"Not especially—but what he doesn't know he can't blurt out by accident to someone who is."

"Jamie, he's in charge of negotiating on behalf of

humanity with the Kendari *and* the Vixa. I think we can assume he's capable of *some* discretion."

"I don't want to assume anything I don't have to. But anyway, according to Ambassador Stabmacher, Milkowski found the body, locked down our side of the building, then immediately contacted Stabmacher, who brought in the other two BSI agents, had the tamperproof seals put up on the outside of the human-side doors, then contacted the Kendari ambassador, or xenologist, or whatever they call him."

"Right. Except Brox *also* claimed to have found the body—and got pretty emotional about it. If he's that good an actor, he shouldn't be wasting his talents as an IS Inquirist. He ought to be back on Earth, in Hollywood or Mumbai, playing the bad-guy Kendari in some vid series."

Jamie thought it over. "They could both be right," he said. "There's nothing to exclude that. Supposedly each of them went in, saw the body, left it completely undisturbed, then left immediately and sealed the entrance, and the next time either door was open was when we went through it—first coming in on the Kendari side, then leaving on the human side."

"*Except* that Stabmacher then immediately contacts Xenologist Flexdal—and for once shows some good sense and records the call with a time-and-date stamp—and informs him that one of their people has been found dead. Flexdal doesn't say 'yeah, we found her too' or anything like that. He lets Stabmacher think that's the first they've heard of it. Or else maybe he directs Brox to go see if there is anything wrong inside the ops center, without giving him any details. He goes and checks, and discovers the body."

"That would work," agreed Jamie, "but Brox sure

made it seem as if he was the very first one there, without any sort of warning or notice."

"And there's nothing to indicate that he wasn't," Hannah pointed out. "Brox comes in, sees his intended mate dead. He immediately leaves, goes back to the head of his embassy, and reports. Then just enough time goes by for the Kendari to get good and damned suspicious. Maybe it's in the split second just before Flexdal is going to call Stabmacher—or maybe contact the nearest Kendari strike fleet—when Stabmacher calls *him*. Flexdal has had just enough time to get paranoid *before* then, so he gets all cagey and plays dumb to see what the humans are up to. That could work."

"And both Brox and Milkowski are reported to have gone in, seen the body, and left immediately," said Jamie. "That would increase the chances of their not overlapping."

"Plus it fits with the idea of the Kendari not jumping in immediately to explain whatever it is they know about that handprint," said Hannah.

"What it *doesn't* fit in with is the idea that Brox has been completely forthcoming with us," said Jamie. "Unless he was unaware of the call from Stabmacher to Flexdal, he's been yanking our chain as well."

"And don't tell me it hasn't crossed your mind that he has to be on our list of suspects—and pretty high up."

"I know. Want to get in a fight over which one of us doesn't like it more?"

"Let's just assume it would be a tie."

"Fair enough," said Jamie. "New topic. The ambassador's lockdown plan. Is it just me, or does that really take the cake?"

"It's not just you," said Hannah. What was obvious

to both of them was that the lockdown was just the sort of idea that would appeal to a layman and be rejected by a real police officer out of hand, for any number of reasons. The first and foremost problem was that, except for the chief engineer, no one had actually been locked up. Anyone who wished could have gotten out, done whatever they liked in the night, then returned.

The ambassador's second mistake was in seeing the tamper-detecting tape seals as infallible and the answer to everything. As Jamie had pointed out, it was far from uncommon for a shipboard cabin to have more than one way in and out—and there were plenty of ways to get around tamper-detecting tape.

There was, for example, second-chance tape. It looked and behaved almost exactly like standard tamper-detect, except that it had a second, outer layer of adhesive. You could peel it back once without any effect—but the second time it went on, it would behave exactly like the conventional material. Supposedly there were also sources for the second-chance adhesive itself. Paint it on a surface before the tamper-detecting tapes went up, and an hour after the seal went up, it would simply slide off of its own accord. The list of tricks and stunts and workarounds went on and on. The moral of the story was that tamper-detect wasn't anywhere near as unbeatable as the vid shows made it out to be. Only an amateur would assume that slapping tamper-detect on everything was a foolproof solution.

But there was another and more subtle problem: Confinement on the honor system would work fine—so long as everyone, including the killer, was honorable. The ambassador seemed to understand, on an intellectual level, that everyone, including him, had to be treated as a suspect. But somehow, at the same time, he seemed to be taking steps that would only be effective if everyone agreed not to cheat—including the murderer. His failure to secure some sort of cross-verification with the Kendari, and his failure to ensure proper surveillance could easily wreck the investigation.

Hannah swallowed a mouthful of dubious bacon and went on. "The tamper-detect over everything and locking everyone up tell me that either he's seen too many bad murder mystery vid shows, and actually thought he was doing some good, or else he's involved in some really oddball conspiracy and they needed the lockdown to give the conspirators time to operate without being observed by the rest of the embassy staff."

"Observed doing *what*?" Jamie asked. "Killing Emelza 401 some more? The victim was already dead by the time of the lockdown, as witnessed by Milkowski and Brox—who, in case you hadn't noticed, is working for the other side. Or is this conspiracy of yours going to be *really* oddball?"

"*I* don't know what the plotters didn't want observed. Maybe they were preparing to flee undetected, leaving the simulants in their place so they can get away unnoticed."

"No one this side of blind drunk would mistake my simulant for me from less than twenty meters away—I hope. Ten times that distance if they saw it walking or moving."

"But we haven't seen your simulant yet this morning. They adapt. They get better. Your simulant might be your exact double by now. Who knows how good they get? For all we know, we were talking to the ambassador's simulant last night."

Jamie snorted. "Yeah, right."

"Hey, you asked for oddball. Obviously, a simulant substitution is a crazy idea. They'd never ever really try it. Let's forget it and move on. We've got about six hundred things to do, and we need to make decisions about who does what and in what order."

Not so many hours later, Hannah had reason to think that "never" didn't last as long as it used to.

THIRTEEN

BAD IMPRESSIONS

There had never been any thought of Brox meeting with Hannah and Jamie to talk out strategy over breakfast, or any other meal, for that matter. It was a given that they would meet after mealtime. If absolutely necessary, a Kendari could sit there and watch a human eat, or vice versa, but it was a duty to be avoided whenever possible. It wasn't just that caffeine was deadly to Kendari, or that there were common ingredients in Kendari food that were equally toxic to humans. Each species found the other's food absolutely nauseating in appearance and smell, and neither found the other's table manners all that attractive, either.

The meeting location was also obvious—if awkward. The joint ops center was neutral territory and had facilities for both species. It was, however, also the crime scene—and, to state the same thing on a more personal level, the place where Brox had found Emelza dead. But Brox was the one who suggested the ops center, and if he could take it, so could Hannah and Jamie.

They were on the way to the meeting when an odd sight greeted them. The ambassador and Zhen Chi were walking across the compound toward a small shed. Hannah and Jamie paused, then shifted course a bit to trail after them. They watched as the ambassador fished some small object out of his pocket and passed it over the door of the shed. It was obviously a keywand of some kind. The door swung open—and the ambassador and Zhen Chi stepped out of it, to greet the ambassador and Zhen Chi, followed by four other figures.

"Okay," said Jamie, half-under his breath, "the simulants *do* get better and better."

"Yeah," said Hannah, in an equally stunned tone of voice. "I recognize Milkowski from his simulant. And judging from the sim, it looks like he's put on weight and gone greyer."

The illusion was good—but it was not perfect. It took only moments for Jamie to spot a half dozen subtle differences between the two humans and their simulants, and not very much longer to spot flaws in the other four as well—big enough flaws for him to be sure that he'd never again mistake any of them for human.

They were further surprised to see Jamie's simulant emerge from somewhere and home in on the group. Jamie had completely lost track of his own sim at some point during the previous evening. He had no idea where the creature—or robot, or android, or whatever it was—had spent the night. That might be a worrisome point.

He didn't think his simulant looked all that much more like him than it had the day before. He was a little irritated to note that it had a bit of an oddly shaped little potbelly. Jamie caught himself patting himself on the stomach, making sure *that* wasn't copied off *him*. He had to laugh at himself. Maybe he was a bit more vain about his appearance than he realized.

For the moment however, his sim clearly wasn't worried about improving its similarity to the original. It was much more focused on herding together with the other six. That suited Jamie. Anything that got that creepy mirror image out of his hair.

The ambassador and Zhen Chi turned their backs on the sims the moment they emerged from their holding pen, paying not the slightest attention to them, any more than a farmer would stay and chat with his cattle after letting them out into the pasture for the morning. Jamie couldn't blame them. Spending time with them meant you were equating them with humans—and, whatever the grand exalted and mysterious Vixa might be, the simulants were far, far less than human.

"Good morning to you both!" the ambassador called out when he saw them, studiously ignoring the fact that his simulant and Zhen Chi's were trailing after them. "Did you sleep well?"

"Well enough, yes," said Hannah, her tone formal.

"Have there, ah, been any developments overnight?" the ambassador asked.

"Not that we're aware of. We're just off to meet with Brox. After that, we're going to do a full-court press on getting everyone out of confinement as soon as possible."

"Yes, good, I'm glad of that. I, ah, can see that I might have created at least as many problems as I thought I was solving with the lockdown—but the damage is done, and I take it you might as well take advantage of their being in isolation. No, ah, chance of simply, ah, letting them out before they're questioned?" It was hard to miss the hint that the ambassador would very much like to have them set loose at once.

"No, Mr. Ambassador, I'm afraid not," said Hannah. "There still might be some value in keeping them isolated from each other—and, frankly, *I* wouldn't want to be the one to tell them that they'd been cooped up all this time for nothing."

The surprised and worried look on the ambassador's face made it plain that he hadn't thought of that angle at all. "Ah," he said. "Ah, yes. A good point."

"Was the info on the handprint of any use?" Zhen Chi asked, speaking for the first time.

"What info?" Jamie asked

"On Kendari rigor mortis. I found it last night and gave it to the ambassador. Since we're still suspects at the moment, I figured I'd better go through channels."

"We got no such information," said Hannah. She looked hard at the ambassador, who seemed to be turning an even paler shade than he had been. "Ambassador?"

"Oh, yes, well—ah—Zhen Chi got it to me after you had turned in for the night, and I, ah—well, I didn't wish to disturb you, and, well—"

"You thought it might be fun to get even with us just a little, after we didn't show sufficient and due respect to you last night," said Hannah. It wasn't a question, and the ambassador made no denial, no reply. "Let's make this clear—news comes in, you get it to us. Direct. This is no game. This is about a murder and a pair of planets. You wake us up, you chase us down, and if we've gone off, you stand in the rain for hours to make sure we get it the *second* we return."

"I'll, ah, yes, of course." The ambassador reached for his datapad. "I can transfer Zhen Chi's report to your data system immediately—"

"No you can't," said Jamie. "We don't want the report beamed around through the air to give the Kendari and the Vixa and who the hell knows else a chance to practice their decryption skills. Besides, if we get it from you, we have to verify it against Zhen Chi's report anyway, because you might have a reason to diddle the data."

"What! How dare you—"

"I dare because you're a *murder suspect,* Ambassador! In a criminal investigation, we don't get information 'through channels,'" said Jamie, bulldozing right over the ambassador's protests and making no attempt to mask his annoyance. He turned to Zhen Chi and spoke to her alone, as if the ambassador wasn't there. "We get it direct from the source, or as nearly direct as we can manage. *Especially,* as you say, since you are *all* still suspects." He paused and looked at both of them. "Maybe I'd better be very blunt about this. You people seem to be treating this as some sort of pro forma thing. Going through the motions to show you respect the process, but thinking it's all for show. It's *not.* Someone is really dead, and someone really killed her on purpose, for motives unknown, and we have *no* information that excludes *any* person at this embassy as a suspect. So if you have anything to tell us, you *tell* us—you *don't* go through channels and pass the information *to a suspect in the case.* Is that clear?"

Jamie's blood was pounding so hard that he barely heard their fumbling replies. He wondered what had gotten into him, tearing the ambassador's head off like that. He wasn't even sure how much of that had been real anger and how much had been theater. He didn't care. Pulling a stunt like this demanded a little theater in response. Hannah looked as infuriated as he did, but he also had to wonder if she was going to tear *his* head off in private—or agree with him. He had no idea. But his gut told him that these people needed a good swift kick or two—and that Hannah would feel the same way.

"I'll get—get the report to you, a secure paper copy, into your hands, in five minutes."

"No you won't," said Hannah, "because we are going to meet Brox in three minutes. But you *will* be cooling your heels outside the joint ops center, report in hand, when we're done. We want this to be a quick meet, but if we're in there until nightfall, you're planted outside the door until then. Clear?"

A flash of temper played across Zhen Chi's face, but then she calmed herself, nodded, and swallowed whatever protest she had been about to make. She glanced around at the ambassador, at Hannah, and at the simulants who had gathered around, plainly interested in seeing the show. Jamie couldn't help but spare an errant thought for them. What would those creatures—and whoever was watching through them—make of this scene? "Clear," Zhen Chi said at last. "I will be there."

"See that you are," said Hannah. "Jamie, we've got a date with an enemy agent. Let's go."

Hannah stalked away from the ambassador and Zhen Chi, fast enough that Jamie almost had to run to catch up, and a couple of the simulants had to scatter to get out of the way. She didn't care. She was angry enough that she felt more like tearing the outer blast door off the ops center with her bare hands rather than opening it normally. But she calmed herself down enough to punch in the right keycode and hear the dead bolt unlock. She pulled the heavy door open far enough for Jamie to get through, then followed him in—and slammed the door shut and rammed the dead bolt closed with as loud a crash as she could manage.

"Okay, boss," Jamie said. "I was about to ask if I went too far out there, but I guess maybe not."

"You did fine, Jamie," Hannah growled. "Let's just say those two characters out there ought to be glad you spoke up first." The inner blast doors were still shut. She checked the time. They still had a minute or two before they were due to meet with Brox. Good. She could stay in the dim antechamber and simmer down for a bit before the meet. "Do they really not *get* it? Have they really suffered that great a failure of imagination? Don't they understand that this isn't bureaucratic paper shuffling and covering your backside and scoring points? This is life and death, and then some!"

"Weirdly enough, I think it all gives us something," said Jamie. "I think what the two of them have told us without realizing it is that they are both innocent. The ambassador knows *he* didn't do it, and Zhen Chi knows *she* didn't do it—and therefore they assume *we* must know it too. They'll cooperate, but it *is* pro forma, because no one could really think *they* did it. They'll go along, but they expect us to know that they know it's all for show."

Hannah laughed coldly. "Like the ambassador's very democratic coffee mug that everyone knows he'll never use. Hang the window dressing well enough, and everyone can pretend they think it's real, and no one has to lose face."

"Yeah. Except sometimes guilty people are very good at finding elaborate ways to act innocent. One—or both of them, I suppose—could be putting on a very brilliant and sophisticated act. But maybe they haven't really allowed for the way reality musses up the window dressing sometimes."

"It sure as hell did this time. And the damnable thing is that I'm sure our little chat with Brox would go better if we had had a chance to read Zhen Chi's report first. But we don't dare postpone the first meeting, or everyone on the *Kendari* side will go even *more* paranoid. So, here we go in, not knowing everything our side knows. Ain't it grand, how everything always works out for the best?"

She stepped to the lock panel on the inner door and started punching keys.

FOURTEEN

THE LAND OF MIRRORS

Inquirist Brox 231 greeted his two rivals and colleagues, who were obviously relieved to be led to a side room of the ops center. That suited him as well. *He* certainly didn't want to have their meeting in the crime scene area itself. The side room was for small secure meetings. It had a split-height table—one side suited to a comfortable Kendari working height, and the other, slightly higher, intended for seated humans. They all went in, sat down, and got right to it.

"Here," said Brox, pulling out a human-built datapad, "are the first fruits of our collaboration, at least from our side of things."

"Good. Thank you, Brox," said Special Agent Hannah Wolfson.

Brox felt his insides go just a bit cold. He prided himself on his knowledge of human gestural language, voice tone, and other clues to emotional state. And every cue he was picking up from Hannah Wolfson told him that she wasn't happy about what she was about to say—and that he wouldn't be happy either.

"But before we get to that," Wolfson went on, "we need to talk motive just for a moment. Some sort of theory of the crime. Based on what we've got so far— the identity of the victim, the location of the crime and who had access to it, the timing and circumstances surrounding the crime, and apparent means used to kill the victim—take all that together. You've had more time to think about it than we. What does it all say to you? What's *your* theory of the crime?"

Brox froze up, staring straight at Hannah Wolfson, his eyes locked with hers. Brox's ancestors were pack predators, and Wolfson's were little better than scavengers, gatherers of roots and nuts—but in that moment, he felt as if he were the prey, frozen in the gaze of the hunter who was about to take him down.

He forced himself once again to reach into his rapidly depleting reservoir of cool and calm, and the moment passed. "The obvious, surface motive would appear to be to cause a rift between your people and mine—or rather, to make the existing rift wider. It was made to appear that one of your people killed one of mine in a particularly cruel way that would be easy for a human to manage but much more difficult for a Kendari—if for no other reason than that your people ship coffee and tea to all of your posts a thousand kilograms at a time—while we of course do not. A Kendari *can* get caffeine, and *can* handle it safely with reasonable precautions—but it would be much more difficult, and the safety precautions themselves would add to the risk of detection. A discarded pair of surgical gloves, or a respirator mask that had caffeine dust clogged in the filters, for example."

"So you think a human did it."

"I did not say that. I was careful to speak of the *surface* motivation. The manner in which the murder was committed was so crude as to be unbelievable—to the point where one could posit the theory that the means of murder were meant as a double-blind—a human, perhaps one of the BSI Special Agents, kills Emelza and leaves clues that point so obviously toward a BSI agent that no one can believe it because we assume no

BSI agent would be fool enough to leave such obvious clues behind."

"Is that what you believe happened?"

"No. It's simply too elaborate, too complex. And I would suggest it would require a contrary mixture of political and personal motives. If the motive was to disrupt human-Kendari cooperation, and the goal was to make it look like one of you killed one of us, the killer, whoever it was, would want the clues to point unambiguously at a human assailant, preferably one with a direct connection to the human government. A BSI agent would do nicely. But the idea of making the clues so obvious that no one believes them would be counterproductive to that goal."

"Unless the killer concluded that creating uncertainty, and destroying the small amount of trust between the two sides would do the job equally well," Hannah Wolfson suggested.

"And then we are off into the land of mirrors," said Brox, "where every move is a feint and a deception, where every arrow that points north is meant to fool us into trotting south, but we know that, so we gallop north, but our enemies know *that,* and therefore the gambit to make us gallop north was meant to prevent us from walking south—"

"Until we are so frozen by indecision that we fail to move at all," put in Hannah, "and perhaps *that* was the goal of our enemies, and so we dare not stay still—"

"And by then we have forgotten that our original plan was to march west," put in Jamie Mendez in a voice so low it was almost a growl. "We should pursue our own goals and not be herded about by ghosts and phantom conspiracies."

"I agree," said Hannah Wolfson. "But even that is far from easy." She looked back toward Brox. "Do you see any other motive for committing this crime in this way?"

"If someone wished to—to kill Emelza for some other reason—this is difficult for me—perhaps for a personal or emotional reason—then that person might well seek to disguise it as a political murder in order to avoid detection." He took a deep breath and stamped his right forefoot on the floor. "Let us not play a game. If *I* were to commit this crime because—because—"

"Because of whatever," said Hannah, in an oddly gentle voice. "Because we are investigators who know how many murders are committed by family members and lovers and the like. Because it is a fact, and a statistic. But not because we know of or suspect anything dark or difficult between you and your intended. Because we are obliged by duty to examine the possibility and for no other reason."

"I thank you, most deeply, for those words. They help. If *I* were to commit this crime for whatever reason, or if another Kendari were jealous, or perhaps some other Kendari or human had some other deep, personal, emotional motive, it is possible they might choose to disguise the crime as political."

"It would take a very rare and dangerous sort of human to commit what might be considered a crime of passion in this cold and calculating a manner. Would that be true of Kendari?"

Brox clenched his fist and fought down the impulse to shout, to scream, *This was my intended, this was my Emelza*. He dared not indulge that desire. "Most definitely," he said in a calm and dispassionate voice. "I have studied human crime, and murder, and found much that was familiar. As with your people, our crimes of passion are—are passionate. An impulsive act, driven by the need for emotional release, the drive to let something *out*."

Jamie leaned forward toward Brox and looked from him to Hannah. "Hold it, both of you. Let's save some time and stop torturing ourselves and each other. I'll say it short and fast and we can move on. Assume for the moment that we don't believe a BSI agent would be dumb enough to leave that many clues pointing to himself, and the most likely possible motives we're left with are someone trying to break up the negotiations—but what you two *haven't* said was that making it look like a human killed a Kendari would *have* to improve the odds of the Kendari snagging Pentam.

"Alternately, perhaps Emelza knew something, had some bit of knowledge, that might sway the decision. Maybe someone, on one side or the other, felt she needed to be silenced. We could dream up a bunch of other political motivations, but that's a good start. Then there's the personal angle—and I don't know enough about Kendari mores and customs and love affairs and so on to speculate. But someone could have killed her for personal reasons, and made it look like a political murder to throw us off the scent.

"We also have to look at who had easy access to the crime scene and the victim." Jamie Mendez slumped back in his chair. "The short form is that we all know perfectly well you're the best fit for all of that stuff. I believe very strongly that you didn't do it, and that goes for Hannah too, I'm sure—"

"It does," Hannah Wolfson agreed.

"— But it's not about what we *believe*—it's about what we can *prove*. And, I have to say, Hannah and I have both believed things that turned out to be wrong. We *can't* exclude you as a suspect—but we can't

exclude you as an investigator, either. We trust you—
but we can't trust you absolutely in this situation."

"I thank you for your frankness, and your under-
standably limited support," Brox said. "I would point
out that it would be quite difficult for me—or any
Kendari—to steal coffee and a coffee mug from the human compound. I'd remind you that no caffeine products of any kind are permitted in this building, for
obvious reasons. We were not exactly given free rein of
the rest of the facilities—and, as you say, we dare not
deal with anything containing caffeine without taking
very careful precautions."

"Those objections are quite valid," said Hannah
Wolfson, "but whatever the motive for this crime, if we
assume it wasn't just Frank Milkowski grabbing a
Kendari and forcing coffee into her mouth—and I
wouldn't want to try that with a Kendari—this was a
carefully planned crime, staged to make it look like
something it wasn't. Whoever did it took his or her
time, and chose the moment. If it took forty days to collect the materials—pilfer a cup someone had left out,
filch a jar of instant coffee from the trash—so be it."

Hannah Wolfson went on. "Or else the killer came
upon the cup and the coffee accidentally, or from some
other source outside the embassy compound. There
are any number of humans living just up the road.
Buying or stealing coffee from them would be no problem. And I've seen at least four of those BSI souvenir
mugs floating around the embassy compound. My
guess is they are given out to all sorts of people as sou-
venirs. They're very popular with visitors to BSI HQ."

Brox cocked his head to one side and turned his
hands upward. "You might as well know now that I
have one at my workstall back in our main embassy
building. And Emelza had one as well. They are a con-

venient size for holding writing instruments, and there is—or at least was—a certain ironic humor in decorating our workstalls with the sign of the enemy. Both of those mugs are still there, as of this morning. I checked. But certainly there could be others in our embassy. There probably are. Your people seemed to enjoy handing them out. So yes, I could have done it. But I didn't."

"I am not calling you off the case," said Hannah. "I don't see how I can, in the situation we're in. But you know as well as I do that you should not be investigating this matter, for all sorts of very obvious reasons."

"I agree. But it was bad enough that Flexdal had to send a QuickBeam message reporting Emelza's death. He did not wish to face the further dishonor and loss of face that would be involved in making the slightest suggestion that I might be a suspect. That would be extremely difficult on a professional level, but that is only part of it. He is a distant connection of both my family and Emelza's, and was part of the group that arranged for us to be espoused. To take me off the case would, in effect, be to admit to a large group of high-social-status Kendari that he had introduced her to her killer, and arranged for them to be together. He also has family ties to the office that would have dispatched a replacement investigator and would have faced grave embarrassment there as well, on similar grounds. He was instantly convinced that Milkowski did it, or that some other human made it look like Milkowski did it. There was also the time element. The Vixa were going to give us one round-trip on the *Eminent Concordance*—but not two. As I understand it, it takes a dozen or so days to replenish the ship between journeys. That meant we had to choose, quickly, between getting in human or Kendari investigators.

"For all the reasons I just listed, my Superior chose humans. He dispatched me to collect you in order to assert his official confidence in me, and to establish me as the senior, leading partner in the investigation. My job, as he sees it, is to force you to reach the conclusion that a human did it and force humans to absorb the full humiliation of declaring yourselves guilty. He is, obviously, a fool, but those were his intentions."

"And maybe you should do what he says," said Jamie Mendez. "If that's the way evidence is pointing, and we're heading another way, you push us back. You keep us honest. But your boss is right, at least up to a point. You can't be the lead investigator on this."

"Agreed. I can assist. I can provide support. But you two are the only ones here who *aren't* suspects. You must lead the investigation. And if you conclude that the best way I could help would be to lock me up in solitary confinement starting right now, so be it. If I am innocent—and I am—then I have the strongest possible motives—personal, professional, and patriotic—for wishing you to succeed."

"I think we can find better uses for you than locking you up," said Hannah Wolfson. "But you remind me of another point. Your xenologist and our ambassador both put all of their personnel in voluntary confinement. I've got a few ideas about how we're going to deal with it, but it's going to be a huge nuisance. I frankly don't see how we can manage interviewing your people as well—and I don't think it would be such a bright idea for either side to have enemy aliens in the room for those sessions. I'd like to suggest that we simply do sight-and-sound recordings of all interrogations and provide the recordings to the other side."

"Agreed. I was planning to suggest the same idea to you."

"How are you going to deal with interviewing your entire staff?"

"It is actually a fairly trivial problem. It is our custom for all of our staff to take their last meal of the night together. Only three embassy staff Kendari—myself, Emelza, and a maintenance worker—were not present at the meal. What that means, of course, is that everyone else has the rest of the dinner party to provide an alibi for the period around the time of death. I was present for the entire meal myself—except for when I went to collect Emelza. I planned to chide her for working late again. Instead, I discovered her body."

"So you have an alibi as well," said Hannah Wolfson. "That's certainly something."

"Unfortunately, I left for about twelve minutes just about at the time of—of the murder. There will be several witnesses who noticed my departure, I am sure."

"Where did you go?"

"I spilled some bloodsauce on myself, and went to my own quarters to clean up before it could stain my body felt." Brox looked from one human to the other, and decided to press ahead, play no games. What point in pretending not to notice what they would see instantly in any event? "And you are not fools, and are of course well aware that staging an accident like that—especially one that would account for my returning with mussed body felt, or with damp, recently washed portions of my body—is exactly what someone wishing to provide himself with a chance to slip away and commit a crime that might involve violence or struggle might do."

Jamie Mendez frowned. "You said it. We didn't."

Hannah Wolfson spoke up in a brisk tone of voice. "Getting back to your own people. How do you plan to proceed?"

"I will work up a written interview form for all of them to fill out, describing where they were and what they did during the evening, without drawing any sort of special attention to the time during which the murder was committed—and see if I can determine who else went away from the meal and came back, or arrived late. I'll then go back and interview the appropriate parties directly."

"That's more or less how we'll be proceeding. We'll want to see copies of all your interview forms, and recordings of the live interviews."

"Will you wish to have them translated first?"

"Frankly, our security rules say we can't rely on outside translation. We'd have to have our computers translate them anyway. The translator programs might miss a few things that we'll need clarified, but otherwise, don't waste your time."

"Likewise, provide us—or, rather, me, I suppose—with your materials without bothering to translate."

"It looks as if we're all going to have a lot of boring written statements to wade through," said Jamie Mendez in a cheerful tone of voice. "But speaking of information—that datapad you've got—you mentioned something about first fruits of the investigation?"

Brox slid the human-made datapad across the table. "I'd appreciate it if you'd get that information transferred as rapidly as possible and get that datapad back to me. We don't have many of them."

"I should be able to do it here and now," said Jamie Mendez, reaching out to take the pad.

"Hold off on that just a moment, Jamie," said Hannah Wolfson.

"Why?"

"Just indulge me for a little bit." She turned to address Brox. "What is the data on that pad?"

"Medical tests and studies concerning the cause and time of death. All the raw data is there, along with a discussion of the procedures used by Medical Technist Remdex 290 to arrive at his conclusions. I would expect that in your service, the medical technist would normally just give you final numbers, without going into a great deal of detail about how they were obtained. However, given the current circumstances, I assumed your people would want to work through from the raw data and confirm our procedures."

"They will, if our people are still speaking to us," Hannah said. "Thanks, Brox."

Brox looked from one of them to another. "Might I ask why your own people might *not* be speaking to you?"

"We just had to tear a couple of heads off," said Hannah.

Brox jerked his head back in surprise. "I beg your pardon?"

"It's just an expression," Jamie said with a smile. "It means we had to yell at the ambassador and Dr. Zhen Chi. Let's just say they weren't following proper procedure."

"And *I* will just say that sometimes your experiences parallel my own," Brox said, allowing himself a small moment of entertainment. "But getting back to the matter at hand, I can give you a verbal summary of the hard data. Your side can, must, and should verify all this, and we'll preserve the evidence for later confirmation and so on—but the matter is so straightforward that I doubt there will be any difficulty."

"Before you do—have you got anything on the coffee mug yet?" asked Hannah Wolfson. "Were you planning to brief us on that right now? Is the data on it in that pad?"

"Medical Technist Remdex is doing that work now, I believe." *And Medical Technist Remdex is practically at the boiling point, ranting that his working conditions are intolerable, and he can't work for such long periods without rest.* "I was not aware that you wanted the data on the container first." Brox's tone of voice made clear the unstated and annoyed addendum *because you never told me.*

"No, just the opposite. I *don't* want the analysis of the coffee mug just yet. We're not going to be ready for that information for a bit anyway."

"Ready for it?" Jamie Mendez echoed.

"Indulge me, Jamie, indulge me," Hannah said again. "It would be useful to our side if you kept the medical data separate from whatever you get on the mug and delivered all the information on your analysis of the coffee mug in its own package. I place no restrictions on our analysis of the samples we took from the cup, and of the broken chip of cup. You may have that information as soon as Dr. Zhen Chi has completed it."

"Forgive me, Special Agent Wolfson," said Brox, "but I must point out that you are being a trifle mysterious."

"Yes I am," Hannah Wolfson agreed. "I wish to avoid planting preconceived notions or causing misdirection. It is because I wish all sides to proceed with open minds, and open eyes, that I do not say more. It is for the benefit of the investigation."

"It doesn't *sound* like it's for our benefit," Jamie Mendez said. "That evidence is important."

"It certainly is," said Hannah. "And we'll get to it. I'm even going to risk the wrath of the catering staff and get the ambassador's permission to make use of the food supplies in the canteen to make sure we can make the best use of the information we get off that coffee mug—and how's *that* for being mysterious? For the time being, you just go ahead and pull everything off the datapad Brox brought in."

"Yes, ma'am. Whatever you say, ma'am," Mendez muttered in English as he reached for the datapad.

Brox observed that the two human investigators were not in perfect harmony. One had ideas or information the other did not. That in and of itself was of interest. "I will handle the report on the coffee mug in the manner you have requested," he said. *Remdex will be glad of the break.* "Shall I proceed with the summary of our other information?"

"Please," said Hannah Wolfson.

He exhaled, and forced himself to speak with the same calm and professionalism he would have brought to any other case. It was not easy. He consulted his information plaque and read off the data it displayed. "Emelza 401 did in fact die of acute caffeine poisoning, brought on by a massive dose of the substance received through the mouth. The time of death can be fixed fairly sharply. She died at roughly 1950 hours, in your units of duration measure. Converting to your units once again, Medical Technist Remdex estimates there is a ninety-two-percent chance she died within plus or minus twenty-two minutes of that time, and a ninety-seven-plus-percent chance she died within plus or minus forty-four minutes of 1950.

"One slightly unusual feature of the case was that she apparently did not have time to swallow. There were chemical burn marks and so forth in her mouth and oral cavity, but not in—I am sorry, I don't know of a good word for this term in Lesser Trade—her swallowing tube. I expect we'll run into a few problems with technical and medical terms as we go."

He paused to steady himself, and continued. "The absence of any damage to any tissue below about this point"—he gestured to about a handbreadth below where his neck met the base of his jaw—"suggests that death was quite rapid, and came about as a result of direct absorption of the caffeine through the membranes in her mouth and oral and nasal cavities."

"Just a moment," said Hannah Wolfson, speaking carefully. "Forgive me for discussing unpleasant details, but it is necessary. In humans, at least, many sorts of trauma are not possible after death. There are other definitions for other purposes, but if this was a human who had been murdered by a fast-acting poison, we'd declare the moment that the person's heart—the person's circulatory fluid pump—stopped as death. The poison would travel around the body in the circulatory fluid, the blood. Once that heart, that pump stopped, the blood would stop moving almost instantly. The poison would therefore also stop spreading through the body. It might be transported by some other means, but only very slowly, and probably not very far."

"All that is quite similar to how things work in the Kendari body," said Brox. "I do not quite see what you are leading up to."

"Forgive me once again. Perhaps your personal involvement has caused you to miss a point. Perhaps it is a nonissue, and I am assuming Kendari are too much like humans. But let me be careful and thorough." Agent Wolfson checked her datapad and her handwritten notes. "Here we are. I wrote down some notes, and I have photos as well. I don't think you need to see them again, but if you do, I have them. I noted down 'apparent chem burns on the skin around back of mouth, also on visible int. mouth tissue. Inside of mouth, extensive inflammation.'"

"That is all just what I got done saying."

"Yes, but my notes go on. 'Also some discharge/irritation around visible eye and ear,'—she was lying on her side and I couldn't see the other eye and ear—'and inflammation and discharge from nasal openings.' It's pretty significant damage in all three areas. My photos show that."

Agent Mendez checked his datapad. "Mine too," he said. "I guess what Hannah is asking is, if death was that fast, and if the Kendari equivalent of a heart stopped and the circulatory system stopped, how did the poison get transported to the eyes, ears, and nose fast enough to do that much damage? In humans at least, that sort of inflammation and discharge is driven directly or indirectly by the flow of blood, or else by things like breathing and blinking and swallowing that can serve to move fluids—and whatever poisons are in those fluids—around. And none of those things happens after death."

Brox was stunned. How had he and the medical technist missed that? They had seen the discharge and inflammation, of course. Only a blind fool could have missed those. But they had forgotten that the processes that caused them ceased at death. How? "You are quite right," said Brox. "If anything, it sounds as if human bodies might be subject to more postmortem trauma than Kendari. For us, at least, they stop in effectively the same moment that circulation stops."

"Okay. Again, my apologies for dwelling on unpleasant details, but if she doesn't have burn marks in her throat, which means she didn't swallow, yet she *does* have trauma to her eyes, nose, and ears, which means she was alive for some time after the poison got in her mouth—that can only mean that she was holding the poison, the caffeine, the coffee, in her mouth for a fairly extended period before she died. Or am I missing something?"

"No, you're not," said Brox. "But it would appear I was."

Hannah Wolfson drummed her fingers on the table—a common signal of agitation and uncertainty among humans. "All right," she said. "I'm probably about to divulge something that's classified. It's one of those damned fool things where *we* know something that you *know,* and we even know that you *probably* know we know it—but they slap a secret label on it anyway.

"Here's the thing. We know various of your guys carry suicide pills on this or that sort of mission. The pills are pure caffeine—but they're coated with some sort of material that dissolves in about five seconds after it is swallowed. That coating is there because Kendari don't have internal nerves that respond to the sort of damage done by caffeine. The stuff will still kill you—it just won't hurt. The reason the coating is there is that the burning sensation in the *mouth* is so painful that no Kendari can suppress the gag reflex. The body instantly insists on your spitting the stuff out because it hurts so much. Is that all about right?"

"I don't know your sources," said Brox, "but they don't appear to have let you down."

"And you can report back to the Inquiries Service that the BSI has made the startling discovery that being poisoned can be very painful. I don't think I've just given away anything much. The point is that Emelza somehow or another held this stuff in her mouth long enough to cause damage to her eyes, nose, and ears without spitting it out. That might have happened if the killer held her mouth shut or something—but I didn't see any sign of any sort of struggle. Her fur—sorry, body felt—wasn't even mussed. Or was there something I missed?"

"No. There were no signs of a struggle. The various distortions of the body—the arched back, the rigid fists, the fixed grin, are all common features of a phenomenon that, once again, I don't believe even has a name in Lesser Trade. 'After-death paralysis' would be close enough."

"Human bodies often react in very similar ways after death. We call it rigor mortis, two words from an archaic human language that translate more or less as 'death stiffness.'"

"Excellent. I doubt the processes in humans and Kendari are identical, but near enough. But in any event, there was nothing about the body that indicated any sort of fight or attack."

The room was silent for a moment. "And here I thought we were getting together to clear up a few questions," said Jamie Mendez. "Instead we invent new ones."

"Wait a second," said Hannah Wolfson. "What about that handprint? *That's* a sign of a struggle."

"A battle with the dead, perhaps," said Brox, deeply puzzled. Then he understood. "Another mistake on my part," he said. "Something so well-known among Kendari we assume that all others know it. There are even sayings that derive from it. 'A touch only the dead would notice,' meaning something that happens late that is noticeable but doesn't change things, and 'a light touch leaves a deep mark,' meaning that even doing something small can have a big result later on."

"That's all very interesting Kendari folklore," said Jamie Mendez, "but what are you talking about?"

"It's a phenomenon related to death stiffness. If left undisturbed after death, the skin of a Kendari becomes rigid and tends to swell up a bit—but it is only when something happens to disturb the swelling that it becomes noticeable.

"The amount and duration and severity of the phenomenon vary depending on a number of different conditions, but everyone knows not to touch a dead body between, oh, let's see, in your measures it would be a period starting no sooner than a bit less than two hours after death, and lasting about three to five and a half hours from that time. If a body is touched during that period, some hours later, when the postmortem swelling and stiffening of the skin takes place, any place where the skin was disturbed *won't* swell up. The touch induces a set of subskin adhesions. The result is just what we saw—any point where the body was touched in that period after death will later show as an indentation when the postmortem skin swelling sets in."

"So *that's* why your people weren't surprised when that handprint appeared," said Hannah. "Human bodies don't react that way after death. We'd never seen that before—and we hadn't seen any marks on the body when we got there. *Our* people all assumed that, somehow, someone must have come in and poked at the body *after* we first examined it."

"But wait a second," Jamie Mendez protested. "Who *did* poke the body?"

"Obviously, Special Agent Milkowski," said Brox. "He enters the joint operations center shortly after I discover the body. He sees Emelza on the floor. He leans over her and touches her. Perhaps he is checking for signs of life or trying to awaken her."

"We haven't interrogated Milkowski yet," said Hannah, "but we have a hearsay version from the ambassador that contradicts that. According to our ambassador, Milkowski finds the body before you, touches nothing, and immediately retreats out the blast doors on our side of the joint ops center. The ambassador is then a witness and participant in what happens next. He calls Diplomatic Xenologist Flexdal, who sends you in to confirm the body is there."

So. Flexdal had started things out by deceiving the humans—and Brox himself. Brox knew he should have figured that out. *I didn't want to know,* he admitted to himself. But he also had to admit it—or at least hint at it clearly enough for his colleagues to understand—if he were not to cause even worse damage. "Clearly there was some error in communication. I was in the act of informing Flexdal of Emelza's death when the call came through from your ambassador."

"Right," said Jamie with an odd little smile. "We figured there might have been that sort of mix-up."

"But if the, ah, 'mix-up' happened that way, Milkowski and the ambassador could easily have believed that Milkowski was the first on the scene," said Hannah. "He wasn't lying. He was just wrong. Why would he lie about poking or not poking the body?"

"Maybe he didn't even realize what he was doing,"

said Jamie Mendez as he examined something on his datapad. "Maybe he was embarrassed about doing something as dumb and unprofessional as poking at a corpse. And maybe he didn't do it."

"I beg your pardon?" said Brox.

"I got a look at his simulant just a little while ago," said Jamie. "Judging from what his sim looks like, he's a pretty big guy, isn't he? A hundred-eighty centimeters, or maybe a bit under that. Bigger and taller than me, by a pretty fair bit."

"That's about right," said Hannah. "What of it?"

He passed his datapad to Hannah, and let her see what was on it. "Then how is it that the handprint he supposedly left is about one-third smaller than mine, and also smaller than yours? Okay, *maybe* he's got the hands and feet of a teenage girl, but I doubt it. People would notice."

Hannah handed the datapad to Brox. It was displaying various shots of the handprint, with scaling data overlays. Jamie silently held up his own hand, fingers spread out, to make the comparison. "And before you can ask, Brox," Jamie said, "I'd say it's essentially impossible for a human with large hands to compress or distort his or her hand or fingers to make a convincing small handprint. Unless there is something seriously weird about Milkowski, there is no way he made this print."

"You are quite right. We'll have to check, of course, and measure Milkowski's hand. But he didn't make this handprint." Brox laughed wearily. "When we worked together on Reqwar, it was a spurious human footprint that caused trouble."

"No," said Hannah. "It was a *shoe*print. Big difference—especially because it is vastly harder to create an even remotely plausible print of a bare foot—and harder still to make a real-looking fake handprint. We have to presume that this handprint is legitimate unless and until we have reason to believe otherwise."

"Let me back up on another point," said Jamie. "Remdex reports that Emelza died at about 1950, and he's more than ninety-seven percent certain that she died no later than forty-four—call it forty-five—minutes after that, or, 2035 at the outside. What time did you find the body?"

"At about 2140 or 2150, I'd say."

"The ambassador's statement and his comm log show Milkowski calling him at 2200. We don't have any proof that he's speaking from the joint ops center, but we have no reason to believe he isn't. Then the comm log shows our ambassador calling your Diplomatic Xenologist at 2204."

"And I was present when that call came in. I had just about finished reporting that I had found Emelza, and Flexdal was questioning me pretty sharply about it. He was instantly convinced that the humans had killed her. He had just gotten through saying so when your ambassador called. Let us say it was not a moment in which he was eager to share much information with your people. He was not entirely forthcoming with Ambassador Stabmacher, and he let him believe that the humans had found Emelza first, and that I was going to go see for myself—when I had already seen the body, sealed our side of the ops center, and reported to him. Before I departed to summon you here, I reopened the outer blast doors, put my crime scene kit inside, and resealed the doors. That was witnessed and recorded. I did not go past the antechamber between the blast doors. I did not disturb the inner door seals."

"All very good. Except that you said it takes a while

after death for the body to be sensitive to this delayed-imprint phenomenon. If she dies at 1950, or even at 1905, how likely is it that her skin is going to be susceptible to the delayed-imprint syndrome at 2200? Or what if she died at 2035?"

Brox frowned and worked it through. "It would be essentially impossible for her skin to produce a delayed imprint before 2200 if she died at any time after 1950. It would be very unlikely—a chance in a thousand—even if she died at 1905."

"Let's assume she did die at 1905. What would be the earliest moment, in a normal case, for her skin to be susceptible?"

"At the very earliest, about 2230, but 2300 would be more likely. Especially considering the very clear, distinct handprint we saw. It takes some time for the full susceptibility to build up."

"And by 2200 hours, all the entrances to the joint ops center were locked down and sealed with tamper-indicator strips," said Hannah.

They were all silent for a time. It was Jamie Mendez who finally spoke.

"So—now that we've gotten together to clear these points up, we've established that Emelza somehow or another got a massive dose of poison in her mouth, but did not spit it out or swallow it, but instead held it in her mouth, despite the extremely intense pain, long enough for tissues around her eyes, nose, and ears to become inflamed, then died. Her body was discovered at about 2150, and again, ten minutes later, at 2200. The inner door to the building was sealed from the Kendari side by about 2200. The human side wasn't sealed immediately, but there were multiple witnesses observing the human-side entrance from about 2204 until it *was* sealed, so we can treat 2204 as the terminal moment.

"After that moment, to all intents and purposes, no one had access to the building. Yes, it takes a while to get everyone pointlessly confined, but according to the ambassador, they're all locked down by about 2500 hours. During that three-hour period, no one was really keeping watch over the embassy staff, but I think someone would have noticed a person breaking into the ops center. It's locked down and it's got tamper seals on the doors. And from that moment to when we collected the ambassador and Zhen Chi, the entire embassy staff was confined to quarters."

Jamie looked around the table. "So, with all that in mind, let's get ready for another nice long silence as I ask—who, exactly, made that handprint, and when?"

FIFTEEN

COLLEAGUES

Frank Milkowski woke up instantly the moment he heard the sound. He had been waiting for that noise—a faint rustling and scratching from outside the hatch of his shipboard compartment—for a long time. Endless hours. It seemed like endless years.

And suddenly he had only a few seconds. He threw back the cover and swung his feet out of bed to sit there in his underwear. There was no time to get properly dressed, let alone shower or shave. He pulled his pants on, stepped into his shipboard slippers, pulled on yesterday's—or was it the day before's?—badly rumpled work shirt, and stepped into the tiny cramped refresher unit.

He splashed some water on his face, gargled for a moment, ran wet fingers through his hair, and stepped back into the main compartment. He stripped the sheets off the bed, stuffed them and the pillow in their storage box, and refolded the bed back into its other incarnation—a semicomfortable one-person couch.

He just barely managed to sit down when the scraping stopped. Thank God it took a while to peel off that tamper-detect stuff—and more thanks that the chief engineer had warned everybody going into confinement that it had to be removed completely for fear of jamming up the doors.

Suddenly he remembered another bit of evidence that needed to be concealed. He scooped up the empty pair of gin bottles that were sitting on the floor in the corner. He had managed to smuggle the booze in with his food supplies during the confusion of getting everyone billeted aboard the ship. He shoved them deep into the recycler bin and made sure they were completely buried under all the food wrappers and other junk before he sat himself back down.

Frank had spent all of the last day and a half in that small compartment—and used nearly all of that time trying to think through the moment that was about to happen, the door that was about to slide open. He had been locked down early. Any number of things could have happened. He had no way of knowing who would be behind the door.

Perhaps Ambassador Stabmacher coming in to tell him all was well? One of the other two BSI agents, Singh or Farrell? If either or both of them had managed to clear themselves of the charge, obviously they would be on the case. Or had Stabmacher changed his mind, found some way to convince himself that letting the Kendari or even the Vixa investigate would be for the best? Neither Vixan or Kendari would fit comfortably in the ship's cramped corridors. Some human would have to escort him to where the xenos would sit in judgment.

Or had they actually managed that loony idea of sending for an outside investigator, setting interstellar speed records to bring in someone else? If so, who? What species? What organization? What individuals? There were only a limited number of plausible possibilities once you evaluated all the variables.

Even as half his mind was telling him it was pointless to speculate, since he would know in another few seconds, the other half was frantically working the problem, desperately trying to work the inaccurate, sketchy, and dated information he had for all it was worth and come up with the right answer, be ready to deal with whoever it was right off the bat.

He could hear the low *beep-beep-beep* tones of someone entering a combination into the lock-pad, and decided it had to be a stranger, but a human. The embassy workers all used the same model of lock-pad a dozen times a day. They'd have worked it faster. But an alien would be much slower. It would have to decipher the human number symbols, and might not even be sure whether to press the buttons or do something else.

He could hear the cheerful *boop-boop* tone pair that indicated that the right code had been entered, then the dead bolt sliding back. But the door did not open. Instead there was silence. Why? And then, of all improbable things, the annunciator, the *doorbell*, rang. And who would bother to push *that* button?

Frank wasn't much for making intuitive leaps, but he made one then. He knew, in the half heartbeat between the annunciator tone and speaking, the answer to that question, who it had to be. "Come on in, Hannah," he said, in the most casual voice he could muster. "You should know better than I do that it's open."

If he had just guessed wrong, he was about to look very foolish. But if his guess was right, then maybe he had just scored enough points, shown himself to be smart enough, on the ball enough, to win the coming interrogation before it ever began. That was the secret, Frank firmly believed. An interrogation was not just one person asking and another person answering. It was a game, a fight, a battle. Zero-sum stuff. If you win, I lose. If you get what you want, that means you took it away from me.

The door slid open—and sure enough, there was Senior Special Agent Hannah Wolfson. She stepped inside, carrying the breakfast tray he had figured was the thing that was slowing her down. Food and drink for the prisoner, playing the good cop to win him over. "Hello, Frank," she said. "I guess I won't bother asking if you're surprised to see me."

"You know me," he said, not bothering to stand up. Let her stand in his presence, show her that he felt no need to defer to her. "A regular junior Sherlock Holmes. Only an outsider who didn't know our lockpad by heart, and who was going to play this extra, extra nice would push that doorbell button. Brox talked my ear off about his adventures working with you and your poodle-boy. If he went for help, and it was going to be a human—who else would it be? Elementary, my dear Watson."

"Supposedly that line doesn't even show up in the real Sherlock Holmes stories," Wolfson said, still standing with the tray. She glanced at the walls, spotted a pullout table panel, balanced the tray with one hand for a second, pulled out the panel, and set the tray down on it. She reached for another foldout and pulled down a chair facing Frank. "And if you're ever up against my poodle—I assume you're talking about Mendez, and yes, he's here too—I'd be careful," she said, being very calm and casual herself. "He's got some pretty sharp teeth and claws—and he tends to go for the throat. More of a Doberman, really."

"Goodness, I'm scared," Frank said in a deadpan. "Thanks so much for the warning." He looked Wolfson in the eye as he considered her opening moves. All very nice, very friendly—but also pushing in on his space, taking over the compartment, telling him he had his facts wrong and that she had a goon she could sic on him if need be. She wasn't bluffing either. Frank had seen a couple of after-action reports about how Mendez handled himself in a firefight. Truth be told, Frank *was* a little scared of the guy.

And of Wolfson, too, for that matter. She had a hell of a reputation—and she was looking the part, sharp and confident. Her hair neat, her tunic and slacks fresh, clean, and neatly pressed, showing every sign of being rested, relaxed, and in control. Frank spotted a pen-sized video camera in her pocket, with a small blinking light indicating that it was running. She didn't draw attention to it, but on the other hand she was making no effort to conceal the fact that she was recording their conversation.

Maybe Wolfson knew how to play interrogation too. Frank decided he should push back a little harder. "Don't try scaring me," he said. "You work at making me happy. You're going to need me by the end of this."

"I hope so, Frank. I truly do. And I *am* trying to make you happy. I brought you breakfast."

He turned his attention to the tray—and realized that was a mistake as he tried to keep his mouth from watering. Eggs, bacon, toast, coffee—all of it fresh, all of it hot. He hadn't seen anything but low-grade emergency medpacks for two days. It was an act of will to keep from lunging for a fork. Instead he pointed a disdainful finger at the BSI coffee mug, full of fresh, steaming-hot coffee, that sat at the corner of the tray.

"Am I supposed to see you brought me a cup just like the one at the crime scene, burst into tears, break down, and confess that I did it?"

Wolfson grinned coldly. "First off, I'm here to ask questions. You don't ask, you answer. Second, I'll cut you a break and answer that one. You're supposed to be polite and say 'thank you for bringing me breakfast.'" She paused for a moment. "On the other hand, Frank, if you did do it, yeah, it would save me a lot of time and paperwork if you'd just let me know right now."

"Well, I didn't do it," he said. "I had nothing to do with it, period. And I had all of thirty seconds to look at the crime scene, so I'm guessing you know more than I do. Next question."

"I haven't asked the first one yet," Wolfson said mildly. "And I won't spoil your breakfast by making you answer questions while you eat. You go ahead. I'll catch up on my case notes while you shovel those eggs in."

And with that, she pulled out a datapad and started scrolling through whatever information it was showing. Frank couldn't see any of it from his angle. For all he knew, it could be last week's sports page—or a full forensics workup from the crime scene.

Another good-cop move that also served to get him off-balance, he noted as he added milk and sugar to his coffee and stirred it. He would have much preferred eating while being questioned. Chasing a piece of egg around the plate, chewing on a piece of toast, sipping coffee—even just having a knife and fork to play with—would all have been first-rate stalling tactics. Instead she sat there calmly, quietly, ignoring him, while he felt obliged to eat as quickly as possible to keep from wasting her time. It would be damned hard to bark and bluster at her five minutes after she had managed to put him oh so deftly in his place.

"What's on the datapad?" he asked. "Forget to file in a requisition for your new pencil with the Bullpen Admin officer?"

Hannah gestured with the datapad. "Sure. You bet. If you're trying to say I just hang around the Bullpen dodging assignments, maybe you're mixing me up with your buddy Kosolov. If it was a slag to make me feel like a wimp for following all the rules, let's just double-check who's been in solitary for two days. And if you're just angling in on a question that would let you know where I came from—yeah, we were flown in straight from the Bullpen to here, nonstop. Damnedest ride I've ever been on. And if it was just a clumsy attempt to make conversation, loosen things up, get things friendly so it's tougher to make them rough in a minute—well, we can find out how well it worked real soon." She glanced at his plate and powered down the datapad she had been reading—or pretending to read. "Finished eating? Good. Then let's get on with it."

"I didn't do it," Frank said stolidly. "There's your beginning, middle, and end."

"That's twice you've denied committing a crime no one has accused you of committing."

"Sure they have," said Frank. "Otherwise, what am I doing here?" he asked, gesturing around the room. "You're off to a good start. Don't blow it with cheap mind games."

"Point taken, point scored," Wolfson said drily. "But I'm going to go out on a limb here and guess you understand that cooperating with me will help prove you're in the clear. Let's reset and start from the beginning. You be the BSI field agent and I'll be the debriefer."

"Sure. Let's pretend. And we can even pretend it's not going to be my neck that gets whacked at the end of all this."

Wolfson ignored the snide comment. "Two nights ago, then. It's after closing time, after dinner. You decide to head back to the joint ops center."

"That's right."

"Why work such late hours?"

"There's a lot of work that piles up, and in case you hadn't noticed, there isn't a lot to do around here. Might as well work instead of staring at the wall. Though I've been doing plenty of that, these last two days."

Once again she ignored the barbs. "And that's it? No other reason?"

"Well—all right. One other. Two, if I want to go easy on myself. The second reason was that there was a big meet with the Vixa and the Kendari that people thought might happen two days from then—today, I guess it would be—and I wanted to make sure we had all our ducks in a row. The first reason was that—here's a stunning surprise—I don't much like Kendari, and they're never around the ops center that time of night. They have their grand ceremonial dinner right about then. I figured I'd have the place to myself, without some half-wolf half-ape centaur-thing growling and muttering to herself right in front of me. Brox was—is—not so bad, but Emelza just can't—couldn't—keep quiet. It drove me batty."

Frank realized a moment too late that he had just handed Wolfson another little bit of motive for his killing the damned Kendari. He waited for her to slap him down for making such pejorative statements about Kendari. She didn't say a word—but the expression on her face spoke volumes. She just scribbled a note into her datapad, and that only served to make Frank even more nervous.

"I'd say that's enough reason for going in after hours. What's your usual procedure for entering the ops center?"

"Well, the scanlogger is supposed to detect my ID badge and release the outer door automatically. I just pull it open and pull it shut, then enter the combo on the inner door, pull it open, and go on in. The doors are rigged so you can't open them both at once—so if you get past the outer blast door on a phony ID or something you're stuck in the vestibule if you don't know the combo or the keypad unit doesn't like your fingerprints. That's the theory. But we get so much interference on so many frequencies that the scanloggers hardly ever work the way they're supposed to. Maybe the Vixa are jamming them on purpose—or maybe the Vix just like messing with us. So most times I have to punch in the combo on the outer door too."

"That what happened two nights ago?"

"Yeah."

"Okay, so you pass through the outer blast door, and then the inner door. You enter the main, central room of the ops center."

"Right. We just call it main ops, usually."

"What's it look like?"

"Excuse me?"

"Are the lights on? Is the room orderly? Is there anyone there? Was there anything unusual?"

"Are you trying to play cute?"

"No, I'm trying to walk you through this without asking leading questions. Are you trying to play dumb?"

Frank hesitated, thought for a second. It was precisely the sort of question he should have been asking himself—and somehow, he hadn't. "Everything was pretty much normal," he said. "The joint ops building is built like a tank—built to be defensible against one side or the other attacking it. It's much stronger than the section of wall between the compounds that it replaced. But one result of that is that it's windowless. No light or air from the outside, so that means the

lights and environment system—the air circulators and
heating—pretty much have to be on at all times—or at
least all times that someone is there. The Kendari like
to set the lighting a little different than we do, and they
like it a little warmer in there than we do—but no big
deal. We argue a little over the thermostat, that's all.
So the lights and air were on. I can't swear, but I'd say
that the lights and temps were set to Kendari mode, if
that means anything."

"Any odd sounds, or smells, anything like that?"

"Not that I noticed."

"Was there anyone else there?"

"You mean, besides Emelza—"

"Yeah. Besides Emelza and you."

"No. No one that I saw."

"If there had been anyone else in the building,
would you have noticed?"

"Why do you ask?"

"*I* ask the questions, Frank. Some to get information, some to distract you from a theory I'm working
on, some to get you in the right attitude, willing to cooperate. Maybe it's absolutely vital that I get a clear
answer to that question. Maybe I'm just asking it to
jog your sense memory a bit, get your brain to think
back to what it looked and smelled and felt like that
night. So—if there had been anyone else in the building, would you have noticed?"

It couldn't be that casual a question. She had asked
it the second time in exactly the same words as the first
time. "Not necessarily. It's a fair-sized building—more
like two buildings that meet in the middle, really. A
Kendari side and a human side. Main ops is almost
like the lobby that links them. But there are side rooms
and storage rooms and so on. I've hardly ever been on
the Kendari side. On our side, we're built to withstand

a siege, if it came to that. Crazy, paranoid stuff—but that was the requirement that came down when the ambassador sought permission to build our half of the thing. So we have bunkers and food supplies tucked away in the lower levels. My understanding is that the Kendari have pretty much the same deal on their side. So, yeah, someone could have been in the building without my hearing or seeing it, easy."

"Would you have heard anyone come in or out of the building?"

"Oh, yeah. That's for sure. When the blast door on either side opens and shuts, it's like a bass drum in an echo chamber. They rumble along on their tracks, and slam into place, and you definitely hear it. You *feel* it."

"No other entrances? No secret tunnels or anything like that?"

Frank snorted derisively. "Not outside of vid shows. There *is* an escape tunnel—but they deliberately left it incomplete when they built it."

"What happened? They run out of money?"

"No. Just no place to hide the exit. The compound is completely surrounded by roads. No private or hidden spot to put the tunnel exit. So the horizontal tunnel ends in a vertical shaft, and the vertical shaft ends in a metal lid, a meter below the surface of the road. If anyone used it, to get in or out, they'd have to dig or blast that meter of rock and dirt and road surface. There would be a hole in the road surface a meter across. Someone just might notice that. And, by the way, just because we are paranoid, we do a seismic perimeter check once a week—and we detect it when the Kendari do a seismic check once every twelve days. If someone dug a hole in the ground, we'd know it."

"Okay, fine. Good. Let's get back to what you saw and did. You arrive in the ops center, and walk into main ops. The lights and temperature are basically normal. Did you note anything else unusual other than Emelza?"

Frank thought for a moment and shook his head. "No."

"All right then," said Hannah. "Walk me through the rest of it."

"I closed the inner human-side blast door, walked into main ops, and I saw her—Emelza—at once. Pretty hard to miss."

"Describe her appearance."

"Different from what you've seen, or will see," Frank said at once, instantly knowing he was saying it too eagerly. But it was too late, and he plowed on. "I wanna start off with that. I've had some brushes with the Kendari before. Once I was part of the team that went in and tidied up after an encounter between them and a Human Supremacy cell. You can check my record on that. I've seen Kendari corpses before, and they undergo a lot of postmortem alteration, if you want to use the technical terms. They stiffen up, and their bodies twist around in kind of odd ways."

"Okay, what's your point?"

"The point is I've been locked up here for two days thinking this thing through. I don't want to get nailed to the wall because someone who doesn't know corpses sees my description is different from what was there later on, yells 'aha' and decides they've caught me in a lie."

"Fine, corpses change. So describe what you saw."

"Not a great deal, because I didn't have much time. I saw her lying on the floor in the center of main ops the moment I looked over. I went over and knelt beside her, being careful as hell not to touch anything. I could see at once she was dead. Not breathing, not moving, eyes fixed and open."

"She was a xeno, an alien. How could you be so sure? For all you could know, she was in a trance state, or a coma, or some weird sudden-onset hibernation."

"Hey, Senior Special Agent Wolfson, I'm not all that much dumber than you. Yeah, I thought of that—but what was I supposed to do? Shake her and wake her up? You're right. I don't know aliens. If she was in a coma or something, I would be as likely to kill her as revive her. The best I could do for her would be to notify her own people and let them deal with it."

Frank glanced at the camera peeking out of Wolfson's shirt pocket, and wondered what sort of sensors were hooked up to it. There were probably some sort of stress detectors that would do pretty fair work as lie detectors—and he might have just given them something to detect. Nothing he had just said was, strictly speaking, false—but it was plenty misleading. He *had* thought of the possibility that she was in a coma or altered state. And it was no doubt true that the best thing he could have done in the absence of real knowledge or expertise was to call in her own people. But the minor detail he was leaving out was that he had thought of all that a full twenty-four hours after the fact. At the time, he simply assumed she was dead.

"All right," said Wolfson. "We've got you kneeling down in front of her, deciding not to touch anything. Then what?"

"Then, not much of anything. I gave it another twenty seconds—I counted it out—just to be sure I didn't see any sign of breathing. I didn't."

"What *did* you see?"

"I told you—a dead Kendari!"

"And you gave me a long song and dance about how Kendari bodies change appearance when they die. So tell me how the body looked when *you* saw it, and everything else you saw."

What was she after? Did she just want to get a good description at a known time, so as to zero in on time of death? Or was there some detail she was watching for, something he had to include to prove himself? Or was it that something big and obvious happened, and she needed to give him every chance to mention it, because his *not* knowing about it would prove something? There was no way to know. She wasn't kidding about not handing out leading questions. He had no choice but to play it straight and hope for the best. He thought carefully, and began to speak.

"She was lying on her side, the right side of her body facing up," he began. "I couldn't see any marks or indications of struggle or violence on her body. No—not quite true, now that I think of it. There was one small bruise or bump right at the back of her neck. Unless it was just Kendari acne. Just a little red mark, less than a centimeter across. She was lying stretched on her side, with her legs fairly relaxed. Her tail was sort of curled in toward her legs, almost as if she were sleeping on her side—though I don't think Kendari do sleep in that pose. I could see a discharge from the eye and the ear that were visible, and from the nose. The skin was drawn back from her mouth, in sort of a snarl or a grimace, and the inside of her mouth was badly inflamed. And, of course, there was that coffee mug right by her. I couldn't know for sure, of course, but it sure looked like caffeine poisoning to me."

"You know how to spot the symptoms of Kendari caffeine poisoning?" Wolfson asked skeptically.

"Are you kidding? Zhen Chi briefs us once a month

at least. There are posters up in all the offices. There are huge restrictions on eating or drinking anything with the slightest hint of caffeine in it. Yeah, I know. Everyone here knows it in their sleep."

"Glad to hear it," said Hannah. "Bear in mind I said I was avoiding leading questions. I didn't say anything about *mis*leading questions. All right, keep going."

"That's about it, really, in terms of what I saw."

"Sometimes people see more than they think they have. Was there anything else? Any other marks or indicators on the body?"

Frank frowned and shook his head. "I don't think so. I didn't notice anything else unusual."

"How about the mug, the cup? Talk to me about that."

"I didn't look at it all that carefully," Frank lied. That mug could be nothing but trouble for him, and he wanted to stay away from it. "It was white. I think it had the BSI logo on it. It looked like it broke in the fall. That's about it."

"What about what you just said about caffeine safety rules? Was having coffee mugs in the joint ops center normal?"

"No," said Frank, as emphatically as he could. "No, and no again. That was one reason none of us much liked the duty in there. A total ban on caffeine in all forms."

"So what was that mug doing there?"

"I got no idea. Ask whoever brought it in."

"Part of the caffeine safety rules seems to be everyone having their own personal cup or mug. Where's yours?"

Oh, hell and damn, thought Frank. *Why did she have to go there?* "It's missing," he said. No point hiding that anymore. Not when she'd find it out anyway. "I lost track of it about a week ago. It was in my office—not in the joint ops center, my office in the main groundside embassy building. It could have gotten pushed off the edge of my desk, and fallen into the trash can. Or maybe somebody broke it by accident and just threw it away without telling me." *Or maybe it got hidden away so it could be prepared for use as a murder weapon.*

"Describe it," said Wolfson.

Frank allowed himself a moment of annoyance, and the luxury of letting it show. "Don't tell me you're not playing cute, Wolfson," he said. He tapped the mug she had brought him that morning. "Just like this one. And just like about fifty or sixty or a hundred or two hundred that we've handed out to visitors and members of delegations and so on in the last year."

"There's the same and there's identical," said Wolfson. "That mug is brand-new. I swiped it out of a case of them in the back of the Snack Shack. Was yours old? New? Worn-looking? Chipped?"

"Yeah, my mug was worn and chipped—two weeks ago. But *that* one I dropped myself. Smashed to bits. I threw it away. So I got a new one. Stole it from the same place you stole that one."

"If there are so many of them around, how did you tell yours from all the others?"

If that wasn't a leading question, it sure as hell was the next best thing to one. "I marked it, of course. But you knew that."

"How? How did you mark it?"

"I used an indelible marker pen and wrote my name on the bottom of it."

"Your full name?"

"Yeah. Right. 'Special Agent Francis Xavier

Milkowski.' With smiley faces instead of dots on all the 'i's. And I drew in pink and blue flowers all around my name."

Wolfson just sat there, staring at him, waiting. Finally he gave in. "I wrote my nickname. 'Milk.' What my *friends* call me."

"Something tells me you want me to stick with 'Frank,'" she said.

"For the time being," he said. "Anyway, I'm not feeling that friendly toward *you*, right now—Hannah."

"I'll bear up somehow—Frank," she said, her voice stiff, but not unkind. "For what it's worth, I might be the best friend you've got in the world—in all the worlds—right now." She glanced down at her notes, but Frank had no doubt that was just to make him sweat for a beat or two before the next phase of the duel. But it worked.

"All right," she said. "Back to the narrative. You see Emelza. She looks pretty dead. You see the coffee mug. All correct?"

"All correct."

"How closely did you examine the coffee mug?" she asked.

I saw it was mine. I saw my name written on the bottom and I broke out in a cold sweat and stayed the hell away from it like it was radioactive and covered with plague germs. That part I didn't expect. Frank kept his poker face on and shrugged. "I saw it was a coffee mug. A white BSI mug. I think it was a little broken. Maybe a chip had come out of it. I didn't look at it that close. There was this dead alien right in front of me that sort of drew my attention."

"Nothing else about the mug?"

"Nothing," he said, and instantly wished he hadn't said it quite so belligerently.

Wolfson looked at him closely for longer than he would have preferred, and then spoke. "All right, then, we'll move on. You see the body, you see the mug. What next?"

"I grab my commlink and call the ambassador."

"From right there? From the main ops room?"

"Right there. Kneeling over the body. Maybe thirty seconds after I got there."

"Why so fast?"

So no one could possibly think I had time to do it, dummy! "What was I going to do instead that should have come first? Conduct a funeral service? And yeah, I gotta say, I was a little in shock. I figured I'd better do something, and fast, and that seemed like the best thing. Besides, like I said, she looked dead, but I'm no expert. Maybe she's not dead, and the Kendari could do something fast." And he hadn't thought of that explanation until a day too late either, but Wolfson didn't need to hear that.

"Why didn't you call the Kendari? I know the embassy commlink doesn't connect with the Kendari embassy directly, but there you were in the joint ops center. There must be some sort of comm system that would get you direct to the Kendari."

It was his turn to stare long and hard at Wolfson. Didn't she get it? If not, then, okay, he'd run it all past her. "One—the joint ops center is suddenly a crime scene. I don't want to touch anything I don't have to. I don't want to shed a hair, or lose a drop of sweat, or plant a shoeprint anywhere I don't need to. I might muss up whatever evidence is there—or leave behind misleading evidence that might implicate me.

"Two, I pick up the phone and say 'Hello, deadly enemies of humanity. It's me, the BSI agent who obviously hates your guts. You know, the one you don't much like either. I'm standing over your dead cop. Please come take a look.' *Then* what happens? Maybe two minutes later I'm lying dead next to her.

"Three, I couldn't call my normal liaison officer. She was lying dead on the floor at my feet. I could call in Saint Brox—but he doesn't like me too much, and the deader is his girlfriend. That might make him a little *extra* angry at me—plus it also makes him a pretty good suspect. Four, the ambassador is my direct superior, it's blindingly obvious right off the bat that this thing is going to mushroom into as big a deal as it has—and I'm supposed to advise him first in an emergency. Something that might blow the doors off the Pentam negotiations and maybe start a war ought to go into that category. Good enough reasons?"

"Good enough," Wolfson said evenly. "And that answer gets all those very reasonable reasons on the record right away, instead of leaving the point hanging for six months until the board of inquiry or whatever. So you call the ambassador. How does that conversation go?"

"The ambassador can be a little—well, not slow on the uptake, but sometimes if he doesn't like the news, you have to give it to him more than once. It took a minute or two for him to really understand what I was telling him."

"What, exactly, did you tell him?"

"As much as I knew, which wasn't much. That Emelza 401 was dead, sprawled out on the floor of the main ops room. He asked me 'are you sure?' two or three different times, and I kept telling him yes, I was. I think he was hoping it would all be a misunderstanding. If he kept double-checking enough times, somehow Emelza would wake up and that would be that. Finally I convinced him that I wasn't mistaken. Then he got decisive. He ordered me to leave everything untouched, to do nothing else but get out of the joint ops center and meet him at the entrance. He said he was going to call the Kendari whatzit—whatever they call him instead of ambassador."

"The diplomatic xenologist."

"Yeah. Him. So our ambassador cut comm with me. I stood up, went through the inner and outer blast doors, locking up behind me, and waited there at the human-side entrance for the ambassador."

"Did you photograph the corpse or the crime scene? Do any sort of crime scene work at all?"

"No. I didn't have a camera, or any other equipment with me, and even if I had, the ambassador gave me a direct order to get out of there at once. Once I was out of the ops center, it was sealed off—at least from our side."

"And that's it." Her voice was flat, hard, unconvinced.

"That's it. I know it doesn't seem like much, but you and I have spent about ten times longer talking about my finding the body than it took for it to happen."

"All right," she said. "We're done. At least with that topic. Let's play a new game. Let's say that we all totally agree that you didn't do it. So now we're not interrogator and sort-of-suspect. Now it's agent to agent. Talking shop. Who did it? You've been locked up here with nothing to do but think about it. What's *your* theory?"

"Zamprohna," Frank said instantly. "I have been thinking about it, a lot. Maybe not him, personally, but maybe one or two—or three or four—of his true believers." This time, he didn't care if he sounded eager. He *was* eager. If she was pumping him for information, trying to get him to make a slip, so be it. There were things she needed to hear from an agent with local knowledge and experience. She obviously knew it herself.

"Why him?"

"Look, all the info I have is from that thirty seconds over the body," said Frank. "You probably know more. I *hope* you know more. But from what I know, it's not just that Emelza was killed. It's *how* she was killed, and where. She died from ingesting a substance associated with humans, and literally right in the middle of the building that symbolized cooperation with humans. It's a cold-blooded attempt to bust up not just the Pentam deal, but any shot at human-Kendari cooperation."

"I thought you didn't like aliens that much yourself."

"I don't. I really don't like the Kendari. I've cleaned up after a few fights with them. But there's such a thing as dealing with the available reality. They exist. We have to live with that. What are we going to do? Kill them all to give ourselves *lebensraum*? My family was on the receiving end of that a zillion years back in World War II. Most people these days barely know what the Nazis were. Good. Better than our deciding to imitate them." He fiddled with his empty coffee mug. "Bet you're surprised to hear me talk like that, huh?"

"Not so surprised as you might think, Frank. But go on. Why Zamprohna?"

"It *could* have been one of the other xenophobe groups, but Zamprohna's got the biggest group, the most money, the loudest voice, and the shadiest past of all of them. And he's got thirty or forty of his people with him—including some guys I won't call goons, because they're too smooth for that. Ex-military. Special

Forces types. They could know how our security works, what our procedures are, that sort of thing. Heck, they could be the ones screwing up our entry key systems. Getting us used to not trusting it could be part of softening us up so they could pull this stunt. Those guys are *good*. I think probably three or four of them working together could bypass our security, get in there, do the job, and get out."

"Three or four team members making it look like one person did it?" asked Wolfson. "Maybe. It would make a few impossible-looking details easier to arrange. Plus Zamprohna doesn't like the BSI any more than we like him. If they could blow up human-Kendari cooperation, making it look like one of our guys did it would just be the icing on the cake."

Aside from breakfast and coffee, the hints in those words were the first things Hannah Wolfson had given away since she came through the door. She stared at him thoughtfully for about the count of five. "All right, then," she said. "You might want to be ready for us to have another little chat—on the off chance that I just happen to think of some tiny little detail in your story that doesn't *exactly* make perfect sense. But one last not-quite-leading question. It might seem a little strange, but bear with me."

She reached into her pocket and dumped a pile of pens and pencils and markers and so on out on the table. "I tried to grab one of each kind I found in the main embassy BSI office," she said. "And please notice I've had them in my pocket and touched them and so on if you're afraid of my trying to get your prints on something incriminating. You don't even have to touch them. Just point. If you remember—what kind of marker did you use to write on the bottom of your mug?"

Frank looked at Hannah, not at the pens. "I hope it looks like I'm staring at you and wondering if you're nuts," he said. "Because that's the expression I'm trying for."

"You're about the third or fourth person I've asked to indulge me this morning," said Hannah. "And I'm asking very nicely. *Very* nicely. And I hope it looks like I'm staring you straight in the eye, and telling you that I'm trying to save your life—because that's the expression—and the goal—*I'm* trying for."

They locked eyes for a count of ten, a count of twenty, before Frank looked down, looked away, looked anywhere but at her. He shifted his eyes to the clutter of pens on the table, and grabbed at one, very deliberately touching it, holding it, making all the fingerprints anyone might want. *If she's inviting me to demonstrate how little I trust her, why play along?* "This kind," he said. "That's the kind I use to mark stuff."

Wolfson snatched up that pen, let the camera have a good look at it, then stuffed it in her shirt pocket right next to the camera. The rest she scooped up and dumped on the tray. She gathered up his plate, his eating utensils, hooked his coffee mug through the handle with one finger, and got them all back on the tray as well. She stuffed her datapad in her pocket, picked up the tray, and stood.

"Thanks, Frank," she said. "Thanks for everything. It's been great." She turned and headed for the door. She paused, a bit theatrically, just as the door slid open. "Oh—by the way," she said. "Stay clear of the joint ops center, and your own office. But other than that—you're free to go." And she turned back, and walked out, and the door slid shut behind her.

Frank gave it the count of ten before he exhaled in a

long, drawn-out sigh of relief. Well, he had *thought* he knew how to play interrogation. That was, beyond doubt, the most polite, most friendly, most respectful working-over he had ever gotten. Like being skinned alive during a massage.

Thank God she's on our side, Frank thought.

But that only brought him up face-to-face with one more uncomfortable question. *What about you, Frank?* he asked himself. *Whose side are you on, exactly?*

SIXTEEN

ENGINEERING RESPONSE

Jamie scraped the tamper-detecting tape off the door to Chief Engineer Subramanian's stateroom, entered the unlock code into the keypad—and didn't get any further than that on his own.

The door slid open, and a young, very tall, very thin, eager-looking man with South Asian features was looking down at him. "Greetings!" he said. "Please, please do come in."

Jamie stepped in cautiously and looked around the tiny stateroom, half-expecting the real chief engineer to be tucked away somewhere. This fellow looked too young to be chief of anything. "Ah, you're Dr. Subramanian?"

"Yes, yes, that's right. Of course. Otherwise, why would I be in his room?" Subramanian asked as he pulled out a chair for the visitor and gestured him into it. "And you're the BSI agent they sent the *Eminent Concordance* to fetch. Am I right?"

"Ah, yes you are." Jamie also felt as if he had to think back to the flight. So much had gone on since then that it seemed like something that had happened long ago. "Is there, ah, somewhere I could set this down?"

"What? Oh, yes, of course." Subramanian cleared books and paperwork off the cabin's tiny worktable, and Jamie set down the tray. "Ah, breakfast! So very kind of you. Will you join me?"

"Ah, no, thanks. I've already eaten. But you please go ahead."

"Oh, I will—in a moment. Please, be seated."

Jamie got himself a chair, and reflected this was the most enthusiastic interrogation subject he had ever met. "I suppose you know why I am here," he said.

"Oh, yes indeed," he said, reaching out for the teapot to pour himself a cup. "I've been here waiting like—like a child whose birthday party is about to start. I have been so eager to get my present."

"I beg your pardon?"

"My present. Well, of course not mine, really. Ours. For all of us." Subramanian suddenly looked worried, alarmed. "You do, ah, *have* something for me, don't you? That *is* why you came."

"Ah, I'm, ah, sorry, Dr. Subramanian. I really don't know what you mean. I'm here to question you about what happened two nights ago."

"What? Oh dear. This is terrible." He looked down at the table, pulled his hand back from his teacup, then looked up at Jamie. "But I have read your standard operations manual. I have looked into the history. I know what equipment is supposed to be in your Ready-To-Go duffel. The whole reason your service *has* RTG duffels is to provide a cover story for Operation Paw Washer. In fact, if you look into the history, Paw Washer is half the reason there is the BSI. The whole *Bureau* is really just there as a cover story for Paw Washer."

Jamie was starting to feel distinctly alarmed. "Ah, Dr. Subramanian," he said slowly. "I don't know anything about anybody in charge of washing paws. I really have no idea what you're talking about."

"You don't know about Paw Washer? You didn't activate the device? I thought you were trained and trained and trained to activate it whenever you were in the vicinity of advanced xeno technology."

And then the light went on. "Oh!" Jamie said. "The gimmick. The gadget in the lining of the duffel bag."

"Yes—the Passive Wide-Spectrum Sensor Recorder. PWSSR, pronounced Paw Washer."

"I've heard that one pronounced a little differently," said Jamie.

"Which is why the program is called Paw Washer," Subramanian said primly. "There is no need for anything rude or unpleasant. But you may call it whatever you like *if you turned it on* when you went aboard the *Eminent Concordance*. Did you?"

"Now I understand you," said Jamie. "That bit about the BSI just being a cover story threw me off. Yes, I activated it. I made a big deal about needing to get rations and clothes out of my RTG bag, and punched the stud to activate the system. I *think* my partner activated hers as well. She looked at me kind of funny when I insisted on getting things from my bag—but then she did the same herself. We were being observed at the time, and I couldn't ask her about it— and we've been kind of busy since."

"Your partner? There are *two* of you here?"

"That's right."

"So we have a shot at *two* recordings. That is excellent news. You have done very well."

"Ah, Dr. Subramanian—I haven't really done anything about this case yet. We're just getting started."

"The case? Oh, yes, the murder of that Kendari woman. Most unfortunate. But we must not be distracted by side issues."

"I think I just have been," said Jamie. "Listen, there's a lot I have to do today. How about we talk about Paw Washer and get that out of the way—and then we go on to this little matter of a murder that seems to have touched off an interstellar incident, okay?"

"Very well. That seems entirely fair." Subramanian nodded, paused for a second, and then spoke again, very eagerly. "Can you give me the two PWSSR units today?"

"I doubt it," said Jamie. "As I said, we're kind of busy—and the embassy compound isn't exactly a secure area at the moment. And, ah, you seem to know all about the gadget—a lot more than I do—but there's also a whole security procedure I'm required to follow before I turn over the recording to you."

"Yes. Yes, you're quite right. That is true," said Subramanian. "Well, it's not as if I could do a full analysis of the data with the equipment I have here in this cabin. The main thing is that we have the data. It will tell us a great deal."

"Um, it will—if it worked. I pushed the stud and pulled back the tab twice, just the way the training said to do—but I have no idea at all if it worked. It didn't beep or light up an indicator or anything."

"Of course it didn't! It's a passive system. That's the whole and entire point. And you needn't worry. Those units are built to the maximum possible standards of reliability. If you did the activation sequence properly—and it certainly sounds as if you did—then there is nothing to worry about. We'll have one—perhaps two—complete wide-spectrum recordings of a complete flight sequence of the *Eminent Concordance*."

Jamie had a feeling that Hannah and Commander Kelly would be surprised to learn that the Bureau of Special Investigations existed for the sole purpose of providing a plausible excuse for humans to carry around duffel bags with concealed recording equipment, but he did have at least a sketchy understanding of Operation Paw Washer, even if he had never heard of it by that name. The idea was simple: to record all the changes in various local field strengths and power levels produced by advanced xeno technology: everything from simple electromagnetic field strengths to the really esoteric stuff involved in transit-jump technology, in the hopes of using that data to help humans reverse-engineer some advanced gear of their own.

Jamie had the impression that more than BSI agents and their RTG duffel bags were involved in the program. He also had not the faintest idea if the program had produced any results at all. It wasn't the sort of thing you were supposed to ask too many questions about. But, on the other hand, his job was to ask questions. "Does this sort of thing do any good?" he asked.

"Oh, my, yes. I wouldn't be at all surprised if the data you and your partner collected shaves a solid year off our efforts to catch up with Vixa shipbuilding technology."

"Gee, great. So we'll get there in ninety-nine hundred and ninety-nine years instead."

"What? Goodness no. Our projections are that there will be a human-built ship of comparable speed and power within forty years—at the very worst case, within our lifetimes."

"Are you crazy? Do you know the *size* of that ship?" Jamie asked.

"Deadweight, ninety-five percent of it," Subramanian said dismissively. "More than ninety-five. You are assuming that you need something that size in order to go that fast. Quite the opposite. Nearly all of the structure of that vehicle consists of excessive shielding, hyperredundant safety systems, and so on. And that whole business of shunting the command sphere about—none of that actually contributes to the power or speed of the ship. It just adds mass that requires bigger engines and more power. Eliminate all that nonsense, and you can get the same payload and the same performance in a vehicle that's only a small fraction of the size."

"So why did the Vixa build the *Eminent Concordance* so big?"

"Oh, several reasons, I think. One, to impress the neighbors. Two, because they've done it that way for the last few thousand years. I'm certain the *Concordance* was based on plans that are older than, say, the human invention of writing. If it's not broken, why fix it? Three, I am not sure their specialists fully understand their own technology anymore—and they are intensely conservative. They would not be confident of any modification. Four, what they have does what they want it to do. Why would they need anything better? But those points are all almost side issues. The primary reason is their absolutely overwhelming demand for safety."

"What's wrong with being safe?"

"When it rains, you might hold an umbrella over your head. But would you carry a lightning rod, and work out some complex scheme to see to it that it was continuously grounded? A Vixan spacecraft designer would think you should. He might want you to do it even when it wasn't raining. Except he'd prefer to encapsulate you fully for further protection, and I expect he'd want to put some armor plate around you in case the wind blew down some sort of debris. He'd develop a sort of armored car for you—and he might decide to make it an aircar, so you could fly above the weather. And of course, that would mean you'd need acceleration compensators and a pressurized cabin.

"But the whole point was to let you take a walk—so the Vixan engineer would include a treadmill, and, in order to provide you with the visual experience of the walk, he'd provide wraparound video screens, receiving real-time feeds sent from a remote robotic unit that was following the route on the ground you *would* have taken if you had walked. I am barely exaggerating. That is the sort of approach the Vixa take. The goal of a Vixan spacecraft engineer is to keep the occupants safer than they would be staying at home. So where you and I might use an umbrella—which is really for comfort rather than safety—they would likely build an armored aircar."

"I hate umbrellas. I wear a hat when it rains—if it's raining really hard."

"Don't tell the Vixa. You'd scare them to death."

"I sure wouldn't want to do that. They've been so neighborly and everything. But you've just told me why they overbuild. That doesn't mean we can catch up with them any time soon."

"True enough. One is not directly connected to the other. There is a *psychological* element, which you have just demonstrated. You assume that we could never catch up with them in any reasonable amount of time. Let us just say that sort of attitude doesn't make us catch up faster." Subramanian shrugged. "On the other hand, there are many who believe that the survival of the human race requires us to keep very, very quiet about any advances we might make. The last thing we want to do is appear to be a threat before we are able to defend ourselves."

"Yeah," said Jamie with feeling. "I've been deep inside that argument, believe me. So what you're saying is that we're making a great deal more progress than we let on?"

"Oh, I would never suggest such a thing directly," Subramanian said with a smile. "You must draw your own conclusions. But Paw Washer is part of a larger whole. We are learning. And there does not seem to be any fundamental reason why we must settle for merely pulling even with the Elder Races. It would appear that there are technologies far beyond what they have, and not so far out of reach.

"And I will make one other suggestion. There are two circumstances that make our situation unusual, if not unique. One is that we emerged into interstellar civilization more or less at the same moment as the Kendari, giving us someone to compete against. Competition also speeds up technical progress. As does the other circumstance. For various reasons, both we and the Kendari have come to know that other 'Younger Races' have popped up from time to time—and then been wiped out—apparently, because one or more of the Elder Races did feel threatened. Fear is also an excellent motivator."

Jamie nodded absently. Strange for a man who was full of such enthusiasms to scare you to death. But perhaps more to the point, Subramanian had completely derailed what was supposed to be an interrogation— or at least supposed to look like one. "All very interesting," he said. And it occurred to him too late that they were going to have to suppress the sound on the pocket camera's recording and blur Subramanian's voice enough to prevent lip-reading before they shared it with the Kendari. "But I came here to discuss a different subject—your movements two nights ago."

"Ah. Yes. Of course. Quite simple, really. I ate an early dinner at the Snack Shack—where else is there to eat? I got there just about at 1900 hours, then walked across the compound with the ambassador. We went straight to his office to discuss repair and upgrade schedules. We were still there when the call from Milkowski came in."

Jamie worked through times in his head as fast as he could. If Subramanian arrived at about 1900, and you stretched "about" to mean, say, 1910 or 1915 hours, he might have a problem. Medical Technist Remdex had given forty-four minutes before 1950, or 1906 hours, as the earliest plausible time for the murder. Time enough to do the deed, then hurry across the compound and make an appearance at the Snack Shack, if need be. In short, Subramanian didn't have an alibi for the entire period of interest. "You heard the call?" he asked. "You heard what was said?"

"N-n-no, not exactly," Subramanian replied. "I heard the ambassador's words of course, and I could recognize Milkowski's *voice,* but I couldn't quite catch the words he was speaking."

"You couldn't understand the words but you recognized the voice?" It was a commonplace occurrence, of course, but Jamie put a tone of disbelief in his voice. Better to see now how confident Subramanian's identification was rather than find him backpedaling later.

"Oh, yes, I'm quite sure. And the ambassador addressed him by name. No doubt about it."

"Then what?"

"The ambassador spoke with Milkowski for about a minute or so, and became more and more agitated. He said something like 'that's terrible. Are you sure?' He listened, then said 'get out of there and meet me at the entrance' or something close to that and cut the connection. The ambassador stood up, apologized, excused himself rather hurriedly, and left me alone in his office."

"What did you do?"

"I wasn't sure what to do. I decided I didn't feel

comfortable alone in his office—it's supposed to be a secure location—so I got up and left, making sure that all the doors locked after me. I went downstairs and saw there was a crowd starting to gather outside the joint ops center, so I went over there. The rumors were already flying. One Kendari was dead, they were all dead, they were sealing the joint ops center because there was poison gas in it, all sorts of things. It was plain only the ambassador and Milkowski really knew anything."

Jamie concluded that he had reached the end of any useful statement from Subramanian. He quickly established that the rest of his account of the events outside the joint ops center matched what the ambassador had to say, and what Jamie had already heard from other witnesses. Subramanian answered everything clearly and fully and seemed quite eager to cooperate.

There was only one other angle Jamie needed to cover, and the chief engineer was the guy to talk to about it. "We'd know a lot more about this case if we had reliable data on who was going in and out of the various buildings that night," said Jamie. "What about your entry-log system? We need the data off it."

"You're welcome to it," said Subramanian. "But it's going to be garbage in, garbage out. We're in a sealed system here already, behind the compound walls. We've got mechanical and electronic locks on all the secured areas—it's very hard to get into where you shouldn't want to go. All the people here know exactly what they are and are not cleared to see. They understand how high the stakes are, and they take it all very seriously. Plus, there are only twenty or so of us. We all know each other. We're all locked in here together, for the most part. All of that adds hugely to security, as I am sure you know—but it also has the odd effect of *degrading* certain security systems—like entry-log systems. The systems are supposed to read the ID tags that everyone is supposed to wear at all times. But many people don't always wear them—because we don't need ID tags with so few people. The ambassador is wise enough not to bear down too hard on that rule."

"Why is that such a good rule to ignore?"

"People in this confined a space can become rather twitchy about their personal space and their privacy—precisely because those are scarce commodities here. Everyone knows everyone, everyone knows everyone else's schedule. A tracking system that watches your every move, that could tell the ambassador that you're taking a longer break than you should at the Snack Shack, that you're in the same room as someone else's spouse after hours—well, that could lead to real trouble."

"So, for the sake of morale, people aren't tracked at all times."

"That's a large part of it. But another point is that the system simply doesn't work all that well. Two or more people walking through the same door at the same time can confuse the readers. If Person A forgets his badge and Person B sees him through the window, gets up, and lets him in, the system could read that event as B leaving and immediately returning, and not record A at all. You get the idea. And there's one more element—the damned simulants. They're alive, in some sense—but they also pack all sorts of electronics and other gadgetry. And they seem to scramble the entry-log sensors, along with some other systems."

"So let me guess. The system wasn't doing much good anyway, and it was throwing out all sorts of false positives and false negatives and crashing and you had other things to do—"

"So we have not bothered to do full maintenance on it for months," Subramanian said.

"That's not very convenient for us, right at the moment."

"No, not at all," said Subramanian with a surprisingly wicked smile. "And it's also rather inconvenient for the Kendari who died. But *very* helpful to the last person to meet her, don't you think?"

It certainly was, thought Jamie. But he wasn't about to share his thoughts on that subject with the chief engineer. "I think that about covers the main points," he said, ignoring Subramanian's last remark. "But let's run over a few details before we wrap up."

Jamie walked Subramanian through the rest of what he had seen and done that night, from the lockdown to the moment when Subramanian had confined himself, then confirmed the details of the ambassador's escorting him to more comfortable quarters once Stabmacher himself was let out. Nothing new in any of it, but they had to follow procedure. When they were done, he said his good-byes and left the embassy ship, carrying the tray with the remains of Subramanian's meal on it. The chief engineer had been relentlessly cooperative, but Jamie didn't learn anything new from any of it. Which was not to say that Subramanian hadn't left him with a great deal to think about. Things weren't always quite the way they seemed.

Hannah set the tray for her next interview and headed back to the embassy ship. She was starting to feel a little more optimistic. Having a probable time of death, and a narrow range of possible times of death made it far easier to run the interrogations.

Hannah had no hard proof, but she felt morally

certain that the murderer must have been present at the time of the crime.

This was no typical poisoning case, something deadly slipped into the victim's food or drink hours or days before. In a case like that, death could happen long after the killer was far away.

But if the humans were trained and trained and trained again to keep caffeine away from Kendari, the Kendari were trained just as hard to avoid the stuff. That had to be doubly, triply true for a Kendari Inquiries Service Inquirist who had been assigned and trained to work with humans.

Hannah simply could not believe that a Kendari would willingly drink caffeine, any more than a human would willingly drink gasoline. It was known to be such a painful death that even a suicidal Kendari would avoid caffeine.

If suicide was excluded, and there was no plausible way for a Kendari to drink a caffeine-based beverage accidentally, what was left was somehow, someone compelling Emelza, forcing her to drink the stuff—at gunpoint, perhaps. Hannah was willing to bet a lot that the killer was present at the time of Emelza 401's death.

Hannah knew that she was playing a tricky game, trying to make some things happen fast while getting others to happen as gradually as she could. But if she was right about a couple of vital details, providing room-service breakfast to the embassy staff might be the fastest possible way to move slowly toward solving the case rapidly.

A glance at the personnel files told Hannah that, if Milkowski fit one stereotype for the sort of BSI agent that would find him- or herself posted off to duty at a remote embassy, Joginder Singh and Maria Farrell fit just as snugly into the other: first-tour agents, young, eager, ambitious—and more likely than not to have finished in the bottom half of their training class. The higher-scoring new agents—for example a certain James Mendez—were cherry-picked by the Bullpen, or some other high-prestige posting.

Hannah decided to play the game a bit differently with the two baby agents—not exactly playing them off against each other but something close to that. She visited Singh in his cabin, then Farrell in hers. Instead of asking each about his or her own movements and knowledge, she asked each about the other's—and confirmed a good deal of what the ambassador and Milkowski had said—though there were a few details regarding the video surveillance that might be worth running by Jamie.

Having heard what each had to say about the other's movements in private, and knowing something about the habits and living patterns of young and idealistic BSI agents a long way from home, Hannah decided that she might learn more faster if she next talked to them both at the same time—especially as it was clear that both of them were thrilled to be talking, in person, to the one and only Senior Special Agent Hannah Wolfson.

Hannah didn't usually have a great deal of time to spend on hero-worshipping subordinates, but under the circumstances, she was willing to grit her teeth and take it—so long as they didn't try to get talking about her old cases, or ask her what Commander Kelly was *really* like.

She and Jamie had drawn the partition across the center of the Snack Shack. She had assigned the left-hand side of the building to Jamie, and taken over the more private right-hand side for her own purposes. She could hear muffled voices from the other side as Jamie talked yet another embassy worker through the events of the night in question.

Meanwhile, she had the baby agents over on her side. It hadn't taken a whole lot of prompting to get Singh and Farrell in there, chattering away over tea, coffee, and doughnuts Hannah had pilfered from the stockroom.

Hannah was very frankly dreading what Catering Chief Vargas was going to have to say to her about raiding his pantry. It might well be that they were going to have another murder on their hands, once he was released from confinement—and she wouldn't be around to help Jamie to investigate *that* one. But, after all, food *was* important in an outpost like this. Offering the troops a few special treats might make them more cooperative, get her some information she wouldn't get otherwise. So she had decided to risk the wrath of Vargas—but had also decided to spring him as close to the end of the job as she could.

"So," Hannah said brightly, "glad to get out of your cabins, I'll bet."

"And then some," said Farrell as she added honey to her tea. "It's bad enough being cooped up inside the compound most of the time—being stuck in that dinky little cabin was ten times worse."

Hannah considered Maria Farrell thoughtfully. She had jet-black hair and milk-white skin, and dazzling blue eyes framed in a remarkably expressive oval face. She was small and delicate-looking enough that Hannah was surprised that she passed the BSI physical. And, most interestingly, she had the small hands and feet to go with the rest of her body.

"So you don't get out much," Hannah suggested. "Not much chance to tour around, take in the sights?"

Singh chuckled. "*What* sights?" he asked as he poured himself more coffee.

It wasn't anything more than a vague first impression, but Singh struck Hannah as being more grounded, more sensible than Farrell—altogether more likely to hang in there long enough to reach the rank of Senior Special Agent—but he was going to face some other problems along the way.

Round-faced and round-bodied, he was going to bump up against the BSI weight-height ratio limit very soon if he didn't lay off the doughnuts. He wore the turban of a Sikh, and his *kirpan,* his sheathed ceremonial dagger, was held around his waist by a *gatra,* the special cloth belt used to hold it. He had managed a fairly credible beard for one so young, and it did help make him look more mature—but there was still something about him—perhaps his deep and soulful eyes—that made him look awkwardly youthful, puppy-doggish.

"All those gorgeous domes in that big beautiful city, for one," said Hannah. "It must be like walking through a world full of giant Easter eggs to go through the Grand Warren."

"You mean Oakland-on-Tifinda?" Farrell asked.

"Um, you've lost me," said Hannah.

"Maria's just showing off," said Singh. "American writer from way back—Stein, or Stone, or something, wrote about some city called Oakland and said 'there's no *there* there.' That's sort of the standard joke about the Great Warren."

"It looks fancy enough from here," said Hannah.

"Yeah, really impressive conduits," said Singh.

"I still don't follow you."

"The place is totally utilitarian—at least the parts we've been allowed to see. Everything clean, well made, well organized, well kept—but nothing there that doesn't *have* to be there. All the streets in a given sector look exactly the same. There aren't any shops, or stores, or museums, or theaters, or parks. Just living units, sanitation centers, distribution centers. No restaurants—not that we'd dare eat the food—but instead just sort of giant cafeterias issuing standard food from centralized kitchens."

"Yeah, it's a lot of fun," said Farrell, propping her hand on her chin. "But that's all the Nines and Twelves—the worker bees—get, and, at least so far as we can tell, that's all they want."

"Ah," said Hannah. "I get it. I almost forgot they're a hive-living species."

"It's sure hard to forget about around here," said Farrell. "Anyway, Joginder and I shouldn't complain. We get out and around a lot more than most of the staff does."

"You're the security detail," said Hannah.

"Right. Whenever the Vixa want to haul in the ambassador and tell him 'no' we tag along," said Farrell. She frowned for a moment. "And oh, boy! That's supposed to happen later today! We're going to have to get ready fast."

"No we're not," Singh said unhappily. "Are we, Senior Special Agent Wolfson?"

"Call me Hannah—or just Agent Wolfson if using my first name seems a bit too much. And no, you're not going to have to get ready. All the embassy BSI agents are relieved of all duties until this is cleared up."

"I thought that was going to happen," Singh said sadly. He looked to Farrell. "Face it, Maria—we're cops, and a rival cop died in our precinct. We're suspects. We have to be."

"But we didn't do it!"

"Fine," said Singh. "Prove that, and we can get back to work."

Hannah nodded sympathetically. "And until we do prove you innocent—or, better still, prove somebody else guilty—Special Agent Mendez and I have to run this investigation and at least take a shot at handling the duties of three local BSI agents."

"Well, two and half, anyway," muttered Agent Farrell.

"Who's the half?" Hannah asked, knowing what the answer would be.

"Let's just say Maria and I could both tell you how many days, hours, and minutes it is until Agent Milkowski retires," said Singh. "We've heard him tell us often enough. He's actually rigged a countdown display on his desk showing how much time he's got left. And Maria's got a point—he spends so much time on retirement planning and how to reinvest his pension that it cuts into his productivity. And it's not great for morale to have someone wandering around the compound telling everyone that he can't wait to leave. The joke around the embassy is that they'll throw a party for him right before he leaves—and a party for everyone else right after."

"That doesn't make him a killer, though," said Farrell. She glanced at Singh. "Somewhere underneath all that, I think there's still a good agent. It's just that it's been so long since he's been given anything worthwhile to do that he's sort of given up."

"Give him the chance and he'll step up, rise to the occasion?" Hannah suggested.

"Something like that," Farrell agreed.

"If he doesn't trip over a gin bottle first," said Singh.

"Joginder, that's just plain mean," Farrell said, obviously annoyed. "Snide remarks and gossip are one thing," she said. "But Milkowski's our colleague—and Emelza's dead. We can't make a joke out of that—or make jokes that could get people in trouble."

"You're right," Singh said, beating a hasty retreat. "That wasn't fair. I take it back."

Hannah said nothing, but reflected that being unfair was not the same as being inaccurate.

Farrell turned toward Hannah. "You've heard all we know about the case," she said, clearly determined to change the subject. "And that's pretty close to nothing. Isn't there anything more *you* can tell *us*? Emelza's dead. That's really the one fact we have. We can guess it didn't seem like natural causes, or else none of this would be happening. But—well, I know it seems weird and all, saying this about a Kendari—but she is—was—our friend."

"*She* won't think that's weird," Singh said. "Don't forget she knows Brox."

"I know Brox," Hannah said cautiously. She very deliberately didn't call him a friend. Things were complex enough already. "We worked together. And I don't *think* he did it—but he *might* have. I have to treat him as a suspect, every bit as much as I have to treat you two that way—even more so."

Farrell surprised Hannah by nodding in sober agreement. "Crime of passion—or the Kendari equivalent. Throw love and jealousy and hormones and romantic rivals and meddling families and so on into the mix, and who knows what anyone is capable of doing? When one of two lovers is killed, the other has to be a suspect. But that's just us humans projecting our culture and emotions onto the Kendari way of doing things. There are thousands of things we don't know about their traditions and personal lives."

Hannah had expected Farrell to make some breathy protest about how dear sweet old Brox could never do such a thing. Maybe Hannah was underestimating her.

"Can you give me anything more on Brox?" she asked, deliberately phrasing the question as ambiguously as possible. More on him as a being, as a coworker, as Emelza's intended, as a murder suspect? Let them choose.

"Well, xenos are xenos," Singh said cautiously. "And cultures vary. The three of us around this table come from very different traditions. The two sides of Maria's family probably wouldn't have been caught dead speaking to each other, a few hundred years ago."

Farrell smiled. "They still don't like it."

"My family has some stories too," said Hannah. "What's your point?"

"Two points, actually. One, what's perfectly acceptable, even expected or required in one culture, is a sin or a crime in another—as I am sure you know, ma'am."

"If I didn't know it, Brox and Mendez and I found it out together on Reqwar," Hannah said grimly.

"The other is that we humans tend to make the mistake, over and over again, of assuming every xeno species has a single, monolithic culture. *We* don't. Why should they? What we know of Brox and his people suggests to us that he is very unlikely to have committed this crime. But there are endless things we do not know. There could be as many Kendari cultures in that embassy as there are human ones in this one. They could conflict, or interact, in all sorts of ways."

"So maybe that duty and honor would require him to murder his fiancée, and then lie about it?" Hannah asked.

"It sounds off the wall, but xenos are xenos," said Singh.

"But you can use that argument to explain just about anything," Farrell objected. "If something a xeno does seems illogical or unreasonable, just chant 'xenos are xenos' and you can pretend you've got an answer." She turned to Hannah. "The other problem with Brox as the killer is that he and Emelza seemed— well, not *happy*, exactly. I'm not sure Kendari are ever really happy. They seemed content, comfortable. As if they were the two parties to a business arrangement, and each was satisfied with the deal they had made. So, yeah, it might be that they were hiding all sorts of inner turmoil, maybe stuff that all the other Kendari could spot from a kilometer off—but it didn't *seem* like it."

"She's right," said Singh, a bit reluctantly. "No knock-down, drag-out fights. No insults about the prospective in-laws, or the financial arrangements—if there are any."

"Something like that would have come in handy—if we were trying to build a case against Brox. So far, we're not."

"It is very tempting to ask if you have a leading suspect, but of course you cannot tell us that," said Singh. "Is there anything you *can* tell us about the case?" Singh asked. "We understand that we can't work on it—and can't do any work until we're cleared. But I know I speak for Maria too when I say we want to help."

"Well, you can," said Hannah. "Mendez and I are going to have to cover for you at this big meeting with the Vixa today. Walk me through that. What can we expect?"

Farrell's lively, expressive face went absolutely dead, emotionless. "What can you expect?" she echoed. "Chaos. Chaos, and some really massive headaches."

SEVENTEEN

HOME AND AWAY

They were getting there, Jamie decided as he peeled the tamper-proof tape off yet another hatch. Cross-checking alibis was speeding things up significantly. If A vouched for B, and then C said he was with A the whole time, and then D confirmed key details of the statements made by A and B, then either the entire gang of them were involved in the conspiracy, or else they were all telling the truth. Even better were statements that could be backed up by some sort of physical evidence. Each newly established trusted player could be used to expand the net, confirming the statements of E, F, G, and so on. It wasn't foolproof. A skillful liar, or someone who had planned ahead to establish an alibi, might have been able to game the technique. But that was harder to do than it seemed. Complex lies were almost impossible to defend.

And there was often a lot more useful evidence than people realized. Fred made a phone call from a comm unit that logged the time automatically. Ned took a picture to send back home that happened to include Ted and Ed—and a clock—in the background. Maura scribbled a handwritten to-do list in the corner of a printed, time-stamped message sent by Flora to Laura, thereby proving she had been around after the message had been sent.

They had gotten far enough down the list that both Hannah and Jamie felt they could relax the rules a bit and talk to at least some of the people outside their cabins. They had been cooped up for a while, and getting them out of confinement was bound to relax them a bit, make them more willing to talk.

All of which brought him to—he checked his list— Frau Helga Groppe. Motor pool chief, the ambassador's personal driver—or pilot, given that the ambassador generally rode in an aircar—and also the designated commander of the embassy ship, in the event of emergency. He rang the annunciator, and the door slid open at once. She was a tall, stern-looking woman, with a high-cheekboned face, dark hair, and thick dark eyebrows that added drama and emphasis to her expression.

"You are the investigator," she said flatly. "You have come now to question me."

"Yes," said Jamie, a bit taken aback. "Please come with me," he said.

"To the Snack Shack, no doubt," she said.

"Ah, yes."

"It is the only slightly comfortable place to talk in this compound. We go."

Jamie found himself following her down the corridors of the ship. *Well,* he told himself, *you wouldn't want a pilot who wasn't sure of herself.*

Five minutes with Groppe was enough to get her statement and add her to the virtuous circle of people who could vouch for each other, or provide physical evidence, to show they did not enter the joint ops center during the critical period. Groppe had been working in the motor pool, doing maintenance checks, and had logged all the checks in to the admin system, generating multiple time stamps. Three people had seen her, and she had seen two of those three, and two others besides. She had been working outside in plain view of the joint ops center doors from 1900 hours until the crisis. When they opened and shut the doors they were very loud. Of course she would have heard them if anyone had opened or shut them. She had heard or seen no one go in or out, except for the BSI agents coming and going as per usual, and Milkowski going in, then rushing out again.

Five minutes with Groppe was also about as much as Jamie felt like spending. He didn't do well with people who were sure they knew the right way to do everything.

He set her loose and went back to the BSI office in the main building and ran through his list of embassy personnel. Who had they seen? The ambassador. Check. The deputy chief of mission had been sent home for medical reasons. That post was empty. Med officer. Check. Dr. Subramanian, chief engineer. Check. BSI agents. Check. Mutambara, the economic officer, and his wife, the political officer. Korelev, the science attaché, and her husband, the military attaché dressed up in civilian clothes that fooled no one. The ambassador's administrative assistant, another admin assistant, her husband, the chief engineer's. Groppe, the motor pool officer—who was also tasked as the embassy ship's captain in the event of emergency evacuation. Her husband, Ostman, the communications specialist.

Vargas, the administrative and life-support services officer—some places, that meant making sure there was enough bottled air on hand. Here, that meant running the Snack Shack—and keeping human-edible food available fifty gazillion kilometers away from the nearest grocery store. Not an easy job, or an unimportant one. And, thank the stars, Vargas had even been something close to reasonable about the two interlopers invading his domain and making free with his supplies—though that might have had something to with Hannah promising to call in a few favors and arranging to expedite a special shipment of Argentine delicacies that was being held up.

That was everybody. Jamie allowed himself a sigh of relief. They were done with the initial interviews. Based on what they had learned, it seemed clear that no one besides Milkowski, the ambassador, and Zhen Chi knew any of the details of the crime, or was in any position to know anything. Those who knew, it would seem, had kept their mouths shut. No doubt that damn fool business about everyone confining themselves had helped on that. No one who knew anything had had much of a chance to gossip.

Perhaps more importantly, it hadn't taken a great deal of cross-checking the statements to confirm that just about everybody had at least a partial alibi for the crucial time period. The overlap was almost complete—not surprising in a place this small, with only one place to eat if you didn't want to hunker down in your quarters. There were a few loose ends, like the few minutes in which Subramanian might have done the job, but Jamie fully expected that a closer study of the statements, and a few follow-up queries, would resolve them as well.

It was almost, but not quite, too tidy. Leaving aside off-the-wall conspiracies that would require just about everyone in the embassy to be in on the kill, setting up an alibi grid of the initial statements put nearly everyone at the embassy in the clear, at least on a provisional basis.

Jamie stood up and looked out the window. The BSI

office was on the ground floor of the main embassy building with a good view of the compound. It was strange to see it full of people after seeing it as a ghost town. They were going about in twos and threes, all of them no doubt trading all the latest gossip and theories about what had happened.

He spotted Hannah coming across from the Snack Shack, carrying a large, carefully sealed box—the contents of which were no doubt going to be the subject of a good deal of conversation in the days to come. He went to the entrance to help her in through the doors. "Ready to make a delivery to Brox?" she asked.

"Yeah—but you'd better make sure Medical Technist Remdex is there too—and Zhen Chi, as well."

"Neither of them is going to be too happy. We've just invented God knows how much work for both of them."

"More work in the short run, maybe—but with any luck at all this stunt will eliminate a huge number of variables in one swell foop, as the Reverend Spooner would put it."

"You're probably right," said Jamie, "but even so, this move isn't going to make us very popular. Anyway, while you've been working the physical evidence, I've been evaluating the interviews."

"And everyone has an alibi?" Hannah asked, perching on the desk.

"A few question marks here and there, but essentially yes. You get anything out of the junior agents?"

Hannah grinned. "How's it feel, getting to call someone else 'junior,' junior?"

"I could get used to it."

"Don't be in a rush. Being the senior agent present all the time reminds me just how senior I'm getting to be."

"Anyway," said Jamie, "to answer your question, yeah, I got some nice murky contradictions out of part of the ambassador's statements.

"First, the ambassador's statement to us strongly suggests that Milkowski gave him most of the details about finding Emelza when the two of them were face-to-face outside the joint ops center. Milkowski's much more detailed and specific statement has Milkowski leaning over the corpse, giving him the main details over the phone. It's either a minor difference in recollection, or, far less likely, one of them is deliberately misleading us for some reason—presumably not a reason we'd approve of."

Hannah went on. "Next murky contradiction: Singh confirmed the foul-up with the recording surveillance video, but he made it sound as if it would have been a much simpler problem to solve than the ambassador had described. More significantly, Singh reported that he *hadn't* forgotten about changing out the media. According to him, the ambassador ignored Singh when he requested that Farrell assist him on the two-person job, but instead kept both of the junior agents busy running around on this errand and that to arrange the lockdown.

"The ambassador wouldn't even take Singh's call until several hours after the lockdown had started. Singh thinks that the ambassador was sleeping during that time, with his phone off—and kind of hinted that maybe the ambassador was just a teeny bit drunk—or maybe blind stinking drunk—when Singh finally got through.

"But, as Singh pointed out, probably it doesn't matter. We have full video coverage for the time before the death was discovered. That's the good news. The bad news is I just did a fast scan of the video records of the joint ops center, starting four hours before the murder, going until the recording media ran out. I saw nothing at all besides everyone quitting and going home for the day, then Milkowski returning as per his testimony, and everyone milling around as reported in all the statements we have."

"Does that mean the ambassador knew he was going to have something to hide after the recording media ran out?" Hannah asked. "Or that he's a pompous ass who pays no attention to technical problems because subordinates are supposed to do that? Or just that all hell was breaking loose and he made some mistakes, and maybe didn't behave perfectly?"

"Zero data on that point," said Jamie. "New topic." He picked up a paper notepad that he had been using. "Aside from going through the statements, I've been compiling lists of this and that—such as people like Agent Farrell and Zhen Chi who have hands small enough to make that handprint."

"But the handprint couldn't have been made until hours after the murder, by which time they were both confined to quarters," Hannah protested.

"And it couldn't have been made then, either, because the joint ops center was under seal and *everyone* was locked down. No one could get in there and either someone's very slick at manipulating temper-detecting strips, or nobody left his or her compartment. And then you need someone who's about on the Houdini level of getting past locks and seals who makes a beeline for a crime scene, does something as blindingly stupid as planting a handprint on a corpse, and then gets him- or herself locked up again without being caught. You'd have to be a genius and an idiot at the same time to do all that. What all that tells me is that something's wrong. Remdex got the times wrong, or something else made that print, or something. There's a piece missing, or a piece that doesn't fit the way we think it does."

"Okay, I can buy that," said Hannah. "But you're leading up to something else."

"Yeah. Planting that handprint makes no sense—but neither does the murder. Not if a human does it." He turned around the notepad to show the page to Hannah. "This is what all my lists and notes came down to," he said. There were crossed-out lists and scribbled-out queries—and one word written in big bold letters, all capitalized, and underlined with a box around it.

MOTIVE

"Why would anyone working at this embassy kill a Kendari *this* way? It was either Milkowski being incredibly stupid and clumsy, or someone doing an incredibly stupid and clumsy job of trying to frame Milkowski, or someone doing an utterly brilliant job of making the crime scene look like a stupid and clumsy attempt at a frame-up."

"Yeah, so?"

"So it's like our idiot genius who gets past all that tamper-indicator tape and the locks on the joint ops center to poke the corpse. If the motive was simply to kill Emelza, there had to be plenty of other ways to do that. Put a bullet in her head. Strangle her. Bundle her into an aircar and drop her into a large body of water filled with hungry predators. Smother her with a pillow—or whatever Kendari use instead of pillows. This wasn't murder for the sake of killing the victim. This murder was done the way it was to stir up trouble. It *had* to have been chosen expressly for that purpose.

Anyone who killed a Kendari *this way* would have to know it would threaten, maybe even wreck, the human bargaining position. They had to know it might easily cost the human race its shot at the Pentam System. This wasn't just murder. This was close to treason."

"If a human being did it."

"Bingo. Exactly. Right," said Jamie eagerly. "If a Kendari did it—either someone on that side killing for himself, or someone acting on orders—then none of my objections matter anymore."

"Okay. But there's a flaw. You're forgetting that this embassy is not the only source of human beings on the planet. There are all those crazies on file up the street. And some of those groups could easily have an objection to our nabbing Pentam. And, while we're at it, there are plenty of Kendari who don't work for the embassy, right on up the same road on the other side. Let's not forget our buddy Tancredo Zamprohna. Maybe he figured it would be a good idea to throw a monkey wrench into the proceedings—and he wouldn't exactly have our qualms about offing a Kendari. He hops the wall, diddles the lock codes to the joint ops center, and kills Emelza, then escapes in the confusion. Maybe he came and went from the Kendari side, while they were all at dinner, and that's why no one saw him. Or if not him, any of his friends or enemies. Or any of the Kendari crazies."

"I thought we were trying to limit the number of suspects. You've just wheeled in a few hundred more!"

"Sorry about that," said Hannah. "Sometimes reality intrudes. But if it's any help, I agree with your basic premise. We all like to pretend otherwise as hard as we can, but every police investigator knows that, given the exactly right—or maybe exactly wrong—circumstances, anyone is capable of some murder. Push someone hard enough, far enough, and they can snap. Fact of life."

Hannah stood up and went to the window, and looked out at the joint ops center. "But look at the way *this* murder was done," she said. "Then look at the alibi witness information. Look at the physical evidence of the surveillance video that shows no one coming or going through the human-side entrance of the joint ops center at the critical times. And, for whatever it's worth, remember that everyone at this embassy was supposedly vetted and checked and indoctrinated and so on to want to win the Pentam decision. It seems wildly implausible that anyone working at this embassy would have committed this crime this way—and there is strong physical and alibi evidence to suggest that none of them *could* have."

"Let me hang one more angle on it," said Jamie. "From what I know, right now, this feels a lot like a political crime—an effort to sabotage the human claim to Pentam—disguised as a personal crime."

"In other words, trying to frame Milkowski. I don't quite see how that's different from what we were saying."

"On the surface, anyway, what was this crime supposed to look like? What were we supposed to think happened?"

"That Emelza picked up Frank Milkowski's big old cup of hot black coffee from off his desk, stood in the center of the joint ops center, drank it, and died on the spot."

"That's not a murder," Jamie said, "that's a suicide."

"Plus she didn't swallow, plus Milkowski didn't

keep his cup in the ops center, plus that's such a horribly painful way to die that I don't see why a Kendari would choose it." Hannah nodded to the big sealed box on her desk. "Plus the physical evidence I'm hoping to develop from that collection. There's *lots* of holes in that first-glance theory."

"Okay, so were we supposed to think that's what happened—or were we *supposed* to see all of the holes?" Jamie asked. "Or just see *some* of them? Or *any* of them? Because neither our people or their people believed the suicide theory for a second. To the point that no one has even considered the implications of someone trying to stage this as a suicide. The killer had to assume there would be some reaction. The murder was done specifically to *cause* a reaction. Are we doing what the killer expected—or have things gone off script? What does the killer think we're supposed to do next? What will the *killer* do next?"

Jamie turned and stared out the window at the embassy personnel outside. Their day had turned into a weird sort of post-incarceration half holiday. Had one of the people he was watching done this thing, because they hated Kendari, or hated humans, or had some morbid reason for opposing human expansion?

"If we agree it was no suicide," said Hannah, "then I think we can't really buy that the killer was seriously trying to *make* it look like suicide. I think we're *supposed* to read the crime scene as an attempt to disguise a murder as suicide. We're supposed to think Milkowski killed Emelza 401 by somehow forcing her to drink from his coffee mug, and *Milkowski* was trying to make it look like suicide."

Jamie laughed, but there wasn't anything all that funny about the situation. "You've got us up to about three layers of deception right there. Mystery Killer X frames Milkowski so it looks like Milkowski was setting up Emelza to look like a suicide. You're not going to hang anything else on that, are you?"

"I hope not," said Hannah. "I agree that it's damned complicated, but unless we're both missing something, it's the *least* complicated theory that actually fits the known facts."

"In that case," said Jamie, "I hope we're both missing something." He turned to the desk and picked up the box. "Come on," he said. "Let's go find Zhen Chi and Remdex, and get started on ruining their day."

EIGHTEEN

DIRTY MUGS

Fifteen minutes later, Zhen Chi, Brox, and Remdex 290 were gathered in the same side conference room of the joint ops center. Jamie had instructed all three to bring safe-handling gloves, masks, and gowns, but not to put them on.

"Thank you for coming," said Hannah. "Let me start by apologizing to Remdex and Zhen Chi, because this is going to seem like my inventing work for them—but I honestly believe this will get us to the truth faster, and with less effort, than any other procedure I can think of."

"I be worked already very hard," said Remdex in his clumsy Lesser Trade Speech.

"I appreciate that," said Hannah. "But if my idea is right, we can move very quickly to put a great number of current potential suspects all but completely in the clear."

"Those be *human* potential suspects?" Remdex asked sourly. "Limit the field to Kendari only?"

"I'll answer that with 'yes and no,' and leave it at that," said Hannah. She reached out and patted the box. "In here, very carefully sealed and labeled, are coffee mugs, coffee cups, tea cups, and cola beverage containers—at least one from every member of the human embassy staff. A couple of people had more than one cup, and I took all of them. They're used and dirty. I am certain they all have caffeine residue on them.

Some people drank decaffeinated coffee or herbal tea or whatever, but even those can have significant trace amounts of caffeine, so please be careful."

Hannah pulled a Kendari data wafer and a human datapad out of her pocket. "Here are the recordings of all the interrogations we performed. Although they provided some useful information to us, the interrogations themselves were in large part deceptions on our part to allow us to sit down and get people talking over a nice cup of tea or coffee. You are welcome to view the recordings in detail. There were one or two instances where the subjects unintentionally discussed human-ears-only information. We have blurred the speakers' mouths and scrambled their voices in those passages, but we have left the sequences in, because the primary goal was to provide a visual record of each person selecting and preparing his or her own beverage. The recordings also show Special Agent Mendez and me packing and sealing the mugs, and putting tamper-proofing on the seals. The records thus provide a chain of evidence to show that the subjects were unaware of our intent to collect the cups and mugs, that they prepared or selected their own drinks, and that the cups or mugs have not been tampered with in any way."

"And what we to do?" Remdex demanded. "Humans have those finger marks, or prints that you make fuss over for identifying. Have you caffeine marks as well? Do you expect me to compare residue each cup against crime scene mug find a match and culprit?"

Hannah grinned. "If you can find the culprit that way, I will be delighted, and astonished. No. What I ask is that you take a sample of two or three of the cups—or five, or six, or all of them if you see fit, and do two things. First, scan the exterior surface for fingerprints, residue of the beverage, and so on. Then take a swab sample of the interior, and analyze the compounds you find. Do whatever other tests, whatever comparisons you like. I won't try to guide you in that. If, if, you have the facilities, and if your first results intrigue you enough, you might try to get readings of the carbon-isotope ratios."

"And what this all nonsense tell us?" Remdex demanded.

"The best way to find out is to do the tests," Hannah said. "Special Agent Mendez and I were brought into this case without even being told what planet we were going to. We were not told who the victim was, or how or where she died—or if in fact there was a murder—*until we were at the crime scene.* We were kept in ignorance to prevent our preconceptions from misleading us, because the case was so delicate, so important, and the evidence so potentially misleading."

That might not be one hundred percent accurate, but close enough for a rhetorical argument. She decided to hit him from another angle and play on his ego. "I ask you to work by that same principle, on a much smaller scale. And there is also the question of politics, and your reputation. It would be best if you found the truth without being told what to find. If *I* tell you what to look for, and you find it, you might easily spend the rest of your life being pointed at as the medical technist who did the human spy's dirty work for her. Do you want that?"

Remdex made an odd little strangling noise and gestured vaguely. Perhaps a Kendari could have read his emotions, but Hannah certainly couldn't. "I'll take that as a no," she said sweetly. "I look forward to your cooperation. Dr. Zhen Chi. You will assist and cooperate, yes?"

"Hmm? What?" she said distractedly. "Yes, yes, of course. I wouldn't miss it." Either Zhen Chi was starting to put the pieces together for herself, or else she was plenty smart enough to recognize an order disguised as a question.

"Thank you both," said Hannah. "One last small point. The cups and mugs aren't really evidence in this case. It is the residues left on the mugs that we're interested in—and even that is only to provide a sort of statistical base, a general sampling. Once the analyses are complete, I would ask that the various beverage containers be returned. Many of them are personal property, and the owners likely have strong sentimental attachments to them."

"Definitely," said Zhen Chi. "I sure want mine back. It'll make a hell of a souvenir after this."

"All right, my fearless leader," said Jamie as they left the joint ops center. "Now what?"

Hannah checked the time. "Now we hope and pray they get that analysis done fast—miracle-level fast."

"You want to walk me through that?"

"From what we've been told by the BSI agents and the ambassador, everyone is expecting the Vixa to convene an important meeting with Flexdal and Stabmacher some time today. The local BSI agents are supposed to provide escort service—but they can't while under suspicion of murder, so you and I have to do it. If that analysis does what I think it will, it ought to clear the BSI agents of all charges. Then they could do their own jobs—or at least come along with us."

"Not all of them," said Jamie. "Milkowski's out of it."

"But—"

"But what?" Jamie asked. "He's only been *slightly* deceitful? He only told two or three lies meant to protect himself in his statement? And he only looked *somewhat* hungover when I saw him at breakfast?"

Hannah paused and looked around the compound. It was still strange to see people in it—and just at the moment, she'd just as soon it was deserted. But at least there was no one in earshot. "All right," she said. "Point taken. He's screwed up. He's dug himself deeper into a hole that he never needed to dig in the first place. And it's probably not smart to tempt fate and let him near the Kendari or the Vixa in the state he's in. I'll go that far. But no further."

"He's no prize," Jamie said brutally. "Why defend him?"

Hannah felt her temper flare, and fought to tamp it down. Jamie could be so *young* at times. "I'll tell you why—partner. Because *I've* had *good* luck. I got good assignments, and I made career decisions that turned out to lead to good things. Because maybe, just maybe, that's the *only* difference between Frank and me. My luck has been better. Maybe I'm scared my luck could *change,* and *I'll* be blamed for something I couldn't control—like this case going bad, everything falling apart, and the whole human race pointing to *me* as the woman who lost Pentam. Maybe I'm scared that five years from now I might look in the mirror and see someone a lot like Frank Milkowski looking back at me. And I'm hoping that someone will give me a break when I need one. That reason enough?"

Jamie was taken aback. "Yeah. Yeah, Hannah, okay. Okay. We lay off."

"Good," Hannah said sharply. "Then let's go find

the baby agents and pick their brains. You'll enjoy it. They're even younger than you are."

Jamie was distinctly relieved that Hannah managed to calm herself down by the time they were settled into the BSI office with Singh and Farrell, and getting briefed on procedure. She must be a lot more on edge than he had realized. Were they that close to losing the Pentam System for humanity? Suppose they found the killer, and the killer *was* human, despite all their logic? Would history, or worse, the Bureau's Office of Personnel, somehow find a way to blame Hannah— blame *both* of them—for losing Pentam, instead of blaming the killer? He had never really thought over the huge career advantage he had gotten from being partnered with Hannah. Singh and Farrell hadn't seen a tenth of the action he had seen. Were Hannah and he one misstep away from the partnership being broken up? *Three months from now, I could be the resident agent on Cinder, with nothing to do for entertainment but watching the crops die.*

And staring into space during a vital briefing would be a great start toward making that happen. He blinked and forced himself to focus on what Farrell was saying.

"The first time you went into the Grand Warren, you were going in for yourself," she was saying. "Not this time. This time you have no status—you *are* the status. You're not going to be escorted. You're going to *be* the escort. Go armed. Loaded weapons, prominently displayed."

"Are you sure that's wise?" Hannah asked.

"No," said Singh. "We're not at all sure. But it is

necessary. All the other escorts will be carrying deadly-force weapons—their stingers. You should do the same. The surest way to avoid attacks is to be prepared to repel them. You will be at a considerable disadvantage as it is. Any escort Vixa you encounter will be controlled by a higher-caste Vixan who regards the escort as expendable—and the escorts themselves regard themselves in that way. They will not hesitate to get themselves killed if it is to the slightest benefit of their superior. You, I assume, won't feel quite the same way about it."

"No, we won't," said Jamie.

"So a Grand Vixa could and would send twenty escort-caste Vixa to attack you, forcing you to kill them all, just in order to empty your weapons. You would be of no account, but that would leave the *ambassador* defenseless, and thus more likely to agree to their proposals in the negotiations."

"So maybe we pack some extra ammo and a backup gun or two," said Jamie.

"I'd advise it," said Singh. "And carry it all where it can be seen."

"Let's get back to routes and locations," said Hannah. "The more we know about where we're going, the better I'll like it."

They were still at it a few minutes later when Ambassador Stabmacher walked in, dressed in an immaculate business suit of absolutely conservative cut. Farrell and Singh instantly got to their feet, and Hannah and Jamie did as well. *We never did that before for him,* Jamie thought. *Should we have?*

The ambassador smiled at them all, and gestured for them to take their seats again. "Just checking in," he said, standing at the head of the meeting-room table. "We don't know for sure when—or if—we'll be summoned today, but we believe we will be. And we *think* this is going to be a significant meeting. It seemed very much like all the pieces were in place—at least, before the, ah, incident. We were on the verge of getting a settled framework for an agreement. So this could be big. Special Agents Mendez and Wolfson, I know you'll do your best, and I know our local agents will give you the fullest and best briefing possible."

"We will, sir," said Singh.

"I know," said Stabmacher. There was something sad about him in that moment. Somehow the small pomposities of the man, the fumbling good intentions, all seemed to melt away. Jamie suddenly understood Stabmacher, and the airs he had seemed to put on. On Tifinda, to the Vixa, he stood for Earth, for humans, for Humanity with a capital H. He suddenly regretted yelling at the man, and felt shocked and ashamed that he could have done such a thing. Berndt Stabmacher was about to stand up and speak for them all, speak to the Vixa, speak whatever truth he had to more power than any of them could imagine. They owed him their respect, and much more besides.

"Speaking of the local agents, however, I only see two of you," said Stabmacher. "The senior local agent should be present. Where is he?"

Singh and Farrell exchanged looks, Hannah frowned and looked down at the table, and Jamie winced inside. "He's, ah, not feeling well, sir," said Singh. *You don't lie to the ambassador,* thought Jamie, *but sometimes it is wisest to let the truth out in gradual stages.*

"I see," said the ambassador, his face hardening. "He's drunk again. Or still. Passed out in his room?"

Singh and Farrell both muttered something inaudible, but they might as well have shouted out loud.

"I see. Special Agent Farrell, I believe you are the more senior. As soon as possible, I would ask you to draw up a list of charges against him for my signature. I think it's time we put an end to that man's trouble-making—and his career."

"No, sir," said Hannah.

"I beg your pardon?" said the ambassador.

"No, sir," said Hannah. "Forgive me, sir, but *I* am the most senior agent present—and I am senior in rank to Milkowski as well. I should be the one to draw up that list of charges. But I would respectfully request that you withdraw your order."

"He is the lead suspect in your murder investigation, Special Agent Wolfson. Or has that changed?"

"Not yet, sir. Not officially. But it might at any time. And I don't think that matters so much."

"How could that not matter?" Stabmacher was obviously struggling to keep his temper. He pulled out a chair and sat down. "I am not a fool—though I know perfectly well I have managed to come off looking like one in the past few days. But I know how the machine works, how an agent like Milkowski ends up at a post like this. I even know some of the specifics of his story. How can you defend him? He got here by being swept under the rug. Now you're giving him a chance to do even more damage! Incalculable damage!"

"No, sir!" Hannah said heatedly, slapping her palm down on the table. "Sir, I can't give you facts and numbers and precise explanations—not yet—but I can tell you with virtually absolute certainty that all he is guilty of is being framed. Maybe he's not the best agent in the Bureau. Maybe he never was or will be. But he's *put in his time*. Twenty-plus years of service—with screwups and mistakes and maybe some really serious rules badly broken, yes—but balance that against the man's service. He gives the Bureau his life, and what has he got for it? No wife, no family, no settled home, and he's out here on the edge of nowhere, with nothing left to him but the Bureau—the Bureau that might just take away everything he has left."

Hannah turned her palms upward, almost pleadingly. "He's been relieved of duty, told to stay away from his workplace, told we don't trust him. Why *shouldn't* he get drunk? If you want to throw the book at someone, throw it at Singh and Farrell! *They* were relieved of duty and told to stay away as well—and yet here they are in the BSI office briefing me. Going strictly by the book, Milkowski's the only one actually following orders. But we're *not* going strictly by the book because everyone involved has the sense to look the other way, bend a rule that doesn't really apply."

"If—*if* he *was* framed, then there must have been a reason he was chosen," said Stabmacher. "And that reason must be that his past actions make him by far the most plausible suspect in the murder of a Kendari agent. He's an embarrassment to the embassy. One we can't afford right now."

"Sir, by that logic, you're asking us to defer to the judgment and opinions of the real killer. Don't let the fact that Frank Milkowski was framed for a crime he didn't commit result in wrecking his career," said Hannah. "Think of the humiliation he's feeling right now. He's had punishment enough—nearly all of it self-inflicted. Sir, I know Frank Milkowski. I don't *like* him all that much, but I know him. Punish him more, and he'll be ruined as an agent for the remainder of his posting, and his career. Let him off with a well-phrased warning, let him apologize, let him feel that justice has been done, that you stood up for him—and he'll be the best damned senior agent the embassy has ever had."

"Slap his wrists?" Stabmacher asked. "Let him go with a warning?" He gestured toward Singh and Farrell. "What sort of signal do you think that will send to the younger agents?"

"That we take care of our own, sir," Jamie said, almost before he knew he was speaking.

"What?" Stabmacher asked sharply, looking around at Jamie, almost as if he had forgotten he was there.

Jamie swallowed hard, and leaned in across the table, toward the ambassador. "It sends the signal that the superior does not have an unquestioned right to kill the inferior at any time. That the escort is not expendable. That's what the *Vixa* do, sir. And the hell with not judging other cultures. There *are* limits. There *are* absolutes. That's what *they* do. We're *better* than that."

And the room was silent for a long time.

The aircar they were to fly in appeared to be the luxury version of an armored personnel carrier. It had three sections to it. Frau Groppe, the pilot, was in the nose section, and Ambassador Stabmacher chose to ride in the aft section by himself, with the door shut. That left Jamie and Hannah in the middle section—jammed in with the embassy simulants. Powered-down, rag-doll-mode copies of the ambassador, Zhen Chi, the three local BSI agents, and Jamie's simulant cluttered up the compartment. The Vixa flatly insisted that they attend the meeting but offered no explanation for it.

"I made a mistake," said Hannah.

"What? By standing up for Frank—for Milkowski?"

"Possibly, yes," said Hannah. "But certainly for doing it when I did." She gestured toward the aft section of the vehicle. "The ambassador came in to give us a pep talk—and instead I picked a fight with him. He's about to go into—well, if it's not battle, it's something close. He's about to state our case for a star system— and I tripped him up, distracted him about playing fair with one man who just barely deserves fairness, if he deserves it at all."

"You were right to do it," Jamie said. "And you treat everyone right for the benefit of the society as much as for the individual."

"Yeah, but this isn't a civics lesson," said Hannah.

Jamie looked out the window. "And it's not the time to distract us from *our* game, either. It looks like the party started without us. And they didn't bother to tell us who else was invited."

Hannah joined him at the window. They were already inside the main city dome, and were just entering either the same inner cluster of domes they had been in before, or one just like it. They weren't coming in through the lower-level cargo entrance this time, but straight through a hatch in the upper-level dome. They came to a halt in midair in preparation for a vertical landing.

But they weren't going to be making that landing just yet. The part of the dome floor directly beneath them was swarming with humans. Shouting, chanting, angry-looking humans. Farther off, Jamie could see that a large and much more orderly contingent of Kendari was surrounding an aircar there.

"Why the devil did the Vixa bus all of them in?" Hannah asked. "There wasn't anything like this at other meetings, was there?"

"No," said Jamie, having to raise his voice a little. "If there had been, Singh and Farrell would have mentioned it."

"*I* would have mentioned it," said Ambassador

Stabmacher as he emerged from the rear compartment. "This is new," he said to no one in particular. "This is unprecedented, and not part of the arrangements. We have been tricked. Again." He turned and looked at Hannah. "Should we abort? Cancel the meeting and head back?"

Hannah nodded to Jamie. "Ask him. He's the tactical expert."

"Well, Mendez?"

"Sir, I can't answer that. I can see the Vixa security guards clearing the landing zone. That tells us they can control the mob—if they want to. But will they want to? Special Agent Wolfson and I are packing lots of firepower. We could defend you, and ourselves, from a mob if we had to. Probably a warning shot or two would do it. But that puts us in the position of shooting at humans on the way to a meeting with xeno diplomats."

"But that mob is there because the Vixa want it there," Stabmacher said, still talking mainly to himself. "Are they using it to send us a message? We've never been able to do any good vetting of who, exactly, they brought in. That could be a rent-a-mob hired by the Vixa. Or it could be human beings expressing their sincere opinions."

"Sir, that's a fine democratic sentiment. But it won't really matter if they're sincere or not if they tear you limb from limb."

Jamie was startled to see a broad grin suddenly appear on Stabmacher's face. "Ah! But if they tear us limb from limb, the Vixa won't have anyone to negotiate with. They'll have to send for another human ambassador—and that would be very inconvenient for them, and therefore they won't allow us to be harmed." He went to the comm panel and pushed a stud. "Take us down, Frau Groppe. Take it nice and easy, be careful, but take us in."

The armored aircar moved slowly toward the ground. They heard the humming and the clunking of its landing gear deploying and locking into place.

The sound of the mob grew louder as they descended. When they were about twenty meters off the ground, the simulants came to life just as disconcertingly as ever, standing up and looking about.

"Escorts," said Jamie. "That's got to be it. You and I, or the three local BSI agents, weren't escort and status enough. The simulants have been hanging around to copy us, so they can serve as proper extra escorts."

The ambassador looked at the simulants thoughtfully. "I think you've got hold of part of it, Agent Mendez. Maybe a big part. But I have a feeling they're with us for lots of reasons. Some we might never learn."

The aircar landed with a *thump* and a *bump*. The ambassador pushed the comm key again. "Frau Groppe, you are to stay with the vehicle and listen in on the audio from my commlink. Activating commlink now. Button up as soon as we're outside. Stay on the ground if it makes sense, but you're authorized to go to hover if you see fit."

"I want her ready to do a dustoff and pickup and immediate takeoff," said Hannah. "You should be able to vector in on our commlinks. She should have trackable signals from all three of us. Use the ambassador's commlink for location, and we'll home in on him."

"You get that, Frau Groppe?"

"Got it, sir. Sit tight here, go to hover on own judgment, be ready for dustoff extraction at real-time track of location Stabmacher."

"Very good. All right then. Opening hatch. Wish us luck."

The side up-and-over door swung open, and the noise of the mob was instantly overwhelming. The demonstrators were behind a solid line of Vixan security Twelves, and it looked like they had already received a couple of lessons in staying back from Vixan stingers. Hannah could see two or three demonstrators half-collapsed on the ground, obviously in pain. Farrell and Singh had told them that the security-caste Vixa could generate any number of toxins—including one that was the rough equivalent of a severe bee sting. It looked as if they had used it.

Hannah and Jamie stepped out first, hands near their holsters but weapons undrawn. The ambassador came out next, and Hannah and Jamie moved in to stand to either side, and just behind him. The ambassador was followed, uninvited, by the six simulants. They instantly formed up on Hannah and Jamie, three of them in line behind each of them. But were they additional protection or additional threats? It didn't matter. The humans were stuck with them.

The demonstrators were shouting, and some of them were chanting, but Hannah couldn't make out the words. She spotted a couple of handwritten signs, written in English, reading FREE FRANK NOW! and MILKOWSKI WAS FRAMED! and HUMAN SUPREMACY LEAGUE SAYS FREE FRANK NOW!

And where the devil were they getting their information? Hannah asked herself. But she knew the answer. She glanced at the simulants. It had to be them, and whatever more conventional snooper systems the Vixa were using. But why were the Vixa feeding information to Zamprohna's group? How many sides were the Vixa playing on?

The Vixan cops had formed a cordon around either side of the delegation's path to the conference dome. The ambassador started walking away from the ship and toward the designated meeting place. Hannah and Jamie kept pace, watching the crowd, watching the simulants, trying to watch everything.

"Something's changed!" Stabmacher called out. "The building for the meeting has been altered somehow."

But did it matter? The Vixan cops were starting to herd the crowd of humans toward the same low dome that they were headed for. It was off by itself, pale blue in color—but beyond that, not much different from the one Jamie and she had visited on their way in.

Hannah could see a crowd of Kendari forming up on the opposite side of the dome, with the Vixan cops keeping the two groups very thoroughly separated. As they walked closer, she saw that large video displays had been set up outside it, and seemed to be showing a view of the interior. She could see two Grand Vixa, and two Kendari, seated and facing each other across two sides of a triangular table. It looked like Flexdal and Brox. It looked as if they had just gotten there and were still settling themselves in.

She spotted Tancredo Zamprohna just by the entrance to the conference dome. That wasn't really surprising, under the circumstances—but his appearance was. The smug, cocky wheeler-dealer pose was gone. He looked gaunt, and worried. That famous mop of red hair was disheveled. He caught her eye, and shouted something at her, but she couldn't hear it—and she had other fish to fry. She pointed to her ear, shook her head, and shrugged. *I can't hear you, but it's not my problem.* They were nearly at the entrance, walking straight down the corridor formed by the lines of Vixan security. *They import a riot, and then protect us from it,* Hannah thought.

When they were about ten meters away, the door opened. Hannah paused, and judged their surroundings. "Hold here just a minute, sir," she shouted in Stabmacher's ear. She lifted her commlink to her face. "Wolfson to Groppe. Capture my present location coordinates under name Static Dustoff One. Confirm."

"Present location captured as Static Dustoff One. Coordinates captured and confirmed."

Hannah nodded, then gestured for Stabmacher to stay put a moment longer. She went in through the door, saw no immediate threats, and gestured for him to come inside. He did so, Jamie at his back, and the simulants trooping in, single file. The door shut itself behind them, and suddenly they were in silence.

The interior of the dome was much the same as the one Jamie and she had visited on arrival—a shallow bowl-shaped floor and a raised dais in the center. There was even the blast of heat, and the same rotting-meat smell. There were differences. The dome color was blue, and the lighting was more or less of normal color and brightness.

On the dais, as they had seen on the video displays outside, were two Grand Vixa. One of them was Zeeraum. The other was nearly twice Zeeraum's size. His dorsal surface was bright orange, and his underside a pale pink. She saw Brox and Flexdal, already at the table and waiting for them. There were two unoccupied human-style chairs placed at the empty side of the triangular table. There was a ramp in front of them that led from about halfway down the bowl-shaped floor up onto the dais. She saw two other Vixa, security-caste, stationed at either side of the bottom of the ramp. They stood with their backs to the dais, facing Hannah.

She noted more details. There were two rows of six human-style theater seats, set facing the dais. A small table, with a table-chair identical to the ones set before the table on the dais, stood in front of the theater seating. The floor under that table had been slightly raised and leveled, so it didn't follow the slope of the rest of the floor. A transparent dome covered the dais itself. She glanced at Stabmacher's face, and saw at once that something was wrong. This was not the way he expected to find things.

Hannah half expected the simulants to slump over into rag dolls, or to break ranks and hustle over to the feeding trough that was, sure enough, right by the door, but neither of those things happened. Instead, five of them moved forward and sat in the back row of human-style seating. The sixth one—Stabmacher's simulant—trooped forward on his own, straight toward the stairs leading to the dais.

"What's going on?" Stabmacher asked himself under his breath. "Something's very wrong," he said in a slightly louder voice, so Hannah and Jamie could hear it. "The crowds outside, the video displays, the dome over the central dais, the chairs for the simulants—all the arrangements have been altered."

The Stabmacher simulant moved forward, stepped onto the ramp, and walked up and forward. A section of the dome over the dais shimmered out of existence for a moment, and the simulant moved through, the dome closing after it.

And then, suddenly, as abruptly as a switch being thrown, the simulant twitched, shifted its stance—and took on precisely the same pose as Stabmacher himself. Stabmacher jerked his head back in surprise. The simulant's head jerked back the same way. Stabmacher raised his arm, as if to ward off an attack—and the simulant did the same. "What is the meaning of this?" Stabmacher demanded—and his voice echoed down, reproduced perfectly, a split second behind the original.

"I am Kragshmal, foremost Subhouseholder of the Preeminent Director, who shall be forever nameless," said the larger Grand Vixan. "Things have come to the point where I saw fit to involve myself directly in these negotiations. I have made changes and improvements to the process. First of these is, of course, a step that relieves Grand Vixa from the necessity of encountering humans directly. Our laws require us to be in the same space at the same time with those with whom we bargain in situations such as these. But all those who have dealt with your kind have complained of the same thing—the dreadful *odor* that emanates from your people. We have consulted our laws, and found that this solution is permissible."

"What solution?" the ambassador demanded. Once again, the simulant echoed the words with uncanny speed. Stabmacher started to move toward the ramp, toward the dais. The simulant copied his body movements, modifying them just enough to remain in one place instead of actually walking. The two Vixan security guards stepped forward toward Stabmacher. Both of them extended all three manipulator arms, the sheaths around their stingers retracted, the stingers themselves glistening with venom.

"No farther!" shouted Kragshmal. "Remain where you are. Do not make any further attempt to approach the platform!" He paused, then spoke again, in a warm and kindly voice. "We mean you no harm," he said, "but we must protect ourselves from your presence. After much thought and long effort, we have found this just, equitable, and civilized way of resolving the issue." He gestured toward the Stabmacher simulant. "Turn it around so they can see it better," he said to no one in particular. The simulant wheeled around to face the audience area.

And the audience outside, thought Hannah. *They're seeing all this. This is for their benefit. All of it arranged to humiliate Stabmacher. No. To humiliate us. All of us. All humans.*

"This modified escort drone has re-formed itself into a splendid simulacrum of you, Ambassador Stabmacher. We have arranged matters so that everything you say and do, it will say and do. You may observe from your place there." Kragshmal gestured toward the small table between the theater chairs and the ramp. "Speak as you wish to speak, gesture as you wish to gesture, and your simulacrum will do the same."

Stabmacher stood absolutely stock-still for the count of ten, of twenty, his arms straight down at his sides, his hands balled into fists, with no motion other than his chest rising and falling as he breathed, his nostrils flaring, the blinking of his eyes. And the simulant echoed all of them perfectly. The only flaw was that its rubbery, mannequin-like face couldn't manage much in the way of expressions. *The Vixa don't have faces,* Hannah told herself. *They wouldn't know how important facial expressions are to us.* She kicked herself mentally for being distracted by minutiae at such a time. Everything, everything hung in the balance in that moment. She knew, with utter certainty, that they could all die in the next few seconds if Stabmacher got this one wrong.

"I refuse. On behalf of and in the name of the human race, I absolutely refuse," he said in a cold, controlled voice, still staring straight ahead at the thing that stared back at him, mocking him, echoing his words.

"My colleague!" Flexdal called out. "I was not consulted. I had no part in it. I learned of it as you did!"

"I believe you, my colleague," Stabmacher said. "You and I have always treated each other as well-respected enemies, worthy adversaries. This insult is not your way."

"This is no insult!" Zeeraum growled, speaking for the first time. "This is an excellent solution that will let us move forward."

Stabmacher did not move. "I speak now to those who are viewing this outside, or recording it, or witnessing it here, beside me. On my honor as a human and a diplomat, *never* have I heard any complaint from any Grand Vixan concerning the so-called problem this nonsense is intended to solve. It is a sham, an empty claim."

The simulant continued to echo every word, speaking as loudly and clearly as Stabmacher, a puppet speaking the words of the man its masters sought to control.

Stabmacher ignored it and spoke. "Were I to accept this humiliation, I cannot even guess what would follow—but some humiliation, some trick, some fraud *would* be next. Those who actually control the simulacrum would put their words, not mine, in its mouth. I would be told to remain at the embassy, and participate from there, without being able to witness directly what my puppet was doing in my name, but against my will. Or perhaps our generous hosts would conclude that there was no need to negotiate at all, and they would merely dictate the solution to the puppet— and make puppets of us all. No proper agreement could be made in those circumstances, and no agreement made could be respected or upheld. No. I refuse. Humanity refuses." He turned his head slightly, to look directly at Zeeraum. "Turn that *thing* off, remove the inner dome, remove your guards, and permit my access to my proper place. Now."

"This will not be done."

"Then we shall depart. If my conditions are not met, there will be no further negotiations on the matter of Pentam at any time in the future."

"Then your opportunity to state your claim is forfeit!"

Stabmacher laughed, but the sound that came out was closer to a snarl. "It is plain now that our opportunity was forfeit long ago. Forfeit, fraudulent, and as bankrupt as these talks." He paused, and then spoke in a louder voice, the voice of a proclamation, not a speech. "All simulants and simulacra are henceforth banned from the Embassy of Humanity to the Grand Warren of Tifinda. None will be permitted to enter. Those who attempt to enter the embassy or interfere with the personnel or the business of the embassy will be subject to destruction without warning. This policy is effective immediately. Wolfson! Mendez! We're going." He began to turn toward the door.

"You will remain!" Kragshmal roared.

"Either open that door and permit our departure," said Ambassador Berndt Stabmacher, in a calm, cold voice, "or kill us now."

That did it, so far as Hannah was concerned. "Weapons out!" she called, but Jamie was a heartbeat ahead of her. She pulled her sidearm with one hand and keyed her commlink with the other. "Wolfson to Groppe! Static Dustoff One! Now, now, *now*!" She left the comm keyed open so Groppe could hear. "Jamie! Cover the rear!"

"On it!" Jamie called.

The Stabmacher simulant seemed to have frozen up, or been shut down, and the guards at the base of the ramp—and the two Grand Vixa—were nearly as motionless. Flexdal and Brox were both standing, and Brox seemed to be shouting something, but Hannah couldn't understand him.

The other simulants were standing up, moving. Jamie covered them with his sidearm and placed the ambassador at his back. He started backpedaling up the ramp, watching the simulants, glancing behind himself every few seconds.

Hannah concentrated on her end of things. If there was any sort of manual door control, she couldn't see it and there wasn't time to play games and ask nicely.

"Ambassador! Shield your face! I'm going to shoot the door!"

"Do it!" he called. "Get us out of here!"

Hannah raised her weapon, set it to shotgun mode, pointed it at the center of the irised-shut door, and fired.

NINETEEN

DUSTOFF

The noise of the blast was fantastic. The dome seemed to echo and reinforce it endlessly. Jamie felt as if his head had been rung like a bell. The air was suddenly full of dust and smoke, and just as suddenly, it all rushed out the gap where the door had been. Now there was just an ugly torn-out gap two meters across, the remains of the irising mechanism shriveling around the edges.

Hannah was guiding Stabmacher through the opening. Jamie could hear the whistling roar of the aircar coming in on emergency power. He put his back to all that and covered the dome interior with his sidearm. Zeeraum and Kragshmal were bellowing something unpleasant, Flexdal had dropped under the table, and Brox was standing, watching, worried—but calm.

None of them had changed position. None of them were following. But the five simulants in the chairs had moved—and they were moving plenty, straight for him, walking stiffly, awkwardly, with no attempt to imitate the gaits and postures of their originals. Without the body language and the mannerisms, they suddenly looked a lot less like their originals—and a lot more menacing.

Hannah and the ambassador were outside. Jamie retreated upward, toward the hole where the door had been, the simulants moving steadily for him. "Time to get moving," he said to himself, and ducked out through the opening.

The aircar was almost directly overhead, and coming in so fast Jamie had to fight the urge to dive for cover. The mob outside was equally spooked. Groppe had to abort her first landing attempt for fear of crushing the humans who were scrambling to get out of her way. She sidled over about twenty meters and came down again, landing gear down and doors open as she bounced to a touchdown.

Hannah wasn't playing nice. She grabbed the ambassador by the collar of his coat and hauled him forward, dragging him forward when he wasn't moving fast enough. She reached the access ramp and half threw him on board. She turned back to Jamie and shouted, "Let's get out of here!"

Jamie was inclined to agree—but the simulants were still coming. He jogged backwards toward the aircar, keeping his gun trained on them.

He was only a step or two from the aircar when a figure suddenly broke from the mob and started running toward him. Jamie turned, aimed, and was within an eyeblink of firing when he recognized Zamprohna. For a flickering moment, he was tempted to shoot anyway, but he fought down the idea. Zamprohna was shouting something, waving his arms, wildly agitated. Jamie realized the man probably had no idea what was going on. "My daughter!" Jamie heard him yell. "What have you done with my daughter!"

Zamprohna grabbed his arm, pulled at him, completely ignoring everything else. There wasn't time to sort things out, and Jamie needed to get clear. He folded his elbow in and rammed it into Zamprohna's gut. The man gasped in shock and collapsed onto the landing ramp as the Farrell simulant grabbed for his legs. Hannah appeared and lunged for Zamprohna, pulled him aboard, threw him to the deck—and then gut-punched him herself. He jerked upward, dropped backwards, banged his head against the deck, and went limp. "If we live, I'll apologize to him later," Hannah shouted. "Now get aboard!"

Jamie scrambled up—and felt another set of hands on his arm. It was Farrell's simulant, grabbing at him.

"Kill it!" Stabmacher yelled.

Jamie didn't argue. He twisted away from the simulant's grasp, kicked it hard in the chest to push it back, and dialed into shotgun mode, all in one movement. He lifted his gun and fired point-blank at the thing's head. The blast was nearly as loud as the one inside the dome. It took the simulant's head clean off, or rather the fleshlike material pretending to be the head. Underneath was what looked like a steel skull held up by a plastic neck embedded in the main body of the creature. That was all. No blood, no flesh, no bones, no nothing.

The loss of its head didn't seem to bother the thing at all. It just kept coming, moving for him, reaching out blindly—or maybe not so blindly. He saw something sharp peeking out from the sleeve of one arm. *Simulants are just modified Vixan escort-caste Sixes,* he reminded himself. *And Vixa have a lot of eyes. The head's a fake. Just two arms fused together and reformed into a head shape.*

"The gut! The central body!" Hannah shouted.

Jamie shifted his aim and fired again, right at the little potbelly that had always seemed to be out of place. The shotgun tore off the simulant's simulated flesh and ripped into the digestive chamber concealed underneath. The simulant toppled over. There was another blast, over his shoulder, as Hannah fired at the

Milkowski simulant, toppling it over. Jamie chose another target, aimed and fired—and didn't realize until his target had dropped that he had just shot his own simulant, blasted his own double.

But Jamie didn't have time to think about that. The aircar lifted off, the ramp door swinging up and shut as it boosted, and there was plenty happening on board.

"Frau Groppe!" Stabmacher was saying. "Direct course, standard speed, for the embassy. Follow all rules while we are in the dome. Do not violate traffic rules. Give them no excuse to attack us. Attempt normal departure of government and city domes. Once through, go to emergency speed. I'm betting they won't try to stop us—but be ready to hedge that bet. Contact the embassy. Order standby prep for immediate evacuation. Sensitive materials ready for destruction, and the embassy ship *Kofi Annan* ready for boost."

"Yes, sir," she called out through the open door of the pilot's compartment. "Sir, a reminder that I am our only qualified pilot for the embassy ship."

"I am very well aware of that, Frau Groppe. You worry about that once we're back in the compound. Send the order. And if you would be so good, emphasize that this is *standby* for destruct and evac. Let's make sure no one starts pouring igniter fluid just yet."

Stabmacher turned to Hannah and Jamie and shook his head. "Well," he said. "It would appear you two have a ringside seat on a first-class diplomatic disaster."

"The disaster wasn't of your making, sir. You had no choice," said Hannah. "You did the right thing."

"You think so? Perhaps you can be a witness when they convene the review board. They *do* tend to con-

vene them when an ambassador orders an embassy
evacuation—or hands a strategic two-habitable-planet
system to the Kendari."

"The fix was in, sir. They were either going to humiliate us, then give it to Flexdal—or watch us refuse
humiliation and do just the same."

"I agree," said Stabmacher. "But there are a lot of
armchair diplomats who won't see it that way if
they gain some political points by blaming me.
That one, for example," he said, gesturing toward
Zamprohna. "What is he *doing* here, anyway?"

"My fault, sir," said Jamie. "He came for me the
same time the simulants did. I had to sucker punch
him to get my weapon clear—"

"And then I hauled him aboard to make sure
Mendez had a clear shot," said Hannah. "So call it my
fault."

"How about we compromise and call it *his* fault?"
the ambassador suggested. "Maybe we'll be able to
make some sense of it when he comes to."

"Sir, we are coming up on the access port for the
main government dome. How am I to proceed if they
refuse to allow us to exit?"

"How are they going to play this?" Stabmacher
asked himself. "Kragshmal doesn't have everything his
own way, because if he did, we'd all be dead by now.
But he's still Preeminent Director, apparently, so he's
got *some* control. The real question is do the rules say
he can or cannot close the portal?"

"I thought Kragshmal said he was some kind of
householder of the Preeminent Director," Jamie said.

"And it's just barely possible he is merely that. We
may never know for sure. They do keep the name of
the P.D. very quiet. But it's not at all uncommon for

the P.D. to pretend to be his own assistant, so he can go out and do things, be involved, rather than stay sealed away in the residence all the time. I think Kragshmal wants to get rid of us, kill us if possible, merely throw us out if that's all he can get away with. The insults today were very carefully chosen. A species that lets its meals ferment in its mouth and smells of rotting meat doesn't usually go around complaining of other species' fragrance. The interesting question right now is, did I respond properly, or was there something in what I said or did that was improper, and will give Kragshmal the right to detain us, or kill us? The dome-access control points would be convenient places to do the Director's bidding."

Stabmacher made his decision. "We were entitled to defend ourselves at the conference dome. We are *not* entitled to damage their installations without permission. Slow down and await normal exit approval, Frau Groppe. Don't attempt a crash-through or other emergency move without my explicit approval. We have followed the rules, and we are alive. We will continue to follow the rules."

And then, thought Jamie, *we will find out if we continue to stay alive.*

"Milkowski! Wake up!"

Frank Milkowski coughed, grumbled, and rolled over.

"Frank!" It was Farrell, grabbing at his shoulder, shaking him. "We need you!"

"Huh? Wha?" He sat up in bed, coughed again, and blinked. He checked his watch. He must have been out for about an hour or so. "What is it?" he asked. "Leave me alone!"

"Believe me, we'd like to," Singh replied, with a glance around the disordered room and the bottle lying on its side on the floor. "But we can't. The ambassador is at the meet with the Vixa, and we just had flash traffic in. It's bioscan-locked for head of security only. Your retina-scan or the ambassador's."

That woke him up. Things had to be plenty hairy for anyone to send a message that rated bioscan status. The bioscan locks were automatically inserted by the embassy's own communications system on any message flagged with appropriate and sufficient security tags. He swung his legs out of bed and stood up. He was in his boxer shorts and nothing else, but that didn't matter. "Gimme," he said, holding his hand out blindly, not really seeing anything. Something big had gone wrong. That was for sure. Singh handed him the retinal-scanner-equipped datapad. He was about to put the scanner up to his eye when he hesitated.

"Wait a second," he said. "Didn't anyone reprogram the comm system? Why is this on me? Wasn't I relieved of duty?"

"Would have been," said Farrell.

"Maybe should have been," Singh put in. "But it's on you. Wolfson stood up for you. And Mendez too. They thought you still had something left."

Do I? he asked himself. Almost without thinking, he put his eye to the scanner. A heartbeat later, the unit beeped approvingly, and the decrypted message appeared on the datapad's main screen.

He read it, allowing the others to read over his shoulder. Shock gave way to fear as he read—but then anger shoved them both out of the way. "They're hanging us out to dry," he said. "Setting it up so it's nice and legal to kill us all, if they feel like it."

And suddenly, somehow, in that moment, the anger dropped away too. Anger and fear would be what distracted them, got them killed. What this situation needed was coldhearted, clearheaded thinking. Organization. Quick, sharp decision-making.

Frank sat back down on the bed and worked it through. Suddenly he realized that he did have something left—or more likely that he had, in that moment, just gotten it back. He knew exactly what needed to happen.

"All right," he said in a voice that was deeper, stronger, more sure than it had been in a long time. "This is what we're going to do."

The aircar had come to a halt in midair, maybe ten meters away from the dome portal. Everyone held their breath, not sure what they would do—or could do—if it stayed buttoned up. But then it irised open, and Frau Groppe piloted them smoothly through it—and, a minute or two later, the main city dome portal as well.

"We are clear of the city," said the ambassador. "Speed and heading at your discretion, Frau Groppe."

She immediately started accelerating, up to and beyond all the local speed limits. Jamie was just about to breathe a sigh of relief when Frau Groppe shouted. "Ambassador! I'm tracking an aircar right behind us. Same course, same heading, same altitude—and speed. And we're at emergency."

"*Now* what the devil?"

Jamie scrambled back into the aft compartment and took a look through the viewport. "It's a Kendari aircar! It must be Flexdal and Brox—"

"Something coming through on comm channel seven!" Groppe shouted. "Putting it on the overhead!"

"—o hostile intent. Repeat. This is Kendari embassy aircar, Brox 231 speaking. We are not in pursuit. Repeat, we are not in pursuit, but performing emergency return to our own embassy. We have no hostile intent. Do you copy?"

Hannah scrambled over to the middeck comm center and patched herself in. "This is human embassy aircar. We copy and acknowledge no hostile intent. What happened?"

"No comment on this feed. Brox out."

Three alert buttons on the comm system picked that moment to flash. "Ambassador!" Hannah called out. "We're getting your-eyes-only traffic from the embassy."

"The hell with that," said the ambassador, standing up and making his way over to her. "We don't have time to play around with procedure. Open the message file yourself. Groppe! How far out are we?"

"Twenty kilometers. Estimate four minutes to landing. Higher speed might cause Vixa security or the embassies we have to overfly to activate their defenses."

"Very well. Wolfson?"

Hannah read. "FLASH TRAFFIC MILKOWSKI REPORTING. IN RECEIPT OF AUTHENTICATED DIRECTIVE FROM HOUSEHOLD OF PREEMINENT DIRECTOR QUOTE CREDENTIALS OF PIRATE (SIC) EMBASSIES OF HUMAN AND KENDAL ARE HEREBY WITHDRAWN EFFECTIVE LOCAL DATE CODE (CONVERTED) 1943 HOURS TODAY. ALL AND ONLY ACCREDITED EMBASSY PERSONNEL MUST EVAC EMBASSY PROPERTY AT THAT TIME. EMBASSY PROPERTIES TO BE PUT UNDER PROTECTIVE SEAL TO

AWAIT LEGITIMATE DIPLOMATIC REPRESEN-
TATIVES ENDQUOTE. REQUEST INSTRUCTIONS
MILKOWSKI OUT."

Stabmacher was silent for a moment before he
spoke. "Well, one piece of good news. It sounds like
the man picked the right moment to sober himself up.
But what the hell happened with the Kendari? They
were the fair-haired boys when we left."

"The Vixa picked a fight with us, sir. Why not
them?" asked Jamie.

"Why not indeed? But why pick fights with *either*
of us?"

"Ah, sir—can they just kick us out like that?"

"It's their planet," said Stabmacher. "If the host
government doesn't want you, there's no point in trying to stick around."

"Isn't there any appeal? Any way to protest or
something?"

"On some worlds, with some species, yes. You might
call some friendly official, or diplomat, and call in favors. Have X have dinner with Y, and see what arrangements might be made. Not with the Vixa. Decisions
flow from the top down, and never the other way."
Stabmacher thought a moment longer, then turned
to Hannah. "Acknowledge the signal and instruct
Milkowski that our arrival is imminent. Instructions to
come in person. Send that and cut comm."

"Yes, sir."

The ambassador found a jumpseat, folded it out, sat
down, and looked at Jamie. "Can you think of anything that hasn't happened yet?"

Jamie was about to reply when he got his answer
from a source they had all forgotten for a moment.

"Whaa. Uhh." Zamprohna was waking up. Jamie
knelt and helped him sit up a little. "Mmm. My

daughter," he said. "What have you done with my daughter?"

"Who is your daughter?" Jamie asked. "What are you talking about?"

"My *daughter*," Zamprohna said again, in a groggy tone of voice that made it clear that everyone knew who his daughter was. "Where is she?" He shook his head mournfully. "I lost time. So much *time*. Too' me th' better part of a day t' be sure she was in th' embassy when it was locked down. What did you do with her? Where is she?"

Jamie was about to protest that he had no idea what Zamprohna was talking about—but then he realized that wasn't true. He remembered a missing-person report that he had decided that he didn't need to follow up on. And then all the pieces of the puzzle suddenly dropped into place. Jamie *did* know who his daughter was.

He knew exactly where she had to be.

And he knew what she had done.

TWENTY

DUNGEON

If Jamie had thought that too much was going on aboard the aircar, he had his mind changed for him once they landed. Groppe powered the vehicle down in record time and had it safed and sealed for storage almost before the passengers were off. She shouldered the ambassador out of the way without a word of apology and made a beeline for the *Kofi Annan*.

But the ambassador wasn't paying any attention to her, either. The moment he was inside the compound and his commlink could patch into the embassy's secure net, he was on the comm to the Stanlarr and Pavlat embassies, activating a contingency plan for those two powers jointly to oversee and look after human interests on Tifinda—including the far-from-minor task of looking out for the welfare of the humans who would remain on the planet.

Meantime, Milkowski, who not only seemed to have sobered up but also to have turned ten years younger—was passing Stabmacher dispatches to read, actions to approve, checklists to authorize, and at the same time keeping Singh and Farrell hopping, juggling a dozen details of the situation in his head. Hannah had been right. Give the man some real work—and he would really do it.

Most important was the formal order to evacuate. Once Stabmacher had signed that, everyone just reached for their contingency plans and started in on them. Fires lit up in the center of the compound as the staff found papers that needed to burn. There were small *bumps* and *thumps* popping off here and there around the compound as small self-contained self-destruct units were activated. Farrell and Singh were already at work inside the joint ops center, burning and wrecking and shredding all the sensitive material on the human side of the structure.

Just as all that was getting under way, the Kendari embassy aircar came in for a landing, dropping in hard, sharp, and fast. Jamie couldn't imagine why they were being kicked out too. They sure looked to be the flavor of the month an hour or so before, when the humans were shooting their way out of the conference.

The armory was unlocked, and everyone, including the ambassador, was issued a sidearm. But they all knew if it came down to the embassy staff defending themselves in a shoot-out, the fight was lost already.

Hannah and Jamie had no part to play in any of those contingency plans. The best service they could perform would be to get out of the way. Besides, they had their own job to do. Their biggest problem was what to do with Zamprohna while they did it. Jamie decided to settle it in the simplest way possible. He ducked into the Snack Shack and came out with a chair no one was likely to need between then and Evac Hour. He carried it along back to where Zamprohna was waiting with Hannah at the aircar. "Come with me," he said to both of them. They made the short walk to the joint ops center. Jamie planted the chair on the ground directly in front of the entrance, facing the door. "In a minute, you're using that chair. But first I'm going to search you. Arms out from your side."

"I'm not going to—"

"It's our job to find your daughter and get her to

safety," Jamie said. "We have to do it. We don't have to let you see her. Arms out."

Zamprohna cooperated. Jamie patted him down, even running his fingers through the famous head of hair.

"Looking for bombs in there?" Zamprohna said. "Or you figure this is your big chance to find out once and for all if it's a wig like the gossip sheets say?"

"I don't read gossip sheets," said Jamie. "But if it'll make you feel better, I'll tell all my friends that it's really all your own hair after all. Feet forty centimeters apart." Jamie did a quick, smooth, professional check of the lower half of his body. Zamprohna flinched away when Jamie's hand slid over his ankle. Jamie pulled Zamprohna's trouser leg up to his calf, and pulled down his sock—producing another flinch from Zamprohna. "Nasty bruise or something there," said Jamie. "You bang yourself up getting into the aircar or something?"

"I don't know. Maybe. I don't remember how it happened all that well."

"Wise choice. It wasn't your finest moment. Keep on forgetting it. All right," said Jamie as he stood up. "There's your chair. Now sit," he said.

Zamprohna did so. He was still a bit subdued, and Jamie wanted to act on that before the man started feeling his oats again. He crouched in front of the chair, his nose ten centimeters from Zamprohna's. "Now then," he said. "Special Agent Wolfson and I are going to go find your daughter. I have a very good idea of where she must be. Then we're going to talk to her. We might have to talk to her for a long while. When—and if—we think we can let you see her, we will come back to this chair and tell you. But all hell is breaking loose around here, and we don't have time to cut people any slack—especially you. So if I come back, and I find that you aren't in this chair, that you've wandered off, or started to try and talk your way out of the compound, you *won't* get to see your daughter—because I will find you, and then I will shoot you. Is that clear?"

Zamprohna looked at him angrily, but said nothing, made no gesture.

"Okay," said Jamie. "One. I need a yes out of you right now. And two, you're not one of my favorite people, and I really wouldn't suggest trying to see if I'm bluffing. Talk to me. Is it clear? Do we have a deal?"

"Yes. Yes! We have a deal. I'll stay right here until you come back."

"We'll make it as fast as we can," Jamie said. "Hannah? Let's move."

They moved through the inner and outer doors in record time, Jamie growling and cursing at himself the whole time.

"*I'm* starting to wonder if you weren't bluffing with Zamprohna," said Hannah.

"I'm starting to wonder too," said Jamie. "But the one I'd really like to slap around is *me*. How could I miss that? Rule one in a locked-room problem— search the room. You'd think if anyone should have learned that by now, *we* should have."

"Well, slap me around first," said Hannah as they came through the inner door. "We had plenty of hints. They mentioned interns that came and went. Her coffee mug was—is—still up on the shelf in the Snack Shack. There were plenty of clues, if we'd bothered to put them together. Here. Gimme that building plan." They bent their heads together and studied it. "In our defense, this place is bigger than it looks. Two underground levels that run the full length of the building. I had no idea." She tapped the most remote of the survival bunkers on the lowest level. "That one," she said. "Let's start there."

They got lucky on the third try. It was locked from the inside, but they had the security codes. They went in quietly, with weapons drawn, not sure what they would find.

The survival bunker was a mess. Mealpacks were everywhere, and the ventilation wasn't all it could have been. But she was there. She was unconscious. *No. Just asleep*, Hannah decided. So exhausted by her own fears that even two cops breaking into the place didn't wake her. They had gotten the whole story out of Zamprohna in three minutes, once they got him talking. *And why couldn't we have gotten that three minutes a day sooner?* Hannah asked herself. Just a few little scraps of information would have stopped them from chasing their own tails.

She was Linda Weldon, the very determinedly apolitical daughter of Tancredo Zamprohna and his belligerent, highly political wife Helga Weldon-Zamprohna. And she had been an intern at the embassy for a month, doing routine filing, some data entry, running for coffee. Nothing classified or sensitive. Nothing that required clearance, or vetting. Probably she had taken the job for the express purpose of rebelling against her parents. Her own father hadn't known she worked there until after she had gone missing. And no one at the embassy, not even Ambassador Stabmacher, who had taken a particular liking to her, had known or thought to ask who her father was.

Jamie knelt next to her, and cleared his throat. "Ah, Ms. Weldon? Linda Weldon?"

It was a very tender moment, even a romantic one, Hannah decided. The brave, gentle, and handsome young police officer rescuing the terrified young woman from the underground bunker. And it lasted until the split second when Linda Weldon woke up, saw Jamie, and screamed.

They should have had Brox there, but there had been no contact since Brox had called them from the Kendari aircar. They should have had Zhen Chi there, but it seemed she was, in spite of it all, still in the med lab in the Kendari embassy compound. The ambassador should have been there, but there could be no disturbing him—and they were very definitely on the clock, with the hours until the Vixa's evac deadline slipping away. They settled for setting up every sort of recorder they could find in the same conference room they had been using.

"All right," said Jamie as he handed her a glass of water. "There's a lot going on around here, and there isn't much time. I'm not going to lie to you—I haven't the slightest doubt that you're going to have to go through all this again—quite possibly several times. But we need to get through the first time now."

"It's—it's bad, isn't it?" she asked.

"Yes," said Hannah. "Yes it is. The situation is complicated, and very serious."

"My father—do you know—is he—is he all right?"

"Your father is fine," said Hannah. "We'll let him know you're safe." She prayed that Jamie had the sense not to tell this semihysterical girl that her father was thirty meters away, just outside, waiting for her. Then they'd get into a bargaining session. *Let me see my father first, and then I'll tell you everything.* But the first sight of her father would make her feel safer, less vulnerable, less obliged to tell them what they needed. And Jamie might well give in.

A glance at Jamie told Hannah her fears weren't misplaced. She gave him a quick, imperceptible shake of the head to warn him off, and he nodded back just as imperceptibly.

The boy needed to get out more. He always did fall to pieces and get all overprotective when it came to interrogating young women. And this one would be pretty enough, if she got cleaned up and put in fresh clothes. She was just eighteen, according to what her father said, and she'd inherited his bright red hair, though little else of his appearance. Her face was streaked with tears, and a little grubby-looking. She was thin, pale, gangly and coltish, and even looked a little fretful—but many a lovely young swan grew out of an duckling uglier than this one. Hannah fought down a smile. *Cool it, Wolfson,* she told herself. *Are you feeling maternal, or just a wee bit jealous? Face it. Our dear little baby agent is all grown-up and getting interested in girls.*

She was tempted to step in and take over. But it was too late for that already. Weldon had zeroed right in on Jamie. He had to take the lead on this one.

"Look, let's just start with you telling us what happened, in your own words. How was it you started up at the embassy?"

"There—there were a bunch of us. It was something to *do* instead of hanging around the residential compounds they had for us, listening to our parents argue the same politics over and over."

"But, ah, no offense, pretty much every one of the groups that the Vixa brought in is considered radical in one direction or another. Why did the embassy let you work here?"

"We weren't spies or anything like that. They never let us near anything confidential. Half of what I did was work in Zhen Chi's garden, or in the motor pool. Stuff like that. And the ambassador kept saying that if we saw what was really going on, what the embassy really did, what the Vixa and the Kendari and everybody were really like, got a different perspective, then maybe that would do us some good."

"And did it?"

She shrugged in classic teenage fashion as she stared fixedly at the water glass and fiddled with it. "I don't know. I guess."

"But the joint ops center is nothing *but* sensitive material," Hannah objected. "What were you doing *here*?"

"Finding an empty desk," she said. "Simple as that. Madame Mutambara, the political officer, had just finished up doing this big report on Vixan history and politics, and asked me to proofread it. There wasn't any room in the pol office, so she walked me in here, and said no one ever used half the space in the place. She told me to leave the work in the room when I was done for the day and that then I could come back to it in the morning. She showed me how to key myself out when I was done, and left me to it."

"Where, exactly, were you working?" Hannah asked.

Linda hooked her thumb out the door. "Down the end of this hall. Third or fourth door on the left. All the stuff I was working out still ought to be there if you want proof or something."

"We'll check on that later," said Jamie. "When did

all this happen? When did Madame Mutambara let you in?"

Another teenage shrug. "They use a funny clock system around here. It was about 1500 hours."

Nearly five hours before 1950, the best estimate on the time of the murder. And they had only done that fast-scan check of the surveillance video for the last *four* hours before.

"So you sat down and got to work at about 1500," said Jamie. "Then what?"

"I worked," she said, as if that was too obvious a question. "I thought it was going to be dull, dull, dull, but there was all sorts of cool, creepy, interesting stuff in the report about their biology and history and stuff. I sort of got hooked on it, and just kept going at it."

"Until when?"

"Maybe 2230 or so."

"You worked through for six and half hours?"

"Well, I went to the bathroom once or twice. It's right next to the office I was in. You can go look. And I brought my own dinner." She paused, and looked from one of them to the other. "I know that's a little weird, staying alone checking a book for that long. But I don't *get* much time alone. The residential compounds are really crowded. Not much peace and quiet. Besides, the stuff in the book was really *interesting*."

"Did anyone see you, or hear you while you were here? Did you see anyone, or hear anything?"

"You mean, alibis and stuff?" She shook her head "no" very solemnly. "I didn't see anyone at all. I heard voices once or twice, from the big room in the middle, but just ordinary talking. No shouting or fights or anything. And I heard the outside doors opening and shutting. They make a lot of noise, big rattling booms. But that's just ordinary too. I didn't pay it any attention."

And when they were shut, the doors made for superb soundproofing.

"Okay, keep going."

"Well, finally, I *did* check the time, and realized that I had been there way longer than I had planned, and that my dad would be getting worried."

"When was that?"

"Like I said, about 2230. Yeah. It was just about then, because I remember thinking I only had half an hour until my curfew—and that's at 2300."

Hannah worked through the sequence of events in her head. By 2300, Emelza had probably been dead for more than three hours already. Brox and Milkowski had both been in and out of the building—some of those booming door noises Weldon had heard. By 2300, the lockdown was already well under way, and the joint ops center was sealed and locked from both human and Kendari sides.

"So I straightened up the papers, and got my things together, and walked down the main hall—and—and—"

"It's the tough part, Linda, but you have to go on."

"And—and I saw him there."

"Him? Who?" Hannah and Jamie exchanged sudden panicky looks. Another dead Kendari? A male? Was their case going to take another hairpin turn?

"The Kendari. The dead Kendari. I don't know the name. Dad didn't like me talking to them, so I never really met any of the ones here. But he was dead! Slumped over on his side, dead!"

Hannah let out a silent sigh of relief. No, not another, male, dead Kendari. Just an ignorant, thoughtless teenage human who couldn't tell the difference. Probably she assumed all dogs were boys and all cats were girls.

"How could you tell?" Jamie asked. "I mean, ah, that the Kendari was dead?"

"He wasn't *moving*," she said, suddenly agitated again. "Not breathing or anything. And there was this sort of slime on his ears and mouth and stuff. But I thought that—that maybe he was just asleep, or passed out or something. I—I—"

She burst into tears.

"Drink some water," Jamie said. "Take it easy. We're almost there. You what?"

"I—I touched him. Sort of poked at him. Pushed at him with my fingers, and then with my whole hand, pretty hard. He was *cold*, and he didn't move—and he was dead." Tears were running down her cheeks. "And then—then I realized that my dad—I love my dad, he's a good guy and everything—but he *hates* the Kendari. Says all sorts of terrible things about them trying to trick us and attack us and how we have to get them before they get us—and there I was in this super-secure place with a dead one, and they'd say I killed him because of my dad—"

She stopped, gulped air, and grabbed at the edge of the table, as if she was afraid of flying off into space. "I tried to get out on the human-side doors, but the key-code Madame Mutambara gave me wouldn't work. It would just flash ENHANCED SECURITY MODE IN EFFECT CONTACT SECURITY OFFICE. I—I almost did that. But then I thought of my dad again, and the dead body, and started thinking about how they—you, I guess, would think I did it—and—and just went a little panicky-crazy, I guess. I decided to hide. I went to the survival bunkers in the basement."

"How did you know about the bunkers?"

"Safety orientation," she said. "They made every-one take it who was going to have to work at the embassy. They even walked us through one of them. I thought it was cool—back then. A private dungeon. Plenty of peace and quiet. And the longer I did it, the longer I stayed down there—the worse it got. The more I was sure that you'd find me, sooner or later, and figure that I must have done it, because why else would I be hiding? But I didn't do it. I didn't."

"Okay," said Hannah, a little harshly. "We got that. Quick follow-ups. Did you see or notice anything around the body? Anything odd or unusual."

"Just the dead alien! That was unusual enough for me!"

She burst into tears again, and Hannah gave it up. She stepped out into the hall while Jamie calmed the girl down again. Linda Weldon wasn't going to be describing broken coffee mugs or appearance of stains on the carpet or hard flooring. It didn't matter. They had confirmation of all that evidence, and her story fit into the narrative perfectly.

Hannah walked down the hallway, idly checked the layout of the rooms, and found the one with a pile of reference materials and a neat stack of printed pages. She checked a page or two, and sure enough, it was an historic analysis of the Vixa, with neat proofreading marks on nearly every page. Weldon had done good work. Madame Mutambara would want to recover it before the evacuation.

Weldon had as much as said she was alone in the same building with the victim for an extended period that included the time when the murder must have taken place. That meant they had her placed in the main ops center, just at the time of the murder, with nothing to stop her from killing Emelza 401. All she had to do was take a break from reading her fascinating Big Book of the Vixa, commit the murder, then go back to her work for however long she judged would best suit the cover story. And it didn't hurt at all that her father was her father. All they had to do was uncover one lie in her story, catch her being wrong in one significant detail, and they'd have themselves a big, fat, juicy, very solid suspect that would make everyone very happy indeed.

The only trouble was, Hannah didn't buy it at all.

Hannah stepped back out into the hallway and spotted Jamie just coming out of the conference room. They walked toward each other. "Hey, Hannah. Well, there's our handprint."

"Yeah."

"Under the circumstances, do you see any real harm in letting her see her father?"

Hannah thought for a moment. "No. The hell with interrogation procedure, and the hell with not liking Daddy's politics. Let's be decent human beings instead of cops, just for a moment. Go get her, and let's take her out to her dad."

"Right. Thanks."

Hannah waited for him to retrieve the wan, tired, frightened girl. They were just about to take her through the inner human-side doors of the ops center when the interlock system kicked in.

"Oops," said Jamie. "We're stuck here for a minute."

"What? Why?" asked Weldon.

"The Kendari-side doors are in use," said Jamie. "They rigged the system so only one set of doors can be used at once, and only one door on each side can be opened at the same time. Paranoid security thing to keep us from rushing straight through the building and attacking them, or vice versa."

"I don't want to see any Kendari!" Weldon protested. "I don't!"

Hannah bit down on the half dozen or so replies she was tempted to make. They wouldn't do any good anyway.

"We don't always get to choose what we see," Jamie said.

Weldon did her best to prove him wrong by covering her eyes with her hands and turning her back on the door—and bursting into tears yet again. *Reminds me of her daddy's politics. Nothing is so big or important that you can't pretend it isn't there, if you try hard enough.* Hannah knew that the girl had been through a hard time, but she had just about had her fill of Linda Weldon.

The Kendari-side inner door rolled open. Brox, Remdex, Flexdal, and Zhen Chi came through the door, Zhen Chi carrying the same large box that Hannah had handed to her earlier that day. "We need you two, and the ambassador, in the conference room, right away," said Zhen Chi. "And yes, it's important enough to interrupt evac preparation. I'm pretty sure we found what you expected."

Hannah stepped forward eagerly. If Zhen Chi was right, that would be the best news she'd heard in a while. *And maybe the worst news too, but one disaster at a time.* Hannah nodded at Jamie. "Let's get her out of here, then go find Stabmacher. We can get him up to speed on what Weldon—Miss Weldon—told us on the way." She turned to the new arrivals. "A lot's been happening today," she said. "We'll get you caught up as soon as we're back."

Hannah followed a step or two behind as Jamie led Linda Weldon through the human-side door, and out into the human embassy compound.

"Daddy! You're here!" Linda spotted her father at once, and he was as fast on the uptake as she was.

Zamprohna jumped up, knocking over his chair, and rushed to his daughter.

The two of them embraced, and Tancredo Zamprohna comforted his child, ignoring the chaos of the world around them as he stroked her hair and rocked her gently in his arms. "You're safe," he said. "It's all right. You're safe now."

Hannah wasn't impressed, but plainly Jamie was.

"That's it," he said quietly, gesturing toward them. "That's our job, right there. To hell with the politics and the plots and the investigations. That's what we're out here for, at the end of the day. To find people. To get people home. To put families back together."

Just for a moment, Hannah allowed herself the luxury of feeling it. Right then, Zamprohna wasn't a pol on the make, or a con man working both sides against the middle. He was a father, and they had found his daughter, and they had given them back to each other. That *was* worth doing.

And it would be even more worthwhile if we can keep all of us from being blown apart, she told herself. "Okay," she said to Jamie, patting him on the shoulder. "Break's over. Time to go back to being cops. We have to go find Stabmacher."

TWENTY-ONE

DISCUSSION

Finding the ambassador didn't take long. Two minutes after leaving Zamprohna with his daughter, they found him in his office, at his desk, dealing all at once with a dozen details related to the evacuation. Hannah left Jamie with him, tasked with the job of peeling Stabmacher away and bringing him in at the earliest possible moment.

She returned to the joint ops center conference room that was rapidly becoming her home away from home, and filled the time until Jamie got Stabmacher to them by briefing the others on what they had learned from Zamprohna and his daughter.

"You should not have let her see her father," Brox said, when Hannah had finished.

"Maybe not, but we did," said Hannah.

"You will be holding her, of course," Brox said. "She is, at the very least, a crucial witness, and she is also the leading suspect at the moment."

Hannah leaned back in her chair and sighed. "Brox, somewhere, on one of the human-settled worlds, there is a tough, hard-edged, cunning, calculating cold-blooded killer of an eighteen-year-old girl. A girl—and I emphasize that I mean girl, and not woman—who is capable of forcing a fatal dose of caffeine into a Kendari who outweighs her two to one at least, planting evidence carefully designed to implicate someone else, then hiding out for hours. A girl who knows her

Kendari postmortem effects backwards and forwards and takes advantage of them by sneaking out of her hiding place, poking and prodding a corpse to make it look like she came upon it accidentally. A girl who has the raw, unvarnished—I won't say character, call it amoral strength of nerve—to then lock herself up in a survival bunker for days on end in order to simulate a case of blind, unreasoning panic. Given the size of the human population, probably there are hundreds, even thousands of them out there. But Linda Weldon is not one of them."

"I would point out that, in order for a young girl to carry out the scheme you have just described successfully, she would have to be able to play the *part* of someone incapable of doing all that. I would also suggest that, for anyone with the internal resources required successfully to carry out so elaborate a scheme, playing the part of a hapless and guileless child for a few hours—or days, or longer—would be by far the easiest part of the job. I must insist that you hold her."

"We will," said Hannah, *at least so long as there's an embassy to hold her in.* "I grant the point you are making, and we will not be casual about checking her story. But she didn't do it."

"I'm inclined to agree with all of that," said Stabmacher as he came in, trailing Jamie behind him. Stabmacher had changed out of his suit and into a set of shipboard overalls. A holstered sidearm dangled from a utility belt that sprouted half a dozen other equipment pouches. There was nothing costumelike or dress-up about any of it. He had been a diplomat a few hours ago. Now he was a field commander, ready for action.

The humans in the room stood up for him, and the Kendari shifted to a pose of equivalent deference.

After the morning's adventures, it would be a long time before Hannah would hesitate about granting him that small sign of respect. "Be seated, everyone," he said as he took his own seat. "She's not going anywhere, except with us, in a few hours' time."

"That might be a problem," said Brox. "We are both instructed to evacuate 'all and only accredited' personnel. The Vixa are likely looking for excuses to cause even more trouble. They would be within their rights to stop and search the outbound embassy ships—and I expect they will exercise that right and take full advantage of any anomalies they might find."

"We'll solve it," said Stabmacher curtly. "We have a great deal more to deal with. I want to start with why *you're* being kicked off the planet. When we left the meeting, you seemed to be in a position of high favor."

"That changed the moment your party departed," Flexdal replied. "Kragshmal, our not-so-nameless Preeminent Director, instantly and very grandly awarded us the Pentam System—subject to Vixan basing rights and Vixan rights of passage through all Kendari-controlled star systems, indemnities to be paid in recompense for Vixan expenses incurred during the negotiations—and, as the climax of their demands, they insisted on our, in effect, paying one of the planets to them as a fee. All of it ignored the terms and agreements and procedures that we had worked out long ago. The conditions of what Kragshmal proposed would essentially turn the Kendari into a Vixan dependency or, at best, a Vixa client state.

"When I pointed this problem out, and declined the offer as politely as I could, and suggested that we revert to the previously agreed framework, he accused me of deliberately wrecking the negotiations and of conspiring with humans to insult the grandeur of the

Vixa. He demanded that I accept his proposal then and there, without any modifications. I pointed out that there was not so much as a written text to consult, and that I could not agree to something I could not even read. Then—well, it went on in the same vein, but not for long. We very quickly reached a situation nearly as acrimonious as the one you faced, and we too departed—though we managed without the gunfire," Flexdal added drily, looking at Hannah and Jamie.

"*We* couldn't have managed without it," said Stabmacher. "I don't know if the simulants were trying to pull us out of the aircar, or board it themselves, or simply trying to force us to a violent response, but it doesn't matter now. The short form is that the Vixa imposed impossible conditions on us—and then on you. Our refusals serve as the pretext for breaking off negotiations and ejecting us from the planet. The negotiations grind to a halt. And yet neither of us can simply abandon the Pentam issue. It has to be resolved before much else of importance can be done. Therefore your people and mine have no alternative but to restart the negotiations about the negotiations that we thought we had resolved."

"And so the Vixa get what they want," said Flexdal. "A Pentam System that remains vacant for that much longer, which improves their odds of scooping it up for themselves in the end—and meanwhile they grind our muzzles into each other's throats, goading us on to fight."

"Your imagery is—vivid, Xenologist Flexdal," said Stabmacher. "And I believe your summing-up is accurate. But I was brought in to hear something else." He turned to Brox. "Forgive me, Inquirist Brox, for saying this—but the sudden ejection of both our embassies makes the question of who killed Emelza 401 suddenly seem almost academic. We will pursue the investigation with vigor, of course—but her murder was a crisis because it could wreck the negotiations—and now the negotiations are wrecked in any event, through unrelated causes. We will have to suspend the investigation until the evacuation is complete, and things are more ordered. We will seek justice for the dead—when the demands of the living permit us the time. We simply do not have that time now, with the evacuation deadline hours away."

"I had foreseen that the changed circumstances might have the effects you have described, Ambassador Stabmacher," said Brox. "I regret the necessity of suspending the investigation, but I appreciate the courtesy and frankness with which you express the situation. Your words are both comforting and upsetting," said Brox.

"And they're also flat wrong," said Zhen Chi. "From beginning to end."

"What!" Stabmacher looked stunned, and every face around the table looked at Zhen Chi in some degree of shock and surprise. "What, exactly, are you accusing me of, Doctor?"

"Forgive me, sir, I did not mean to accuse you of anything. I'm just tired, and strung-out. I think my tactfulness circuit shut down. What I should have said, more respectfully, is that your assumptions are, in fact, quite faulty. Technist Remdex will confirm that."

Remdex, far from happy about being put on the spot, made a gesture of reluctant assent. "I agree must," he said in his sketchy Lesser Trade. "With respect."

"And what, of my assumptions, might be at fault?"

"That the death—the murder—of Emelza 401—is

no longer relevant," said Zhen Chi, "and that it is unrelated to the incidents of today. I, at least, believe that
is absolutely central to the current crisis. I further believe that it is urgent that the case be resolved at once,
even if it means missing the evacuation deadline."

"How is this so? How could it be so, when the Vixa
have sent a clarifying message in the last few minutes?
You might not have received your copy yet, Xenologist
Flexdal, but I expect you will. We are informed that if
the *Kofi Annan* is still on the ground after the evacuation deadline, she will be declared an enemy vessel.
Precision-aimed bursts will target the ground coordinates of the embassy ships immediately after the deadline, whether they are there or not—just to keep us
moving along. We are assured that, if the *Kofi Annan*
departs on time, she will not be molested. I'm sure that
is a great comfort to us all. Are you still willing to risk
missing departure, and put all our lives in grave peril,
in order to solve this one murder?"

Zhen Chi nodded expressionlessly. "If, as I believe,
the missions of this embassy—to represent humanity,
to defend the interests of humanity, and to defend the
honor of our race—are in fact more important than
the embassy itself, then yes. And if that mission is not
of greater value than all our lives, we might as well
give up now."

"I see," said the ambassador, working to hold his
temper. "You view the stakes as being rather high. All
I am aware of is that you found some sort of evidence."

"Urgent, vital evidence."

"If it is urgent, then please present it at once."

"We will. At the suggestion of Special Agents
Wolfson and Mendez—and I have to say, we weren't
thrilled to get the suggestion—we went a little past

Remdex's earlier analysis of the coffee mug found at the scene, and my analysis of the chip broken off it. Remdex had merely confirmed that the cup contained a residue of caffeine, and that the interior surface area of my chip was really too small to get anything more reliable than a confirmation that caffeine was present.

"The central thing that the BSI agents had us do was get swab samples from this collection"—she tapped the box—"of beverage containers that had been used by the various members of the human embassy staff. We were also provided with video imagery that confirmed that the containers had been used—and what had gone into them."

Zhen Chi looked around the table, and raised one eyebrow. "One of our key findings was that humans are a bunch of slobs. The exteriors of the mugs from the human embassy were covered with all sorts of residues and compounds, covered with fingerprints, handprints, lip prints, and so on, along with drips and dribbles of residue of the contents. The crime scene mug had no exterior prints or marks at all, not even glove marks. Indeed, it almost seemed as if its exterior surface—and the interior surface, for that matter—had been lightly etched by some sort of strong acid or solvent. The samples we took from its interior surfaces confirm that the mug had held caffeine. It might be more accurate to say the mug had been *saturated* with chemically pure caffeine dissolved in distilled water—and *nothing else*.

"None of the other mugs we compared to it were even remotely similar. They contained all sorts of things—many of which I had to help Remdex identify, as Kendari just don't ever deal with them. Esters and sugars and suspended milk solids, saliva residue, bits of tea leaf, tiny bits of ground coffee—the list goes on.

"But there's more. Extrapolating from the residue, the crime scene mug originally contained, at a minimum, *ninety times as much caffeine* as the next strongest sample. The contents of that cup would likely be a sufficient dose to kill a human, if taken all at once."

"Caffeine can kill a *human*?" asked Xenologist Flexdal.

"Enough of practically anything can kill you," Jamie said. "You can die from drinking too much water."

"And it gets better. Also at the suggestion of Agents Wolfson and Mendez, we did a quick-and-dirty measure of the ratio of isotopes of carbon 14, carbon 13, and carbon 12. I'll skip a lot of details, but due to variation in how the parent stars form, the local intensity of gamma rays, and a bunch of other factors, the ratio of isotopes of a given element vary by star system, or sometimes by planet. Take the carbon from anything on Earth, and do a ratio check, and the result will be different from the ratio found on Center, or Reqwar, or Kendal, and so on.

"The basic fact is this: The results from the crime scene sample are totally different from all the other samples—and all the other samples we ran break down into three groups. One group matches the isotope ratio for Earth. Another matches Center. Another matches Cinder. And we're talking precise, three-decimal-place precision. As individual as fingerprints. It just so happens that those are the three planets where coffee and tea are grown for export."

Zhen Chi paused, and looked around the room. "However, the crime scene mug's caffeine sample has carbon-isotope ratios that *precisely* match those of standard samples taken on Tifinda. The caffeine had to have come from Tifinda, and not from any supply brought in from Earth, or any other human- or Kendari-inhabited world."

"You realize what you're saying?" Stabmacher asked.

"Yes, sir," said Zhen Chi. "Suddenly the Vixa are the prime suspects in the case."

Brox pounded both his fists into the table. They could hear his feet stamping against the floor and his tail lashed wildly. "The Vixa did it?" he demanded. "They engineered all this?"

"Yes, Inquirist Brox. A Vixan committed this crime."

Jamie grunted and reached for his investigative notebook. "That reminds me of something. I jotted it down after I heard it, because it really struck me. Where is it?" He flipped back several pages. "Here we go. It's something the Grand Vixa Zeeraum said during our first little get-together. 'Strange idea, crime. Only for individual-centered species. Vixa have no crime. We have no problems.'" Jamie looked again at his notes, and frowned at them, as if he had seen something else, something that worried him.

"Zeeraum was right," said Zhen Chi. "If you define crime as an act by one or more individuals against the state, then you need to have individuals. They don't. They rule by the consensus of the hierarchy. Everyone down below does what they're told to do by those up above. Everything is done by the group as a whole."

"In other words, there is no crime in the Vixan *state*," said Stabmacher, "but the Vixan state can commit crimes against others. And it has. The Vixa, collectively, committed this crime."

"Yes," said Zhen Chi. "Unless you can tell me why a human or a Kendari would go get chemically pure caffeine from a Vixan chemical lab, then use it as planted evidence by pouring it in a human coffee mug, we must conclude that a Vixan—check that, a Vixan being ultimately acting on behalf of the Preeminent Director—did this thing."

"But—why?" Remdex asked. "What could they hope to gain by killing one of our people?"

Brox spoke, visibly struggling to regain control, act calmly, professionally. "The simplest explanation is that the Vixa have been trying from the first day to instigate a war between humans and Kendari—let us wipe each other out, and the Elder Races wouldn't have to bother with us anymore. I don't know Elder Race law well, but I believe that, with the official recognized claimants out of the way—in other words, if humans and Kendari exterminated each other in a war—there wouldn't be anything to prevent the Vixa claiming the Pentam System. That's quite a fine motive. A star system with two habitable worlds would be a prize for us. Why shouldn't it be one for them?"

"And so, one fine day not so long ago," said Jamie, "one Vixan looked at another and asked, what do you have to *do* to start a war between the damned Younger Races? *Kill* someone? And they liked that idea. They had learned through the simulants that humans—at least most of the humans at this embassy, anyway—were walking caffeine sponges. They learned caffeine could kill Kendari. The plan for causing trouble was obvious. But then they didn't sweat the *details* of how to stage the murder, or how to administer the caffeine, or how to conceal it or what it should look like. Why bother? The Younger Races are primitive, unadvanced, their cultures far less developed, far more chaotic than Vixan civilization. The Vixa got sloppy— and they still nearly got away with it."

"So they killed Emelza, then were ready and willing to 'assist' the investigation in any way," said Brox. "They were probably delighted when we requested a human investigator. They assumed a human would refuse to blame a human for the murder, and that we Kendari would be sure it was a human."

"One diplomatic incident is not enough to start a war," Stabmacher objected.

"But it was a part of the whole—and a big part," said Brox. "Plus the huge effort they made to be 'helpful' after the murder was a way of showing the other Elder Races how reasonable, how generous they were being. But my guess is that the whole intent of the Pentam negotiations was to get us fighting. Who was actually granted the use of the star system was incidental to them. What would it matter, when they expected both species to be extinct in a few decades at most—and perhaps much sooner? The Vixa could just engineer the start of the war, sit back, and watch us destroy ourselves—while perhaps arranging some sort of covert support for whatever side was losing at any given time. The longer they kept the fight going, the more even the match was, the weaker both sides would become."

"And it would be a mistake to look only to the Pentam negotiations, or only to the Vixa, for evidence that many of the Elder Races have no great desire to see us get along," said Flexdal.

"That's bordering on pure paranoia," Zhen Chi objected.

"Doesn't mean they're not out to get us," said Jamie.

"Let us stay focused!" said Stabmacher. "Technist Remdex, Zhen Chi—how certain of your data are you? How solid is the evidence?"

Zhen Chi gestured for Remdex to speak first. *Is she deferring to his expertise, or letting him stick his neck out first?* Hannah wondered.

"It definitive," he said. "It certain as anything can be. Crime scene mug contained pure caffeine in solution, not caffeine-based drink from humans. Caffeine in question chemically pure, and from on this planet."

"I concur," said Zhen Chi, and left it at that.

Stabmacher turned to Hannah. "Are these the results you expected, or were hoping for, when you had the medical personnel do the tests?"

"Simply put, yes."

"What made you think of it? What pointed at the Vixa?"

Hannah gestured toward the door of the conference room and the crime scene area out in the main ops room. "The spills on the carpet and the floor around the cup were whitish, and not dark brown or black."

"And that's *it*?" Stabmacher said.

"Every human at this embassy knows what a coffee spill looks like—and I'll bet that every Kendari in their embassy has been trained to recognize drinks with caffeine, and their residue."

"Oh yes," said Remdex. "They get training. Every sixty-four days. They no enjoy it, but they get it."

"So neither a human nor a Kendari was likely to make that mistake of leaving a whitish residue. And that only left the Vixa."

"A very slender reed, Special Agent Wolfson."

"Yes, sir. I agree. That's why I collected that boxful of cups and mugs and asked them to run the tests. But I did have something else. Not much, but something. I noticed that the writing on the bottom of the crime scene mug was faded. I wanted to know how that might happen. I took five fresh BSI coffee mugs, and wrote MILK on the bottom of each one, and numbered them for future reference, using the same type of marker Milkowski said that he had used.

"I washed all of them five times in the Snack Shack's auto dishwasher. Then I pulled one of them and washed the rest five times, and so on, until I got up to twenty washes on the last cup. None of the lettering on any of the cups was even slightly faded, and the finish on the mugs was identical to ones fresh out of the box."

"Very thorough tests, and I hope Senor Vargas doesn't mind so much about your abusing his equipment, now that it must be abandoned. But what of it?"

"The word MILK on the crime scene mug was badly faded and partially worn away—and the exterior of the mug looked slightly abraded, almost as if it had been sanded or scoured. What all that told me was that the mug had been exposed to some very strong acids or solvents. We'd seen Zeeraum having a bite to eat, so we knew what the Vixa digestive cavity was like. We'd noticed the slight, odd, potbelly on the human simulants—and it was hard to miss that Brox's simulant had a little bit of a hump on its back. But I think what Jamie put together was the key."

"And what was that?" Stabmacher asked, turning to Jamie.

"We got to be pretty sure that the simulants—at least the one that imitated humans—were actually highly modified variants of the escort Sixes. When I blew what I thought was the head off one back at the government dome, when I thought they were trying to grab at us, I saw something else that didn't really register until I thought about it later. Something sharp peeking from the sleeve of a simulant's arm when it was trying to grab for me.

"And I remembered that Zamprohna just folded up and passed out seconds after another of the simulants got their hands on him. He hit his head on the deck, and I thought that accounted for it. But that was pretty dumb of me. No one outside of old movies gets knocked out cold from a little bump on the head like that. And when he woke up, he was very groggy, disoriented. Almost like he was drunk. When I searched him, the back of his head wasn't sensitive to touch at all—but the ankle that the simulant grabbed at was red and inflamed."

The room was silent as everyone worked out the implications of that. "Those simulants, the human simulants, have stingers," Jamie said. "Stingers that were envenomed with some sort of fast-acting stuff formulated to knock humans out. They were coming after us to knock us out and drag us back. One of them managed to sting Zamprohna. That's why the simulants were chasing us and not the regular guard Vixa that had, after all, threatened the ambassador. *Their* stings would have killed us, and they weren't quite ready to risk that. And then I read the transcript of Hannah's interview with Milkowski. He described a small bruise or bump at the back of Emelza's neck. A little red mark less than a centimeter across."

"And if the human simulants had stingers, why not my Kendari simulant?" asked Brox.

"Exactly," said Hannah.

"But Emelza wasn't stung to death," Remdex objected.

"Most species on Earth that hunt for food with stingers don't actually use their venom to kill," said Zhen Chi. "They use it to paralyze their prey. Special Agents Mendez and Wolfson witnessed Zeeraum doing just that on their first day here—though they weren't aware of it at the time."

"I see it—or nearly see it," said Stabmacher. "Walk me through it."

"Brox's simulant," said Hannah. "That's who—or more accurately what—was used to do it. But Brox's simulant was either being directly controlled in real time, or executing a set of preprogrammed instructions. The simulant itself was the weapon, not the killer. The simulants have slightly more independent thought and free will, volition, than this table," Hannah said, patting its steel surface, "but not by much."

"Go on," said Flexdal.

"It would have been dead easy for Brox's simulant to get access to the joint operations center. It either goes in tagging along behind someone, or uses some sort of Vixan hardware to defeat the door security— the simulants apparently jammed some of our systems just by being present. They could easily have some means of manipulating them. Most likely the sim just keys in a combination it has seen already. It comes up behind Emelza. Maybe it relies on its resemblance to Brox in order to let it get close—or maybe Emelza was so used to the simulant by then that she recognized it for what it was but didn't pay it any attention.

"It stings her with a paralyzing agent that disperses so quickly that it didn't show up in the postmortem toxicology. Then it pulls the coffee mug and a container of dissolved caffeine from where it had concealed them, in its digestive chamber. Possibly it has been carrying them around for several hours, or even days, waiting for its chance. It would have been absurdly easy for one of the human simulants—probably Milkowski's—to steal Milkowski's mug and pass it to Brox's simulant. Brox's simulant pours some of the caffeine into the cup, forces it into Emelza's mouth, then drops the cup to the floor, either breaking it accidentally, or deliberately trying to do so. In any event, that drop spills the contents and breaks the cup. And the deed is done."

"The only really surprising thing is that Milkowski's mug survived at all in a Vixan digestive chamber," said Jamie.

"The chamber isn't always filled with digestive fluid," said Zhen Chi. "Probably it wasn't there for long, or with the chamber full. Besides, ceramics are very resistant to most acids and solvents."

"So even that isn't surprising," said Jamie. "And then, of course, the ever-helpful Vixa dispatched Brox to Center—accompanied by my unimprinted simulant—*and* Brox's simulant. The killer rode all the way to the Center System and back with the Kendari Inquirist tasked with *finding* the killer. I'll bet that appealed to the Vixan sense of humor."

Hannah turned, and looked at Brox. His tail was lashing furiously, the finger-claws on both hands were extended—but his face was calm, unreadable. Even as she watched, he got himself more fully back under control. But that did not mean the rage was gone. She was feeling a pretty fair share of that rage herself.

She looked around the room and suddenly realized that something was happening. Something important, that all of them were too busy to notice. The meeting had turned into a council of war, a consultation between allies—or at least, temporary cobelligerents of convenience. Whatever else the Vixa had accomplished, they had managed to get the Kendari and the humans on the same side in the fight that neither Younger Race had even known was going on until the Vixa got careless.

"That's all theory," Stabmacher said. "It is convincing. It holds together. But do you have any proof? Any evidence?"

"There is the abrasion to the coffee mug," said Hannah. "And, of course, the sting injury sustained by Emelza. It was so faint, and the body so altered by the time we examined it, that all of us missed it—but a close examination ought to reveal it. Remdex wasn't searching for neurotoxin residue in the samples he took from Emelza's body. I very much would suggest that he do so now. And we should be able to do the same sort of carbon isotope match on the caffeine residue taken from the scene, and from the victim's body."

"That's still not much," said Stabmacher.

"We're not going into a court of law, sir," said Jamie.

"Agreed. We're dealing with something much bigger than that—our relations with one of the most powerful Elder Races—and with all the other Elder Races as well. If we make an accusation against the Vixa, it must be convincing. Convincing enough that it will stand up against Vixan denials. It must be utterly solid, indisputable."

"We have the evidence we have, sir," said Hannah. "Considering the situation, I'd have to say we've done pretty well."

"Agreed. No question at all about that—but that doesn't solve my problem."

"One thing might," said Zhen Chi. "Having a little chat with Brox's simulant. It's not all that smart, all on its own. If we could cut it off from its links to its base, isolate it somehow, and keep it from dropping into rag-doll mode, maybe we could question it, get something out of it."

"I'm afraid that is no longer possible," said Brox. It was the first time he had spoken in a while, and his voice was not altogether steady.

"Why not?" Flexdal asked.

"Because," he said, "I destroyed my simulant earlier today, as soon as we returned from the government dome."

TWENTY-TWO

DISSECTION

"Back at the conference dome, we saw your simulants quite literally turning on you," said Brox. "They chased you out of the inner conference dome. We could see them continuing to pursue you. Our driver witnessed their pursuit as you made your way to your aircar, and described it to us. We even overflew the bodies of the two simulants Special Agents Mendez and Wolfson destroyed. Kragshmal started threatening us, as well—and as we have observed, the simulants don't act on their own. I recommended to Xenologist Flexdal that I destroy my simulant at once before it could be turned on us."

"And I concurred, very strongly," said Flexdal. "Perhaps I would have done otherwise if I had known the simulant was the, ah, weapon used in the attack, but perhaps not. I couldn't leave the thing running around loose where it could attack my people."

"I must admit that I am quite pleased to have destroyed it," said Brox, "but I am also glad I destroyed it *before* hearing what we all just heard. I can know, and all of you can know, that I acted out of duty, not for personal reasons."

"But it is—unfortunate—that we have lost a potential source of evidence," said Stabmacher.

"I am not sure that we have," said Jamie. "No offense, Zhen Chi, but I don't think we could have gotten the simulant to talk before the evac deadline—and

I don't think our Kendari friends would have wanted to bring it along to question on your ship after we left—and I don't think the Vixa would have allowed that anyway."

"It might be things aren't as bad as we think. Maybe our medical and investigative specialists can get more from a dead simulant than a live one," said Hannah. "We should examine it. And we should do it now—before anything else can happen."

"I shot it in the far corner of our compound," said Brox. "The body is still there."

"Ambassador Stabmacher?" Hannah asked. "Xenologist Flexdal? Permission granted?"

"Most certainly," said Flexdal.

"Make it fast," said Stabmacher. "But go get us what we need."

Brox stood guard, weapon in hand, ready if the corpse should suddenly come to life—not altogether unlikely, considering that the simulant was in large part robotic. Jamie set one video camera on a tripod to get an overall view of the scene, and moved in and around getting close-up views with a handheld camera. Remdex and Zhen Chi performed what amounted to a field dissection, emphasizing speed over precise technique. They all wore protective clothing, gloves, face masks, and eye protection. No telling what toxins or acids or solvents might come spewing out at any moment.

And they all watched the clock.

"I gotta say, that was some nice shooting, Brox," said Jamie, looking over the corpse. "I wasn't thinking. I went for the phony head. You went right for the thorax. Were you aiming for the braincase, or did you just get lucky?"

"A little of both," Brox said. "There was a lot of guessing involved as to where it would be on a Vixan body that was this severely modified, but apparently I guessed right. And I might add that I had the benefit of your experience to guide me—and I was not shooting in the midst of a near-riot situation. You did quite well yourself."

"Well, we're both still alive," said Jamie. "That must show something."

Remdex and Zhen Chi were working fast to strip off the false Kendari skin that hid the half creature, half machine underneath. It was a grisly job, but Zhen Chi seemed to be pursuing it with real enthusiasm and was gloating over every new tidbit of information they gleaned on the subject of how to build a simulant. It was startling to see how much of the simulant hadn't really been there at all, how much the creature inside had relied on artificial structure, how much of its interior was given over to electronics of one sort or another.

"Don't get too involved in detail work," Hannah warned. "We've got to hurry."

"I know, I know," said Zhen Chi. "But we might have another murder to deal with if Dr. Subramanian finds out we had a chance at these electronics boxes and didn't grab them." She looked over at Remdex. "I could cut out those two fast. One for you and one for me?"

"Our investigative technists would also be very interested. Yes, please."

Zhen Chi used a cutting laser and sliced the two boxes out of the corpse. Something arced and sparked as the beam sliced through a cable.

"Careful!" Jamie called out. "The simulant is dead, but there are still lots of live power sources."

"Now he tells us," said Zhen Chi, calmly extracting her prizes. She handed them to Remdex. "We'll split these up later," she said.

Hannah checked the time again and swore. "Zhen Chi! The digestive chamber!"

"All right, all right. We've been working toward it. We have to do this with at least some degree of order if we're going to make sense of it later." She stood well back from the half-dissected body. "I wanted to get some information about the rest of the body before I sliced that thing open. From what we can tell, there must be some hellacious acids in those chambers. The stuff might just slosh out and dissolve half of what's left of the body."

"Or us," said Jamie. "Everybody back, and watch out for fumes as well."

Zhen Chi adjusted the cutting laser. She lifted it to her shoulder like a rifle and sighted down its length. "A little off the top," she said, and fired. The beam lanced out and sizzled into the top of the chamber. The flesh twitched and drew back, either simply shriveling in the heat or through some sort of creepy postmortem reaction. Zhen Chi kept firing, moving the beam slowly across the top of the chamber. Suddenly a plume of greenish gas jetted up, and an unpleasantly familiar smell of rotting meat filled the air. A nasty-looking fluid dribbled out, and whatever it dripped onto immediately started fizzing and spitting.

Remdex was ready with a long pole with a hook on the end. He eased it into the hole Zhen Chi had cut, and pulled hard.

The digestive chamber came apart with a crack. Remdex reached in again with his pole—ignoring the plume of smoke rising from the pole itself—and pulled out what looked like a sealed package of some sort. He dragged it over away from the ruined body of the simulant. "Water," he said. "Clean it up."

Brox slung his weapon, trotted away, and came back moments later dragging a flexible hose behind him. A jet of water played on the package. Remdex made sure it had a good long soak, then used a surgical knife to slice it open.

Inside was a Kendari sidearm, the twin of the one Brox was carrying, along with two packs of ammunition for it.

"Well, they weren't done with us yet," said Jamie. "I wonder how many of us would have had Kendari bullets in our guts? How many would they have left alive? They'd need a *few* of us still around to investigate."

"Get some good shots of this, Jamie," said Hannah. "I think we have proof enough to make the ambassador happy."

Except, of course, that the ambassador was going to lose his embassy in another two hours. Even if they got out of this alive, it was possible that nothing would ever make him happy, ever again.

TWENTY-THREE

DEADLINE

They stripped off their protective clothing and left it all next to the eviscerated simulant corpse. No time left to clean anything up, and no point in dragging all over both compounds whatever acids or solvents or toxins that had splashed around. After a hurried discussion, it was agreed that the humans would take the protective package that had been around the Kendari sidearm, plus one pack of the ammo. The Kendari would take the gun itself, and a sample swatch of the material that made up the package. It took a few minutes they couldn't really spare to photograph everything in detail and get their prizes into evidence bags, but everyone was very aware of the clock, and they got it done in good time.

Brox escorted the humans back through the Kendari-side doors and into the joint ops center. Milkowski, Farrell, and Singh were all there, very obviously back on duty, very obviously frantically busy. Milkowski was bellowing in Lesser Trade to whoever was on the other side of the phone. The two younger agents were running through some sort of security checklist. Zhen Chi instantly made a beeline to the human-side doors. Hannah was about to follow her when Jamie pulled her to one side. "Listen," he said. "We might have a problem. I don't know if we will or not—but if we do, we have to decide what to do about it."

"Here? Now? Jamie, there's a lot to do before we get on that ship."

"That's the point, Hannah. I'm not so sure we're *going* to get on that ship."

Milkowski was on a new call, shouting in English, by the time they finished talking. "Yes!" he yelled. "For real. Right now. Yes, the whole embassy staff. No, ma'am. We're not in control, ma'am. If we were, we'd say yes to all the kids." He covered the phone and nodded to Hannah. "Hold it a sec!"

Milkowski listened at the phone, and rolled his eyes, and spoke again, his hand still covering the mike. "If we were in charge, we wouldn't have allowed anyone to bring kids to this madhouse in the first place. No, *we're* not endangering them. *You* took care of that when you brought them here." He took his hand off the mike and forced his voice into a more soothing tone. "Of course you do, ma'am. Yes. No, we can't. Because we can't. Believe me, the ambassador stretched every rule as hard as he could to swing the interns. Ma'am, my hand to God, we would take the younger kids if we could. But if the Vixa board the ship once she's in space—which they have the right to do, and they have the firepower to back up the right—if they board, and find someone whose name *isn't* on the list—well, ma'am, that might cost the lives of everyone on board. We have no choice but to play by their rules. Ma'am. Ma'am! Please! I'm sorry. I have to go. The clock is running, and I have other people I must contact. It is your decision—but the ship can't wait. Have—damn, which name is this"—he checked a list on his desk—"Marlana—have Marlana at the pickup point in by 2050 hours—not a split second later. If she's there, we'll take her. If she's not—we won't wait. We *can't*. I'm sorry, ma'am. I'm sorry. I have to go. Good-bye."

He slammed down the receiver, cursing with rage and frustration. "Damn fool!" he shouted at the phone. "If you're so worried about your child's safety, don't bring her to a place that's likely to become a hostage-taker's swap meet." He looked up at Hannah. "Ambassador managed to get that Weldon kid on the evac list. She worked at the embassy as an intern, and somehow he got them to concede that was official status enough to qualify as 'all and only' embassy personnel—and *then* he stretched the point even harder, and got the other five kids who did intern work. Now I have three more idiot parents of smart kids to contact and explain the situation to them."

"What's the pickup point?" Hannah asked. "Is that job covered—or do you need us for it?"

"Zamprohna volunteered. The pickup point is back in the human residential compounds. He's the right man for the job. He knows the area, and he's got a vehicle. He's whacked-out politically—but, well you saw how he was about his *own* kid. He knows the way there and back. He'll do it right. But two things. One—thank you. You got me off the charge."

"No one got you off anything. You didn't do it," said Hannah.

"That wouldn't really matter to *some* agents I could mention. Including me, maybe. You played fair. So fair it hurt. So fair everyone's going to have faith in the result. No gossip. No speculation. Believe me, that helps a guy like me a lot. Second thing. This, ah, evac list. You two have got a situation. Go see the ambassador. Now. He's in the conference room."

* * *

"There's damned little I can do," said Stabmacher. "In fact, absolutely nothing. Less than nothing. I stretched the loopholes as far as I could to add the interns to the evac list. We physically have room for you on board the *Kofi Annan*. But you're not on the list. Officially speaking, you don't now and never have worked for the embassy. The Vixan I spoke with had a particular phrase that he kept using."

Jamie shut his eyes, and could see the words from his notepad, clear as day. "We agreed when we got here that we were 'controlled by a superior, external hierarchy.'"

"That's correct. In other words, the setup was that you weren't under me, so I couldn't interfere with your investigation. Quite proper. Correct procedure. But the Vixa are using it as *their* loophole. The Stanlarr and the Reqwar have both agreed to post observers in and around the human residential compound. That ought to be enough protection for run-of-the-mill civilians. At least I pray to God it is. But you two—"

Jamie swallowed hard and nodded. "We shot up one of their domes, probably humiliated the Preeminent Director, blasted two simulants into scrap metal and dead meat, then helped dissect a third sim—though they don't know about that last one yet. I think."

"An excellent summing-up," said the ambassador. "And I thank you for all of your service. But if you go aboard our ship, they will regard that as canceling all rights of passage. They'll declare us an enemy vessel. And their navy is quite good. They made it quite clear that if I pushed any harder for *you* to come along, they'd cancel the clearance for the interns—and maybe

for the whole embassy staff. They're playing rough."
The ambassador looked exhausted, half-slumped-over
in his seat, the table in front of him buried in a chaos
of papers and datapads. But he made the effort to sit
up straighter, and look them both in the eye. "I said
there's nothing I can do. But that's not true. I can break
the rules. This embassy owes you. The *human race*
owes you. So to hell with the Vixa. We take you along
and smuggle you past their searches, somehow. No
pack of murderous thugs can tell me to leave the two
of you behind."

"No, sir," said Hannah. "But *we* can tell you that.
And we are. Jamie—Special Agent Mendez and I—
have talked it over. Our job—one of our jobs—is to
protect others. We can't do that if our mere presence
endangers everyone else. We stay off the ship. Besides,
there's a job that needs doing. One that we can do best
from here, in the joint ops center. One that I think
you'll approve of. In fact, it will *require* your approval,
and Xenologist Remdex's okay as well. We think we
can work it so we're safe—more or less—in the joint
ops center. Once the job is done, we'll wait for the
right moment, and run like hell for the Reqwar Pavlat
embassy, or call them for a dustoff and pickup. They
owe us some favors."

"They seemed to think the same thing," said the
ambassador. "When I contacted them asking for help
regarding the human civilians, I happened to mention
you by name while explaining the situation. Apparently you know the, ah, chief executive of one of
their planets?"

"You could say that we, ah, got him the job, sir,"
said Jamie.

"That's what *they* said, too," Stabmacher agreed. "I
didn't quite know what to make of it. For what it's

worth—and it may be worth quite a lot—you've both been granted full Reqwar Pavlat citizenship, as well as citizenship on the Pavlat home world, effective as of about thirty seconds ago. If you do choose to stay, they'll do all in their power to protect you—but that might not be enough."

"We'll take the chance," said Jamie. "We've been in tight spots before. We'll manage."

"I'm starting to believe that," Stabmacher said. "But what's this task you want to do?"

"It's pretty simple," said Jamie. "BSI agents have to do a lot of cop work, of course. Some times we have to edge over into your territory—diplomacy. We're thinking of branching out into a whole new area."

"And what would that be?" Stabmacher asked.

Jamie smiled, and gestured toward Hannah. "Hannah and I are going to hang out our shingle on the joint ops center," he said. "We're going to see about practicing a little freelance interstellar law."

TWENTY-FOUR

DEPARTURE

The last thing the embassy staff needed was the well-intentioned but fumbling help of two outsiders who hadn't ever been through an evac drill.

Hannah and Jamie were unwillingly passive observers, shoved to one side once it came down to the crunch. They watched the show from the same bench in front of the main embassy building that they had used on their first night there.

The compound was a mess. Paper blew everywhere. Puddles of cold ash were kicked up by the wind and then thrown down again. Heaps of clothes, abandoned suitcases, books, tools, equipment, supplies were scattered everywhere. Doors were left wide open. A window or two had been smashed in order to save time moving large and bulky objects. The flowers and plants in Zhen Chi's garden were simply gone, with nothing left but heaped-up piles of dirt. Perhaps she had hustled them on board the *Kofi Annan*. Perhaps there was some regulation that required the garden to be destroyed during an evacuation. Perhaps she was just determined to leave nothing behind that might be sullied by the Vixa.

For some reason, one of the tables from the Snack Shack had been dragged outdoors along with four chairs. Four full place settings were arranged on it—including, somewhat incongruously, four BSI coffee mugs identical to the one at the crime scene. It looked as if someone had intended to have one last civilized meal before departure. But that meal was never going to happen.

There were shouts, crashes, and thuds coming from everywhere, then nowhere. The whole place would mysteriously go silent, then abruptly erupt in noise all over again.

People had been rushing in and out of the ship's main hatch, but it was getting to the point where most of the traffic was one-way, into the ship.

Just minutes before the takeoff deadline, the main embassy gates swung open, and a large manually operated groundcar came roaring up. Tancredo Zamprohna was driving, and driving fast. He slammed on the brakes and came to a screeching halt five meters from the main building. He was out of the car before it stopped moving, and immediately set to work hustling a gaggle of bewildered, tearful, frightened teenagers into the *Kofi Annan*. He saw them to the main hatch.

Jamie and Hannah watched as he hugged his daughter good-bye. "Weird to see a guy with ideas as wrong as his work so hard to do the right thing," said Jamie.

"Yeah, well he's only human," said Hannah. "And I don't feel right sitting here watching his good-byes to his daughter. Especially with this camera helmet strapped to my head. It feels downright creepy to be recording this."

"We've got to get it all," said Jamie, reaching up to touch the helmet-cam rig he was wearing. "So everyone else can see it later."

"Some plans sound better than they turn out to be," said Hannah. "I'm starting to think this wasn't our best idea."

Milkowski had come up to Zamprohna, and the

two of them were arguing. Jamie probably could have fiddled with the camera's microphones, and heard what they were saying, but it wasn't really necessary. The gestures and hand-waving, and the snatches of speech that he did manage to hear, told it all. Zamprohna wanted to stay in the compound and see the ship off. Milkowski told him that was a good way to get himself killed or hurt—and probably the last thing that the human civilians who were being left behind needed to deal with was a badly wounded man.

The wind shifted, just for a moment, and Jamie could hear Milkowski clearly. "So get the hell out of here. You won't do your daughter any good by staying, you'll be able to watch the liftoff better from farther away—and you'll have less chance of being shot at."

There were times when there was nothing harder to say no to than a perfectly logical and reasonable argument. Jamie could read it on Zamprohna's face. There was no sense to it at all, but it was obvious the man felt he was betraying his daughter by moving a few hundred meters away. Jamie felt for the man. Jamie knew *he* wouldn't have felt right if Milkowski had bullied *him* into abandoning his post. "I'm almost starting to feel glad we're staying," he said.

"You'll change your mind," said Hannah.

"'Almost,' I said." He checked the time. "Twenty minutes to go. Let's not cut it too close, people," he said, addressing the embassy in general.

With obvious vast reluctance, Zamprohna got back into his vehicle, turned it around, and went out the way he had come in.

Milkowski trotted over toward them, and they stood up as he approached. "Time for me to get aboard," he said. "Listen, Zamprohna wanted me to pass the word. There's at least twenty Vixan defender-caste Sixes out there. It looks like they're just waiting around until the deadline passes."

"What will they do then?" Hannah asked.

Milkowski shrugged. "Ask the Sixes when they get here. Zamprohna also said there was a group of about fifty Kendari marching along the road toward here, carrying what looked like portable ramping gear. And before you ask which compound they're headed for, I don't know."

"Great," said Jamie. "Things couldn't be going better."

Milkowski checked the time and swore. "Look, I *have* to go. Thanks. Thanks again. For everything. More than you know. If you're going to change your mind and come along, this is your last chance. I'll hold the hatch as long as I can—but time is running out."

"Thanks, Frank," said Hannah. "But we've made up our minds."

"Right," said Milkowski. "Okay then. Good-bye and good luck to you." He made a tentative step toward the ship, then hesitated.

"What is this—your imitation of Zamprohna's farewell?" Jamie asked. "We're staying. You're going. It's okay—and you have to go *now.*"

Milkowski opened his mouth, as if to say something more, then shrugged again, turned, and trotted for the ship.

The outer doors of the joint ops center boomed open again. The embassy comm techs had been working frantically to set things up to work from there, but Jamie had thought they had already finished up and gone aboard.

Apparently they had—it wasn't the techs. It was Brox. He stepped out of the doors, looked about, and headed directly for them. Jamie poked at Hannah. "Look who's here," he said, and stood up to go over and meet him halfway. "Brox, you've got to get out of here. Your people will be sealing their ship any minute now."

"They already have sealed it," said Brox. "I am remaining here with you. I have many reasons." He started speaking quickly, before they could object or interrupt. "First, I brought you into all this. Honor requires that I see you through it. Second, without your work, I doubt we would have ever known the truth about how Emelza was killed. That is a debt that cannot be repaid—but it must be acknowledged. Third, it seemed sensible to me that a Kendari be part of what you are planning to do. It can only make the impact greater. And fourth, I felt I had to warn you—"

"About the Kendari marching this way right now," said Hannah. "We just got the word, but that's about all we know."

"Then you need to know more. They are part of a group that is roughly as irrational as your Human Supremacy League. The Vixa managed to convince them that you two—not just any human beings, but *you two in particular*—were at least indirectly responsible for Emelza's death."

"I think we've got a pretty good alibi for that one," said Hannah. "Being in the wrong star system and all. Not arriving on planet until she'd been dead half a day."

"Both our species include individuals who will believe what they want to believe," said Brox. "But delusional or not, they *are* coming after the two of you, and I don't believe the Vixan security forces will be very eager to protect you from them."

"No, I don't suppose they will," Hannah agreed.

"But what about the 'all and only' clause?" Hannah asked. "Suppose the Vixa stop your embassy ship and find out you're not aboard."

"Xenologist Flexdal has prepared a multilayered tissue of lies that should provide an adequate defense. He will cling to each as long as he can, then change his story as required," Brox replied. "It was a misunderstanding. There was a translating error. I was left behind inadvertently in the confusion. If need be, to protect the rest of the ship's company, he will inform them that I was unfortunately killed in an accident just before departure."

"And when they find you're still alive at the end of all this?"

"Assuming I am still alive then, we can worry about that problem later. The worst they can do is kill me for real—after our embassy ship is safely out of Vixan space."

Suddenly they heard a sound like the shriek of a badly annoyed dinosaur. "That's our alert siren," said Brox. "Our ship's departure sequence will start in less than a minute. It will involve the use of various pyrotechnic devices, and there might be some flying debris. I would suggest that we move to someplace less exposed."

"Inside the main building, I guess," said Jamie, pointing the way. "If we hunker down inside, we should be safe enough, and we'll be able to look out through the windows—and stick the cameras up there too."

"I was going to suggest that we head to the joint operations center now," said Brox, "but I gather you want to record everything. Very well. Let us go—and hope the explosion debris is well behaved."

They had no sooner gotten inside the main building

when there was a series of sharp reports, hard and fast, that made the floor tremble slightly. Jamie crouched in front of the window, checking the drop-down monitor of his helmet cam to make sure it was getting a good view. There was a series of deeper, more booming explosions—and suddenly the Kendari embassy ship came into view, just over the roof of the joint ops center. It was a big, thick-waisted, unlovely thing, a dull green cucumber shape lumbering up into the sky. But it was a ship. And it was getting away.

Hannah checked her wrist display. "Our turn in about thirty seconds!" she called. "We're closer, so this is going to be hairier." She went up to the window to kneel next to Jamie, not wanting to miss anything—but not wanting her head blown off, either. "In twenty!" she called out. "Get yourself ready, Brox!"

"How would I do that?" he asked. "What would make me ready?"

He's got a point there, Hannah thought. *Or is he actually looking for practical advice?* Sometimes it was hard to tell the difference between Brox being literal-minded and Brox being ironic.

She checked her countdown clock again. Ten seconds to go. She resisted the urge to chant the passing seconds out loud.

The charges around the embassy ship went off right on schedule, with a rapid series of short, sharp explosions that shook the main building. The blasts cut the ship clear of all the connections to the surrounding buildings. Two or three fires started up instantly as the destruct sequencers tripped incendiary charge circuits to destroy all the remaining confidential materials in the outlying buildings. Almost certainly all of the secret documents were gone already, but destroying them twice could do no harm. Two or three fire alarms went pointlessly off.

Hannah and Jamie had been briefed on what would come next. When it had first landed, the embassy ship had been set down in a pit deep enough to bury the propulsion system, so as to bring the main entry hatch down to ground level. Now the ship had to blast free. The buried base of the ship was inside a gigantic protective cylinder, which was in turn surrounded by a ring of empty underground chambers. More shaped charges went off underground, all around the ship, knocking out the supports that held up the cylinder sleeve sections, causing them to collapse outward, freeing the ship. The ground around the ship fell away, dropping the surrounding buildings, and blasting dust and smoke and debris up into the sky. The embassy ship's reactionless thrusters cut in, and the ship began to move, trembling, shuddering, slowly lumbering upward.

Hannah looked up in the sky to see that the Kendari embassy ship was already almost out of sight, boosting gracefully for high orbit. She hoped mightily that they made it.

The human embassy ship broke free of the ground, kicking up a shower of dirt and rocks and debris. It moved upward, painfully slowly, moving at only a meter or two a second. If it had boosted at full power, the field distortions produced by the reactionless thrusters would have scrambled the guts of any living thing in the compound. The ship had to escape slowly in order to keep from frying Jamie, Hannah, and Brox.

Twenty seconds after the launch of the *Kofi Annan,* there was another explosion. The main gate of the compound blasted inward, and a full squad of Vixan defenders was inside almost before the smoke had cleared.

"Just for the record," Hannah yelled, "I think that's a violation of extraterritoriality."

Suddenly, there was a giant whirring, whizzing sound that seemed to be coming from everywhere—and a hard, sharp blast of sound, more felt than heard. The reinforced glass of the windows starred and cracked but it held. The hole in the ground where the *Kofi Annan* had been was suddenly a sheet of flame and smoke and debris thrown upward. The ground shook hard. Bits of the ceiling broke off. The compound was blanketed with dust, and dirt and wreckage thrown up by the blast came rattling down. Something or other smashed into a window elsewhere in the room and managed to punch through with a crash.

Seconds later, the same whirring noise came again, a trifle farther off, and another giant blast, coming from the Kendari compound.

"And that's another violation," Hannah shouted for the benefit of the recording her helmet cam was making. "The Vixa just shelled the prelaunch ground coordinates of the embassy ships."

Giant ramplike things suddenly came over the wall behind the crater where the embassy ship had been. The lower end of the ramps crashed into place, and Kendari started coming over the wall and into the compound.

"Time to get moving," Jamie shouted in Hannah's ear. She nodded and signaled to Brox, pointing toward the joint ops center.

"Draw your weapon," she shouted at Jamie. "We're going to make a run for it. Do *not* fire at any Kendari unless one of them attacks you directly. In that case, fire *only* at your attacker."

"What is this, the etiquette of self-defense?" Jamie shouted back. "I might not be able to be that selective."

"Do your best," Hannah yelled back. "If you want, you can fire over their heads or into the ground or whatever."

"Oh, I'm going to want to," he said. "Very much indeed."

"If it makes you feel any better, the Vixa you can shoot at as much as you like."

"Wrong again," Jamie shouted back. "We don't want them to know we're here, remember? I'm gonna lob smoke grenades between us and them before we leave the building and hope they don't notice us at all."

"Okay. Get ready with the smoke." Jamie immediately started pulling apple-sized grenades out of his pockets and setting them out where he could reach them easily.

Hannah peeked out the window again and checked the situation. The Vixa seemed to have gotten themselves distracted by the arrival of the Kendari. Hannah couldn't blame them. It was a confused situation. The Vixa were holding the Kendari back, at least for the moment, keeping their fighting arms held high, their attack talons unsheathed, the neurotoxin oozing very obviously from the stingers.

Everyone was busy. It looked like a good moment to leave.

"Jamie! Make with the smoke bombs." He immediately starting pulling pins and heaving the cylinders out the window and into the compound. She turned to Brox. "Okay," she said. "Nothing fancy. We run like hell, we give each other whatever mutual cover we can, and we get through the blast doors, then get them shut behind us. Understood?"

"Understood."

"Okay, on the count of three," Hannah said, drawing her own sidearm and checking it. "Ready, Jamie?"

"Are you kidding?"

"Close enough. One. Two. Three!"

They sprang to their feet and starting moving, legs pumping, heads down. Hannah glanced behind them. The embassy ship was still crawling into the air, only a hundred or so meters in the air, clumps of dirt still falling away from it, the reactionless thrusters pulsing violet and purple as they strained to lift the massive vehicle on minimum power. The smoke was a solid, swirling, dirty grey wall that concealed the far side of the compound. It ought to hide them from the Vixa. If it didn't, there wasn't anything they could do about it.

The noise was not only overwhelmingly loud. It was impossibly complex. The roaring hum of the embassy ship's engines, the *crump* and *thud* of secondary explosions, the shouts and cries of the mob, the *crackles* of the fires that were starting to spread, the dull *thuds* of debris dropping out of the sky, and any number of other sounds did not merge into one another—instead they seemed to interact, resonating, amplifying each other, weaving in and out so that one would be heard, then another.

Jamie yelled something toward Hannah, turned, fired at someone or something, then turned back again, all without breaking step—and Hannah couldn't hear any of it at all.

The smoke was starting to spread, and dust was everywhere, making it hard to see, and a little hard to breathe. Brox was moving faster than any of them and got to the ops center first.

Hannah reached the ops center's blast doors after Brox and fought off a coughing fit as she worked the lock controls. Jamie put his back to the wall and fired into the ground and into the air, doing his best to add to the chaos and confusion that were their best and only protection.

The door unlocked, and Hannah hauled it back just far enough for them to scoot through. Jamie followed after, firing off one or two last potshots before he dove in. Brox brought up the rear. Hannah slammed it shut behind and instantly started to work on opening the inner blast door, trying not to think how long they were going to be able to hold out.

Except that was the wrong question. The Vixa had all the hardware and weapons and cutting beams and so on they could ever need. The question wasn't how long it would take the Vixa to break in—it was whether they would decide to do so, and how hard were they willing to try. *So let's hope they don't find out we're in here,* she told herself.

They got through the inner door and rolled it shut, then turned and faced the main ops room. It had been a crime scene, not so long ago.

"All right then," said Brox in a perfectly calm tone, as if running for his life through a pitched battle were his morning commute. "It's time to go to work."

TWENTY-FIVE

UNDERGROUND CELL

"What do we do first?" Jamie asked.

"First we think this through," said Hannah. "We threw this together in a hurry, and we're going to be down in the bunker a while. The bad news for you, Brox, is we didn't know you were coming. We set up the gear in the bunker under the *human* side of the joint ops center—and we didn't think to make any arrangements for Kendari visitors."

"Plus which, the entrance to the bunker needs to be sealed to give us proper blast protection," said Jamie. "Sealing it is about a five-minute job. Opening it is a little faster, but not much. Once it's closed, it's camouflaged pretty well. The idea is that no one is supposed to know we're in the bunker, or even that the bunker is there in the first place. Given the mob we just left outside, I like that idea. We can't go back and forth through that hatch ten times a day without exposing ourselves to a lot of needless risk. Once we're inside, I don't want to open that hatch again until we're ready to leave for good."

"Splendid," Brox said sourly. "So I may look forward, not only to being underground most of the time, but to dealing with hallways that are too narrow, tables that are the wrong height, and all the other conveniences of working in areas designed for human use. Needless to say, steep, narrow stairways, such as the one leading to your bunker, are a favorite with Kendari."

"Not just working on the human side," Hannah said. "*Living* there. I don't think we can count on being able to come up here to the main level at all. The Vixa could decide at any moment to flatten it, or blow it up, and we're not going to get much in the way of warning if they do. *I* don't want to be topside if that happens. And what with the two bunker systems being designed to protect *us* from you and your people from *us*, no one thought to put in any connecting passages between the underground levels."

"So I must go over to the Kendari side, collect food and supplies, and take them into the human bunker," Brox said. "I was in need of exercise anyway."

"I'll help you," Jamie said.

"No," said Brox. "I can manage. You two get started on the reason we're going down there."

"Fine," said Jamie. "*You* take the easy job." He watched as Brox headed off to find food and supplies—and couldn't help remembering being locked in with a Kendari once before. The memories were vivid.

"If it's any comfort to you," said Hannah, "I just happen to know the Kendari have a portable sanitizer in storage on their side. My guess is that Brox wants to do the hauling job alone because he's going to have to haul their portable sanitizer down into the bunker and he doesn't want an audience. He's on the prim and proper side, even for a Kendari."

Jamie breathed a sigh of relief. Kendari sanitizers were extremely powerful and effective—because they had to be. "Being buried alive just started sounding a whole lot less unpleasant," he said. He was about to say something more when a shudder passed through the whole building, strong enough to kick up a cloud of dust.

"What do you say we do the rest of our thinking in the bunker?" Hannah asked.

"Sounds good to me," said Jamie.

"We have the facts," said Brox, some hours later, once they were settled in and sealed up. "We have absolute proof of many things, and compelling evidence of additional items, that show that the Vixa deliberately murdered Emelza."

Hannah nodded and let out a weary sigh. "And you care about that, and *we* care about that—but the Elder Races won't care about the death of one Younger Race cop. How does it affect them?"

It had been a long argument already, and they had only been underground for a few hours. The bunker had seemed cramped, musty, and unpleasant when they started, and it hadn't improved in the interim. "Look," said Jamie. "I think we're losing track of something. Telling the truth is all well and good, but that's not the point. We're trying to build a *case* against the Vixan government, against the Preeminent Director. A case that will convict him in the court of Elder Race public opinion, at the very least."

"You're not suggesting we fabricate evidence," said Brox.

"No," said Jamie. *We'd never get away with it anyway.* "Of course not. We're trying to *prove* a fraud. *Creating* a fraud would be suicide. What I'm saying, and what Hannah is saying, is that murder—or rather proving murder—is not enough. It's part of the whole. We want to prove charges of incitement to war, intent

to seize the Pentam System by fraudulent means, interference with a diplomatic mission. Grand-scale stuff."

"But we don't even know if those are *crimes* to the
Elder Races," Brox objected. "Your people always talk
about the Great Game, as if it were all some sort of
sporting competition. If the Elders view it that way,
why would they even care?"

"Some of them would," said Hannah. "The Reqwar
Pavlat certainly would, and I'd bet the rest of the Pav
governments would feel the same way. It's okay to kill
someone as long as you do it properly. Honor is a very
big deal."

"But on the other hand the Stanlarr Consortia are
so hard to kill, and live so long, they barely know what
death is, let alone murder," said Jamie.

"But they *would* care about planet-theft," said
Brox. "Even if it was a plot that was going to take
many twelves of years. They feel strongly about honest
dealings."

"The Metrans and the Bruxa wouldn't like the
planet-theft," Jamie said. "Or the stalling, the playing
for time. They know all about being short-lived. They
take it as a deadly insult when another race tries to use
that against them in negotiations."

"Wait a second," said Hannah. "All of that is good.
Very good. Step back a bit, and what we're telling each
other is that we should build a case for each race,
based on what that race cares about. Or at least try.
We're going to be awkward about it, we'll get some of
it wrong, but some of it will work. And it will get attention."

"And there's one other race to think about," said
Jamie. "What about the Vixa? They're the ones who
did it. They're the ones who are probably going to try

to do us in once they figure out we're here. What about them?"

"You know," said Hannah, "Special Agent Singh made a pretty interesting observation to me. He pointed out that we humans always assume every alien culture is monolithic. But just about every one we've come up against has had factions and groups and bickering and all the rest of it. We always think of you Kendari as a unified whole—but I don't think your government agrees with the guys who came over the walls with ramping equipment."

"No," said Brox. "We don't. And I assure you that if you ever visit Kendal, you'll find all the bickering factions you would ever care to see. You won't have to look any further than my family."

"Stop by our house some time," said Hannah. "That's a whole other angle. Maybe the most dangerous one for us. How will our people, and yours, react?"

"With anger," said Brox. "Extreme anger, that might tempt one or both of them into doing something foolish. I would suggest that we *don't* try and contact any human or Kendari worlds or groups, just at first. We do not wish to incite any rash reactions."

"I think you're right about that," said Jamie. *And just how crazy are we to be trying to dabble in Elder Race politics when we don't dare tell our own home worlds what's going on?*

"Getting back to the point I was about to make, we know the Vixa aren't monolithic, either," said Hannah. "One clan maneuvers against another. Kragshmal became Preeminent Director very recently—and they moved the Grand Warren back to Rivertide because of it. One of the Cities on the Founder's Pillar lost the Warrenship. Presumably they weren't happy about it."

"And we've heard a phrase a few times," Jamie said

eagerly. "Flexdal used it. 'The consensus of the hierarchy.' If it was a complete, absolute, hierarchy, that idea would be meaningless. Everyone would always agree with what their superior did, and that superior would always agree with his superior, and so on right up to the big boss. But if there's a consensus, that means there has to be some wiggle room, *some* chance to disagree."

"Okay, great. You're telling me we're going to have to think through the politics of what amounts to a caste-based hive mind," said Hannah.

"A place to start would be to ask the same question you've asked regarding every other species," said Brox. "What would the Vixa care about in all this?"

"Easy," said Jamie. "Getting caught."

"Don't get cute, Jamie. This is serious."

"I *am* being serious. They're the lord-high Vixa, mightiest of all the Elder Races—according to their own publicity, anyway. The craftiest, the most cunning, the cleverest schemers in the sky. And they got caught—caught by the two bumbling, dopey, clumsy idiot Younger Races they were trying to cheat. Caught in the attempt while trying and failing to take candy from a baby. How's *that* for humiliating?"

The others were quiet for a long time. Hannah broke the silence. "I think you've got hold of something there, Jamie. Maybe something big."

"Something big, yes. But even that would be more effective if it were, as you put it, part of a larger whole. I suggest the following," said Brox. "We put together a complete package of all our evidence. Everything from the isotope ratio of the carbon atoms in the caffeine to the Kendari weapons inside my simulant's digestive cavity. Make it as orderly, as detailed, as complete as we possibly can. All facts, with no opinions or conclusions."

"Seems pretty obvious," said Jamie. "Then what?"

"Then we craft an introduction, a summing-up, that will appeal to each particular species. Let them all have the truth, the proof, the evidence—but for each one, present an argument, state a case. A case that is supported by the facts, but that will appeal most strongly to that species. Then we do what you had planned—transmit it to all the embassies of all the species here on Tifinda, using all the means at our disposal. Assuming this bunker's communications system survived the Vixan attack."

"Getting all that together shouldn't take more than, what, two or three years?" asked Jamie. "How long you figure we've got, Hannah?"

"With one thing and another, it's going to be a lot harder to keep control of the situation once the two embassy ships make their transit-jumps," said Hannah. "Once they do, and they reach their home systems, word is going to get out. The *Kofi Annan* ought to reach its transit-jump point in about five days. Once it does, the story is going to start leaking."

"Our ship will likely be about a half Earth-day slower. But if we're to have any hope of affecting the situation, we'll need to transmit well before they boost," said Brox. "For one thing, the longer we wait, the longer the Vixa will be able to get out their version of events, unchallenged. Two embassies evacuating, and the compounds fired upon. All the other embassies saw it. How could they not? They'll *have* to come up with some explanation. The longer we take to make our case, the more Elder Races will find reasons to accept whatever nonsense the Vixa put out. Furthermore, the sooner we transmit, the more chance the other ambassadors on Tifinda will have to contact our embassy ships directly. They'll want to ask our people follow-up questions, and so on."

"A big part of the idea here is that the accusations are *not* coming from the embassy ships," Hannah pointed out. "We don't want to give the Vixa any excuse for declaring them pirate craft or something and blowing them out of the sky. If they start getting queries from the other embassies, answering the questions could lead to them being targets again."

"Leave that to Stabmacher and Flexdal," said Brox. "They will know how to answer questions—and confirm our accusations—without giving the Vixa any excuses for being unpleasant. In short, they will be— well, diplomatic."

"Whereas there's a good chance there will be a smoking crater where we are now, five minutes after we transmit," Jamie said. "I doubt we'll get more than one shot at this. It'll have to be the absolute best we can do. We'll have to draw on all the data both species have. In other words, Brox—if you show us yours, we'll show you ours."

"I beg your pardon?"

"I think—I hope—he's talking databases, Brox," Hannah said with a smile. "Of xeno species. We've got ours. If we integrate it with yours, we're bound to wind up with better data overall."

"I don't need to tell you how many security violations that will involve," said Brox. "Ours and yours."

"No, you don't," said Hannah. "And I don't have to tell you all the reasons we should do it, either."

Starting with Emelza, Jamie thought. *But we don't dare say that directly.*

"The integration will take some time," Brox said. "We had better get started."

*　*　*

It wasn't work any of them was trained for, or even very good at. But, in a sense, that didn't matter. It even worked in their favor. There were times, Hannah soon realized, when telling the truth too slickly, too smoothly, was counterproductive.

They created a written report of the facts and a visual record of everything that had happened. It offered no analysis or opinion—just the bald facts, and evidence that supported them. The death of Emelza. The chemical analysis of the residue in the crime scene coffee mug. The isotope-ratio evidence. The attempted humiliation of Stabmacher by Kragshmal. Recordings of Kragshmal's improper offers regarding the Pentam System made to Flexdal, and his brazen demands for payment in return. The pursuit of the humans by the simulants, and Zamprohna's getting in the way and getting stung. The dissection of Brox's simulant. Linda Weldon's statement. Imagery of the evacuation, and the shelling of the embassy ship coordinates, and the attack by the Vixan assault force. They had that from a dozen camera views—and they even had shots of the Vixa systematically going around the human compound and destroying the cameras, one by one. Brox was able to contribute an authenticated recording of the brazen lies told to the Kendari to get them to attack the human compound. The first draft of the report was rushed, but it led to a better, tighter second draft.

With that job completed, they set to work on accompanying communiqués, tailoring each one to appeal to a particular Elder Race.

To the Pavlat they spoke of honor. For the Metrans, they emphasized the evidence that the Vixa were hoping to stall the process for a century or two. The message to the Stanlarr Consortia pointed out the Vixan frauds and deceits. They told the Unseen Race about the underhanded attempts to instigate a war, and spoke of the dangers of an unstable political situation. They made sure the Bruxa and Tlzeskez were aware of the violent attacks on the diplomats and diplomatic property.

All the messages asked if the Vixa could be trusted to treat the recipient's diplomats properly. Would it be a small matter if the Vixa next arranged to kill a Metran diplomat, or a Pavlat, and planted evidence to implicate the Tlzeskez in the crime? Would it be a minor issue if the Vixa attempted to foment a war between the Stanlarr and the Unseen Race?

To the Vixa went a taunting description of all the sloppy work that had been done and all the mistakes made in the name of their Preeminent Director, along with a cheerful reminder of how thoroughly humiliated they were about to be, once the news spread. That one they all read over most carefully. They wanted to embarrass the Vixa. They did not want to enrage them.

All of it had to be written in the ponderous, careful, precise phrases of Greater Trade Writing, then checked, and rechecked, and checked again for errors.

They worked against the clock, knowing that the Vixa might find them at any moment, that every hour that passed was time the Vixa could be using to get their version of events out there, making the humans and the Kendari the bad guys in the story. And every hour brought them closer to the time when the embassy ships would be making their transit-jumps, and the chance for some garbled version of the story to leak out on the human worlds, or the Kendari planets. It didn't even bear thinking about how many ways the situation might spiral out of control from there.

Brox found himself to be mainly an observer much of the time. Nearly all of the equipment they were using had been designed for humans, and it was almost always faster and easier for the BSI agents to do something themselves rather than wait for Brox to struggle with the awkward keyboards and datapad displays.

He was able to make himself useful enough using his own portable gear for various forms of research, but there was no disguising the fact that he was very much the junior partner in the enterprise.

It gave him a chance to observe Wolfson and Mendez—no, Hannah and Jamie—at work. He thought of all the Kendari's stereotyped ideas of humans. Humans were impulsive, disorganized, argumentative, unable to work together, or stay focused on a job long enough to do it properly.

That was the thing he had not really seen in action before. Their persistence, their endurance, their focus on the job. Brox was not assuming that all humans were like these two. But they were revealing traits and abilities that, according to most Kendari, *no* humans had.

They were flawed, irritating, and most un-Kendari-like aliens. There was no denying that. But they were tough and determined as well. With every hour that passed, Brox felt more sure that he would not wish to find himself in a fight against them—and more certain that fighting alongside them was the right thing to do.

But all such high-minded thinking could not mask the central irony of the situation. Brox knew perfectly well that a great deal of that sleepless determination was coming from the bunker's tiny kitchen, where the coffeepot was in almost continuous use. At Brox's best estimate, each of the two BSI agents was going through approximately one pot of coffee drenched with deadly caffeine every twelve hours.

Any species that could put itself through that level of chemical abuse was bound to be hard to kill.

Jamie yawned tremendously as he shoved the datapad away from him. "Okay," he said. "That's it. I just caught myself starting in on reading over the same section five times in a row. I'm too tired to read, let alone proofread."

"Me too," said Hannah. "How are you doing, Brox?"

"Mppmh? Me? I stopped being able to do much of anything fourteen hours ago. Either we stop, allow ourselves an extended period of complete rest, and then go on—or we stop now, accept that we have done the best we could in the amount of time we had, and send what we have."

"The risks on that side go up and up and up with every hour that passes," said Jamie. "What we're checking for now is big, dreadful mistakes that some xeno or other will take as a deadly insult. We haven't found anything. There's a chance we've missed something—but I think we're at the point where there's more risk in delay."

Hannah rubbed her face. "I agree with Jamie. How about you, Brox? Do we rest up?"

"Yes," said Brox. "*After* we send our reports. Let us make our marks of authentication and responsibility and get them on their way."

"Fine by me," said Jamie. "Slide that thing over here again, will you?"

He took the datapad from Hannah's hand and went rapidly through the authentication procedure. "Okay, there," he said. "A blurry fingerprint, a scan of my bloodshot retina, plus my illegible signature. If anyone can read any of that, they ought to be able to prove it's me. Hannah?"

Hannah went through the same steps, a bit less theatrically, and handed the datapad to Brox. "Here," she said. "This thing is rigged to do Kendari authentication as well."

Brox let the unit scan his front teeth, the pattern of whorls in his snout, and do a voice match. He used the stylus to draw his personal mark on the input screen, and the job was done. "The weapon is loaded and energized," he said. "Now all that remains is to fire it."

"Let's just check to make sure it's aimed the right way first," said Jamie. "Let's just run through the list of recipients and make sure each one is getting the right version." They quickly confirmed that everything was in order, but Jamie paused over the last line on the list. The Vixa. More specifically, Founder's Column City, the presumed center of opposition to Kragshmal.

Jamie tapped at that entry. "Before we do this, let's think it through one more time. We have no idea at all how the Vixa will react. We've set things up to hide where the messages will be coming from, but they might be able to trace them back to here, to the bunker under the joint ops center. They might be able to do it very fast, and they might decide to vaporize us. They might think it over for a week, and *then* decide to wipe us out. They might decide to blast away without bothering to look. Or they might never find us."

"Are you changing your mind about staying here?"

Hannah asked. "Are you saying we ought to make a run for it after we send the message, try and hole up somewhere?"

"No. If they attack us here, at least there's no one else around who might get hurt. If we run to one of the embassies, or to one of the human or Kendari groups, we'll be exposed while we're running, and we'll be endangering whoever agrees to take us in. They blew up *our* embassy. Why not someone else's? We stay here, and hope that things break our way, or at least calm down enough after a while so we can come out with some degree of safety before our food runs out."

"So what is the point you are trying to make?"

"We send the messages out. We immediately cut all our links to the comm net to reduce the chances of the Vixa tracing us back to here. But that means we can no longer send or receive messages. We won't know anything. The Vixa already have a mass mind. They don't exactly have a need for a continuous all-news video feed. We can't just turn on the news or read the text updates. We *might* be able to eavesdrop on radio frequencies that the Kendari and humans on-planet use. Maybe we'll learn something from that. My point is that once we send the message, we're down here for the duration—and we'll have almost no way of knowing what's going on, or how long that duration might be. Are you both prepared for that?"

"I'd like to think so," said Hannah.

"How could one prepare?" Brox asked. "But I am ready to endure the consequences. The weapon is now loaded, energized—and aimed. Are we ready?"

"Go ahead, Brox," said Hannah. "Pull the trigger."

The Kendari Inquirist reached out for the datapad, took it in his hands, and brought up the command sequence that would first send the messages, then cut the comm links. He paused, only for a moment and activated the sequence. Silently, quickly, invisibly, it was done.

The three of them stood there for a minute or two, half-expecting the Vixa to be able to do the traceback and vaporize them at once. But nothing happened.

"All right then," said Jamie, yawning and stretching. "I just hope that if the Vixa do zap us into dust, they at least have the decency to let me get some sleep first. Good night, or good morning, or whatever time of day it is."

None of them got any sleep at first. They were all too wound up—and also half-expecting that the Vixa would strike back at once. Every small noise in the bunker, every shift in the ventilator noise brought all of them back to instant alertness. But after a while, even being scared can get boring. With the comm links cut, and the exterior cameras destroyed, they had no way of knowing what reaction there had been to their messages. They didn't even have any way of knowing for sure if the messages had gotten through.

They monitored the radio frequencies used by the human and Kendari, but the signals were weak and intermittent at best. Besides, it was unlikely to be any news from there because they had decided not to send copies of their reports to the enclaves. The humans and Kendari on-planet were all pretty radical in their views to start with, and even the bits and pieces of the story they already were likely to get them angry. There seemed no point in providing further incitement. What if the news started a riot that got humans or Kendari killed?

Keeping their own people off the send list was a sensible decision, but it did leave them with no good way to find out what was going on. About all they could do was wait until there was news over the human or Kendari radio that suggested it was safe to come out, or until someone came and got them, or until their food ran out and they were forced to come out of their hole and make a run for it.

And so they slept, and ate, and read whatever books and texts happen to be available in the bunker. Jamie tried to teach Brox chess, and Brox tried to show him a roughly similar Kendari game, but neither attempt really went anywhere.

Nothing at all happened.

Until something did.

The first sound was far off, distant, and low, almost more a vibration than a noise. But it was enough to wake Hannah up at once. She rolled out of her bunk, flipped on the lights, and went to find the others. The bunker had been designed to hold the entire staff of the embassy. It would have been a tight fit for that many, but it meant that Hannah, Jamie, and Brox could each have the luxury of a private room.

But Hannah didn't want that luxury at the moment, and it would seem that neither Brox nor Jamie did either. She found them out in the hallway, looking up at the ceiling—and watching the dust that was suddenly being kicked up everywhere.

Something was happening over their heads. That much was obvious.

"What have we got here, Jamie?" she asked in a whisper, as if whoever was overhead could hear her.

He shook his head. "I dunno," he said, whispering

back. "It's not an attack. At least not yet. No explosions or anything. It could be they're setting up for an assault. Or not."

"That is not particularly comforting," said Brox.

There didn't seem to be more to say, or much more to be done about the situation. The sounds overhead grew louder, and seemed to get closer. The vibration grew more intense. There were *crashes* and *thuds* that sent low shudders through the bunker, and then relative quiet for a while, before another series of *bangs* and *thuds*.

"They're right overhead," Jamie said at last. "I *think* it's demolition. But I don't know for what reason. They might be looking for us, or just clearing the site to put up a new restaurant—or this might be a deliberate attempt to dig us out or entomb us."

"All right," said Hannah. "Time to think about the escape tunnel." There was a second way out of the bunker, an emergency tunnel that climbed all the way out of the compound and ended in a vertical shaft under the street outside. The top of the vertical shaft came to an end about a meter short of the surface, with a metal cap on top. There were shaped charges rigged to it that would blast the top of the tunnel clear, opening the way for those inside to make a run for it, if need be. There were also shovels and picks stored in the shaft, in case there was time to make a more leisurely, if less spectacular, exit.

"Hannah, I checked that tunnel out," said Jamie. "After the first three meters it's a hands-and-knees crawl all the way through a round pipe eighty centimeters across and maybe a hundred meters long—and the vertical shaft is the same diameter, with ladder rungs set into the side of it."

"So?"

"So Brox simply can't fit inside a tunnel that size, let alone crawl through it. It was designed to keep Kendari out, not let them in."

"Then the two of you should go," said Brox.

"Very noble of you, Brox, but even if you weren't here, I'd say no," Jamie replied. "It'd be suicide. If we set off the charges to clear the tunnel, whoever is up there trying to dig us out is going to hear it, and probably see the dust and smoke from the blast even over the wall. If we try digging, they'd probably hear that too—and it would take us so long to break a person-sized hole through the street surface that they'd be bound to spot that."

"So what do we do?" Hannah asked.

"We sit here and wait," said Jamie. "And hope the bunker entrance is as well camouflaged as we think. One thing we have going for us is now *we* know that *they* don't know we're here. If they did, they would have been here a lot sooner. With some luck, that should mean they won't be as thorough as they would be if they knew for sure this was the place."

"That all sounds very relaxing," said Hannah. There was another *boom*, deeper and harder. A new cloud of dust was kicked up, and the lights cut out for a moment. "Handlights," said Hannah. "Let's make sure we all have handlights. I don't want to be down here in the dark if the lights die for good. And let's find some clothes we can tie up into dust masks."

The booming and crashing went on. The lights cut out momentarily two more times in the next ten minutes, and then went out and stayed out. Jamie checked the breaker panel. It looked as if all they would have to do was reset the system—but they decided to wait on that. Whoever it was topside might have instruments that could detect electric systems turning on and off. They had their handlights, and the air would be okay for a while without the ventilation system or the scrubbers.

The crashing and the banging got louder still—and then, suddenly, it wasn't coming from overhead—but from alongside.

"Our bunker," said Brox. "We did not think to conceal the entrance. They must have found it and decided to destroy it."

There was another sharp *bang,* and a low, rumbling, shuddering *boom* strong enough to knock them all over. They climbed back to their feet, coughing and wheezing in the darkness. "Okay," said Jamie. "Back to the utility room. It's on the far side from the Kendari bunker, and that's where the tunnel leads off from."

"You can't be thinking of trying for a breakout now!" Hannah shouted. "And what about Brox?"

"I'm not thinking of a breakout," said Jamie. "But if this place collapses, and we live through it, we're going to want to be near the tunnel exit. And maybe we can push and pull Brox through the tunnel, or send one of us out to go for help—or to offer our surrender."

"Surrender?" Brox asked.

"Buried alive and starving to death, or prisoners of the Vixa," said Jamie. "Which would you choose?"

"To be honest," Brox said, "I am not quite sure."

"Let's get to the utility room, and we can debate it later," Hannah half shouted to be heard over a new series of rumbling crashes.

Jamie led the way as they staggered down the hallway and into the utility room. They slammed the reinforced door shut. Hannah and Jamie sat down on the floor with their backs to the far wall while Brox curled himself up into the smallest space possible in the corner.

The noise and vibration reached a climax, then began to ease off. Within a few minutes, they had dropped to almost nothing. There were a few low thuds and bumps that seemed to come from overhead. Even those stopped after a while. Whatever had been happening was over.

"I think your bunker might have saved us, Brox," said Hannah, speaking into the silence. "I think some gang of Vixa had orders to tear down the joint ops center to make sure we weren't in it. They found a bunker and wrecked it, as well—and managed to bury the entrance to this one and churn up the ground so much that they didn't notice there were *two* bunkers. Maybe we might be okay for a while."

"If you don't mind being buried alive," said Jamie.

"They've tried to find us here," said Hannah. "They've failed, and made such a mess that maybe they won't even think of trying again. This doesn't change our plan. It just improves the odds that it will work. We hold out here as long as we can. A few days. Maybe a week, if we can make it. Then we try and get the main bunker door open. It's got some heavy-duty hydraulic jacks on it. It might still be possible to get out that way. If it isn't, we use the escape hatch and send for help to get Brox out of here."

"You make it sound almost easy," said Brox in a sarcastic voice.

"It might be," said Hannah. "It might be. The hard part is going to be the waiting." She shined her handlight on the ceiling, looking for cracks and breaks and not finding any. "We sit in the dark for twelve hours," she said. "That will give the Vixa plenty of time to get bored and leave. Then we can risk turning the lights and air back on."

Jamie's eyes opened. He was in his bunk, in his room, in the bunker. The same place he had woken up for—how many days? He resisted the urge to check the time. He had decided to stop keeping track of time a while back. He hadn't noted the time in days, or even longer. The whole point of it was that he didn't know anymore.

The whole point of it is that you're starting to crack up, Jamie told himself.

He got out of bed and made his way down the hallway. The bunker had actually come through the demolition assault in fairly good shape. There was a layer of dust on everything—including Jamie—but the structure still seemed solid.

But how long is that going to last? Jamie asked himself. *How long is anything going to last?* It seemed as if all his questions, all his thoughts and fears, centered in on time. *That* was why he avoided checking any of the dozens of clocks, watches, and data displays that could have told him, to the split second, exactly what day and time it was. What was the point of that when time itself had lost its meaning? Time measured the rate of change in things, and nothing ever changed in the bunker.

He found Hannah in the main workroom. "Good morning or evening or night or whatever," he said.

"'Hello' would cover all the cases," she said. "I've been checking our supply status. We're fine on food and water, but all the air-scrubber systems have been working overtime since the demolition attack.

It's like the ventilation system is pulling in as much dust as air."

"Probably the air vent to the surface got buried or filled in and that's exactly what's happening."

"Probably. But the point is the filters are going to fail and we'll be choking on solid dust clouds in about four days. We've got to start preparing now for our breakout. I don't want to have to start digging out the escape tunnel exit when we're already near passing out."

Jamie was about to answer when Brox rushed into the room. "I just heard something!" he said excitedly. "Scraping sounds, coming from the other side of the main bunker entrance!"

"Grab weapons and handlights," Hannah said. "Let's go."

The three of them hurried down the main hallway and into the armored, right-angled vestibule that led to the bunker entrance. They could all hear it clearly. A slow, careful, methodical scraping and rasping, the sound of shovels biting into dirt.

"Whoever it is, this time they knew right where to dig," Hannah whispered.

"Yeah," said Jamie in a low voice. "Maybe that's a good sign. Maybe."

"Kill the lights or keep them on?" Hannah asked, keeping her voice down.

Jamie shrugged. "I don't know. Leave them on, I suppose. If it comes to a fight, we'll go down swinging, but I don't think the lighting will change how it comes out. Just make sure you've got some sort of cover, and a clear line of fire—and hope we don't need either."

They set themselves around the corners of the vestibule, guns drawn but not raised, and listened to the digging sounds get louder and louder, until it was metal-on-metal, the shovels striking the camouflaged upper access door itself.

The upper door lay flat on the ground and led down a narrow set of stairs to the vertically oriented inner door they were staring at.

There was more *clanking* and *banging,* and the sound of gears grinding and protesting metal—then louder, sharper *bangs* and rattling *crashes* that could only be rocks and debris falling into the chamber between the two doors.

There was a brief silence, then the inner door started to move, sliding back into its wall niche.

Frank Milkowski stepped inside and looked around. "My God," he said to the three scarecrows aiming guns at him. "You're all still alive."

They staggered up into the light, and looked around at the rubble field that had once been two embassy compounds. Simply put, everything had been utterly flattened. "Boy," said Jamie. "Will you look at this place? I'll bet this is the last time they let *us* house-sit."

They walked forward a bit. Stabmacher and Flexdal and a mixed group of embassy staffers were there, standing ready to give them a helping hand. But they didn't need it. Just being outside was cure enough for what ailed them. It was good to see the sky, the sun, familiar faces.

But what Hannah, at least, was gladdest to see was Zhen Chi, down on her knees, scrabbling in the dirt, industriously and determinedly replanting her garden, putting her plants back in the place where they were supposed to be growing.

TWENTY-SIX

FINAL INQUIRIES

"So," said Ambassador Stabmacher, standing in the rubble of his once-and-future embassy, "how does it feel to have brought down the government of one of the most powerful planets known to the Elder Races?"

"Strange," Hannah said, peering around. It was strange just to be *outdoors* again, after spending endless days in the bunker of the joint ops center. "Disconcerting. I know they deserved it, I know it was for the best—but, somehow, I even feel a little guilty, like I broke someone's window playing ball."

"*They're* the ones that broke the windows," said Jamie, looking around the ruins of the Embassy of Humanity. "And pretty much everything else."

"We'll rebuild," said Stabmacher. "The interim government has offered us a more prestigious plot of land in a better part of town, but we'll rebuild *here*. This is our place. If nothing else staked our claim to it, your work certainly did."

"Thank you, sir. But in the grand scheme of things, I can't really believe that sending out a few press releases could have really done the whole job. Kragshmal couldn't have had that firm a hold on the Directorship, if what *we* did could bring him down."

"I beg to differ," said Flexdal. "I suspect that it was precisely because he had *too* firm a hold on the office that everything collapsed. 'The consensus of the hierarchy' we all keep talking about. He pushed it too hard, too fast, and in the wrong direction. And the rest of the Grand Vixa stopped following."

They came upon the bench that had stood outside the main embassy building. The building itself wasn't there anymore, but the bench had merely been tipped over. "Why don't we just sit here for a moment?" Hannah suggested. "It feels good to be out in the sun and the air."

Hannah and Jamie righted the bench, and dusted it off, and the three humans sat down on it, while the Kendari cleared the rubble from a large enough space to sit back on their haunches. They watched as small groups of humans from the embassy staff wandered over the compound, touring the wreckage.

The ambassador spoke. "The grand irony of this whole affair, at least so far as I'm concerned, was that it brings us back to almost exactly the same point as when we started. In an earlier phase of the meetings, held in the Founder's Pillar Column City, Xenologist Flexdal and I had just about reached an agreement wherein we would propose *sharing* the Pentam System—one planet for humans, the other for the Kendari. It would be a difficult and awkward arrangement at first—perhaps for a long time. We both knew that perfectly well. But it certainly beat the winner-take-all deal that the Vixa were insisting upon. Our analysts said turning it into a question of one side winning and the other losing was practically a recipe for war."

"Ours said the same thing," said Flexdal, "and, apparently, so did the Vixan analysts. Which would explain why they insisted on arranging matters that way."

A rare thing, to hear a Kendari make a joke, thought Hannah.

Ambassador Stabmacher smiled and raised one eyebrow, as if he were thinking the same thing. "It was only when the new Preeminent Director came in, and the Grand Warren, the city designated as the capital, shifted back to Rivertide, that we had problems. We got assigned adjoining embassy space—supposedly for the convenience of proximity but probably just to put us at each others' throats. I suppose nearly all of the things they did to facilitate matters were really meant to make things worse."

"But you didn't go for each others' throats," said Hannah. "You built the joint ops center instead. Then the Vixa invited in all those interest groups to 'observe,' and made sure to skew the representation to the most radical human and Kendari groups on both ends of the spectrum. But you managed to keep *that* from derailing the negotiations. So the Vixa decided to try blatant favoritism. Forcing the simulants on us, and not on the Kendari—with the eventual goal of performing the humiliation ritual they staged for our benefit."

"That day didn't go according to plan for them, did it?" Stabmacher asked. "I think we—I—was supposed to accept the insult, sit outside the inner dome where my odor couldn't offend, and let myself be represented by a puppet." He gestured toward Flexdal. "They'd force concession after concession out of me, then grant your people whatever they took from mine—but always at a price. An indemnity. A right to bases. Access to this, or that. And then we'd both go home to our governments with deals they could not support, and the two sides further apart than ever. Everything meant to goad us into distrusting each other, into seeing the negotiations as a failure. Sooner or later, it would all add up—to war. And favoring one of us over the other was part of that."

Jamie spoke, nodding toward Brox and Xenologist Flexdal. "My guess is that they chose to favor the Kendari because, well, you *are* just a bit more orderly than we are. You tend to like things in nice straight lines, and you work as a group more easily than humans. And, two other points. You have more legs than we do, and while the underlying Kendari body plan is utterly different from that of the Vixa, you move a lot more like Vixa than a pack of strangely balanced bipeds do. That made you just that little bit more similar to them."

"More slender reeds," the ambassador objected.

"There's more. Our embassy's deputy chief of mission was sent home for medical treatment. Our ambassador had no one with him of roughly similar rank when he went to the meetings. The BSI security detail didn't count. The Vixa saw the detail as being what it was—the precise equivalent of their escort groups. The BSI agents didn't provide security—they provided *status*. But in certain cases, a smaller escort can confer greater status on a Grand Vixa than a larger one, and it seems escorts that are roughly your size also enhance your status. Xenologist Flexdal, you and your assistant were escorted by two Inquiries Service agents that were about his size. We had one lone—and very tall—diplomat escorted by three fairly short BSI agents. It would be subtle, perhaps even subconscious—but it added up to the Vixa instinctively reading the Kendari as being of slightly higher status than humans."

"And we played up to that," Brox admitted. "And why not? It seemed a reasonable way to curry favor with our hosts, who stood in judgment over us."

"There were more than just clues to hint at our

lower status. We were also unknowingly sending clues showing *scrambled* status that must have confused them—and given them a low opinion of us. The simulants—and whoever was watching through them—saw Jamie and me yelling at our ambassador and Zhen Chi about that whole Kendari rigor mortis issue. But we were from an external and superior hierarchy, so we had that right. At that time, we acted as if we were their superiors. We gave them orders as to how to turn over the evidence." She turned and looked directly at Stabmacher. "Then they saw us treat you, Mr. Ambassador and Zhen Chi—your subordinate—as if the two of you were both *equally* subordinate to us, which would reduce your status in their eyes, Mr. Ambassador. Later they saw us acting as your escorts. We permitted ourselves to be treated as being in the same status level as the simulants and the escort castes *after* seeming to show we outranked you. Your superiors were willing to be disgraced, and to act as your subordinates. It probably was dreadfully offensive to them."

"I want to circle back a bit," said the ambassador. "Senior Agent Wolfson. You're suggesting that the simulants were put here for the sole purpose of insulting and annoying us?"

"I spent a lot of time while we were holed up in the joint ops center thinking about all the angles on the simulants and the Vixan biocastes and so forth. I started seeing a lot of interesting second- and third- and fourth-order effects, on both sides, caused by mutual misunderstanding. If you look for it, you'll see a pattern of the Vixa tending to do a thing for multiple small reasons, rather than one big reason. But yes, insulting and annoying us was a goal. Secondary functions, but from the Vixa point of view, quite useful ones. After all, they were trying to generate tension. That said, most likely, the simulants were mainly meant to observe. No one paid them much mind on that account, as you all quite rightly assumed that the Vixa had far more effective and efficient means of spying on us.

"*My* theory, and it is only a sketchy one, is that the simulants were *also* intended to *imitate* us, to simulate us for the benefit of the Vixa themselves. They hoped that, if the simulants became similar enough to us, that they would be able, on some level, to serve as guides, explain us to the Vixa who controlled them. However, the Vixa weren't anywhere near as good at that as they thought.

"But I think there might have been another psychological effect, one that colored a lot of what happened, in ways that not even the Vixa expected—or even consciously noticed. Our people hated the simulants from the start, but they gritted their teeth and endured them. The embassy staff tolerated them so as to avoid insulting their hosts."

"That's about right."

"*But the superior may kill the inferior at any time,*" said Hannah. "In a species that has multiple natural and engineered castes, many of which aren't really sentient, that rule makes a certain cold-blooded sense. The nonsentient castes are viewed as being somewhere between tools and work animals—and there are lots of them, and as best I can see, each worker caste consists of effectively identical clones. They're all the same, and any vestigial survival instinct was bred or engineered out of them long ago. If you have to kill ten or twenty of them in order to get your dinner on time, so be it. There's plenty more where they came from, they won't even mind dying, and you'll get your dinner without any significant cost or harm to you."

"What are you saying?" the ambassador asked.

"That by *not* killing the simulants the first time they caused trouble, we were failing to assert our superiority over them. In Vixa eyes, we were equating ourselves with the simulants. And that certainly made the Vixa *our* superiors."

"I should have done more than just obey orders under protest," said the ambassador. "I should have refused the simulants, point-blank."

"And I should have done the same," said Flexdal.

"Ah, not exactly on point," said Jamie, "but I've been thinking about the groups representing the various humans and Kendari fringe groups that the Vixa brought in. I think they were here for the opposite, the converse, of that same reason. This is just a dumb junior cop guessing, but the Vixa have at least a rough general idea that neither of our societies has castes, that everyone is more or less equal to everyone else. Okay, I know the ten thousand ways that *isn't* true—but it's a lot truer for both our peoples than it is for them. Humans are all at least *supposed* to be equal before the law, even if we don't reach the ideal."

"I don't quite see what you're getting at," said Hannah.

"The Vixa must have as much trouble dealing with the subtleties of our more-or-less-but-not-exactly equality as we have understanding and dealing with their biocastes. They brought in a whole mob of politically active humans and Kendari who were, as best they could see, the *equals* of you diplomats. You represented all of humanity, and Zamprohna represented his brand of the Keep Earth Flat society. But all the Vixa could see were the representatives. On a gut level, an instinctive level, they might have asked, What's the difference? That would tend to depress their view of our status as well."

"But there's another part to that," said Brox, almost eagerly. "The Vixan castes operate on the consensus of the hierarchy. We keep coming back to that. There's a strong pressure to agree with each other, especially with the people who outrank you. Both our species have that impulse too, of course—but the Vixa have it a thousand times more."

"So they brought in representatives of external groups to put pressure on us," said Flexdal. "But they deliberately brought in groups with wildly divergent opinions to make it impossible for us to fully bow to that pressure. We could and did tolerate that, but the Vixa couldn't have. In short, they brought in our own people in hopes of driving us mad."

"We should have refused something besides the simulants," said Stabmacher. "We should have refused to continue the negotiations with all those damned delegations present."

"There's one other huge and fundamental difference of perspective in all this," said Hannah. "We all thought they wanted to make Emelza's death look like a suicide. The concept of suicide must be alien to Vixa. Individuals are expendable in service to the whole. Death of a Grand Vixan isn't the death of an individual, either. It represents the collapse of the entire household devoted to caring for the Grand Vixa. Suddenly the other castes have no home, no purpose, no leader. It never would have entered their minds to stage a suicide. They wouldn't really know what one was."

"And if the superior can kill the inferior at any time, murder isn't such a big deal either," said Jamie. "There are economic reasons not to do it. You might have to pay compensation, and that can run into real money after a while. But killing someone else's escort Nines wouldn't be considered that serious an offense. Probably the Vixa had experts and advisors who assured them we would react very strongly to the apparent murder of Emelza 401—but that was just expert talk. My guess is that the Zeeraums and Kragshmals of the hierarchy never quite understood what all the fuss was about. They never really had an emotional understanding of why the humans and Kendari were so upset."

"They are quite alien to us, aren't they?" asked Flexdal. He pulled his head back in puzzled surprise. "And I think I just meant both our peoples when I said 'us.' That's rather disconcerting, in a way."

"That's the way I felt the first time I did it," Brox said.

"That brings me to something I was thinking about while we were in that bunker," said Jamie. He stood up, to face the group, looking very young and unsure of himself—but going on ahead anyway.

"What would that be?" Stabmacher asked.

"Well, I'm no diplomat," said Jamie. "But just an idea. A thought. It couldn't hurt to listen, sir."

"Go on," said the ambassador, as he leaned back on the bench and looked out across the ruins of what had been and would be his embassy.

"From what you've been saying, without the Vixa trying to sabotage everything, the negotiations for Pentam ought to move forward pretty smoothly."

"Negotiations rarely run smoothly," said the ambassador. "But go on."

"Share the Pentam System, but *don't* divvy up the Pentam planets," said Jamie. "Leave one of them— well, leave it fallow. Whatever the word would be.

Leave it alone for now. Save it for later. Just settle *one* of the worlds—and *don't* build separate Kendari and human cities, either. Build *one* city. One place that can—that can be a sort of giant joint operations center. A place where we're *forced* to work together. Where we can *learn* to work together."

No one spoke for a while. The sun was setting. The reddish dirt caught the gathering twilight and seemed to glow with color.

"I like that," the ambassador said at last. "Even putting the high and noble purposes to one side, it would actually be a far more practical solution. No duplication of effort, building two of everything—and if we're right in each other's laps—though of course Kendari don't have laps—it would be a great deal easier to keep an eye on each other. That in itself would help build trust. I wouldn't go so far as to call it the start of a potential alliance—but it would give us a huge head start on finding ways to work together, find the interests we have in common. What do you think, Xenologist Flexdal?"

"I think it will never work," Flexdal replied, rising up off his haunches. "We'll never get along. We'll never understand that we are natural allies, not natural enemies. We'll never see that we have far more in common with each other than with any of the Elder Races—or that *they* have far more reason to suppress us *both* than either of *us* has to harm the other. It will never work—unless we all fight like fury to *make* it work."

He paused, and stamped his rearfeet and forefeet, and twitched his tail. "But *I* like it as well. And if—*if*—it can be made to work—then I think it's just possible that the Elder Races *will* have to get used to having both of us around, after all."

"I've always liked your ideas, Jamie," said Hannah. "Well, maybe not every single one of them. But this one, I could definitely get behind."

"Forgive me for indulging in a bit of sentiment," said Brox, "but I believe that Emelza 401 would have liked it as well. She was coming to enjoy working with humans."

Jamie Mendez looked down at the ground and kicked away just a bit more wreckage, clearing the way for just that little bit more of something new to go in its place. He looked up at all of them, and smiled at Brox 231, his enemy, his friend, his colleague. "Well," he said, "if the Xenologist is right, and the Elder Races will have to get used to both of us—then maybe *we'd* better get started on getting used to each other."

THE END

ABOUT THE AUTHOR

ROGER MACBRIDE ALLEN was born on September 26, 1957, in Bridgeport, Connecticut. He is the author of twenty-two science fiction novels, a modest number of short stories, and two nonfiction books. His wife, Eleanore Fox, is a member of the United States Foreign Service. They married in 1994. They were posted to Brasilia, Brazil, from 1995 to 1997, and to Washington, D.C., from 1997 to 2002. Their first son, Matthew Thomas Allen, was born on November 12, 1998. In September 2002 they began a three-year posting to Leipzig, Germany, where their second son, James Maury Allen, was born on April 27, 2004. They returned to the Washington area in the summer of 2005, and live in Takoma Park, Maryland.

Learn more about the author at www.rmallen.net, or visit www.bsi-starside.com for the latest on the BSI Starside series.